I Didn't Think You Existed 2:

A Fool in Love

I Didn't Think You Existed 2:

A Fool in Love

Hazel Ro

www.urbanbooks.net

Urban Books, LLC
300 Farmingdale Road, N.Y.-Route 109
Farmingdale, NY 11735

I Didn't Think You Existed 2: A Fool in Love
Copyright © 2022 Hazel Ro

ISBN 13: 978-1-64556-335-8
ISBN 10: 1-64556-335-9

First Trade Paperback Printing September 2022
Printed in the United States of America

10 9 8 7 6 5 4 3 2 1

This is a work of fiction. Any references or similarities to actual events, real people, living or dead, or to real locales are intended to give the novel a sense of reality. Any similarity in other names, characters, places, and incidents is entirely coincidental.

Distributed by Kensington Publishing Corp.
Submit Orders to:
Customer Service
400 Hahn Road
Westminster, MD 21157-4627
Phone: 1-800-733-3000
Fax: 1-800-659-2436

I Didn't Think You Existed 2:

A Fool in Love

Hazel Ro

Acknowledgments

Here we are again, and I'm just as excited about this book as I was the first. There are so many individuals who supported me during the completion of the first project and then this one, and there are no words that can ever convey my gratitude.

First, I thank God, simply for being you. Thank you for trusting me with the gift of writing and creativity. You didn't have to choose me for this, and I am so thankful for this opportunity. I pray that readers not only find entertainment but also see my heart throughout the pages of this book and others.

From there, I have to express my sincere gratitude to Mr. Carl Weber. You have made my dream come true by giving me this opportunity, and I thank you from my heart for that. I also want to thank the entire team at Urban Books. Thank you all for getting me and this project where it needed to be and for your patience through it all. I appreciate each and every one of you.

Of course, I owe everything to the best literary agent in the business, N'Tyse. Thank you for believing in me and continually guiding me through this process. You are the definition of a female boss, all wrapped in elegance, style, and class. I can only hope that we will have many more successes to share in the future. Thank you.

And a heartfelt thanks goes to my family and friends. There are far too many to name, but please know that I thank you and appreciate each and every one of you.

Acknowledgments

Thank you to all my readers and supporters! I can only hope that I have once again created a quality read that captures your heart, mind, and soul. Thank you from my heart for allowing me to have a small moment of time in your world.

Last but not least, a special thanks goes to a very special person, and you know who you are. Thank you for your friendship, encouragement, love and support. You are truly valued and appreciated more than you'll ever know.

With all the love in my heart,
Hazel Ro

CHAPTER 1

TIFFANY

My nerves were a complete wreck. My heart was pounding so hard that it felt like it would come through my chest. All I could see was the look of betrayal and disappointment written across Terrence's face as he looked back at me before stepping onto the elevator.

With the help of my best friend, Keisha, he had prepared an amazing night for us here in suite 1307 of the Ritz-Carlton in St. Louis. Everything was perfect. Roses and lit candles were all throughout the suite. Champagne and chocolate-covered strawberries were waiting near the filled Jacuzzi tub. And even the bed was adorned with rose petals, in the shape of a heart. Terrence hadn't left out one single thing. This was supposed to be our special night, when we confessed our love for one another without any inhibitions—despite the fact that he had a wife. I wasn't sure if he'd already told her that he wanted a divorce or that he was in love with me. That wasn't my concern. All I wanted was to share the first night of the rest of our lives together.

But now it felt as if my dream had been ripped away from me.

I'd waited patiently at the suite for Terrence's arrival. I'd longed for his scent, the gentleness of his touch, and the warmth of his body next to mine. Fantasies had even danced through my mind: I'd envisioned him removing my black silk robe, laying me down on the bed, and having his way with me while giving me all of him. It was going to be a beautiful dream come true for both of us. But when he'd reached the suite, he'd found me here with David—wrapped in his arms, no less. And in a matter of seconds, that beautiful dream had turned into a big, dreadful nightmare. After roughing up David, he'd turned on his heels and left the suite without uttering a word. I'd run to the door and watched him charge down the hallway to the elevators.

I could only imagine what was going through Terrence's mind. Did he really think I'd invited David here? Did he honestly believe there'd been more to my and David's embrace than an expression of friendship?

My heart literally felt like it was in the pit of my stomach as I tried now to concentrate on what to do next. Oblivious to everything around me, I grabbed my phone from the nightstand and tried calling him, but just as I figured, he didn't answer. In fact, his phone didn't even ring. The call went straight to his voicemail, so I knew that he'd turned off his phone. After trying several times more to reach him, I shot him a couple of texts, begging him to at least return my call.

"God, if only he would just hear me out and let me explain. I know that we can fix this," I said aloud to myself.

"Listen, I know you don't want to hear it, Tiff, but maybe this was all for the best." I was surprised to hear David's voice, as I had forgotten all about him being here. He walked from the bathroom while wiping his face with a towel as he continued sharing his unwanted thoughts. "I mean, did you see how he attacked me? That man's temper is outrageous, and you don't need a guy like that in your life. And, hell, he better damn well hope I don't press charges either."

My mind was so caught up with what had happened with Terrence, and David was the furthest thing from it. Although, when I thought about it, *he* was actually the one to blame for everything that had happened. As I glanced over at him sitting comfortably on the bed, my anger started to boil deep down inside me. Had it not been for David, Terrence would have never left the way he had, and we'd probably be making love by now. Yet as I looked at David, I was suddenly reminded why he was here in the first place. With everything inside me, I tried to muster up a little compassion for the man I had once been engaged to marry. Of course, I never would have imagined that David would be diagnosed with cancer, and my heart truly went out to him. But in all honesty, that's as far as it went. All I wanted was to get rid of him so that I could be alone and try to find Terrence. With that in mind, I took a deep breath and considered the best way to let him down.

"Uh, David, look, I know that you're going through a pretty rough time right now, but tonight was just not the night for this, all right?" I said as I paced back and forth. "If you haven't noticed already, I had plans here, with Terrence, and his seeing you here may have messed up everything. I have to find him and somehow try to explain this and fix things, so I hope you won't mind leaving."

"All right, sure. If that's what you want, then I'll leave," he said, still not budging from the bed. "I guess I probably shouldn't be here, anyway, but I was so desperate to see you, Tiff. It was like I said on the phone when we spoke yesterday. I *needed* to see you face-to-face."

"And, like I remember telling you, I *needed* to think about that. So, this just wasn't the time or the place to pop up on me the way you did, David. And now everything is ruined."

Then, as I was speaking, it finally dawned on me. All at once, I stopped pacing and looked at him firmly.

"Wait a minute. How exactly *did* you know I was here anyway, David? Because if I recall correctly, I said nothing more than I'd come back to St. Louis when we spoke. I didn't even know that I was coming here until earlier today. So, how is it that you showed up at *this* hotel, at *this* very suite, tonight, knowing I'd be here? And please don't say anything stupid, like it was all some big coincidence, because we both know that's not the truth."

His behavior suddenly seemed odd. He started to wiggle around, refused to look directly at me, and struggled to get his words out. "Well, I . . . I . . . I hope you don't get upset, Tiff, but since I already knew you were here in St. Louis, I hopped on the first flight. All I planned on doing was meeting you at your old house to talk to you. But then I saw a post on Facebook that Keisha had made. She posted something about taking her bestie to the Ritz and hoping all your dreams came true. That's when I decided to get an Uber here instead going to the house. I wasn't even positive about what I was doing, but I thought it was worth a shot."

He took a deep breath and went on. "Anyway, I lied to the young lady downstairs and told her I had an emergency and had to speak with you. I even gave her a hundred-dollar bill for her trouble. Then, after confirming you were here, she gave me the room number. But you really have to understand, I felt so hopeless when I found out about my illness, Tiff. All I wanted was to right my wrongs with you from the past in case anything happens to me." He paused for a second as he met my gaze. "I'm sorry. I truly feel miserable about everything, but I felt like I had no other choice. But, please believe me, I had no idea about you meeting up with this Terrence guy. I promise," he pleaded, his hands raised, as if he were surrendering the whole truth and nothing but the truth.

"David, I can't believe you. Tracking me down here? And lying and paying the desk attendant downstairs? All of that is damn near considered stalking. And you're talking about pressing charges against Terrence? I should press charges against you."

"Listen, I did it only because I *had* to see you. It couldn't wait until you came back to Texas." Out of nowhere one lonely tear began to creep down his cheek. He reached out and grabbed my arm, then took both my hands in his. His tone softened when he said, "I needed to see your face again, Tiff, and look into your eyes. I had to know that despite everything that's happened between us, I'll have you by my side while I try to battle through this illness. Please, you have to understand."

My heart sank further as I watched the man whom I had once planned on marrying wallow in his grief in front of me. As much as I wanted to be angry with him, I couldn't. Besides, I knew I would live to regret it if things didn't turn out the way I hoped. So, I released my hands from his, tightened my robe, and walked a few steps away from him to put some distance between us.

"David, I already promised you that I would be here for you. I meant it when I said I would try to help you in every way that I possibly can, as much as I can. But I also gotta be totally honest with you too. That's really all that I can offer. If you're expecting anything more than that, then you need to know that I can't give it to you. I mean, what we shared was special in its time, but that part of my life is over, and I've moved on."

"I know. I guess a small part of me hoped that I could somehow win your heart back before, well, you know . . . before it's too late." He dropped his head in his hands.

It crushed me to see him that way. I started to feel like maybe I was being too rough. I had to admit that he *was* dealing with a major illness, one that could possibly have a negative outcome. I had no idea what he was truly going through or feeling inside. So, as much as I wanted and *needed* him gone, I decided to ease up a bit and be a little more compassionate. I sat down next to him on the bed, placed my hand on his knee, and tried to offer a sense of comfort. However, I couldn't help but keep my eyes focused on the door, still praying that Terrence would show back up.

"Listen, I'm sorry, David. I know that finding out you have cancer has to be a lot for you and that you're trying your best to make amends for past mistakes. But to be truthful, when it comes to you and me, too much has happened between us that I still can't forget just yet."

"Or that you can't seem to *forgive*, you mean."

"Well, I guess that's kind of true too. It's just that forgiveness takes time. It's not something that happens overnight. And, unfortunately, not enough time has passed since you did what you did to me."

His eyes locked with mine, and I could almost see a hint of sincerity in them. "Look, I know I messed up before, but this whole cancer thing has really opened my eyes to what's most important and to how much I really do love you. I only want a chance to make up for where I went wrong before. And I promise, I'm done with all the lies and deceit. I *need* you right now, and I want you back, Tiff."

I saw his lips moving and heard the words coming from them, but I still couldn't believe my ears as he poured his heart out to me. And, even more so, that it was happening right now. All I could think was that I had to find a way to bring some closure to this situation without hurting him. "David, I don't think—"

Before I could get another word out, I suddenly felt his lips cover mine as he gently kissed me. There was no way he had the nerve to pull a stunt like this, I thought. And as I pulled away, I almost wanted to haul off and smack him, but out of nowhere, there was a knock on the door. Right away both our heads turned in that direction as if in one motion. I knew it had to be Terrence, and I figured he'd come back to straighten this whole mess out. And although I couldn't have been happier, I feared what might happen if he found David still here.

Panicking, I jumped off the bed and started to yank on David's arm while whispering to him, "David, you have to get out of here before Terrence sees you again." My eyes went from him to the door and back to him when another knock sounded. However, instead of reacting like I hoped he would, David just sat there, looking like he could care less.

"I'm sorry, Tiff. I don't feel comfortable leaving you here with that guy," he said, his volume of voice at a normal level, and I was sure Terrence could hear him.

"It's not what *you* feel comfortable with, David. So, please leave," I whispered.

As I watched him get up in an unconcerned manner, knocks sounded once again. Suddenly, I had a change of thought. "No, no, wait. The closet. You have to hide in the closet, okay? Then I'll distract him, and when he's not looking, you can go ahead and sneak out." I pushed his back toward the closet, not giving him a chance to offer up any rebuttal. The more I thought about Terrence being on the other side of that door, the more I knew that I was doing the right thing. There was no way on earth he would ever be able to understand David still being here. And to tell the truth, I still didn't understand it myself.

"David, please, if you love me the way you say you do, then you'll get in the closet and leave quietly when you get the chance." I was using his same manipulation on him, and that was when he said the one thing that made me feel sorry for him all over again.

He stopped in his tracks and turned to look me dead in the eyes. "Tiff, I know you want me to go, and I will, but I also have to be honest with you. I'm scared. I mean, what if the doctors can't cure this? What if I don't have much longer to live? That's *really* why I came here tonight. And that's why I kissed you. It might be my last time with you."

Being between a rock and a hard place was an understatement. Just the mere thought of him dying from this illness turned my mind completely away from Terrence and back to him . . . but for only a moment. I wanted to be encouraging. I even wanted to be supportive. But the truth was, I just could do that right now.

"David, listen, neither of us knows what the future holds, but you're not going anywhere anytime soon if I have a say in this," I said softly so that Terrence wouldn't hear us. This way when I finally answered the door, I could act as if I had been sleeping and hadn't heard his initial knocks. "You can fight this, and I'll be here for you every step of the way. I promise, we'll fight this together."

"You really mean that?"

"You have my word, okay?" I said, reaching out to embrace him and praying in the back of my mind that I wouldn't end up regretting my words. "But listen, right now I need to handle this with Terrence, so I'm asking you to hide in the closet and then leave peacefully."

David hugged me again, and with a slight hesitation but not putting up a fight, he walked toward the closet as I went to the door. I just stood there as I allowed my robe to fall off one of my shoulders, smoothed down my hair, and took a deep breath. Then I opened the door.

"Terrence, I—"

"Good evening, ma'am. I have room service that was ordered by Mr. Montgomery. He requested for it to be delivered at this time."

"Oh, um, of course. Mr. Montgomery isn't here yet. But please bring it in, and thank you so much," was all that I could say, hoping he couldn't read the disappointment written all over my face. I had wanted it to be Terrence so badly, but now I had to be honest with myself and face the fact that he might not return.

I watched as the gentleman pushed the cart into the room. When he turned, I gave him a fake smile as I handed him a tip. He wished me a good evening and left. I closed the door, and feeling stuck in place, I stood there, allowing the tears to flow freely from my eyes. I couldn't move. I couldn't blink or even swallow. The tears had taken over when out of nowhere I was reminded of my unwanted guest and the very reason that my night had turned out this way.

"Come here. It's okay. Everything's going to be all right." I felt David's arms surround me. I wanted to hate him for all that had happened tonight, but the truth was, he was my only solace at that point. He took me over to the bed, laid me down, lay beside me, and held me.

"I love you, Tiffany, more than you'll ever know," he softly whispered in my ear.

I heard his words, but there was no way I could form my lips to return them. Mostly because I blamed him for the pain I felt at this very moment. Did I still care for David and want the best for him? Of course. But anything more was an impossibility. I loved him, but not in the same way that he loved me.

He must have noticed my overall discomfort with this entire situation, because not another word came from his lips. Instead, he pulled me closer and held me tighter. Lying there, I kept trying to make sense of things. However, after a few minutes, I closed my eyes and allowed my body to find relief with the one lying next to me. With both our worlds in such turmoil, I knew it was what we both needed at that very moment. So, I stopped putting up a fight and simply exhaled.

CHAPTER 2

TERRENCE

My cell phone buzzed for what seemed like the millionth time within the past few hours. When I glanced down at it, I noticed the alerts I'd received for several text messages. My eyes zeroed in on one from Tiffany. The second I saw her name, the anger inside me started to build. Vivid images of David holding her flashed before my eyes, and my aggression almost got the best of me again. Instantly, I thought back to having him pinned against the wall and wanting to choke the life out of him. However, I'd known that if I did, I would be walking out of there in handcuffs instead of as a free man.

Rather than responding to Tiffany's or anyone else's messages, I pressed the END button and turned my cell phone off completely without giving it a second thought. I was still so hurt and angry that all I wanted was to take out my hostility in the worst way. In fact, I wanted Tiffany to feel the same pain and sense of betrayal that I felt at that very moment. That was the reason why I'd texted Patricia from the airport, asking her to meet me here at the house. I wasn't exactly sure if what had happened with Tiffany tonight was a sign that I needed to fix my marriage, but here I was, waiting anxiously for my wife's arrival.

Standing in the middle of my empty living-room floor, I looked around at what used to feel like a home to me and tried to understand the turn that my life had taken out of nowhere. When I first left to see Pops in Memphis and then to St. Louis for Tiffany, I had envisioned things turning out in the complete opposite way that they had. In the back of my mind, I had seen Pops making a miraculous full recovery. As for me and Tiff, I had thought it would be the beginning of our life together as one. And never would I have imagined that I would be entertaining life with Patricia once again. But in just a few hours, things had taken a turn for the worse, and I was questioning everything: my marriage, my future, and even God.

As I tried to make it all add up, I realized that as crazy as it sounded, the only person that remained constant and consistent in my life was Patricia. Even with all her madness and the drama we'd gone through, she had never cheated on me, that I knew of, and had never talked about divorce. She truly wanted to be with me *for better or for worse*, whether I felt the same or not. I guessed that was why I had started feeling that maybe I owed her this much. Maybe I hadn't given our marriage a fair chance, because of her dramatics and, more so, because of my feelings for Tiffany. But still, I wasn't totally sure.

My mind was so boggled that my head began to throb harder and harder. I couldn't focus on one thing as the entire night's events circled through my mind. Then all I kept hearing was my stepmother's voice ringing in my ear, telling me that he was gone, as I stepped onto the elevator at the hotel. I still had the same dryness in my mouth, which had made it difficult for me to talk. And my chest had a lingering heaviness, making it hard to breathe no matter how I tried to gather myself. It was like a nightmare had been replaying repeatedly, one that I hadn't been able to wake up from.

The strangest thing, though, was that I thought I'd prepared myself for this moment, since the doctors hadn't given Pops long to live, but now that it was happening, it all seemed so sudden. Especially because I felt like he and I were just beginning to rekindle our relationship. And now I no longer had a chance to make up for all the lost time. Suddenly, my thoughts of Pops were interrupted by a sound coming from the other side of the front door. I stood still and watched closely as the doorknob twisted open and Patricia walked into our dark, empty living room. She came to a stop and looked at me with confusion written all over her face.

After what seemed like hours but was only a minute, she began to speak. "Terrence? What's going on? Why did you ask me to come here?" Her tone was soft and sweet. She had abandoned that nagging voice, which I'd become accustomed to.

I didn't answer her questions, though. Instead, I took her face between my hands and began to kiss her. They weren't mere kisses of love between a husband and wife either. They were strong, forceful, and wildly passionate. With each touch of our lips, I tried to convey just how much I missed her and wanted her. Her scent, her body, her warmth, her tenderness—all of her. I knew it may have been for the wrong reasons, but I needed Patricia in the worst way. I needed a release from all the pain I was feeling inside, and more than anything, I knew that she was ready and willing to receive me.

All at once, she pulled away from me, and we both gazed at one another long and hard. I could read in her eyes that she was questioning if this was real. That was when I began to undress her slowly while kissing her body from head to toe. My mouth slowly made its way from her neck to her nipples to her belly button and, finally, to her ultimate treasure. I could tell she longed for me as much as I did her, as she moaned over and over while grabbing the top of my bald head the entire time.

"Ooh, baby. Please, don't stop," she whispered.

Fulfilling her request, I pulled her down on the bare floor with me and laid her on her back. With all the madness that had gone on for so long between us, I hadn't admired her body in its purity in what seemed like an eternity. She was beautiful, and I had to pause for a moment simply to take her in. Then after pleasuring her a bit longer, I climbed on top and thrust all of me inside her. However, as my manhood found its home, my mind drifted off to a totally different place than where I was at the moment. All at once I saw Tiffany's face staring back at me as I stood at the elevator doors.

Don't you still love me, Terrence? I could hear her asking me.

"Yes, baby. Yes, I do," I said out loud.

Then don't leave. Please stay and just tell me that you still love me, she said and reached out to me.

"I love you, baby. I promise, I love you." I began moving toward her, until I heard Patricia's voice.

"Oh, Terrence, I still love you too," Pat said back to me.

What the hell is happening? I thought. It was Tiffany's face that I could see, but Patricia's voice was speaking back to me. Right away, I was reminded of where I was and what was truly taking place. Then, all at once, my heart started to beat faster, and my strokes became more aggressive when the visions of Tiffany's face turned ones of David's. There he was, looking at me and smirking, as if he'd won the war. I wanted to hurt him for destroying my night with Tiffany, but she stood in the middle of us, begging me to calm down. That was when my aggression took over even more. The harder I pushed myself inside Patricia, the louder her moans became as she tightened her legs around my waist. All I wanted was for all of it to be over and for this night to be what it was supposed to be, with no David or Patricia around, only me and Tiff. That was when I realized that I wasn't supposed to be here now with Pat, or ever, for that matter. What we had was over, and that fact became painfully clear to me in the heat of this very moment.

As the sweat poured off my face and onto her, my manhood began to swell. My legs tensed up when I felt my release was in sight. Not even a second later, everything that had built up inside me came pouring out into her. Happily, she took all of me with pure satisfaction. Then my body, limp from being physically and mentally drained, sagged on top of hers. There was so much that I had to figure out, but it was clear that the one thing on my mind was getting back to Tiffany. I rolled my large frame off Pat's helpless yet satisfied body and came to a rest on my back. I could feel her hand begin to rub my chest as she cuddled next to me.

"Terrence, thank you. Thank you so much for this and for giving our marriage another chance. I don't know what made you change your mind, but the fact that you're here right now means the world to me. I know we can fix things. And I'm so sorry about my behavior and all the threats I made. I love you, baby, and I promise to do better at showing it. As a matter of fact, as soon as the sun rises, I can call the movers and have them bring all our things from the storage back to the house and—"

I honestly hated myself for this, and I really couldn't find the words at that moment to say anything. Rather than responding, I cut her off by pushing her hand away and hopping up. "I have to go Pat," I said without even looking at her. I picked up my clothes and headed toward the bathroom.

"Wait a minute, Terrence. What's wrong? Baby, where are you going?"

Still, I didn't say anything back to her. I simply closed the bathroom door behind me and turned on the shower. I knew that Patricia would never understand, because I didn't understand it all myself. Yet the last thing I needed tonight was another argument. I had to figure out things with my father and Tiffany, and now that there would be no more second-guessing myself, I had to determine how quickly I could have my divorce from Patricia finalized.

nity to get out of there. Then, once outside, I envisioned myself pounding the steering wheel while yelling at the top of my lungs. Half of me wanted to go back inside and rip the jerk to shreds, while the other half craved to be next to Pops and somehow miraculously bring him back. I couldn't make sense of anything other than taking off at full speed.

For a while, I wrestled to see clearly while bobbing and weaving in and out of traffic as if I were in a high-speed chase. The entire time, I drove with a sense of urgency while headed in no real direction. I thought about going to the nearest casino, but my pockets decided against that for me. Then I thought of calling Tiffany's best friend, Keisha. I knew that she had to know something since she was the one who helped me put the whole surprise together in the first place. However, as quickly as I thought about it, I decided against it even faster. My intuition told me that she would only suggest I go back to the hotel and try to work things out with Tiff. But that just wasn't anything I was able to handle at that moment. All I really wanted was to ease the tension I was feeling from the night's events. So, before I knew it, I had Google lead me to the nearest cigar bar.

At first, my plan was to drown my sorrows in one stiff drink after the next. I wanted to get so wasted that I would pass out in my truck until the sun came up. But after pulling my Escalade into the parking lot of the Black Room Cigar Lounge, I parked in a spot farthest from the building and took a deep breath as I pressed my head back against the headrest. I was sure that's when I dozed off and had that dreadful dream of Pat and me. I couldn't believe that for a few moments I started to wonder if God was really telling me to try to salvage whatever piece of marriage I had with her. I thought that maybe I owed her and the boys that much. But honestly, I knew if I did go back, it would be for all the wrong reasons. Of course, I couldn't deny that once upon a time I did love her, but somewhere along the way, that love had turned to a strong dislike. Over the years, she'd just become so insecure that it sucked the life right out of me, her, and whatever remnant of our marriage we had left. I felt like I tried my best to love her, care for her, and provide for her as a husband should. Yet nothing I'd done had stopped the constant madness that she'd been putting us both through all this time. That was why before coming to St. Louis, I was positive that there was no way I could continue this charade. But that experience in that hotel room tonight almost made me have second thoughts altogether. Thankfully, the dream had merely confirmed what I already knew, and I no longer had any qualms about shooting down the entire theory of working things out with her. What we had shared was completely over, especially since my heart was elsewhere.

Glancing at my cell phone, which was lying on the center console, I noticed it kept lighting up and vibrating. Hesitantly picking it up, I saw I had missed back-to-back calls from my stepmother and Tiffany. I knew that I needed to call my stepmother and let her know that I was all right, but the way I felt, I didn't have the energy to do even that much. Part of me also figured that she was calling because she wanted and needed consoling as much as I did, especially now that we had only each other. However, I honestly had nothing left inside me to give to anyone. I felt completely wiped out, and I owed my exhaustion to the very person I loved the most. The one who had caused most of my pain from the last hour or so.

"Dammit! How could you do this, Tiff? How could you allow this creep back into your life, especially with every-thing between us?" I hit the steering wheel again as hard as I possibly could. "I always had a gut feeling that sooner or later he'd try to slither his way back into your life. I just never thought you would actually allow it. Why couldn't you just leave him in your past, where he belonged? What in the hell made you entertain this jerk after all that he's put you through?" I muttered, as if Tiffany were sitting beside me. My stomach began to rumble from the disgust that I felt from reminiscing about it all.

My thoughts then drifted back to a year ago when she and I first met. She was dealing with a nasty breakup from David at the time, while I had been putting up with Patricia's daily shenanigans. There was no denying the immediate attraction, but because of our situations, our meeting had happened at the most *inopportune* time. With that in mind, we'd planned on being nothing more than friends and coworkers, yet we'd soon found that it was much easier said than done. We began talking on a regular basis, spending time together outside work hours, and allowing ourselves to be vulnerable and to smile again. Needless to say, in our weakness, we found peace and comfort in one another. I wanted desperately to get us back to that. I wanted every day of our future together to feel just like the very beginning, when things were new, innocent, and good. That was what tonight was supposed to be all about. I'd planned this amazing evening for the two of us, during which I would confess my love to her. Of course, I still had the issue of divorcing Patricia, but in the meantime, I needed Tiffany to know exactly how I felt before we allowed another minute to slip by. I had assumed she felt the same too, but from the looks of it all, the joke was on me.

As my thoughts meandered from Tiffany and then to David, what I didn't seem to understand was how he'd ended up at the hotel with her in the first place. She knew I was on my way there, so none of it made any sense at all.

"Maybe I should call and talk to Monica," I said, reasoning aloud. She was my and Tiffany's boss at the school, but she had also become a close friend, as well as a voice of reason for the two of us. She knew about all the craziness I'd dealt with, with Patricia over the years, and she certainly was well versed in the drama Tiffany had experienced with David. Which was why she'd been the main one rooting for us to finally be together. With that in mind, something inside me told me that if anyone could help me clear things up, she could. Not to mention, I needed to tell her of Pop's passing. But then my eyes glanced at the time on the dashboard.

"No, no, Terrence, it's way too late to call and disturb her at home," I told myself, still speaking aloud. Plus, I knew there was no way I'd ever get out the words to say that Pops was gone.

I finally decided to lay everything aside until I returned home. My mind was made up: I would head back to Texas on the first flight out in the morning. But for the moment, I lacked the willpower to continue fighting the urge I had inside. All I wanted was to sit alone and drown my troubles in booze. When I stepped out of my truck, I could almost taste the alcohol sliding down my throat. For the next few hours, I didn't want to think about anyone, talk to anyone, or be bothered with anyone. This moment was all for me, and I would simply deal with everything and everyone else once I stepped on Texas soil tomorrow.

CHAPTER 4

MALAYSIA

Why I continually allowed Toni and Larisse to talk me into going out was beyond me. I could just as well stay at home and watch reruns on the HGTV channel, which had become one of my favorite pastimes.

Well, I guess this will have to do. I mean, we're only going out for drinks anyway. I reasoned with myself while looking at my outfit in my full-length mirror. I had decided on some simple dark denim jeans, my favorite graphic tee, and sandals for the night. Fortunately, I didn't have to fuss with my hair much, because I'd just had it put in a protective style of braids. And as for makeup, plain ole eyeliner and lip gloss were it for me. After going over to my jewelry box, I threw on a pair of earrings and bangles, and voilà, I was ready in twenty minutes, with no fuss. However, I could already hear Toni's mouth when I got into the car.

Girl, where are you going dressed like that? And where's your makeup? How do you ever plan on catching a husband like this?

Toni was my best friend, but she could be a little demanding most times. I laughed to myself. She and Larisse were sisters, and both had been with their husbands for quite some time. Come to think of it, Toni and Charles were high school sweethearts, while Larisse and her husband, Damon, met during college. So, of course, since they were both married and had families of their own, they wanted the same for me. It was not that I didn't want a husband and children too. It was just that after things went sour with my son's father, I stopped looking or even considering marriage. Besides, most of the men that I had bumped into didn't have many of the qualities that I desired in a potential mate. Things like an established career, a home, transportation, and a savings account. These things were the mere basics, in my opinion. However, I'd come across more and more adult men *without* them, and I just didn't have time to take care of or raise a grown-ass man.

Anyway, I had way more important things to focus on in my single life right now. I needed to get my eighteen-year-old son through college, work a lot of overtime to pay off some old debt, and simply get back to life as I knew it after a relationship gone bad. With all of that going on, I just didn't feel I was in the right state of mind to meet anyone new. Although, let Toni and Larisse tell it, I'd been single long enough. And Toni constantly reminded me that if I didn't want to grow old alone, then *now* was the time to find the perfect mate. *If* he existed at all, was what I thought.

I knew that wishing they would change their minds and stay home tonight with their husbands was for naught, and sure enough, I suddenly heard Toni blowing her horn outside. The damn girl was blowing that horn like the police were after her or something, so immediately, I had a gut feeling it was going to be one of *those* types of nights. Grabbing my bag and heading toward the door, I hoped that the night would hurry to an end. I also prayed that not one man with a bunch of gold chains around his neck and a grill in his mouth tried to talk to me. As of late, it seemed like that was the only type of man to approach me whenever we went out, the wannabe-rapper type of guy, and I was completely over it. If there was a Mr. Perfect for me, he would have to be perfect in every single way. And although I wanted to be optimistic, I couldn't help but feel like that he would be too good to be true.

Anyway, after I set my alarm system and my feet hit the porch, I heard Toni yelling at me from her car, just as I had figured she would.

"Malaysia, what the hell do you have on? We're not going bowling or anything. Honey, we are trying to catch you a man. So, go back in the house and change clothes."

Trying to tune her out, I kept walking toward them and got inside her white Malibu. Her husband must have had it detailed, because it was as clean as a whistle and was shining in the evening light. Making myself comfortable in the back, I peeked at Larisse, who was sitting there quiet as a mouse in the front passenger seat, while Toni continued to do all the talking, or should I say yelling.

"Hey, y'all," I said in a nonchalant and dry tone.

"Hey, y'all nothing. Where's your formfitting clothes? Your heels? Why aren't you showing a little skin or something? And where on earth is your makeup, Malaysia?" Toni shouted.

I inhaled and exhaled while gazing out the window, wishing I'd never answered my phone earlier. But had I done that, I knew I would never hear the end of it at work tomorrow. Not only were we best friends, but we were also co-workers in the medical billing department of Centene Corporation in St. Louis. Toni and Larisse had grown to love their careers there, but for me, it was only a J-O-B to keep the bills paid.

"Tee, I didn't feel like all of that tonight, all right? We're only going to have a couple of drinks, and I'm not looking for anybody anyway. So, I wanted to be comfortable, casual, and cute, okay?"

"Look, maybe *you're* not looking, but the men definitely will. Ain't I right, sis?" she said and gave Larisse a high five, like she'd just made the statement of the year.

"Yep, you sure are, sis."

My lips folded because I had expected that from Larisse. She was the older one of the two sisters, but she basically went along with anything and everything Toni said. Tee, as we both affectionately called her, was known as the drill sergeant, and we were her army.

I tried changing the subject from my wardrobe. "Where are we going tonight anyway?"

"Girl, just sit back and relax, all right? We're going to a new spot over on Clayton. Charles said it's real smooth and laid back, and some nights they even have a live band playing. He said we'll love it," Toni replied.

"Well, live band or not, girl, I really don't feel like being surrounded by a lot of heavy smoke, half-naked women, and a bunch of horny-ass old men all night. So, can we just go somewhere and pick up a couple bottles of wine, grab some wings or something, and go back to my place instead?"

She rolled her eyes at me in the rearview mirror and kept talking like I hadn't said a word.

"Malaysia, look, we are only going to be there for a minute. We'll look around and see what kind of chocolate is in the place while letting the men get a good look at you. And if it's nothing going on, then we'll leave, all right?"

"Yeah, I guess. But you almost make me feel like I'm nothing more than a piece of meat or something . . . letting the men get a *good look* at me."

"Well, that's because in this case, honey, you are. And trust me, they are going to be ready to get them a bite of Ms. Malaysia."

Yeah, that's what I'm afraid of, I thought, without saying it out loud. She and Larisse both fell out laughing while giving each other high fives again. I, on the other hand, didn't see anything funny. Then my mind wandered off, and I scolded myself, because I remembered a new episode of *Love It or List It* was airing tonight. However, instead of being a sourpuss all night, I let it go and told Toni to turn up the music as I let my window down to take in the night's breeze.

Twenty minutes later we were pulling into the parking lot of the Black Room Cigar Lounge. I was confused yet thankful all at the same time. Confused because for it to be one of the newer spots to go to, it appeared to be pretty empty. And thankful for that exact same reason. This way we could go in and have a couple of quick drinks, and then I could hurry home to watch TV.

Larisse finally spoke up. "Damn. I wonder where the crowd is?"

"Definity not here," I said from the back.

"Well, we're still going in to take a peek around, and lucky for you, I have some heels in my trunk that are just your size," Toni told me.

"C'mon, Tee. Give me a break already. I don't feel like tiptoeing in heels all night."

"Girl, listen, I didn't have much control over that outfit of yours, but at least you are going to put some heels on. And trust me, they'll make your legs and butt look a whole lot better," she said, giving me a smack on my rear as we exited the car.

"Whatever."

Despite my better judgment, I went ahead and did what she said and threw the heels on. Then the three of us swished our tails inside, and I could see immediately why they called the place the Black Room. It was extremely dark, to the point where it was difficult to see what was right in front of you. There were mahogany-colored leather recliners throughout, and they had old-school music playing on the overhead speakers. Toward the middle of the room, I could see a bar, and farther back were a few pool tables and a small area in which to throw darts. Off to the right side was a small stage, where, I assumed, the live band would play. As we continued to look around, I started coughing from the thick smoke hitting my throat.

"Are you all right, girl?" Toni asked, scowling at me.

"Yeah, I think I'm good, Tee," I assured her while taking off my foggy glasses and wiping them the bottom of my T-shirt.

"Oh, and give me those glasses too," she said, quickly snatching them away from me. "You will *not* be needing these tonight."

"But wait, you know I really can't see without them, and it's already dark as hell in this place." I'd already begun squinting and trying to make out what was in front of me.

"And you don't have to see. Just hold on to my arm and follow me back to the bar. Then simply sit and look cute while the men see you."

I grabbed her arm, and we walked over to three stools at the bar and sat down. That was when I snatched my glasses right back from her, so that I could get a better look at what was going on. In my opinion, it didn't make sense to find a man if you didn't even know what he looked like. After getting comfortable, we all ordered our drinks and began to laugh and talk, mainly about things that had happened at work.

"Girl, did you see the way Pam bent over in front of Will yesterday at the copier?" Toni exclaimed. "I was surprised that booty of hers didn't rip her skirt right up the back. She practically scared the life out of the poor boy."

Larisse and I fell out laughing as we recalled the incident Toni spoke of. Our co-worker, Pam, was always on the hunt, flirting with anything in the building that looked halfway decent. I had to admit that she had a nice, voluptuous figure, but she wore clothes that were so tight that she resembled a popped-open can of biscuits. Will, however, was the new maintenance guy who had started a week ago. In that short amount of time, Pam already had the young man scared to come to our floor of the building to take the trash out. We were still laughing and talking about her when a fairly nice-looking guy walked up to the bar and approached us a second later.

"Well, thank God he doesn't have a gold grill," I whispered to Larisse.

His cologne was so heavy that it spoke for him before he even said a word. Not to mention his Versace shirt and matching Versace shoes, which you could spot from across the room. I would bet my last dollar in my pocketbook that he was wearing every dime he had to his name.

Sticking out his hand and flashing his Versace watch, he said, "Hello, ladies. I'm Aaron."

We all said hello in unison.

"I had to come over when I saw all three of you beautiful ladies sitting here by yourselves," he told us.

"Really?" Toni said.

"Yes, really. I have a table over there if you would like to join me. And I can buy you all another round of drinks if you like."

We presumed Toni was the spokesperson for the group, since she answered him first, while Larisse and I remained quiet, sipping our drinks.

"Well, Aaron, I think we're all right with getting our next round of drinks. Besides, we kind of like the view from over here at the bar. But maybe we'll make our way over to you a little later, okay?"

"Now, c'mon, don't make a man beg, ladies. You're not going to let me sit all alone over there, are you?"

"Did you come here alone?" I asked.

He gave me a look that said if he wasn't trying to flirt, he would tell me exactly where to go.

"Let me ask you something," Toni said. "Do you always come on so strong? And do you always have trouble accepting no for an answer?"

He laughed inwardly, and I saw that his energy had waned and he felt somewhat awkward. It seemed that Toni and I must have thrown him off his game a bit.

"Yes, ladies, I did come alone, and to be honest, I don't think I came on strong at all. To answer your other question, it is a bit hard for me to accept no when it's something or someone I really want. So, can you blame a man for trying? Besides, I think that I'm the only man in the room confident enough to approach three women as beautiful as yourselves, so why not? And instead of buying your own drinks all night, why not allow me?"

"You're confident, huh, Aaron?" Toni asked.

"Yeah, he has to be confident to wear that shirt and shoes," I whispered to Larisse. We giggled to ourselves again, missing his whole response to Toni's question. Then, to my surprise, instead of urging Aaron to go along his way, she continued to entertain him.

"So, are you single? No wife or girlfriend?"

"Very much single and ready to mingle, baby," he answered before taking a sip of his drink and allowing us to get a glimpse of his empty ring finger, as if that meant anything.

"And what about you?" he asked in return.

"Oh me? Well, I'm happily married, and so is my sister over there." She pointed to Larisse. "But my girlfriend here is single and is mingling as well." She began rubbing her hand across my back.

I could have kicked Toni right off that damn stool for saying that to this creep. And the second she did, he stepped closer to me, grinning from ear to ear.

"My type of woman. So, are you going to tell me your name, beautiful, or are you going keep sitting here looking mean all night?"

"My name is Shaquan, and I apologize for my facial expression, I have RBF," I said, cracking up on the inside while hearing Larisse almost spit her drink out. Shaquan was my go-to name whenever I didn't want to tell a man my real name.

"RBF? I'm sorry, but what's that?" He looked around at all three of us, trying to figure out what the joke was.

"RBF is Resting Bitch Face," I answered. "So, I guess you could say that I can't help the way I look." I rolled my eyes, praying that he would take a hint already and leave.

"Oh, I see. Well, Shaquan is a beautiful name for a very beautiful woman, who I hope to have the pleasure of getting to know a lot better—"

"Whoa, whoa. Slow down now, buddy." Toni put her hands up, cutting him off. "There's some questions you need to answer correctly before you and my friend can talk more."

"Questions? All right, sure. Why not? Hit me with them," he said, shrugging his shoulders and sounding overly confident.

Toni took over from there. She ran down her list of questions that she always asked men before *approving* them for me. "So, do you own your home? Do you live alone? Do you have a car? Any young children under the age of two? Are there any women out there thinking they're your wife, girlfriend, side chick, regular booty call, or anything else? Do you like women all the time? And do you brush your teeth in the morning *and* at night?"

I was so embarrassed by my friend, but Larisse and I laughed until we cried, and we couldn't wait to hear his responses.

"Okay, well, yes, yes, yes, no, no, definitely yes, and hell yeah, of course I do. Does that take care of it for you?"

"Well, Shaquan girl, he passed my test." Toni looked at me and so did he, waiting for my response.

"Um, excuse me. I think I need to run to the ladies' room." I got up and started to head toward the back of the lounge. As I left the three of them at the bar and put my glasses back on to find the bathroom, I prayed that Aaron would take a hint and disappear by the time I returned.

Walking extremely slowly because of the darkness—and plus, my feet were killing me from wearing Toni's heels—I tried my best not to fall or appear clumsy. With that said, I held on to any piece of furniture that was nearby as I went. However, not looking silly seemed to be much easier said than done as I gripped the back of chair after chair. It was at that moment that I realized why I'd never really been a heel-wearing type of chick. They were the most uncomfortable shoes in the world to have on and walk in. Then, seconds later, my life practically flashed before my eyes when I nearly tripped over something on the floor and had to try to catch myself from falling. Luckily for me, though, a kind gentleman sitting on one of the recliners near the restrooms hopped up and offered his hand.

"Hey, are you all right?" he asked, catching hold of my arm before I had a horrific accident.

"Yeah, I'm good. If anything, I only have a bruised ego," I said, looking around at the floor, trying to see what I had almost tripped over. "I guess I shouldn't play around in other people's shoes," I added, making light of the situation, as I finally looked up and saw the man standing in front of me. "Damn . . ." It slipped out before I knew it.

He cracked a slight smile while looking back at me. His skin was dark and smooth, like milky chocolate. He had a bald head and a full black beard, which was groomed to perfection, without a hair out of place. He looked to be anywhere between six feet three and six feet five, and his muscular build held his clothing just right. Unlike Aaron, he wasn't dressed in name-brand clothing from head to toe. He simply wore some nice denim jeans and a crisp cream-colored shirt. And his eyes were by far his sexiest feature. They practically pierced right through me as he stared into mine.

"Well, I'm glad you're okay," he said, sitting back down. Then he focused more on his drink and cigar than on me. I assumed this was his way of telling me he wasn't up for meeting anyone. So, with that said, I gave a mere thanks and again made my way toward the restroom. And that was when it dawned on me. Turning back around, I called out his name, just to make sure it was him.

"Terrence, Terrence Montgomery." I hadn't seen him in ages, but there was no way I could ever forget his face. He still looked as good as he did during our college days, just a little more solid and mature now. I could tell I caught him off guard from the confused look that crossed his face and the lines in his forehead as he tried to figure out who I was.

"Uh, do we know one another? Because I have to be honest, I can't seem to put a name with the face right now," he said, continuing to squint at me, as if that would somehow make him remember.

"Trust me, it's okay. It's been a long time, so you probably wouldn't remember. Plus, I just never forget a face. We went to college together. My name is Malaysia, Malaysia Cole."

"Malaysia, Malaysia . . ." He repeated my name a couple of times, trying to jog his memory. "Wait, I do remember you," he finally said, pointing at me. "You were kind of quiet and always had your head stuck in a book. You also shared a dorm room with Deja Spencer, right?"

"Yeah, I was somewhat of a bookworm all those years ago, and yes, I shared a room with Deja, the one you were pretty crazy over back then."

He let out a modest chuckle as, it seemed to me, he went back to those years in his mind. "Wait a minute. Now, I wouldn't go as far as to say I was crazy over her. But I guess I was young and dumb, and well, she was always down for a good time, so—"

I threw my hands up, stopping him from finishing his thought, because Deja was *not* a topic I wanted to discuss at the moment. "Yeah, please spare me the details. Trust me, there's no need to explain. I get it," I said as I took a few steps closer to him.

"Wow. That was so long ago. How have you been?"

"I've been good, just working and trying to get through this thing called life. How about yourself?"

"Uh, I've had better times, but I guess you could say that I can't complain," he answered.

After getting the pleasantries out of the way, I stood there for a second, trying to come up with a way to remain in his presence for the rest of the evening. Glancing back over at the bar, I knew there was no way I was going back there. Aaron was still hanging around, and I had a gut feeling that Toni and Larisse were stuck on trying to get me hooked up with him. Besides, Terrence seemed to be a much better option than that. Although, sitting here alone, he did appear to be a little withdrawn and in his own world. I couldn't help but wonder if maybe his big and bold personality from college had simmered down that much or if there was more to his story.

Anyway, I looked around to make sure there wasn't a woman nearby who might be there with him. When I didn't see anyone who remotely appeared like they were heading back to his table or had their eyes focused in his direction, I tried to shake off all the nervous energy inside me. Not wanting to appear intrusive, I searched my mind for the right words to say, all the while swallowing the huge lump in my throat. A few seconds passed before I suddenly received my wish without me having to do any of the asking at all.

"So, would you like to sit down and have a drink with me? I could use some good company tonight if you don't mind."

I was utterly shocked that he considered me *good* company and that he had invited me to join him. I wasn't putting myself down by a long shot, but in school he and I had been complete opposites. I'd been the quiet, shy one, the one who was always studying, while he had been one of the campus's star athletes and had always partied. A guy like him never hung out with a girl like me. But now, since he had offered, I wasn't about to pass up the opportunity. After approaching him and taking the recliner next to him, I quickly asked an important question before getting my hopes up too high.

"So, are you married now?"

"Uh, no, not anymore. I'm divorced. And you?"

"Oh, no. I was engaged a couple of years ago, but we ended up calling it off. Things just weren't working out."

"Yeah, I guess it's like that sometimes."

With that out of the way, we both let our guards down and found ourselves reminiscing about the good ole college days at least for the next thirty minutes or so. That was when, all of a sudden, I noticed out of the corner of my eye Toni and Larisse approaching us.

"That bathroom must have been pretty far away, huh?" Toni joked while looking at me and then looking at Terrence. Neither of them had to say a word, because I could see the curiosity written all over their faces. I could only imagine the conversation I was in for at work.

"I'm sorry, y'all. I bumped into an old college friend on the way to the ladies' room. Terrence, these are my best friends, Toni and Larisse. And this is Mr. Terrence Montgomery."

They all greeted each other with hellos and handshakes.

"Well, we were going to head out, but since you're talking, I guess we'll go back over to the bar until you're ready," Toni announced as I gave her a look that said they better go back to the bar or hang out with Aaron or something.

"Or I can take you home if your girls are ready to go now," Terrence offered. I watched his full lips take a puff from his cigar. If only he knew I was more than happy to oblige. That was why I spoke up before giving either one of the sisters an opportunity to shoot down his offer. Knowing Toni as well as I did, though, she would definitely put up a fight before agreeing to leave me there with someone she didn't know.

"That sounds good with me, so you two can go ahead and leave. I'll give you a call sometime tomorrow," I said.

"Um, I'm sorry, Terrence, but can I have a second to speak to my girl privately?" Toni pulled me out of my seat and over to the side, where he couldn't hear us.

"Girl, now you know anytime we go out, we leave together. We come together and leave together. That's always been the pact, and you know it," Toni told me, her tone serious.

"I know, but this time it's different, Tee. I already know him, so it's not like you're leaving me with a complete stranger. Trust me, I'll be fine."

"No, you *knew* him, and the only reason it's different this time is that you like his fine ass. And don't try to tell me you don't, because you're gushing all over the place. I mean, just look at you over here, grinning from ear to ear and damn near drooling over the man."

"Okay, so maybe I do like him a little, but, Tee, please . . . You and Larisse have wanted me to meet someone for the longest, and finally I have, unlike Mr. Versace himself."

"Speaking of Mr. Versace, or Aaron, Larisse and I found that he's actually a pretty decent guy if you would just give him a chance."

"Yeah, he is a really cool guy," Larisse chimed in, following her sister's lead.

"Well, decent, cool, or whatever, he's not for me, all right?"

"Oh, and Mr. College Friend is?" Toni shot back.

"Look, Tee, are we going to stand over here arguing all night about this or what?"

She folded her arms and stuck out her lips, like she was my mother giving it some thought before agreeing to it. "And how do you know this man isn't married, anyway, or involved with someone? As nice looking as he is, there has to be *someone* who believes they're in a relationship with him, because I refuse to believe he's single."

"Listen, I already handled that. I asked him if he was married, and he said he's divorced. So, in my mind that means he's single, free, and very *available*."

"Well, you're an adult, so I guess it's up to you. But you better call me the minute you make it home, and I'm not playing."

"Okay, Mother. I will," I answered sarcastically.

Toni rolled her eyes as we walked back over to Terrence, and then she and Larisse said their goodbyes, leaving him and me to our lonesome. I thought about how I may not have been his type all those years ago and how he'd soon learn that I was far from the quiet, shy girl he had known in college. And if I play my cards right this time, who knows, I might just be the next Mrs. Montgomery.

CHAPTER 5

TERRENCE

Malaysia was far from the norm for me when it came to the type of women that I was usually attracted to. It was not that she was unattractive or anything, but the women I normally became involved with all tended to have a very specific look. Normally, they were tall, with a fair complexion and long dark hair. Malaysia, however, was the total opposite of that. She wasn't any more than around five feet seven, she had a dark complexion, and I wasn't so sure about her hair. It was shaved on both sides, and the top portion was in braids, so I couldn't tell if it was long or short.

Despite that, though, her overall energy was what I needed right now. Although it had been less than an hour since we'd run into each other, she had me feeling extremely comfortable and relaxed. And, more importantly, she'd taken my mind off everything else in my life, including Tiffany. So, I figured, what was the harm? It wasn't like I was trying to date her or anything, anyway. She was simply a welcome distraction from all that I had going on at the moment.

Looking at her body language, her smile, and the way she continued to gaze into my eyes as we spoke, though, my gut told me that she was far more attracted to me than I was to her. It was flattering, to say the least, but there was no way I could even think about getting to know another woman right now. I had to admit to myself that although I hated this situation with Tiffany, my heart was still with her. That was why I wasn't sure why on earth I'd lied and told Malaysia that I was divorced. It had slipped out before I could stop myself. While sitting here, I'd contemplated telling her the truth, but after considering that after tonight we would be hundreds of miles away from each other, I figured there was no sense in stressing over it. She would never find out that I had lied, because her life was here in St. Louis, and mine was all the way in Texas. So, what she didn't know wouldn't hurt her.

We ordered a couple more drinks and took a trip down memory lane, recalling our college days, before she started to ask questions that I wasn't in the mood to answer.

"So, you said you live in Texas now. What brought you all the way here to St. Louis?"

I tried to think of what to say quickly without fully disclosing the situation with Tiffany. "Uh, business. I came in to take care of some business with a friend of mine. At least that was until I received the news about my father's passing. That's why I have to leave and head back home first thing in the morning."

"Oh no. I'm so sorry to hear about your father, Terrence. I'm sure that must be devastating, and I guess that explains your disposition when I first came over. I felt like something was wrong, but I didn't want to intrude."

"It's that obvious, huh?"

"Yeah, pretty much. But now I get it. I mean, even as an adult, I don't think I can imagine life without either one of my parents."

"Yeah, it's all right, though. I'm just glad me and my pops had the chance to see each other and spend time together again before all of this happened."

I wasn't sure if I had soured the mood after revealing my father's death, but all of a sudden, she glanced at her watch. "It's getting late. I guess you probably want to get to your hotel to rest up for your flight in the morning?"

"Uh, to be honest, I don't have a room for tonight. Things were supposed to turn out a lot differently, and now it's too late for me to find somewhere decent to book a room."

"So, where do you plan to sleep? I know you didn't plan on staying in here all night, puffing on cigars and throwing back shots."

"Uh, no, not quite. To be honest, I planned on just crashing in my rental car until the morning. It's only a few hours away, so it won't be that bad."

"Oh no. No doing. You'll come back to my condo with me and get a good night's rest and some breakfast in the morning, before you head out."

"Nah, Malaysia. I can't invade your space like that at the last minute. Plus, I don't want to make you uncomfortable. I mean, I saw the look on your friend's face when I offered to take you home. I don't think she was too keen on that idea."

"Look, don't worry about Toni, all right? She can be a bit overprotective, but what she doesn't know won't hurt her. Besides, I feel *totally* comfortable with you, Terrence," she said in a somewhat seductive manner, which I was slightly aroused by. "It's the least I could do, anyway, in exchange for you taking me home."

"Are you really sure about this?" I asked before taking another sip of my drink. I noticed her eyes were focused directly on my lips.

She closed her eyes and took a deep breath. "I'm positive, Terrence. And I'm not taking no for an answer."

At that point, I wondered if we were still referring to me bumming on her couch or something more. Either

CHAPTER 6

TIFFANY

Feeling David's cell phone buzzing against my thigh, I slowly opened my eyes and peeked over my shoulder. He was still sound asleep, with his arm secured around my waist, and for the life of me, I couldn't believe I had let this happen. All we'd done was sleep next to one another, but even that had been too much for me, and I was sure I'd given him the wrong impression. Not to mention, I felt like I was practically cheating on Terrence with his enemy. Looking up at the ceiling, however, I mouthed a sincere thank-you to God and my guardian angels for protecting me and not allowing anything more to take place.

Snapping out of my moment of vulnerability, I removed his arm from around me and made my way out of the bed. As my feet hit the floor, my eyes shot over to the clock on the nightstand. It was just before midnight. Then I glanced at my phone, which was lying there on the bed, hoping to see it light up from a missed call or text, but it didn't. That was the very reason why I couldn't get David out of the room fast enough. I needed to try to reach Terrence again and somehow plead my case to him. Just then David's phone buzzed again, and he started to stretch and moan as he emerged from slumber.

"Don't you think that you should answer that, David? Whoever it is seems pretty desperate to talk to you," I said, although I could tell he was trying his best to ignore the buzzing phone.

"Where are you going?" He pulled at my arm. "Whoever it is can wait. What's most important right now is you and me, so c'mon and come back to bed."

"David, listen, I'm sorry if I may have confused things for you, but there is no *you and me*, all right? This whole situation with what *almost* happened with us was a huge mistake, and I never should have let you stay here. I was hurt over the circumstances between me and Terrence, but I love him. I'm not going to do anything to jeopardize what we have. So, maybe you should go ahead and leave now because I really need to be alone."

"I don't understand how you can still love that guy, Tiff. I mean, *I* was here for you last night. We were here for each other. And that . . . that punk that you cried yourself to sleep over in *my* arms ran out of here and hasn't once tried to check on you. He hasn't given you a second thought since leaving here. Doesn't that tell you something?"

"That's enough, David, okay? Look, I want you to go." I spoke firmly while walking over to the door and opening it. It was evident that he'd gotten a little too comfortable, and it was way past time for me to draw a huge line in the sand between us, illness or not.

He ran over, though, and closed the door instead of leaving. "Wait, Tiff, wait. Maybe what I said came out the wrong way, but I'm only trying to make you see what's right in front of you. *I'm* here, and he's not. I'm not the one who ran out of here because my ego was bruised. He did. That should count for something, right?"

"Listen to me, David. I can't thank you enough for being here for me, and like I said earlier, I plan to support you wholeheartedly through your illness. But that's it. You never should have been here tonight in the first place, and it's possibly destroyed my future with the man I'm truly in love with. Now, I know you don't like it or agree with it, but it's not your decision to make. It's mine. So, please, it's time that you go." I opened the door right back up.

Without another word, he went over to his shoes and slid them on, threw his shirt over his shoulder, and walked to the door in his wifebeater and jeans. Before leaving, however, he stopped and looked into my eyes. "He's not any good for you, Tiff, and I hope that you don't end up hurt."

With that said, he walked out, and the second I closed the door, I felt like I could breathe again. Immediately, I ran over to my cell phone. I almost dialed Keisha, but then I would have to explain this whole situation with David, which I wasn't up to doing. Instead, I felt it best to call Monica because she would be more than understanding. Upon looking at the time again, I decided to text her first, asking if she could talk, instead of calling first. Rather than texting me back, she called me a few minutes later.

"Monica, I'm so glad I caught you before you went off to bed. I really needed someone to talk to," I told her, thinking how she had become such a saving grace in my life. Monica had become so much more than my and Terrence's supervisor at the school where we worked. She was our friend and, honestly, our biggest cheerleader. I knew she wouldn't be happy with the news I was about to share with her.

"Girl, what is this tone you have? I expected you would be calling with some fantastic news."

"Yeah, something told me that you already knew that Terrence was coming here, but things didn't actually turn out the way either of us planned."

"Oh no. What do you mean? Hold on a sec and let me go into another room so that I don't disturb Todd," she whispered. I held the line for a few seconds. Then she came back on, with a full voice and with several questions on the tip of her tongue. "Now, what happened? Was it that damn wife of his? You know what? You don't have to answer because I'm sure it was. What did she do this time?" Her words spilled out, and I didn't have a chance to answer the first question before she posed the second one.

"Whoa. Slow down, Monica. It wasn't Pat. Actually, it was someone else," I said. I hesitated then, as I was ashamed to tell her the truth.

"What? Who then?"

"All right." I took a deep breath. "I guess I may as well just come right out and tell you. It was David."

"David? That deadbeat ex of yours? What does he have to do with anything?" She sounded more agitated than angry, like I had expected.

"Um, well, somehow, he found out I was at this hotel and popped up right before Terrence got here. And then when Terrence did show up, he saw David and me hugging one another. And, of course, after that all hell broke loose. Him and David had words with each other, Terrence threw David against the wall, and then, all of a sudden, he just left. Monica, he wouldn't even listen to my explanation or anything that I had to say. He just walked away, and I haven't heard from him since." I'd given her the very brief version of events.

"Oh my God, honey! Why on earth would you let David come there? And more importantly, why were you two *hugging* one another? Please don't tell me that you still have feelings for that man, Tiff."

"No, Monica, please . . . Now, you know I don't have feelings for him. It's something much deeper than that."

"Girl, what could David possibly have to say that would make you entertain him in the least possible way after all that's happened between you two?"

"Monica, he found out that he has cancer, all right? And, well, he's afraid of possibly losing his life from it. He said he doesn't have anyone else and asked if I would help him through this."

The phone became quiet, but I wasn't sure if it was from her being shocked by the news of it all or from her biting her tongue, refraining from giving me a few choice words. "Mon, are you still there?"

"Yeah, I'm here, Tiff. But I'm just thinking. If what David is saying is true, then why is he coming to you instead of the other women in his life? I mean, he had a whole other fiancée when he was with you. Where is she? Why is he not somewhere crying on *her* shoulder? And besides, how did he know you would be there tonight anyway?"

"He tried to explain that he saw some Facebook post of Keisha's and made his way here. I'm not completely sure that I believe that, though."

"So, why are you believing him about this whole cancer thing?"

"What? Do you really think he would lie about something so serious?"

"Uh, hell yes, I do. Tiff, the man was engaged to you *and* another woman at the same time. And let's not forget that he had you move into her home. Honey, he has proven himself to be a compulsive liar, and I wouldn't trust a single word from his mouth."

What she said made total sense, but I still didn't want to think that he would lie about something like that. Especially when I'd already made it clear to him that this illness had no bearing on our relationship. However, I also couldn't focus my attention on him anymore. That was the reason why I chose not to tell Monica about me crying myself to sleep in his arms after Terrence left. I would simply keep that bit of information to myself. My top priority now was Terrence.

"Well, I'll just have to worry about David later. Right now, I'm more concerned about Terrence and whether he'll ever speak to me again."

"Oh, girl, don't you worry your little head about that. If there's one thing I'm positive of, it's that Terrence loves you. So yes, he'll speak to you again. But he's also a man, Tiff, who saw the woman he loves in the arms of another man, her *ex*-man at that. I'm sure he's hurt, and his ego is bruised. So, just give him a second. Let him breathe and cool down and process things. Trust me, he'll be back."

I wasn't all the way convinced. "You didn't see the look on his face, though, Monica."

"I can only imagine, but you mark my words. He still loves you, and he'll be back. And when he does come back, just be ready to be totally honest with him, all right?"

"Okay, I will. Thank you for everything, Monica. I think that this is the most relaxed I've been since he left."

"Good. Now, why don't you go and get some rest? I'm going to go before my husband thinks I've snuck off to go talk to some mystery man."

"Oh wow, you're right. It is getting late. I'm so sorry."

"It's okay, but we'll talk tomorrow. And, Tiff, I really hope you will reconsider and go ahead and come back to Texas. I miss you."

"I miss you too, Monica." We hung up, and although I was still a bit anxious and wanted to text Terrence again, I planned to do exactly what my friend had said. I decided to relax and trust that our love was strong enough to withstand this storm.

Instead of dwelling on the situation with Terrence any longer, I allowed my thoughts to go directly to Monica's suggestion that I return to Texas. Little did she know, it was something I'd been considering for the past few days. When I first left the state, I had felt I was making the right decision for both me and Terrence. It had been evident at the time that we were falling in love with each other, but he still had so much left to figure out with Patricia. Everything had started to become confusing between us, and a bit messy where she was concerned. So, I had thought I'd give myself space to figure things out, as well as to allow him to make a rational decision regarding his marriage. However, I didn't realize how much being in Texas meant to me until after I'd left. I missed the life that I had been building there, and I desperately wanted to get back to it. Of course, St. Louis would always hold a special place in my heart, but Texas was now considered home to me and was where I needed to be.

CHAPTER 7

DAVID

"I have to admit it, Patricia, I was a little hesitant about all of this when I talked to you earlier, but seeing the look on his face when he saw Tiffany in my arms was everything for me. I'm telling you, it was hard as hell for me to hold back my laughter," I told her between bellyaching chuckles.

The minute I left Tiffany, I had hurried to call Patricia. She'd been calling me nonstop for at least the past twenty minutes. The way she answered on the very first ring made me picture her standing somewhere, puffing on a cigarette, with her cell phone in hand as she waited for my call. As soon as she'd answered my call, she'd demanded to know every single detail of the evening, starting from the time I arrived at the hotel.

And now, having told her half the story, I couldn't stop laughing at my dramatics to tell her the rest of it. I'd given an award-winning performance tonight, if I said so myself, and I was starting to think that maybe I was in the wrong profession altogether. What was even more amusing was the fact that Tiffany believed every bit of it. I could literally still see the concern all over her face when I'd started talking about dying.

"Would you stop laughing already and tell me what happened? What did Terrence say? What did he do?" Patricia quizzed.

Opening the door to my hotel room, I tried to gain control of myself enough to fill her in on what she was so desperate to learn. Once I was inside, I threw the room key on the table, fell on the bed, and picked up the menu on the nightstand to order some room service the minute I hung up with Patricia. All that lying and acting like a sick man had me famished, and since Patricia was flipping the bill for my stay, I figured I'd have an all-out feast.

"Okay, so, I'm glad I got there when I did, Patricia, because it seemed like I wasn't there five minutes before he came sneaking in the door."

"Really? So, what happened when he saw you there? Did he say anything to you? Did they argue? Did she get all dramatic and start crying? What the hell happened?"

"Calm down already, would you? I'm getting to that. Now, at first Tiffany and I didn't even realize he came in. I was right in the middle of giving her my whole sad sob story of needing to make things right between us before something happened to me. And let me tell you, I really laid it on thick too, Pat. You would have been so proud of me. Anyway, that's when she hugged me, and he came in right in the middle of our embrace. She didn't hear him, and her back was to the door, so she never even knew he was there until he grabbed me and ran me up against the wall."

"Ran you up against the wall? Are you serious? Are you okay? I mean, I know how my husband can be when he's angry."

I could hear the concern in Patricia's voice as she took in everything I said. Although, I wouldn't have been surprised, either, if she was sitting on the couch and eating a big bowl of popcorn while listening to me tell my story, because this drama was right up her alley.

"Look, I am dead serious. But trust me, I'm fine. I let him blow off a little steam, but he quickly came to his senses and let me go. Then, after all of that, he just left."

"Wait, just like that? He just left?"

"Yep, just like that, with not another word said. The man was sick and cowardly, running out of there just a fast as he came in." My laughter started up again, and I almost busted a gut as I doubled over on the bed.

"David, would you please stop laughing! Now, tell me what she said. What did she do after he left?"

"I have to admit that when he left is when I started to feel bad about all of this. Pat, she's really hung up over the man, and she's hurt about all of this."

"And do you really think that I care about her little hurt feelings? Because I don't. If you've forgotten, she happens to be hung up on the wrong man, because he is *my* husband."

"Well, anyway, she called him over and over again, but he never responded, and she ended up crying herself to sleep in my arms. That's why I didn't answer when you kept calling."

"Wow, David, I knew you would be the answer to my prayers. This is amazing news, and believe it or not, you've practically saved my marriage," she said, the sound of redemption in her voice.

"You think so, huh? Just like that, you think the man is completely over her?"

"Trust me, I know so. If I know my husband the way I believe I do, he's completely done with little Ms. Tiffany Tate and her betrayal."

"Okay, good. So, I guess now we can talk about my portion of the million bucks you mentioned to me?"

"Oh no, slow down, honey, because this is far from over. It's only the beginning," she answered.

"But you just said you're sure he's done with her. That's what you wanted, right?"

"Yeah, but I have to make *absolutely* sure, and that means I'll need you a little while longer. So, enjoy your night's stay at the Ritz, and we'll talk more tomorrow."

"Hey, hey, wait. I need money for food and miscellaneous items. You know I was locked up right before coming here, and I don't have a dime to my name. That's the only reason I agreed to any of this."

"Okay, David, all right. I'll Zelle you a couple hundred in a few seconds, and more as we go along, all right? Good night."

She did that thing again where she hung up without giving me a chance to say another word. But as I hung up, it hit me. *What the hell have I really gotten myself into?* I didn't know all of Patricia's plans or what her expected outcome was, but the tone of her voice hadn't sounded good at all. Thinking about it, I almost felt a little bad for Terrence. I couldn't imagine having a wife like Patricia doing all her scheming and conniving antics behind my back. Not to mention, the way she'd offered another man a piece of *Terrence's* money to do it. It was crazy, to say the least, and I guessed I was even crazier to be helping her, but I *needed* the money bad.

"I'm sorry for doing this to you, Tiff, but right now I have to," I said out loud. "I promise, though, as soon as I get my hands on that cash, I'll find a way to make it all up to you."

My phone started ringing, and when I glanced down at the screen, I saw the one number I could do without ever seeing again. It was Sonya, and I knew she was calling only to hound me about that baby business. She had to know I didn't have any words for her, especially after she threw me out of her house and had me arrested. And yeah, maybe I was wrong for taking her money out of her bank account, but what did she expect when she tossed me out like yesterday's garbage, with absolutely nothing in my pockets? I hit the IGNORE button on my phone, and she called me several more times, but I refused to pick up. I thought about calling my mother. But then I decided that she was another person I could go without talking to right now. We hadn't left off on the best terms before I came to St. Louis, and I really wasn't in the mood for her hounding me about how much I needed to get my life together.

Besides, right now I was lying up in the Ritz-Carlton, with a load of money about to be at my disposal. So, my life, as I saw it, was very much together. And if I could somehow finesse my way into Tiffany's life again as more than just her ex, I'd pretty much be on easy street. That was if I could keep Terrence and Tiffany's jealous, hating-ass best friend, Keisha, out of the picture and out of our lives.

I picked up my phone to order some grub finally, and my eyes landed on a disturbing text.

You better watch your back. Because you won't get away with what you did.

Although the threatening words made me a little nervous, I tried to laugh and brush them off. I was positive it was only Sonya, anyway, upset that I hadn't answered any of her calls. Then I figured I would call her bluff, and I shot her a text right back.

Give it rest, Sonya, and stop making threats that might get you hurt in the end. This will be your only warning.

CHAPTER 8

PATRICIA

It was all coming together. Dancing around the room, I was ecstatic at the mere thought of Tiffany Tate finally being out of my and my husband's lives. She'd been a thorn in my side ever since Terrence befriended her, and my wish to have her gone for good was about to come true.

Simply thinking about her plastered all over his Facebook account, on lunch dates and such, was enough to make me angry all over again. In fact, it made me sicker every time I logged on. Knowing my husband as well as I did, I knew that she was his *type* and that he was smitten with her in every way. But there was no way in hell I was going to let her, or any other woman, for that matter, come in and destroy what I'd worked so hard to build. That was why I was so thankful for David. After what he had just shared with me, I knew things were headed in the right direction. Maybe now Terrence would start acting like he cared about me and this family again. Especially if he didn't want me to take more than half of his father's estate from him in a nasty divorce. He was the only one who wanted the divorce in the first place. I didn't. And if he knew what was good for him and didn't want to end up dead broke, then he'd damn sure get his act together.

As I tried to think of my next plan of action for David and Tiffany, my cell phone began to ring. I picked it up, glanced down at the screen, and saw that the call was from an unknown number. Having no idea who it could be at this time of the evening, I chose to ignore the call altogether. However, a minute later the phone rang again, and it was the same number. This time around, I was much too curious and decided to pick up.

"Hello."

"Hello, Mrs. Montgomery?"

"Yes, this is Mrs. Montgomery."

"This is Ashley from the hospital, the nurse taking care of your father in ICU."

I'd almost forgotten that I had called the hospital earlier and pretended to be Pops's long-lost, grieving daughter to get information on his condition. The nurse had completely ignored the fact that I didn't have the family password and had taken my word that I was who I said I was. Luckily, I'd been able to sweet-talk her into keeping me up to date on his condition.

"Oh, Ashley, yes. How is my father doing? Please, I hope you have some good news for me."

"I'm sorry, Mrs. Montgomery, but your father made his transition this evening. I wanted to personally contact you myself and offer my condolences. His body is still here, and you're more than welcome to come and be with him one last time before the coroner arrives."

Somehow, I had to muster up some tears to keep up my charade and not let on that I was completely over-joyed by the fact that the old man had at last croaked. I tried to respond with a soft and somber tone—and without laughing.

"Oh, Ashley, I can't thank you enough for taking care of him and for reaching out to me. It truly means the world that there are still some good and decent people in your profession, so thank you very much. But I think I'm going to let the rest of the family handle everything from here out. I just can't see him in that condition."

"Yes, of course, I totally understand. Well, please know that you and your family will be in my prayers. And if I can offer any comfort at all, I want you to know that he didn't suffer at all. His transition was peaceful. And, Mrs. Montgomery, you are such a lucky woman to have had a man like that in your life. He was so kind and sweet."

"Thank you," I said hurriedly, wishing to hang up, because it was sickening to listen to her talk about him in that way.

"Okay. Well, take care, Mrs. Montgomery."

I hung up without saying another word and tossed my cell phone on the sofa.

"He was so kind. He was so sweet," I muttered aloud. "Yeah, well, the old buzzard wasn't kind and sweet to me. And he didn't even think I was good enough for his son. But that's okay, dear father-in-law, because I'm about to have the pure pleasure of spending every penny you had while you're tossing and turning in that grave of yours."

My thoughts turned to Terrence's return home from St. Louis, and I knew I had to think quick on my feet. Before he'd left, I'd overheard him talking with his lawyer about keeping his father's money away from me if something were to happen to him. Well, now that the old man was gone, I was here to show Terrence that this feat was going to be much easier said than done. I had to act fast, though, and get my whole plan in motion, and that meant giving my old friend Kim a call. We had been friends back in college and touched base from time to time. The last time I bumped into her, about a month ago, she told me that she'd recently become a divorce attorney and represented herself in her own divorce. She also shared that she'd taken her husband for every penny he had for his adulterous acts. I knew she was the right person to call, and it couldn't wait until the morning.

After picking up my cell phone, I made myself comfortable on the sofa, but as I looked around the room, the most unsettling feeling came over me. I realized that there was no way that I could stay at my father's home much longer. In all fairness, his home was nice and all, but it was way too small for my liking, and I was sure the boys felt the same. It wasn't what we'd become accustomed to, and it just wasn't home to us. That made me even more anxious to move things along as quickly as possible. After dialing Kim, I listened to her phone ring a few times before the voicemail picked up. However, there was no way I was about to leave a message. I needed to talk with her tonight, even if that meant calling over and over until she answered. It didn't take long, though, because she answered the phone the second time around.

"Mrs. Patricia Montgomery. To what do I owe the pleasure this time of the evening, honey?"

"Hi, Kim. I'm so sorry to call so late, but I desperately need your help. I need an attorney and some divorce papers drawn up as quickly as possible. Do you think you can help a dear old friend?"

"What? You're joking, right? You're trying to divorce that fine-ass husband of yours? On what grounds, Pat? And you know this could have very well waited until tomorrow, right? It's not like I'm going to hop out of my bed this very minute," she said sarcastically.

"I don't know . . . Would something to the tune of one million dollars wake you up?"

"One million? Oh, wait. Please go on." She suddenly had a perkiness to her tone.

"Well, I believe that my *fine-ass husband*, as you put it, has been cheating on me. In fact, I know he has. However, I'm willing to forgive it and work things out for the sake of our family, but he's been pressing the issue of divorce. And, since that's the case, I want to beat him to the punch. Especially since his father just passed away and his estate is worth at least one million dollars. If my husband is going to keep talking divorce talk, then I want every single cent that I'm entitled to. I want the house, the cars, and everything else, including most of that one million," I explained, noticing that I had her undivided attention.

"All right, and you're totally sure about this?"

"I'm positive, Kim. Either he calls this off or he's left with nothing. The choice will be his."

"Okay, well, say no more. Leave everything to me. Your wish, my dear, is my command. If he wants out of this marriage, then I'm going to make sure he *pays* to get out. And, trust me, whoever he's been cheating with will not want anything at all to do with his broke ass by the time I'm done, no matter how *fine* he is. That will surely make him rethink things."

As I laughed at what she'd said, I knew I'd done the right thing by calling her. She was going to be my ticket to either keeping my husband or getting what I deserved if he still planned on walking away. I gave her a few more details before we hung up with one another. Then I gave some thought to another plan of action that I'd already set in motion, which was the house.

The minute Terrence had left to see his father, I had had everything in the house moved into storage. I'd already told him that the boys and I were moving in with my father and staying there until we straightened out our marriage, but that was all I'd said. He had no clue that the house would be stark empty when he returned home. I was positive he would feel like I was being overly dramatic, as usual, and maybe he was right. But I felt like I had to do something drastic to get his attention, and I'd figured this would do the trick. I needed to show him that divorcing me would basically leave his ass with nothing but the clothes on his back, just like with his first divorce. And knowing my husband, I was sure he would dread the very idea of having to start over from rock bottom. I only hoped that we could settle this matter sooner than later, because I was feeling more cramped by the second at my father's house.

After contemplating whether I had dotted all the i's and crossed all the t's with Terrence, I went right back to thinking about David. Although I was thankful for his help, I didn't like the way he seemed so demanding about getting paid. Plus, the more I thought about it and did the calculations in my mind, the more I really didn't want to part with too much of the money I had coming my way. I was already sure that Kim would take a significant amount for her fee. I didn't want to be left with almost nothing. Not to mention that I'd also been thinking about the fact that I didn't know David well enough to fully trust him. There was no guarantee that he wouldn't spill the beans on me and tell Tiffany everything, or that he wouldn't come sniffing around for more money later. I had to think of a way to keep him quiet—and far away from me once this was all over and done with.

Before calling it a night, however, I decided to log in to Terrence's Facebook account once more. I was shocked to see that he hadn't made one single post about any of the evening's events, not even about Pop's passing. I immediately went to Tiffany's account. Her page was just as deserted as his. I figured that they were both feeling down and out and were not up for posting, which gave me the sense of peace that I needed. David hadn't lied. Tiffany was feeling sad and hurt, while Terrence was left feeling betrayed.

"It's all working out in my favor," I announced aloud. I kicked my feet up and took a sip of my red wine that was awaiting me in my glass just for this perfect occasion. "Checkmate, bitch!"

CHAPTER 9

MALAYSIA

Excited was an understatement, and all I could seem to think about was whether I had on a matching panty and bra set or not. This man was everything I could have dreamed of and more. He was handsome, charming, funny, charismatic—all that I wanted and needed in my life right now. The conversation during the ride to my place had even been light and easy as we talked about things from our past and present and about what we desired in our futures. It seemed strange, because I'd never been one to really believe in fate or love at first sight, yet within the past hour or so, Terrence had completely changed my mind about that. And now I couldn't believe that after all these years, in just a few more minutes, he'd be at my home with me.

We pulled up to my condo, and he got out and came around to open my car door. Just as I stepped out, I could feel my cell phone begin to buzz inside my bag. I knew it was nobody but Toni, so I didn't bother digging through all my things to answer. But I swear, it was like that girl had a radar or something and knew exactly when we made it back to my place. We headed inside, and I led him into my living room.

"Wow. This is nice. Very warm and cozy. You have great style too. Have you ever considered interior decorating as a career?" he asked, admiring my home as he looked around.

"Not so much, because I really don't have that good of an eye for decorating. I just watch a lot of HGTV and steal ideas from that," I answered. I was glad I hadn't left things scattered here and there, as I sometimes did. "But thank you, anyway. Go ahead and make yourself at home. Have a seat. Can I get you anything to drink?"

"Uh, sure. Water would be great. I think I've had enough alcohol this evening to last me for a while," he said, making himself comfortable on my sofa.

"Yeah, I guess you're right. I drank more than normal too, and I wouldn't want either one of us to take advantage of the other." I laughed, as if I was joking around, but little did he know, I was dead serious. He laughed too, but almost in a manner that conveyed that the idea of that was far-fetched. Anyway, feeling as if I had put my foot in my mouth, I made my way to the kitchen to pour two tall glasses of ice-cold water, mainly to cool myself off instead of quench my thirst. Then I came back into the living room and sat down on my love seat, across from him. Immediately, I flipped on the HGTV channel, as I usually did. However, for the first time in forever, I could care less about watching it. Terrence had every bit of my attention.

"So, were you going to call your girls and let them know you made it home safely and that I'm not some lunatic?"

"Nope. I'll shoot them a text later, because if I call right now, trust me, there will be way too many questions to answer." We both laughed.

"It's good that you have friends that care about you so much, though. You don't see that a lot nowadays. I think that women these days are way too concerned with competing against each other instead forming a sisterhood."

"Yeah, well, not me and those two. We've been friends for a very long time, and I trust them with my life. They're just as close to me as my family, and as much as we get on one another's nerves, I wouldn't trade them for anything in the world."

After I said that, it became quiet in the room, the only sound was that of the television, which was on low. My eyelids started to feel a bit heavy, and I yawned non-stop. At first, I wasn't sure where the sudden drowsiness had come from, but then I remembered alcohol always made me sleepy, and a bit horny, to say the least. I found myself sitting there half asleep and moist from the sinful thoughts in the back of my mind. As I tried my best to keep my eyes open and focus on the television, I could feel Terrence's eyes on me.

I glanced over at him. "Why are you looking at me like that?"

"I don't know. I guess because I never would have imagined my night turning out this way . . . here with you right now."

"Yeah, me either," I said softly, trying to force myself not to jump all over this man. "Like I said in the car, I dreaded the thought of going out tonight when Toni and Larisse first picked me up, but now I couldn't be happier I did."

"Wow. Well, I'm glad we bumped into each other again too. You really changed my whole mood around from how I was feeling earlier. Plus, I can't thank you enough for opening your home up to me like this. You are just as sweet as I remember, and I hate that I never actually took the time to get to know you better back then. Who knows where things could have gone."

As he continued to speak, I kept admiring his strong features. Although I was trying hard to listen to his words, my mind started to wander and go on an escapade all its own. All I could imagine was going over and straddling him while his massive hands gripped my ass. I could practically envision his mouth on my breasts as I rode his stick nice and slow. My thoughts drifting further, I could literally feel his hard thickness all up and through me. In a slow and steady motion, I imagined my ass bouncing up and down on him as he grabbed the back of my head and put his tongue in my mouth while sucking mine. I was so hot and wet that I almost wanted to scream when Terrence's voice finally brought me back to reality.

"I'm sorry. You must be tired, and I'm over here rambling about homecoming back in the day."

"Oh, no, trust me, it's okay. I'm just usually in bed by now, that's all," I uttered, trying to play things off.

"I understand. It is getting late."

On that note, I hopped up and said, "Would you like to take a shower? Oh, I mean, not with me, of course, but alone. I mean just in case you wanted to clean up for tonight. But not that anything is going to happen tonight that you need to be clean for, but before you go to sleep. You know what? I am so sorry. That came out all the wrong way, so I'll just get you some towels before I keep putting my foot in my mouth."

Instead of bursting into laughter over what I'd said, he only cracked that same sexy smile and grabbed my arm before I had a chance to walk away. "I'd much rather do this . . ."

He kissed me. His tongue met mine, and at once, I became wetter than I already was from my vision. My mind told me to pull away, but my body told me to stay right there and let him have his way with me. A moment later, he pulled my shirt over my head and started to unbutton my jeans.

Thank God, I have on matching underwear, I thought, but it really didn't matter, because the next thing I knew, he removed those too. Then he took me by the hand, led me into the bathroom, and turned on the water in the shower stall. I got in first, and right away the beads of hot water hit my naked body. At once, I felt his large, muscular body ease into the shower behind me. He pressed himself close to me, and before I knew it, he was inside. Every single inch of him was inside my pleasure zone, and it felt good. I let out a long sigh of relief, thinking that this was something I'd longed to feel for years.

"Malaysia," I heard him say between long, deep strokes. He continued to call my name, his voice growing louder and louder.

"Malaysia? Malaysia? Are you good?" he asked, snapping me out of my daze.

I didn't know exactly when I had blacked out or for how long when I saw him still sitting on the sofa and realized I was seated on the love seat, both of us *fully clothed*. "Damn."

"I'm sorry I woke you, but I was trying to let you know that I'm fine if you want to go inside your room and lie down. I'm sure I'll doze off here any second."

"Oh yeah, of course. It's been a long day, and I'm sure you're just as tired as I am," I said, although I was more embarrassed than anything. "That blanket at the end of the sofa is quite cozy. I'll get you some towels together for the morning, in case you wake up before I do. The bathroom is right back there, and you can help yourself to whatever you need."

"Thank you so much. Again, I really appreciate this."

"No problem." I waved him off. "And, Terrence, have a good night."

"Sweet dreams to you too."

I turned off the lights and went inside my bedroom. The second I crossed the threshold, I could have kicked myself for what had just happened. I felt like a total and complete idiot for falling asleep in front of this man, and I wasn't sure if he had heard me moaning and had realized I was damn near about to cum. Of all the dumb-ass things to do, I'd had a wet dream right in front of him. After falling onto my bed, I kicked and screamed into my pillow, as if I were having a tantrum.

How the hell will you live this down, Malaysia? I asked myself, putting my pillow between my legs, because I could still practically feel him inside me. In fact, my clit was still dancing around inside my jeans. "Calm down, girlfriend. It was all a wet-ass dream."

An hour or so later, I opened my bedroom door and tiptoed into the hallway to go to the bathroom. Peeking in the living room, I saw in the light flickering from the television that Terrence was fast asleep. As I went to turn off the TV, I couldn't help but take a quick glance at him lying there in his boxer briefs, with no shirt on. Noticing that he had kicked the blanket off, I quietly went over to cover him back up. My condo usually got a chill to it during the night, and I didn't want him to end up sick.

My goodness, you are so damn sexy, Terrence Montgomery, I thought as I gazed at him. He was looking as peaceful as could be. I also noticed how everything about him seemed perfect: his long eyelashes, his chest hair, which lay perfectly on his broad torso, and even the size of his manhood poking through his briefs. I knew I had to hurry up and go back into my room before I practically attacked the poor man. After turning around and heading toward my room, though, I heard his strong, deep voice faintly say my name.

"Malaysia."

"I . . . I . . . I'm sorry if I woke you. I noticed that the blanket was off, so I just wanted to cover you back up."

"Thank you." He smiled as he looked at me standing there in my red satin nightie. "Come here."

My heart started to beat fast as I walked closer to him. I wasn't scared of what might happen; I was excited, to say the least. Once I was standing in front of him, he sat up and pulled me close. My heart began to beat faster with the anticipation of the moment. However, a few seconds later, the unimaginable happened: he grabbed me around my waist, laid his head on me and, out of nowhere, began sobbing uncontrollably. All at once, my heart sank, because I knew the tears had to do with the loss of his father. What I didn't know was exactly how to console him, because, honestly, I just wasn't good at things like that. Rubbing the back of his head, I simply chose to let him cry as much as he needed. I wanted him to know that he was safe with me.

"It's going to be all right, Terrence. I promise. Everything is going to be all right."

He held on to me as tight as possible, crying his heart out, and I could just about feel his pain. Wishing there was so much more that I could do, I decided that there was no way I was leaving him in the living room alone for the night. Without a word, I gently pushed him away from me, took his hand, and led him inside my bedroom. We lay down in the bed, and Terrence pulled my body in close to his. Before shutting his eyes, he took my face in his hands and gently kissed my lips.

"Thank you, Malaysia."

CHAPTER 10

TIFFANY

After saying a little prayer while exiting the Uber, I inhaled as I prepared to enter my house. It was still quite early—I had planned it that way—and I hoped that Keisha was still asleep. I knew she would have a million questions regarding last night with Terrence, or basically *without* Terrence. And the way I felt at this very moment, the last thing I wanted to do was answer a bunch of unnecessary questions about him and what *didn't* take place. Especially since there was no way I could explain that the entire evening had gone downhill thanks to David showing up there. Keisha hated his guts and would never understand my wanting to be there for him through his illness. So, being able to sneak in the house before she got up would give me enough time to think about the untruths I would tell her when we finally did run into each other.

After opening the door, I peeked inside to make sure she wasn't passed out on the living-room sofa, something she occasionally did. Once I saw that the coast was clear, I stepped inside, took off my shoes, and started to tiptoe to my bedroom, trying my best not to make any noise. I was literally only two steps away from my room when I saw her bedroom door crack open. She came out in her T-shirt and panties, a bonnet on her head, and her face was all scrunched up, as if I'd disturbed her beauty rest.

"Hey, I thought I heard something out here," she said in a soft tone, her voice a little above a whisper. "What are you doing home so early? Where's Terrence? Did he propose? Let me see the ring." It all came out at once while she was still wiping the sleep from her eyes.

"Keisha, can we please talk about last night later? I'm really exhausted, and I just want to lie down in my own bed."

Instead of letting me off that easy, she grabbed me by my arm before I was able to walk off. "Tiff, look at me."

I didn't answer her at first or meet her gaze until she said it again. That was when I figured I might as well get this over with, because I was positive she wasn't about to leave it alone.

"What, Keisha?" I stared at her, knowing good and well why she was looking at me the way she was.

"What exactly is going on? What happened? Why are your eyes all red and puffy, like you've been crying? And where is Terrence?"

After throwing my bag down on the floor, I headed toward the kitchen to get a glass of water. I debated whether to tell her the truth or make up some off-the-wall tale, but the only problem was, my best friend was as much an undercover detective as I was. I knew without a doubt that she would eventually find out the truth. Taking a sip of my water, I headed toward the living room, with her following right behind me.

"All right, well, you might as well sit down for this," I said. I took a deep breath, preparing to tell her the whole truth and nothing but the truth. She hurried to take a seat on one end of the sectional, and I sat down on the other end.

"Okay, well, first things first. I have no idea where Terrence is. He came to the hotel, and then he left right away, and I haven't heard from him since. He hasn't called or texted, and he hasn't answered his phone any of the hundreds of times that I've tried reaching out to him. So, where Mr. Terrence Montgomery is, is as much a mystery to me as it is to you."

There was total silence for a minute or two, while she sat there with a puzzled expression on her face. Then she finally spoke.

"I don't know . . . This just doesn't sound right to me, Tiff. I mean, why on earth would he go through the trouble of planning this amazing evening only to show up and leave? That doesn't make sense. Unless there's something you're not telling me." I could sense her detective instincts were starting to kick in. "Did you two get into an argument or something? Does this have to do with his wife?"

I sat there with a dumb expression on my face while she continued to weigh the possibilities. And I figured that whatever sounded good was what I would roll with, instead of spilling the beans about David.

"I don't know. Maybe this does have everything to do with her," I finally said, rolling with the wife excuse. "Maybe by the time he arrived at the hotel, he realized that he couldn't leave her, and that's why he left. I mean, it's not like she doesn't have him all wrapped around her finger. I had to be foolish, anyway, to think that the man would leave his *wife* just to be with me. That was the very reason I needed to put some distance between us in the first place when I left Texas."

I hoped that what I had just said sounded legit and that she would leave well enough alone. But as I watched her place her hand on her chin and struggle to figure things out, like it was some tough mathematics problem, I knew that scenario was too good to be true.

"No, no, that can't be what it is, Tiff. You didn't hear his voice when he talked about you and him being together forever. Or the way he said he loves you. I can't see him just up and going back to her after everything he did to get here. There has to be more to it than what we know."

Choosing not to respond to her theory, I became deathly mute, which clearly put more doubt in her mind.

"Unless there is something that you're not telling me." She waited for me to reply, but I kept drinking water until my glass was completely empty. Then, knowing she wouldn't give it a rest, I figured I would stop stalling.

"All right. It was David, okay?"

"What? David? What the hell does he have to do with anything?" she said, sitting up straight.

"Look, please just calm down. David showed up to the hotel, and Terrence found him there with me. He saw us in an embrace, and that's when he left. I haven't heard from him since."

"What the hell was that jerk doing there, and why the hell were you hugging him? Are you still seeing him, Tiff? Do you still love that man, after all he's done to you?"

"Listen, that's not it, Keisha. You know I'm in love with Terrence, but David has a lot going on that he needs my help with."

"A lot? Like what? What kind of scheme has he come up with now to make you feel sorry for him?"

"Keisha, the man has cancer, okay? And . . . and he doesn't have anyone else to lean on right now."

"Oh, give me a break already. Tell him to go and lean on his *other* fiancée."

"Wow, you sound just like Monica."

"Monica? Wait a minute. You mean to tell me that your friend all the way in Texas found out about this before I did, and then you sat here trying to lie to me about everything?"

"Keisha, I called Monica last night because I knew how upset you would be about David, that's all."

"Yeah, well, since it seems like you guys are much closer than you and me, then why are you even here? Why don't you go back to Texas and be with your new *best friend*?" She stormed into her bedroom, then slammed the door behind her.

Everything was such a huge mess, yet all I could think about was Terrence. "Where are you, Terrence? And why haven't I heard from you by now?"

Deciding to bite the bullet instead of waiting for him to reach out, like Monica had suggested, I figured I'd give him one more call. His phone rang at least four times. I was about to hang up when he picked up.

"Hello? Hello?" I said into my phone.

I heard him answer, but I was at a loss of words given what I heard in the background. And even when I thought my ears were deceiving me, I was sure that was *her* giggling. Something inside me told me that he'd run back to Patricia after seeing me with David. Not able to speak due to the sudden nauseousness that came over me, I hung up as quickly as I could. I couldn't believe that all this time, I'd been desperate to hear his voice, crying my heart out all night and praying that he would call, and he had been with her. I didn't want to believe it. I didn't want to think that he would do something so foolish, and trying to understand it was beyond me. At that point, the only thing I was sure of was that I was completely done with Terrence Montgomery.

After walking into my bedroom, I closed the door and plopped down on my bed. The last thing I wanted to talk about or even think about was Terrence. I couldn't believe I'd been putting my entire life on hold because of this man. I'd taken a leave from my job, come all the way back home, and moped around on account of my feelings for him. And now I found out that he had left me and gone running straight back to her, without having the mere decency of a simple phone call.

"Well, this is it, Terrence Montgomery. Not another minute of my life is going to be wasted on you. It's time that I get back to Texas and continue with the life that I'd begun building, without you." As difficult as it was going to be, I planned to behave as if he and our friendship, relationship, or whatever this had been, had never existed.

Tomorrow will be the beginning of a whole new life, I thought to myself as I picked up my cell phone and began to dial Monica's number. I wasn't quite prepared to go into any details about what I'd just heard or about my fight with Keisha. Right now, I simply needed to inform her of my plans to return to Texas. I finished dialing, and Monica answered on the very first ring.

"Tiffany, hey. I've been trying so hard to wait for you to call me. I almost gave in and dialed you, but I didn't want to bother you." She took a deep breath and got right down to business. "Did he call yet? Did the two of you finally have a much-needed conversation?"

"Hey, Monica. No, he didn't call at all, but I really don't want to get into it right now. I'm calling only to let you know that I'm coming back home tomorrow, and I'll be ready to get back to work immediately."

"Oh, all right. That's great," she said, surely sensing the agitation in my voice. "But are you sure everything is okay, outside of the fact that you haven't heard from Terrence? You don't sound like yourself."

"If it's all right with you, I'd much rather wait and tell you everything once I return."

"Sure, of course. That's fine." She didn't press the issue any further, and that was one of the reasons I loved her so much. She knew when to back down, *unlike* Keisha. "Well, I'll have your office straightened up and waiting for you, all right? I'm so happy you're coming back, Tiff."

"Thank you, Monica. Thank you so much. And I can't wait to see you."

I hung up. I could tell that she still had so many questions swimming through her head that she wanted to ask. I planned on sharing everything once we were face-to-face. My only concern was that I hoped she wouldn't develop any negative feelings toward Terrence on my account.

CHAPTER 11

TERRENCE

I'd hung up after saying hello a couple of times and not getting a response. I was positive that Tiffany had heard Malaysia in the background. I was sure that was why she hadn't said anything before hanging up. I started to think that maybe I shouldn't have answered her call at all, but when I'd seen her name scrolling across the top of my phone, I hadn't been able to help myself. Although part of me still didn't have very much to say to her, the other part was curious to know her reasons behind being in that hotel room with David in the first place. I honestly had had no idea, however, that at that very moment I took Tiffany's call, Malaysia would walk into the room, laughing at something her girlfriend had said on the phone. But, maybe now Tiffany would be able to see how it felt to be betrayed by the one you loved most.

Trying not to concentrate on that phone call any longer, I started to go through in my mind everything that I would have to deal with once I touched down in Texas. First and foremost, I had to grapple with everything related to Pops. Although I was dreading it, I'd already begun preparing myself for planning his arrangements with my stepmother. Thinking of him quickly brought to my mind the issue of his entire estate. It hadn't fully hit me until now that once I receive his death certificate,

I would have access to one million dollars, and I had to admit that I needed that money badly. After living in hotels for the past couple of months, hitting up the casinos practically every other day, and splurging on this trip to be with Tiffany, I was more than strapped for cash. With that in mind, I figured I should call my lawyer, Randle, to check the status of my divorce papers. I needed to make sure that I would not be sharing any money with that wife of mine under any circumstances. Malaysia was still on the phone with Toni, so I went onto her balcony for a little privacy.

"Hello."

"Hey, Randle. It's Terrence," I announced, with a sense of urgency in my voice, hoping and praying that he had some good news for me.

"Terrence, hey, how are you, man? Are you back in Texas yet?" He sounded all business, like usual, and I couldn't pick up from his tone if that was a good thing or not.

"Uh no, not yet, but I'll be heading back shortly. I want to fill you in, though, on what's been going on, if you have a sec."

"I'm back in my office now and alone, so go right ahead."

"Okay, well, it's my pops, Randle. He passed away last night."

"Oh no, man. I'm so sorry to hear that. I know you were praying that things would turn around."

"Yeah, I was, but I guess it was his time, you know?"

"Yep, trust me, I understand. So, how are you holding up?"

"Well, things really hit me last night, and it was rough, but I'm doing a lot better today. But now that he's transitioned, I'm sure you know the reason for my call. There's a little matter of one million dollars at stake, and I have to make sure it stays out of the wrong hands, if you know what I mean."

"I know exactly what you mean, man, but right now I can't give you the response you're looking for when it comes to your divorce. I think you need to wait and come into my office when you get back," Randle told me.

"Wait, what do mean? What's wrong?"

"Uh, nothing is *wrong*, so to speak. We may just need to take a different route with things. But I'd much rather you come into my office and we talk more about it then, face-to-face."

"I don't know, Randle. You really have me nervous now, and I don't want to have this feeling the entire time I'm traveling back home. So, trust me, whatever it is, I can handle it. I need for you to go ahead and be straight with me."

"Okay, well . . ." He hesitated and fumbled with his words for a minute before coming right out with it. "I have a strange feeling that your wife already knows about the money."

"What? There's no way she could possibly know. The only people that know about how much his estate is worth are me, you, and my stepmother, and I'm positive that none of us said anything to her," I stated, but I knew he could hear the suspicion in my voice when it came to him. He and Patricia had become friends over time, though he was my friend and my lawyer. And I'd come to know that the term *friends* went out the window whenever money and women were involved.

"Well, Terrence, let me assure you that I didn't say *anything* to Pat about your father's estate," he said, trying to clear up any misconception.

"So, I don't understand. What's going on?"

"Look, I'm not exactly sure, because this has all happened so fast. I mean, when we spoke before you left, I thought things were moving along smoothly. I even had the judge ready to sign off. But this morning all of that changed. It seems that Pat has her own attorney, and she's filed her own divorce papers, which I'm sure you will be served with any day now. And just to prepare you, she's asking for spousal and child support, the house, cars, everything. She's stating that she has become accustomed to a certain lifestyle and that it shouldn't be taken away from her and her children because of you committing adultery. And I have to be honest with you, man, any judge will probably eat you alive after finding out you stepped outside your marriage. I'm hoping she doesn't have any proof of this. Does she?"

I couldn't even answer Randle because I was filled with rage. Of all the low-down, dirty tricks that Pat had pulled, this one took the cake.

"If you consider a few Facebook pictures proof, Randle. But, honestly, man, those were nothing more than mere lunch or dinner dates with my coworker. And as far as her boys are concerned, they are practically adults, and I'm not their biological father anyway. Why should I be on the hook for them? Besides, man, I've been struggling a lot lately with trying to maintain things alone. I'm swimming in debt."

"Terrence, I hear you, all right, but once we submit your income and financial records, the judge isn't going to look at the fact that you're swimming in debt. If she's able to prove that she's lived a certain way all these years, then unfortunately, you're going to have to maintain that. And when it comes to her sons, if you've been acting as Daddy in their lives all these years, then they *are* yours, biological or not."

"This is way too much right now, and I can't deal with all of this," I said, hearing Malaysia get off the phone with Toni. The last thing I needed was for her to come out here on the balcony and pick up on anything that was going on. "Look, I'll just have to see you the minute I get back into town. But, Randle, I'm begging you, man, find a loophole or something to get me out of this mess." I hung up before he said anything further.

Thinking about Patricia and her mischief, I should have known that she was up to something, because she'd been quiet as a mouse ever since I left. I quickly remembered that right before I'd left Texas, she'd made this huge deal of moving into her father's building. The crazy broad had moved all the furniture out of our home, leaving it completely bare but for the personal items that belonged to me. I hadn't had the time or energy to deal with her shenanigans then, but she had better believe that I damn sure had the time and the energy now. If these were the type of games she wanted to play, then I would be a fierce opponent. She'd find out soon enough that I was not about to play nice with her any longer. Either we sat down like two adults and resolved of this situation in a way that benefited both of us, or I would play hardball. My only prayer was that Tiffany didn't get caught in the crossfire of it all and get hurt.

Instead of continuing to dwell on my troubles, I decided to focus on the beauty that was headed my way. A second later she opened the door to the balcony.

"Hey, I'm sorry to bother you out here, but I made us some breakfast . . . if you're hungry," she announced.

I was still in disbelief and completely embarrassed about what had happened last night. To my surprise, she hadn't said a word about it this morning, which I was thankful for. Admiring her morning glow now, I had to admit that I hadn't been the least bit attracted to her when we first arrived at her condo. She'd been gliding around all morning, with a huge smile plastered on her face, humming melodic tunes. And instead of putting a damper on her spirits, I had chosen to play right along with everything, seeing that this would be our first and final meeting.

But having watched her stroll around in her sexy robe and nightgown as she catered to my every whim all morning had my hormones starting to get the best of me. I began praying silently that I would not start anything that I would end up regretting later. Plus, I didn't need her to read into things, though something made me fearful that she already had.

I followed her into the kitchen, and she gestured to me to take a seat at the table, which she'd already set. Then she placed a heaping plate of pancakes and a bottle of syrup in front of me and told me to dig in before they got cold.

I poured some syrup on my pancakes and took a bite. "This is pretty good. I see you kind of know your way around the kitchen, huh?"

"Yeah, well, I'm not a gourmet chef or anything, but I think I do all right," she said, placing her own plate of pancakes and two large glasses of orange juice on the table. Then she sat down across from me.

"I'll be sure to keep you in mind, then, whenever I open Montgomery's Barbecue and Soul Food Restaurant," I said, practically kicking myself right after the words came out, because they made me think of Tiffany again. She'd encouraged me this entire time to start my own business, whereas Patricia had done nothing more than shoot down my entrepreneurial ideas. Tiffany was also the one who had come up with the name for the restaurant. I didn't want to admit it, but she added to my life in a major way. Maybe that was why I loved her so much, which was another reason why I didn't want to start anything with Malaysia.

"Now, don't tell me that you know how to cook too, Mr. Montgomery," Malaysia said, sounding amazed, as she snapped me out of my memories of Tiff.

"I guess you could say I do a little something, something," I responded, and we both started laughing.

The table became quiet for a minute or two, however, and I assumed we both had our own private thoughts circulating in our minds. Then she began to share what she was reflecting on.

"Terrence, I really hate that you have to go back when I feel like we're just getting to know each other again."

"Yeah, me too," I said, without letting on that it really didn't matter to me one way or the other. There was no doubt that I appreciated her for allowing me to stay the night and for comforting me last night, but I refused to allow things to go any further than today. But then she inquired about that very thing, and I felt like I had to say what she wanted to hear.

"So, are we going to keep in touch with one another?"

"Uh, sure. I don't see why not," I lied, then watched a smile come across her face again. Knowing that I didn't plan on keeping my word almost made me feel worse.

"I was thinking that maybe you can even come back to visit when things settle down for you. Or maybe I can pay you a visit in Texas sometime."

"Yeah, that doesn't sound like a bad idea," I was able to get out between forkfuls of food.

"Good, because I'm really looking forward to us getting to know one another outside of our college years, Terrence."

There was a seductive tone in her voice, and I could clearly tell that she had an infatuation with me. If I wasn't mistaken, it had even been there during our time in college, but I hadn't paid much attention back then. Sitting across from her now, though, I was tempted to give it some thought, to get to know the woman she'd become, despite how much I was determined not to. I had to admit to myself that she was quite beautiful in her own way, and she had an amazing vibe about her that made her even more attractive. But coming to my senses, I realized I couldn't consider it even if I wanted to. At present, there was simply no room for her in my life. Not to mention with things being so fresh with me and Tiffany, I couldn't say where everything stood between us. All I knew was that she owed me a huge explanation for last night, and once my anger subsided, I'd be waiting for it.

I also couldn't entertain Malaysia until I got things squared away with my marriage. Although she was believing that I was already divorced, only God knew how long that whole process would actually take, especially now with Pat's ridiculous demands. So, there was no way I could add her to this pot of confusion I already had cooking.

"Uh, I think I better get out of here before I'm late for my flight," I announced, snapping out of my reverie.

"Oh yeah, you're right. I wouldn't want you to miss that flight," she agreed while getting up from the table. "Will you please let me know that you made it safely? And if you need anything at all regarding your pops, even if it's just to talk, I'm here for you," she told me as she walked me to the front door.

"I will definitely let you know when I make it home, and, again, I can't thank you enough for everything."

Before opening the door, Malaysia reached up to hug me, then gave me a sweet kiss on the lips. It was nice, very nice, and any other time I would have been flattered. But oddly enough, it only had me missing Tiff. I wanted to be kissing her. I needed her in my arms more than I truly wanted to admit it. That was why I was already trying to decide when I would break down and call her. We needed to talk, sooner rather than later. With that said, I kissed Malaysia on her cheek. She opened the door, and I stepped outside and waved goodbye. Once I got into my truck, I figured I'd go ahead and bite the bullet and call Tiffany. I pulled out away from Malaysia's condo, drove a little way, then called Tiffany. To my surprise, she didn't answer, which made me wonder if she was still with David. I hung up and dialed again, but there was still nothing, and then her voicemail clicked on. I was becoming madder by the second, so I finally chose to call Keisha.

"Hello?" she answered, with a weird sound in her voice.

"Hey, Keisha. It's Terrence."

"Okay, give me a second and let me step into my bedroom," she said, basically letting me know that Tiffany was near her. I held on, waiting for her to respond again. Then, without her ever taking a breath, she seethed, "Terrence, where are you? And what the hell happened last night at that hotel?"

"Whoa, whoa. Slow down, all right? Look, all I know is that when I got there, I snuck in to try to surprise her, but I'm the one that ended up getting the biggest surprise of us all. I found her in that punk David's arms, hugging him. And I'm telling you, Keisha, I had a mind to strangle his ass."

"So why didn't you?" she shot back. "His pathetic ass shouldn't have been there, anyway, so you really should have hurt him while you had the chance."

"Well, I don't know what he was doing there, but from my point of view, she seemed pretty comfortable with him, which is why I left. After I started to feel like I could have killed him, I came to my senses and decided to leave instead. I wasn't about to get arrested and sit in anybody's jail because of him. Besides, Tiffany was the one that allowed him in. She had her arms around him, and when I threw him against the wall, she pulled *me* off of *him*. So, in my mind, she made her choice. Did she at least tell you what he was doing there in the first place?"

"Trust me, she didn't want to, but basically, I gave her no other choice. She said something about his being diagnosed with cancer and her feeling the need to be there for him. But, Terrence, that man is a lying, good-for-nothing piece of trash, and I have a gut feeling that he's being dishonest about his sudden illness. Yet you and I both know that she can't see through his bull the way we can."

"Cancer, huh?"

"Yeah, that's what he's claiming, but none of this sounds right to me," Keisha replied. "He had no business being there, and in fact, he shouldn't even be in St. Louis. So, I know something weird is going on, and I plan on finding out exactly what it is and what he's up to."

"Well, anyway, after leaving the room, I got word that my pops passed away, and I pretty much blacked out at that point. There was no way I could deal with that whole situation with Tiffany and David after that. So, I left the hotel, crashed at an old friend's place for the night, and now I'm headed back home to start taking care of Pops's arrangements."

"Oh, Terrence, I'm so sorry. I had no idea he was sick. You and your family have my condolences. But don't you think Tiffany needs to know this too? Shouldn't you be talking to her right now instead of me?"

"I tried calling her before I called you, and she didn't answer."

"Oh, so you called me to see if she's here or still with him, right?"

"I guess you're a mind reader now, huh?"

"Oh, you didn't know? It's my second job," she said playfully, I assumed to try to lighten my spirits. "But, really, Terrence, she is here, but that's about all I can give you. We are kind of not speaking right now. But please try to call her again. She needs to know about your father's passing, and I'm sure you need her more than anything right now too. So, one of you guys needs to stop being stubborn."

"I guess you're right, but it's going to have to wait. I'm pulling up to the airport, and I need to hustle before I miss my check-in. But if you two make up, will you please tell her that I'll give her a call when I touch down?"

"Believe it or not, I think you'll be able to talk to her face-to-face. I overheard her talking to you all's boss, and she mentioned going back to Texas as soon as tomorrow."

"Wow. All right, well, in that case, don't tell her you spoke to me. I'll handle it from here."

We hung up, and first I raced to drop my truck off at Hertz Car Rental and then ran through the airport and checked in for my flight in the nick of time. I couldn't wait to sit down and try to process everything I had going on. The first thing to tackle was this divorce. Just before the gate attendants began the boarding process, I looked at my phone. Thinking of the devil herself, Patricia had called me three times while I was on the phone with Keisha. Lord knows what she wanted, but I chose to by-pass the awaiting voicemails for the moment. On top of that, Malaysia had shot me a text saying how good it was to see me again and that she hoped this would be the start of a wonderful friendship. "Damn." With my head cluttered with nothing but drama from each woman in my life, I boarded the plane, crawled into my seat, threw my head back, and closed my eyes.

"God, what on earth have I gotten myself into?" I muttered aloud.

CHAPTER 12

MALAYSIA

"Girl, I couldn't say everything I wanted to say while he was here, but, Toni, this man is fucking amazing," I told my bestie as I fell back on my sofa, where I could still smell his scent.

I had had her come over to my place the minute he left, and although she lived at least fifteen minutes from me, it had seemed like she'd gotten here in five minutes or less. Now, as she sat directly across from me, munching on a bag of potato chips like it was popcorn, her ears were wide open.

"All right, so tell me absolutely everything. And do not leave out a single detail."

"Well, there's really not much to tell, Tee, that I haven't already told you. We came back here and talked for a little while. Then he went to sleep here on the couch, while I slept in my room," I said, trying to remain discreet about what had really happened. Although I knew my friend would never disclose anything we talked about, I wanted Terrence to trust me fully. I didn't need him thinking that I told my friend every single detail about what had happened between us, even though I did.

"Oh no," she said, waving her hand. "I came all the way here, so don't go giving me some watered-down version. I want details. I want to know how he looked at you, if you talked in general or if there was deep conversation. Did he lick his lips while talking, did his tone change, and did that fine-ass man make them panties of yours drenching wet? Girl, tell me everything." She adjusted the position of her legs, making herself more comfortable. Right away, I knew there would be no way around *not* telling her the finer details. I was glad, however, that Larisse wasn't present. Even though they were both my best friends, I tended to confide more in Toni than her.

"All right. Well, while we were still at the Black Room, we mainly talked about college and things from back then. You know, just kind of catching up. Then he told me he was here for business but had to leave because his father passed away."

"Oh no, I hate to hear that. Was his dad sick? Were they close? Did he happen to mention what type of business he was here for?" Toni quizzed.

Knowing exactly where she was headed with her last question, I decided to set the record straight now rather than later. "Look, before you start, I don't care what the man does for a living. He could be a janitor, for heaven's sake, and it wouldn't matter to me one way or the other. He seems like a very decent guy, and that's all I'm concerned with."

Turning her lips up and giving me a sour look, she remained quiet. Although Toni pretty much bossed Larisse and others around, she knew exactly when enough was enough with me. Anyway, I let the minor tension between us die down before I continued.

"So, after talking a bit longer, I suggested that he drop me off so he could to get to his hotel, and that's when he told me he planned on sleeping in his truck for the night."

"Sleeping in his truck?" She side-eyed me.

"Yes, he said it was too late to get a hotel room, and since he was leaving early, he was going to crash in his truck."

"And you believed him?" she questioned before taking a sip of her juice and looking at me in a manner that said I was being naive.

"What reason would he have to lie, Tee?"

She took her hand out of her potato chip bag and began counting on her fingers as she called off the reasons. "Let's see, you're a beautiful woman, you're a single woman, he's a divorced man, the two of you are attracted to each other, and he could have buck-naked, hot, nasty, downright filthy sex with you here in the comfort of your own home. Do you need me to go on?"

I wanted to smack her, but knowing how my friend was, I decided to ignore her instead. "Listen, do you want me to finish or not?"

She waved her hand as if to say whatever, but I knew she was anxiously waiting to hear the rest. "Anyway, I invited him to stay the night here."

She gasped for air while covering her mouth with both hands. I was so tickled by her reaction that I burst out laughing, saliva shooting out of my mouth.

"Girl, what is wrong with you?"

"I'm sorry. I guess I'm just shocked that you invited him over, let alone to stay the night. I mean, Malaysia, we both know how you are when it comes to having strangers in your home."

"Yeah, but that's just it. He's no stranger to me. True enough, it's been years since we've seen each other, and even still, it wasn't like we were close friends in school. But, Tee, I felt so comfortable with him, so relaxed. I haven't felt this way around a man in a very long time, and being with Terrence last night felt good. Really good." I closed my eyes and quickly my mind went back to that moment in my bedroom when his arms engulfed me.

"Ooh, Malaysia, did you have sex with that man?" She got up, pointing her finger at me like kids did when someone was in trouble. My eyes shot back open.

"What? Toni girl, would you stop it already! Now, do you really believe I would have sex with him on the first night?"

"Hell, as fine as he is, yes. Because if you didn't, *I* surely would have. So, did you?"

I rolled my eyes and tried my best to answer her question without really answering. "Tee, what we shared was a beautiful expression of two familiar souls connecting as one."

"Wow." Her mouth fell open and stayed that way as she gazed into space.

"Girl, I swear, there's something about him that makes this feel right. I can't really explain it, but it's like his presence and energy made me feel, I don't know . . . Safe is the only way to put it."

The room had a quietness to it, and it lasted for a few minutes. I kept thinking of Terrence, while Toni stared at me, speechless, I assumed. That was when the one question that I believe both of us were thinking fell from my lips.

"Tee, do you believe in love at first sight?"

"Girl, I sure do and, Malaysia, I believe you are in love with that man."

"Yeah, me too, best friend. Me too."

CHAPTER 13

PATRICIA

"Kim, you are a jewel. Girl, I could kiss you for helping me like this." I'd come to her office bright and early to sign some documents, and I was ecstatic over the news she'd just shared with me. She'd put together an entire divorce agreement overnight, and now I was relishing the fact that Terrence would be served the minute he returned to Texas.

"All right, calm down, Pat, because we still have a ton of legal red tape to get through. But I think the hardest part is done. What we do need to discuss, though, is my fee. Now, I know that we're old friends and all, but, honey, being old friends doesn't pay the bills. So, here is some paperwork detailing my retainer fee and all fees thereafter. You can look it over at your leisure and then get back with me, okay?"

"Uh, okay," was all that I could say, because I was starting to feel that between her, David, and the pile of debt awaiting me from Terrence neglecting the bills, I would be lucky to see a few hundred bucks out of the million.

Speaking of Terrence, I knew he knew that I had called him, yet he had chosen not to call me back. Of course, I never imagined him running home to me, crying about what had happened with Tiffany, but I expected he would have at least called by now and told me about Pops. Plus,

I needed find out what his thinking was when it came to the house and the bills. After walking around this little space at my father's house, I was ready to get back to my home as quickly as possible.

"So, what do we do until he's served or hears back from his lawyer?" I asked Kim.

"We wait. And something tells me that's going to be extremely hard for you. But, Pat, I'm going to be honest with you. If we can get a judge on your side, then I don't need you to go messing things up with a bunch of nonsense."

"Nonsense? Trying to get my husband back home is not nonsense. Trying to get that home-wrecker out of his life is not nonsense. And trying to get him to love me again is surely not nonsense."

Suddenly, I began reflecting on how distant he and I had become with one another. It was like we had turned into two completely opposite people compared to when we first married, and it seemed like we hardly knew each other anymore. While I was aware that my behavior of late may not have been becoming of a wife, I loved my husband, nonetheless. And I placed the blame and the sorry state of our marriage directly on him, along with Tiffany Tate. He never should have started having lunch dates with her, posting pictures on social media with her, or doing anything else *with* her. He should have done those things with me. It was almost like she was his wife, and I was merely the one on the outside, looking in. It wasn't right, and that was why I felt more than justified about my actions, no matter how off the wall they seemed. It was purely my way of slapping some sense into him so that we could get our lives and our family back on track.

"Listen, why don't you go home and just relax, Pat? Like I told you last night, by the time I'm done, either your husband will call this all off or we'll have sucked him dry. You're going to win either way."

"Yeah, well, I can't even get my husband to answer a damn phone call from me, so I'm sorry, but I'm not feeling like much of a winner right now," I said, realizing that my marriage was possibly over. Getting back at Terrence had been all fun and games at first, but now I wasn't so sure about that.

Once I made it to my car, however, I felt it was time I started contemplating my next move. I began to dial the number of my partner in crime to check up on him. It took a few rings, but he finally answered, sounding like he was still sleeping.

"Hello?"

"Rise and shine, sleepyhead. We have work to do."

"Patricia," he mumbled. "What time is it?"

"It's time for you to get up and get started on the next part of our plan. I need you to go to Tiffany's room and find out what's happened since you left. Find out if he's called her or if she called him and just what's going on. I also want to know what her next move will be when it comes to them. Plus, I need you to lay your illness on a little thicker than before. You have cancer, remember, so act like you're not feeling well at all, like you're drained and fatigued. Make her feel so sorry for you that she'll forget all about my husband."

"Patricia, look, I started thinking last night, and I don't know about all of this anymore. I mean, it was cool at first, and fucking with your husband was fun and all, but I kept seeing Tiffany's face in my sleep. It's not right for me to do her like this, because, honestly, I've already caused her enough pain. Besides, I don't know how to go about faking having cancer anyway. What if this comes back to haunt me in some way?"

"Tiffany, Tiffany, Tiffany. I swear, that woman has you and my husband both caught up in that little web of hers, but I think I should make myself extremely clear to you,

David. You don't have a choice in the matter. If you want another dime from me, then you will do exactly as I say, or otherwise consider our agreement officially canceled. Either way, I'll get what I want, and you'll remain dead-ass broke."

There was complete silence on the other end of the line. I suspected he was giving what I'd said some real thought before answering, especially the part about getting paid. A second later, it seemed like he'd come to his senses.

"What did you want me to do again?" he asked in a huff.

I giggled to myself about the fact that I had him right in the palm of my hand.

"Like I said, find out where your girl's head is when it comes to my husband. Once we do that, I'll decide what should happen next. And, David, just a little reminder. Don't fuck this up, because of your feelings for her, all right? We have a job to do, and you can't go getting all soft on me."

He hung up without saying another word, but I believed I had got my point across. There was nothing left for me to do at this point but wait, just like Kim had said. I figured waiting would be easy now. With all the pieces of the puzzle coming together the way they were, I knew they would eventually fall right into place.

CHAPTER 14

DAVID

After hanging up on Patricia, I threw my phone on the bed as hard as I could and let out a long, exasperated sigh. There was no way I could continue to allow this woman to have control over me, no matter how much money was involved.

Once I'd returned from Tiffany's hotel room last night and updated Patricia on what had taken place, I had ordered room service and had drunk until I passed out. I'd tossed and turned in my sleep the rest of the night. I'd kept having visions of Tiffany's face and the way she'd looked at me in her hotel room, especially when I'd confessed how afraid I was of dying. She had shown a sincere concern for me, something that I'd never expected, mainly because of everything I'd already put her through.

Her tenderness toward me was what basically had me now regretting this whole cancer scheme. Not to mention the dreams I had had through the night, which had scared the hell out of me. It made me wonder if this was some kind of warning. So, although I desperately needed the money, I wasn't all the way sure it was worth it. I decided that for the time being, I would go ahead and do what Patricia needed me to do. But I would also find a way to get her out of my life—while at the same time getting my hands on some cash. Even if that meant coming face-to-face with Terrence again.

As I got cleaned up and dressed, I put together a plan
in my mind on how I would approach things with Tiffany
today. Despite what Pat had said, I felt like I'd pretty
much laid the illness bit on much too thick last night, so
this morning would be all about rekindling our friendship. I figured I would head to her room and invite her to
have breakfast with me. From there, I would simply take
her on a trip down memory lane, recalling times when
things were decent between us. I knew that would put her
in the exact mood I needed for her to spill her guts about
her and Terrence. If there was one thing I knew for sure,
she would need a shoulder to cry on, and mine would be
ready and available.

After slipping on my shoes, I grabbed my room key
and headed out the door and down the hall. As I made
my way closer to her room, I could tell that her door was
wide open.

"There's no way she could be gone already. It's nowhere
near checkout time," I mumbled aloud.

Curious to see what was going on, I picked up my
speed. When I reached Tiffany's room, I didn't stop. I
walked inside and found the housekeeper making the
bed.

"Good morning," I said in a friendly tone, so that she
wouldn't think I was up to any funny business.

She smiled, nodded her head, and returned the pleas-
antry.

"Um, the woman that was staying in this room, where
is she?" I questioned.

"Oh, sir, the guest that was here checked out already.
Early this morning."

"Really? Okay. Thanks."

Perplexed, I retreated to the hallway. Why had Tiffany
left the hotel so early, and where had she gone? It made
me nervous to think that Terrence might have made his

way back to her hotel room last night. Quickly, I started dialing her number, only to get her voicemail. I tried her several more times, to no avail.

"C'mon, Tiff, answer the damn phone already." I danced around in the hallway as I kept dialing her number. That was, until the cleaning lady came running out of room.

"Sir, sir, your friend left this inside the room. Can you get it to her, or should I take it down to our lost and found?" she said, standing there, dangling a diamond heart-shaped locket in from of me. I took it out of her hand and opened it, only to find a picture of her on one side and one of Terrence on the other. It pissed me off that she was so caught up with this punk that he couldn't be faithful to his own wife. Tiff had to know there was no way he would suddenly be a changed man for her.

"Uh yeah. Don't worry. I can make sure she gets this back."

"Thank you. Thank you so much, sir. It looks quite expensive, and I would hate for her to not have it."

Little did the woman know, she'd just brightened my entire morning, as the word *expensive* echoed again and again in my head. Immediately, I began calculating how much I could possibly get for the locket if I decided to go that route.

All right, David. You can either use this as a way to reach out to Tiffany or hang on to it for a little cash, just in case Patricia doesn't hold up her end of our deal, I thought to myself. Contemplating the latter scenario, I pulled up Google on my phone and did a search of pink diamond heart-shaped necklaces to see how much this one might be worth. After I got what I needed, I dialed Patricia's number.

She picked up before the phone had completed its first ring. "Hey, what are you doing calling me? I thought you would be with Tiffany right now?" she said, getting right down to business. It made me ask myself if this woman had any type of life outside of torturing her poor husband.

"Look, I tried, Patricia, but it appears that she checked out early this morning."

"Checked out? This early? Where did she go? Did she leave to try to find my husband, or did she leave *with* him?"

Man, this woman was really getting on the last little nerve I had left. "Now, how in the hell am I supposed to know if she went looking for Terrence or if she's with him? All I know is that she checked out of the hotel already. I have no clue about the rest, all right?"

"Wait, are you calling yourself yelling at me, David? Because if so, I have a mind to call this entire deal off, you know."

Tossing Tiffany's locket around in the palm of my hand, I decided to go ahead and call her bluff. "You know what? Do whatever you think you need to do, Pat, because I'm over this. I'm not about to let you keep talking to me any type of way you want just because you have money hanging over my head. So, if what I'm doing is not good enough for you, while all you do is bark orders, then find yourself another flunky. I'm done."

I hung up and immediately Googled the nearest pawnshop. "I'm sorry, Tiff, but right now, I have to do what I have to do."

Following that, I dialed my mother's number, hoping to catch her in better spirits than where we'd left off before I came to St. Louis. I truly wanted to make things right with her. More so, I *needed* to. She was my mother, and we'd never gone this long without speaking. Not to mention, her house was the only place I had left where I could lay my head when I returned to Texas.

"Hello, David," she answered, greeting me in a monotone.

"Hey, Mama. How are you?" I responded, upbeat and chipper, trying to sway her mood to match mine.

"Where are you, David, and what do you need? Because we haven't spoken since you got upset with me for saying that you needed to start behaving like a grown man."

"Mama, look, I understood exactly where you were coming from, but I guess I needed some time to mull things over. I love you, and I hate not talking to you."

"Well, you know I love you too, son." Her tone was lighter now, and I could feel her bending a bit, which was why I felt it was the perfect time to ask.

"So, Mama, I know you have your friend there and everything, but I could sort of use somewhere to lay my head for a few days. That's if you don't mind, of course."

"I already asked him to leave, David, while waiting for you to call. Something told me you would be calling soon enough. So, c'mon home. And you may as well bring all your dirty clothes with you, so I can wash those too. But let me just go on the record by saying that you really need to get your business in order and to stop playing around with all these different women. They don't mean you anything but trouble."

I rolled my eyes, because I had had a gut feeling there was no way we would end this call without her having the final say about my life.

"Mama, Mama, okay, I hear you, and I will do whatever it takes to get things in order." It was then that I knew there was no way I could possibly tell her anything about Sonya and her soon-to-be grandchild. That would have to wait until she was in a much different type of mood.

After she read me the riot act a little longer, I rushed her off the phone before she gave me anymore motherly notions or unwanted advice. But also, I'd just received another text message from an unknown phone number, and I wanted to see what that was all about right away. I was surprised when I opened the text.

You know you're not going to get away with what you did. When I find you, consider yourself dead.

Whoever this was, was making deadly threats now, and I had to admit, this scared the crap out of me. I had two women who hated my guts, but I hadn't been able to judge which one hated me more. Either way, Sonya or Leslie wasn't going to get away with this. The minute I stepped foot back in Texas, I would deal with both of them, even if it meant getting the police involved.

CHAPTER 15

PATRICIA

"How dare he hang up on me and bail on our plan like this!" I was livid, and if David knew what was good for him, he'd better damn sure be thinking of a way to get back into my good graces. I'd given him a little bit of cash so far, along with paying for his trip and his stay in St. Louis, and he hadn't done nearly enough to cover those expenses. And I didn't plan on letting him get away with this. He would work for me until I felt like I had been paid back in full.

I didn't have any more time to worry about him, though, because my focus had turned back to Terrence and Tiffany. First, I checked both their social media pages. Still, there weren't any new updates on hers, but I noticed that my husband had made a post about the passing of his father.

"So, you can go on social media and tell the world about your father, but you couldn't have the decency to call your own wife?" I muttered aloud.

I didn't know why Terrence's behavior continued to surprise me. He was acting like he didn't love me or his children anymore, the way he had shut us out of his life. I began thinking back to our wedding day, when we had vowed to love one another and be there for one another, for better or for worse. We had been so excited and so committed to our future. Now it seemed like I was the only one holding up my end of our vows.

Not really knowing which way to turn at this point, I called our oldest son, Kendall, into my bedroom. "Kendall, Kendall, come here for a second, honey."

He dragged himself into the room, which was normal for him. As much as I hated to admit it, Terrence was right about our son needing to do something more with his life than what he had been doing. I just didn't want Terrence to be the one to tell him that, for fear that Kendall would end up resenting him for it.

"Yeah, Mom?"

"Baby, can I see your phone for a sec? I need to call your father."

He fidgeted around with the basketball in his hands for a few minutes. I knew he always kept that cell phone in his back pocket, so I couldn't understand what was taking him so long to give it to me.

"Kendall, what's wrong? Didn't you hear me ask you for your cell phone?"

"Yeah, but, but maybe you shouldn't call him, Mom." He put his head down after he said that.

"Now, Kendall, I know you're not still upset about when your father tried to put you out. Honey, that was a long time ago, and we're a family, so we don't hold grudges, all right?"

"But that's just it, Mom. We're *not* a family. Terrence isn't concerned about me and Keith. And it's more than obvious that he doesn't love you either. What husband and father goes around posting pictures of himself and another woman all over his social media? So, look, we're not in that house with him anymore, and I think that's a good thing. So why don't you stop making yourself look crazy and just leave him alone and go on with your life already, because clearly, he's gone on with his." He reached into his back pocket and pulled out his phone, then threw it on my bed and stormed out of the room.

"Kendall. Kendall, you come back in here. I'm not done with you yet," I yelled, but he went right outside, completely ignoring me. My mouth was wide open, as I felt dumbfounded by what he had said. Kendall had always been my quiet child and had never said much, but today he'd sure given me a mouthful, and it had caught me way off guard. I almost wanted to cry after hearing him express his feelings about his father that way, but right now I *had* to call Terrence. I was even more determined to do whatever it took to keep our family together, as well as to prove to Kendall that his father did love us.

The only thing I prayed was that Terrence would finally be ready to see how his actions were destroying our family and would be open to change, for all our sakes. I also believed that it was about time I gave Ms. Tiffany Tate a call and spoke with her woman to woman. She needed to know that not only was her conduct with another woman's husband inappropriate, but it was also damaging a father's relationship with his two teenage sons. I would see what she had to say for herself then.

Dialing Terrence's number from Kendall's phone, I prayed that he would answer. At least that would mean that he still cared about his children. The first call went to voicemail, but I wanted to give him the benefit of the doubt, to show myself that he wouldn't ignore his son too, so I called again. After several rings, the second call went to voicemail too. I tried telling myself that maybe he was speaking with someone regarding Pops, so I called yet again. This time my hand started to shake, and a single tear fell from my eye when I heard the voicemail connect once again. Not only had he not been responding to my calls, but he also wouldn't even respond to his own son's call.

It was now time that I made the call I'd been putting off all this time. I didn't have her number directly, but I had previously noticed that she was connected to Facebook Messenger, and I could call her from there. Taking a deep breath, I pressed SEND when her name came up. It rang a couple of times. When the ringing stopped, I was about to disconnect. Then I heard a voice.

"Hello?"

Suddenly, my mind went blank. Before calling, I had had so much pent-up anger, and I had known exactly what I wanted to say, but now that I had her on the line, I fumbled with my words. That was until I heard her say hello again, and I felt it was now or never.

"Hello, Ms. Tate. This is Patricia Montgomery, Terrence's wife."

I heard her gasp before the phone became silent. I knew she had hundreds of questions roaming through her head about what I was doing on the other end of the line. So, I hurried to provide some answers before she hung up in my face.

"Tiffany, I'm calling because I believe it's about time you and I had a woman-to-woman conversation. Now, I know I've done some questionable things in the past, and I want you to know that I'm sorry for that. However, this time I'm coming to you as not only a wife but also as a mother that's hurting about the relationship between her husband and children."

She didn't say anything at first. But then she gave a deep sigh and addressed me.

"Mrs. Montgomery, listen, first of all, I think it's rude that you called me without me ever giving you my number directly. You and I don't know one another, so you shouldn't be calling me. Secondly, yes, you did a lot in the past, unthinkable things that could have damaged my entire reputation and career at the school. But you said you're coming to me now as a wife and mother who is hurting for her husband and children. Trust me, I totally sympathize with you on that. However, that's not my fault or my concern. I didn't have the power to come in and break up anything that wasn't already damaged. And from the outside looking in, your and Terrence's problems started way before I entered the picture. So, the person you need to be communicating with is your husband. Not me. And just a little piece of advice, like you said, woman to woman . . . My mother always told me never to let a man tell you or show you more than once that he doesn't want you. Have a good day, Patricia."

She hung up, and I swore I could have hurt someone with my bare hands. Here I was, letting my guard down, hoping that another woman would understand what I felt. But in an arrogant and snobbish manner, she had practically thrown it all back in my face. Then to tell me that she sympathized with me. "Well, I don't need anyone's pity or sympathy, Tiffany. Not yours, not my son's, not anyone else's," I muttered audibly. However, one thing she was right about for sure was that I needed to be speaking directly with Terrence. I didn't know if I had to go to St. Louis and track him down or if I would confront him at his father's funeral service. One way or another, though, I was going to find my husband, and he was going to make time to talk to me.

As I gathered my belongings together to embark on my search for Terrence, I couldn't forget what Tiffany had said last. *My mother always told me never let a man tell you or show you more than once that he doesn't want you.* I laughed when I realized that this had come from a woman who hadn't been married a day in her life and couldn't even hang on to a pathetic-ass fiancé like David, for that matter. She had no clue about the things a wife had to endure to keep her husband happy and satisfied.

CHAPTER 16

TERRENCE

I'd always been someone who loved to travel, but the minute the plane landed, I took a deep breath, inhaling the fresh Texas air. It was good to be back home, although I wouldn't be here long. During the flight, I'd made my to-do list, and first things first, I needed to get home and to repack. Then I would head out bright and early in the morning to go and see my stepmother, so that we could make the arrangements for Pops. That I would have the house all to myself was one reason I was glad Patricia had gone through with her whole charade of moving to her father's. There was no way I could deal with her today with all that I had going on. Plus, I needed one night alone, to myself, in the peace and quiet of my home.

I headed to the baggage claim and caught an Uber. Half an hour later, the driver pulled up in front of my place. After getting out of the Uber, I grabbed my overnight bag and went to the mailbox first. It seemed as if Patricia hadn't been back to the house once because the mailbox was stuffed with mail, and some of it had fallen to the ground.

"Damn, Pat. The least you could have done was pick up the mail. The neighbors probably think we've abandoned the house," I muttered aloud. I shook my head as I took out as much of the mail as I could manage to hold.

Then I turned on my heels and headed toward the front door, flipping through a stack of envelopes as I went. My heart almost jumped out of my chest when I saw a number of late notices, disconnection notices, and foreclosure notices. I couldn't wait to get inside, because whether I was ready to deal with Patricia or not, it was time.

I stuck my key in the doorknob, unlocked the door, and walked inside. I was still focused intently on the mail when I dropped my bag on the sofa. Or I would have if the sofa was there. I heard my bag hit the living-room floor. After slowly looking up, I canvassed the room. My stomach sank, and my eyes bulged out of my head at the sight of . . . nothing. Not a stick of furniture. I ran from room to room, then upstairs and down to the lower level. When I had left the house, Patricia had taken only a few pieces of furniture. But now my entire home was empty, except for my clothes and some minor things.

"This is just like in my dream. My whole fucking house is empty," I exclaimed as I stood in the empty living room. Then my eyes caught a glimpse of a large yellow envelope lying on top of a pile of my things in a corner. "Your divorce papers, huh, Pat? You are a real piece of work. I don't know what the hell I was thinking ever marrying you."

Just like Randle had said, this heffa had had the nerve to issue her own divorce documents after refusing to sign mine for weeks. Not only that, but she had the nerve to claim that due to my infidelity, she was entitled to the bulk of our estate, so that she and the boys could keep up the lifestyle they were accustomed to. True enough, I'd already heard this nonsense from Randle, but it was an entirely different thing seeing it in black and white with my own eyes.

"You bitch!" I yelled at the top of my lungs, and I heard the words echo through the empty house. I pulled out

my cell phone as quickly as I could to dial Randle and
see what he had possibly come up with. That was when
I heard someone put a key in the front doorknob. Slowly,
I turned around, only to see the devil herself standing
there, with a dumb-ass smirk adorning her face.

"Well, hello, dear husband. Welcome back home."

"You gotta be fucking kidding me, Pat. You know, if I
were the type of man to put my hands on a woman, they
would be around your neck right now."

"Really? Well, it seems like these are the lengths I have
to go to in order to get a peep out of you. I've called you,
texted, left voicemails, and even your sons tried to reach
out to you. But did you answer? No. Instead you were
living it up with your little mistress all the way in St.
Louis, much too busy to care about the well-being of your
family."

"How did you know I was in St. Louis? Are you stalking
me now?" I growled.

"Oh, is that what we're calling it these days? A wife
trying to reach her husband is now considered *stalking*?"

I drew a little closer to her so that she would know
I meant business. "What more do you want from me?
You've taken everything out of the house. You're trying
to get every dime I have to my name. You've just about
taken my dignity away from me. So, what more is there,
Pat? Whatever it is, you can have it, as long as that
means I will get away from you and will live peacefully. I
don't even care anymore." I said this purely out of anger,
because, Lord knows, I had nothing left to give. The
house was going into foreclosure. We had had the cars
for a number of years, and they weren't worth anything
now. I had little in terms of savings. The only thing I did
have coming my way was Pops's money, which I was still
determined to keep away from her gritty hands, married
or divorced.

As I looked at her, she had the nerve to stand there with tears creeping down her face.

"Oh no, no. Don't you dare start the crying antics now. See, that's what the hell you do best, trying to make me feel sorry for you. I'm not falling for it anymore. I'm over it."

She struggled to get out what she needed to say. Then, in a flash, it seemed like the words came spilling from her lips. "Honestly, all I want Terrence is my husband and my family back. The home, cars, or any amount of money doesn't matter. None of it does if you, me, and the boys aren't together."

Before I knew it, I found myself so close to her that I wrapped my hands around her arms and started shaking her. "When are you going to get it? I don't want you anymore, Patricia. I don't want you or this garbage of a marriage," I yelled.

She screamed at the top of her lungs, and all at once I caught myself. In an instant, I started dialing her father's number.

"Who are you calling? Who the hell are you calling, Terrence?" she yelled like a crazy woman while reaching over my arm, trying to take my phone.

"Please, please come around here and get your daughter. I'm trying my best not to put my hands on her. Please come and get her," I begged her father the second he picked up.

His home was less than five minutes from ours, so he was there in no time. When he walked in, Patricia and I were in our separate corners of the living room, as if it were a boxing ring. However, all we were doing was yelling at one another.

I watched as her father went over to her and tried to calm her down. Her complexion was now pale and red all at the same time. Her face was drenched in tears, and she'd sweated out her hair. I'd left marks on her arms when I grabbed her. Anyone who didn't know any better would have sworn we'd been in some type of tussle. Thank God, however, I had decided to call her father instead of the police. Her father took her face between his hands and asked her a simple question.

"Patricia, what's going on?"

"Daddy, I just came over and tried to talk to him. I just wanted to tell him how much me and the boys need him."

"But, baby, you and Terrence have been going through this for far too long now. I know you might want to fix it, but sometimes, baby, it's just not meant to be. So, why would you want to stay with someone and be with someone who clearly doesn't love you anymore?"

A hush that was indescribable came over the house. You could basically hear a pin drop. But then, between her whimpering and sniffing, she stated, "Because I still love him and always will."

He put his arms around his daughter and hugged her tight. True enough, I was angry for all that had taken place, but I hated seeing her that way. Because, despite it all, right now she was still my wife. A second later, right before they left, her father came over to me, surprisingly, and shook my hand.

"Thank you, son, for calling me first and not harming my daughter. I may not like what's going on, but I can respect you for at least doing that."

I shook his hand and nodded my head in return, then watched them walk out the door. Not knowing what to do with myself at that point, I thought about calling Tiffany. As of late, she had been the first person I ran to when I was faced with a serious situation. But I was still confused about the whole David issue, and I wasn't sure how to address it. Besides, after what had taken place with Pat, I was too mentally drained and couldn't afford to possibly have another emotional encounter.

I gazed down at my phone just then, and I noticed I'd received several messages from Malaysia. I'd promised myself that I wouldn't include her in my drama and that our encounters would be limited to the one in St. Louis, but at the moment, I needed to hear a friendly and upbeat voice.

"Hey, you."

"Terrence, I really didn't expect for you to call. I figured you were kind of busy handling everything for your father's service." She sounded shocked, yet happy.

"Yeah, I was, but I had something else come up. Anyway, what are you up to?"

"Uh, my usual. Hanging out with Toni and Larisse, working, and watching HGTV. I guess it sounds kind of boring, huh?"

"Hey, I'd rather be there with you any day, watching HGTV, instead of going through the drama in my life."

"Wow, what a coincidence, because I'd much rather be there with you." I heard that same giggle from her after she said it. Her voice was low and sexy, yet her message came through loud and clear. I gave it a quick run-through in my head and decided what the hell.

"So, what's stopping you?"

"What are you talking about?" She tried to laugh it off, but I knew she wondered if I was serious.

"What's stopping you from being here with me? I mean, I could really use the support of a friend."

"Really? I guess I didn't think you wanted me to be a part of such an intimate time for you. I assumed it would be your family and close friends."

"You're not my close friend?" I asked. I could almost see her blushing through the phone. "It's not like I go around crying my heart out on everybody."

"Terrence, you better stop playing, before you have me on a plane in the next hour."

"I dare you," I said, testing her as well as myself. Half of me was only talking trash to take my mind away from what had just happened with Pat. But the other half of me really wanted someone by my side and, well, she was available.

"Okay, all jokes aside. Do you *really* want me there with you?"

"Will you really come?"

"You already know I will."

We both hesitated, waiting on the other to speak first. Then I made a decision that I honestly couldn't believe I was making.

"All right. So, what I'll do is send you my flight information, and you can see if you can find a flight that will connect with me at the DFW Airport here in Dallas around the same time," I told her.

"Are you sure?"

"I'm positive. And, Malaysia, I can't wait to see you again."

We hung up with each other, and I had to ask myself what in the world I was doing. I knew I didn't want Malaysia in the same manner that she wanted me, but something mysterious and mystifying was happening between us. Something I hadn't experienced with Patricia, or even with Tiffany, for that matter. Something, I had to admit, that I wanted to know more about. Maybe my mind was only playing tricks on me, because of the emotional state I was in. I'd never lost someone so close to me, and I felt confused about how to process what I was feeling. But right then I needed to enjoy some aspect of my life. Since I couldn't do that with Tiff, then Malaysia was a befitting alternative. I continued to reason with myself that she and I were only friends and that my heart was still with Tiffany, or so I hoped.

CHAPTER 17

MALAYSIA

While waiting for Toni and Larisse to show up at our favorite restaurant, I ordered a round of drinks and started skimming the menu. I wasn't too famished, because pure excitement had taken over, so much so that I could literally jump out of my skin. It was still unbelievable to me that I was about to take a trip with an amazing man, even if it was only to make arrangements for a funeral. And I figured tonight was the perfect opportunity to have a little girl time, since I was leaving in the morning.

Having already told Toni that I would be leaving for a couple of days with Terrence, I began debating how much I wanted to share with Larisse. She still wasn't aware that Terrence had stayed at my place that first night, and I kind of wanted to keep it that way. Larisse just had a way of letting things slip out at the wrong place and the wrong time, such as at work, among the nosy parkers. The last thing I needed was to have all of them in my business. With that in mind, I knew that tonight Toni and I would have to tiptoe around the topic of my trip, and I hoped she picked up on my hints.

A few minutes later I saw the waitress escorting them to the table.

"Hey, girl," Toni greeted me first, as usual.

"Hey, girl," Larisse chimed in, sounding like her sister's echo.

"Hey, y'all." I stood up and hugged them both like it had been ages since we'd last seen one another. Then, before I was able to say anything or let on to Toni that we would talk about the trip some other time, she did the precise thing that I was worried about.

"So, c'mon and tell us about this trip," she said, not having a clue about what she was doing.

"Yeah, tell us everything about you and Mr. Wonderful going away for a couple of days," Larisse added as we all sat down.

At once, I was positive she knew all about the first night too.

"But wait, hold on. Because I need to run to the ladies' room really quick. I'll be right back, so don't start without me," Larisse told me.

Larisse got up and left the table, and I immediately went in on Toni. "Why did you say anything to your sister about Terrence?"

She tried to put on an innocent act. "Girl, why not? You know she asked a million questions after leaving the cigar bar, so what was I supposed to do?"

"Shut your big mouth, that's what. You know that girl speaks without thinking sometimes, and I don't need all my personal business circulating around the office, with those nosy-ass women."

"All right, I'm sorry. But I figured you'd tell her sooner or later, anyway, especially since it seems you and Mr. Montgomery are getting pretty close really fast."

I couldn't help it when a huge smile crossed my face as I thought back to a few days earlier.

"Okay, you all must have started without me, the way Malaysia is over here smiling," Larisse said when she reached the table.

"Well, I guess the two of you already know that I'm going away for a couple of days with Terrence, to be there for him while he plans his father's funeral. But, y'all, I'm starting to feel like this is love at first sight. I mean, I haven't been able to stop thinking about him, and the feeling he gives me is insane."

"Chile, tell us something we didn't already know," Toni said. "This is the first man you've let around you in quite a long time."

"So, what is it that you love about him anyway?" Larisse spoke for herself, not waiting for Tee to say it first.

"I don't know . . . He's just perfect. He's nice looking, charming, intelligent, he can cook, and he has dreams and ambitions, because he plans to open his own restaurant. Not to mention, he's about to come into quite a bit of money. What else could a girl ask for?"

"I don't know what else a girl could ask for, but I'm starting to wonder why a man this perfect is single. And who goes around bragging about money he's getting from his father's passing?" Toni had to play devil's advocate, like always.

"Me too, Malaysia. Something just doesn't seem right about that. I mean, all the women in Texas, and no one has caught his eye?" Larisse interjected, trying to have an opinion once again.

"Look, he wasn't bragging, all right? We were having a mere conversation, and it came up. I don't even think he realized that he told me. And trust me, I hear both of you and your concerns, but I choose to trust Terrence until he gives me a reason not to. He's already told me that he's divorced and that he briefly dated some crazy chick afterward. That's it. That's why he is single."

"Okay, and what happened to the *crazy chick*? And besides, what exactly made her crazy?" Toni asked, with a touch of suspicion still in her voice.

"Uh, he didn't quite go into detail about it. He only said that she started behaving crazy and obsessed—well, his actual words were that she was garbage—and that things just didn't work out. Hell, I got to experience a little of her craziness too, because every time his phone buzzed, it was her."

Toni held her hands up in front of her. "Wait, hold up. He said he was completely done with this woman, but she's still texting and calling him?" They both looked at me with doubt in their eyes.

"Tee, he's a good guy. He said he doesn't want to hurt the woman's feelings. He said he knows that she's in love with him, and he's been trying to find the best way possible to let her down. But in the time being, he answers her texts here and there. But you know what's crazy? The woman is from St. Louis too."

"What?" they said in unison.

"Yeah, that's what he said."

"Well, what's her name? Let's look her up on social media," Larisse insisted, not being her normal quiet self at all.

"I kind of promised him I wouldn't, y'all. Besides, he said she's so crazy that if she ever found out that he was dealing with someone else, she might stalk me, so he asked me to block her from my Facebook page."

"Listen, you're my girl, so if you want to believe this man, then I am right there with you," Toni said. "But for me, it still isn't coming together, so I'm going to keep a close watch on Mr. Montgomery."

"Me too, sis," Larisse added, going right back to what I was used to her doing, which was just agreeing with Toni.

I took a sip of my margarita while thinking about what the two of them had said. Obviously, it did seem a little strange that such a wonderful man wasn't with anyone, but I chose to look at it as perfect timing for the two of us. In any case, I wasn't about to let him go, not for an ex-wife, ex-girlfriend, or anyone. I was already dead set on one day becoming Mrs. Terrence Montgomery, and I wasn't turning back now. I must have missed Toni calling my name, because both of them were staring at me like I was crazy when I snapped out of my daze.

"So, back up a bit. How much money is the man supposed to come into anyway?" Toni asked me.

Looking over my glass while indulging in more of my margarita, I decided that before I answered that question, I had to insist that Larisse be as discreet as possible.

"All right. Listen, Larisse, this information at this table better not come up once in the office, at work, understand?"

"Okay, I got it," she answered, almost sounding offended.

"Terrence said he's due to get, like, one million dollars from his father's estate," I revealed.

I had expected some crazy reaction when I shared the amount with them, but they damn near fell out of their chairs.

"Wow! You're going to have a millionaire for a man? I'm so jealous," my best friend said.

I smiled. "I still can't believe it myself, you guys. Me? With a successful, wealthy man, after the type of lowlife I was about to marry? God must be giving me double for my trouble, baby."

We all high-fived each other, and since I was in such an amazing mood, and was about to have a wealthy-ass man, I ordered another round of drinks for the table. Meeting Terrence again was my key to finally having the life I deserved, and that was something to celebrate.

CHAPTER 18

DAVID

"Open up, Sonya." I kept banging on her front door while yelling for her to open it. The minute I had got off the plane, I'd headed straight there. And if there was anything she could say to make me believe she wasn't the culprit behind those threatening text messages, then Leslie was next. "C'mon, Sonya! Don't make me break this door down. I know you're in there because your car is here."

After a few minutes more of my banging and yelling, I finally heard her making her way to the door. She unlocked it and opened it slowly, hesitant to reveal herself. I figured that was because she knew what she was in for.

"What's up, man? What can we do for you?" asked a tall, slender young man wearing a wifebeater, his jeans hanging off his ass, once the door was open. There he stood with the brim of his hat to the back, a square behind one ear, and a gun stuck in the front of his jeans. I also got a good whiff of marijuana smoke from inside the house as he shifted his weight from one leg to the other. Clearly, I must have woken him up because he was still wiping junk from his eyes.

"Uh, where's Sonya, young man?" I asked, wondering if maybe he was some long-lost relative or something.

"She ain't here right now, Pops. Who should I say came by?"

"Never mind all that. I'll just give her call," I told him, refusing to give the punk my name. He was probably the one having her make all those threats to me anyway. In fact, from his looks, I was convinced he was.

"Suit yourself, Pops." He closed the door quickly, I assumed to get right back to his midday slumber. Something about him wasn't sitting well with me. Plus, the young buck had the gall to call me Pops. Well, I had the right mind to show him that this *Pops* could still teach him a lesson, for sure. If he didn't have that weapon on him, I would have pulled him outside and beat the crap out of his ass. Instead, I dialed Sonya's number. Something told me she wasn't going to answer, but to my surprise, her phone hadn't even rung for ten seconds before I heard her voice come on the line.

"What do you want, David?"

"Who's this kid at your house, answering your door?"

"What are you doing at my house to begin with? And that *kid* you're speaking of is much more of a man than you'll ever be. So again, what do you want?"

"Listen, I know it's you behind these messages I've been getting, and it needs to stop now. You're not scaring anyone. And if you keep it up, you're going to have to deal with either me or the police."

"Who the hell do you think you are calling me and making threats toward me, David? First off, no one is scared of your sorry ass, and please trust and believe that I don't have time to waste to play games with a lowlife like you. I have a fatherless child to be concerned about, not you. But I'm sure I'm not the only one that you've done wrong in your life, so go harass one of your other women and see if it was them. Oh, and just to make myself totally clear, if you call me or come near my home again, I'll have Dante' deal with you, and trust me, you wouldn't want that."

She hung up. I was hating the fact that I had ever dealt with Sonya from the start. She wasn't the woman that I had thought she was, and now I was regretting that she was going to be the mother of my child. Thinking about it, however, I had to admit that she sounded very convincing about not being the one sending the text messages. That made me realize there was only one person left who could be behind all of this. None other than Leslie. I wasn't exactly sure how to reach her. She'd had her number changed, and as far as I knew, she didn't live in that house anymore. But I *did* know someone who would know exactly how I could find her, and my next plan of action was to pay them a little visit.

After getting back into my car and starting the engine, I noticed that my gas light had come on and it wouldn't be long before I was on empty. I fumbled through my pockets and pulled out a just few bills. I didn't have much of anything left from what Pat had sent me, but I thought maybe if I got back on good terms with her, she would help a brother out. I gave her a call.

"Hello?" she answered with a very somber tone, nothing like the Patricia that I was used to.

"Hey, Pat. It's your partner in crime, and I'm back in Texas. So, what's our next mission?"

"David, there is no mission, all right? I'm calling this whole thing off, so consider yourself free and clear."

"But wait a minute. What about making sure you keep Tiffany out of Terrence's life? What about the things we've already done, like the cancer I lied about? You set this entire plan in motion, and now you're just going to call it quits just like that? And what about my share of the one million dollars?"

"Look, David, I don't care anymore about any of that, all right? Now, I gave you a few hundred, and that should cover what you've already done for me, but you have no share in the one million. And as far as your lies to your little princess, either keep lying or tell her the whole truth. It really doesn't matter to me anymore."

She hung up in my face, and I was as confused as two left feet. "What the hell am I supposed to do now? Where am I going to get some money?"

I had laid my head back against the headrest to think of what to do next when out of nowhere, it dawned on me. Slowly, I pulled from my pocket the locket that Tiffany had left in her hotel room. "I don't want to do this, Tiff, but I really have no other choice. I'll just have to find a way to pay you back later."

An hour later, after weaving in and out of Texas traffic, I stopped at a pawnshop on the other side of town. I wasn't there a good ten minutes before the clerk agreed to pay me for the locket, and to my surprise, it was worth way more than I had thought. I was able to fill up my tank, get me a decent meal, and have some cash left over, enough to last at least a week or more. But before getting too relaxed from having lined my pockets, I had to deal with my old nosy-ass neighbor, Mrs. Smith. I knew that if anyone could lead me in the direction of Leslie, it would be her.

I pulled up to her house, walked to her door, and stood there, taking a second to admire the house Leslie and I had shared next door. Despite it all, we had had some really good times in that house. And now I couldn't believe I'd been so foolish as to try to move Tiffany there. As I reminisced about the past, Mrs. Smith must have been looking out her front window. The next thing I knew, she was standing at the front door, waving that damn cane around.

"What are you doing here? Who told you to come around here? Leslie isn't there anymore. And even if she was, she wouldn't have anything to do with you," she barked.

"C'mon now, Mrs. Smith. Is that any way to talk to an old neighbor of yours? Especially one that practically treated you like their own grandmother?"

"Well, you went and messed that up when you did what you did. You hurt that poor girl's feelings, and I can just imagine how the other child is feeling too."

"You're right. I messed up big, Mrs. Smith. I just want the chance to apologize to Leslie face-to-face," I lied to her, not wanting to say anything about the threatening texts. "So, can you please tell me how to reach her? Because I know that you know."

"Even if I knew, I wouldn't tell you, son. That girl has moved on and has a wonderful man in her life. Your apologizing won't do her one bit of good, so just leave things where they are."

Before I was able to say anything further, she hobbled right back into her house and slammed the door in my face. Now I felt like I had no other choice but to get the authorities involved, because minutes after leaving, I received yet another text.

Die, was all that it said, and no matter what Mrs. Smith had said, I knew that Leslie was behind it all.

CHAPTER 19

TIFFANY

It might have been only a week since I'd returned to Texas, but it felt amazing being in the place I called home. True enough, St. Louis would always hold a special place in my heart, but after visiting there, I knew where my spirit was most at peace was in Texas. Things had been mainly quiet. After following my regular routine at the school and participating in functions at the church, I generally ended up right back at home. Being curled up with a good book and a nice glass of wine at home was my happy and safe space, and that was where I was at the moment.

In fact, the only thing that was missing was Terrence. I had never realized how hard coming back would be, with everything reminding me of him. The school, restaurants that we'd been too, and even things in my house triggered memories of him. I wanted to text him, just to let him know I was thinking of him, missing him, and wanting him. But I chose to do what Monica and Keisha had advised and let him have his time to grieve his father. I was, however, expecting him to at least text me and tell me about his father, but maybe that was too much for him to deal with at present.

Anyway, speaking of things being quiet, I was shocked that I hadn't heard a peep out of David or Patricia. My

last interaction with her was the phone call. It still bothered me that she had basically blamed me for Terrence's
failed relationship with their sons. Yet, a small part of me
couldn't help but think that maybe she was right. Had I
not entered the picture, I wondered if things would be
different and if Terrence would have tried to work things
out with her.

Then there was David. He'd said nothing more about
the cancer, and that seemed a little suspicious to me,
especially given how thick he had laid things on at the
hotel. I didn't want to think about either of them anymore, though. It was time to crack open my second bottle
of wine, turn up the smooth rhythm and blues on my
Pandora station, and fall in love with by book boyfriend
in Ashley Antionette's latest series.

An hour later, I was feeling right and was about to call
it a night when I heard my cell phone buzzing across the
coffee table. "That has to be either Monica or Keisha," I
told myself, but then I sat up, leaned forward, and looked
down at the illuminated word looking back at me.

Baby?

After immediately hopping up, I started dancing
around my living room. All Terrence had texted was
one little word, but that word meant *everything* to me. I
began feeling all warm and fuzzy inside. Not to mention,
my girlfriend was having a party of her own inside my
panties.

"Okay, God, tell me what to do. Do I break down and
text back, making myself look desperate, like I've been
waiting to hear from him? Or do I wait a day or so and
let him hunt me down? Wait, what was that? Did you say,
'Go ahead and text back'? I hope so because that's what
I'm about to do." I tried to gather myself before I sat back
down on the sofa and keyed in two simple words.

Yes, baby?

Where are you?

Home . . . here in Texas.

I need you. Will you come here?

Uh, where are you?

I'll send the address. And, Tiff, I can't wait to see you.

Lord, have mercy, this man knew exactly how to handle me. He literally had me in the palm of his hand, and I liked it. With that said, I raced to shower, oiled my body down, and sprayed on the sweetest scent I had. Then I threw on something super sexy, just the way he liked. I was going to do more with my hair, but since I had a short, stylish cut, I settled with a messy do. After grabbing my pocketbook, I was out of the house in record time. He had sent me the address, but I was confused as to where I was going.

"Is he actually inviting me to his home? Where's Patricia? Are you really doing this, Tiff? Are you for real about to meet this man at the home he shared with his wife?" I wondered aloud as I drove.

I talked to myself the entire ride, as there were a million questions floating in my mind. I even kept trying to make myself believe that this was all innocent and didn't seem odd, but the truth was it was odd. Yet I was still going to meet up with him. That was the effect that Terrence had on me. I took his word on everything at face value. I wanted to be right by his side, there for every up and down in his life. His mood was my mood. I felt like our souls were connected. Continuing to reflect on me and him, I drove through the darkness, and it wasn't long before my navigational system said I had arrived.

The house was dark. There wasn't a porch light on or any lights on inside. Looking at myself one last time in the rearview mirror, I made sure my lip gloss was just right. Then I climbed out of the car and headed to the door. It was open a crack, and when I pushed it gently, it swung all the way open. I stepped inside stealthily, then paused in the dark foyer. Taking a deep breath, I entered an empty living room. Candles glowed softly around the room, and in the flickering light they cast, I could see a pallet and blankets on the floor. Mellow rhythm and blues played on a small speaker. Terrence was nowhere in sight, and I wondered if this was some type of game, like a scavenger hunt maybe. That was until he came walking down the staircase.

"Terrence, what's going on? Why is your house completely empty? Where's your wife?"

He didn't say anything but instead walked over and put his large arms around my small frame. Immediately a warm sensation shot through me. I felt safe as he held me for at least the next five minutes.

"Baby, are you okay?" I pulled away and stared into his eyes. "Keisha told me about your father, and I'm so sorry. I wish there was something I could do. I know how much you loved him. Um, and I'm also sorry about the entire situation with David at the hotel. I—"

Before I was able to say another word, he placed his finger on top of my lips. Finally, he spoke his first words of the night.

"Tiff, I don't want to talk about Pat, David, or even about what's going on with my father. I have missed you, and I need you. I need you to make the world stop for me, even if it's only for a little while."

All at once, with those very words, he confirmed what I'd been hoping and praying for since that night at the Ritz: that he still loved me and wanted me just as much as I did him. Not a second later, he pulled me down on the pallet, and when our eyes met, his strong hand lifted the back of my head so that our lips could finally meet. After his tongue entered my mouth, I allowed my own to make contact, and our tongues slowly danced to the beat of both our hearts. Without delay, he slipped the straps of my summer dress off my shoulders. My nipples immediately stood at attention, in anticipation of his touch. As he cupped both my breasts with his large hands, he placed his head between them and took a deep breath. I released a slight moan, and my breathing became heavier, as I desired all this man had to give. Then he put one nipple in his mouth and began to caress it with his tongue.

After undressing me and getting undressed himself, he told me to get on top of him, and I practically wanted to scream. My juices had saturated the outer portion of my playground. I couldn't wait to feel his massiveness inside me. We were so in tune that he must have sensed my desire, because all at once, he flipped me over and climbed on top of me, then thrust his manhood inside *her*. Ignoring the soft music playing in the room, we let our bodies groove to their own beat. With his every stroke, my moans became louder and louder. I could practically feel him in the pit of my belly. Then, suddenly, with one motion, he turned me over, and I was back on top again. My juices came pouring out of me. I began to ride Terrence for dear life, until I couldn't take it anymore.

"Baby, I'm about to cum," I screamed.

"Let it go, baby. Let it all come out."

It all happened so fast. It seemed like my body shook for ten minutes or so once it was over. It was hard for me to settle my breathing, and I had no idea when I had last orgasmed like that. Then I glanced over at him. He was lying there peacefully, completely satisfied. I laid my head on his chest, never wanting this night or this feeling to end. And although I hated that she crossed my mind, I couldn't help but wonder where on earth Patricia was.

***

A few hours later, I woke up to Terrence shaking me vigorously.

"Baby, baby, get up!" He grabbed all my clothes, shoved them in my arms, and then pushed me toward the basement door. "Go downstairs and hide inside one of the bedrooms down there. And don't come back up until I tell you to."

"Terrence, you're scaring me. What's going on?"

"I think Pat's outside. Just go downstairs and be very quiet, okay?"

"But—"

Before I could debate things any further, he guided me to the basement door, opened it, and nudged me onto the first step. Then he pushed the basement door shut. It was then that I heard Patricia calling out his name.

What the hell have you gotten yourself into, Tiff? I thought as I stood on that first step, in the darkness, and tried to slide my dress back on. I was so terrified of her finding me there, I could barely contain myself. In fact, I was trembling so much, I was sure that urine would soon drizzle down my legs. Once I had my dress on, I pressed my ear against the door and listened closely.

"What are you doing here, Pat?"

"Terrence, we need to talk. I mean, we haven't communicated since that day, and . . . and we're still married, for Christ's sake."

"Look, there's nothing for us to talk about, and I don't even think you should be here."

"This is still my home too, Terrence Montgomery. I have a right to be here."

"All right. Then I'll leave. I have a meeting this morning, in just a few hours, but right after I'll come back here and get all my belongings. I'll leave the key inside the mailbox."

"Why the hell are you being so difficult? Terrence, I miss you, and the boys miss you too. Can't you understand that?"

He didn't respond. A minute later I heard a door bang, and then a few moments after that, I heard Terrence calling my name.

"Tiff, baby, go ahead and come back up. The coast is clear now. She's gone."

I opened the basement door as fast as I could and stumbled into the room. "Terrence, what the hell is going on? Why would you have me come here if she still has a key?"

"Baby, I didn't think she would stop by here. There's nothing here for her. If you haven't noticed, she left the house almost completely empty. Besides, our last interaction didn't end on the best of terms. I had assumed I wouldn't see her anymore."

"Well, I don't like this. I should have never come over here, especially to do what we did in *her* house."

"It's my house too, Tiffany."

"Yeah, that you share with her. This isn't right. I need to get back home," I said.

He grabbed my arm and pulled me close to him. "Baby, calm down, okay? Now, you're right. Maybe this wasn't the right place, but what happened with us last night was right. I needed it, and I could tell you did too. I'm sorry that I put you in this situation, but I promise to make it all up to you. I have a meeting with my attorney in a few hours, a meeting that will change the whole trajectory of my life . . . and yours. You just wait and see."

He kissed my forehead as I prepared to leave. Despite everything that he'd just said, my spirit was feeling conflicted. Here I was, a grown-ass woman inside another woman's home, sleeping with her husband on the floor of an empty-ass house. Then, to top it all off, I had to hide in the basement, praying that this woman didn't find out I was there. This was pathetic, to say the least, and there was no way I could put myself in this situation again. Yet I *still* loved him.

"How stupid can you be, Tiffany?" I muttered aloud as I stepped outside.

CHAPTER 20

TERRENCE

I looked at myself in the mirror to make sure I was perfect for this morning's meeting. A classic black suit and a creamed-colored shirt were appropriate for the reading of my father's will, I'd decided.

Wow, Terrence. In just a couple of hours, you will be a millionaire, so it's definitely time to start looking like one, I thought.

After the whole falling-out with Patricia a week ago, I'd felt relieved to get out of town for a few days, even if it was to assist my stepmother with Pop's arrangements. Instead of some sad and depressing occasion, we had a really good time reminiscing about Pops and reflecting on his life. My stepmother had shared a lot about my ole man in his younger years with my brother and me, and it fascinated me how I had turned out so much like him. In fact, I was more like him than my older brother was, even though he had been named after Pops. It honestly made me prouder to be his son and hold the Montgomery name.

It had also felt good having Malaysia there with me. I had realized she was a little nervous being around my family at such an intimate time, but I'd assured her that it was what I wanted and needed. Her energy relaxed me in ways that I couldn't explain, so I couldn't see it any other way. And although we'd been there to fulfill a very specific agenda, we'd managed to take in some sights and do some other activities. We really enjoyed one another's company. So much so, that I felt like I had taken a much-needed break from everything and everyone, except for my old but new friend.

It was too bad that our trip had lasted only a couple of days, but she'd needed to get back to work and I'd needed to figure out my life overall, which still included Tiffany. Even when I'd been around Malaysia, I'd still missed Tiff like crazy, which was why I'd texted the minute I got back. Not wanting to pop up at her place, I'd decided to have her over at the house. I knew she would be a little startled, since Patricia had taken all the furniture out and so the house was nearly empty, but I found ways to make it nice and romantic. The lit candles were just the right touch, especially since Pat had had the electricity turned off. It seemed like none of it even mattered to Tiff, until Pat showed up. I hoped that I was able to smooth things over by telling her that after today, everything would change for us.

After the meeting, I would have access to more money than I could handle, and it would change both our lives. The thought of that alone gave me a true sense of peace. Once the meeting was over, Patricia could play whatever games she wanted with the house, the cars, and what-ever else, while Tiff and I would live happily ever after. My only problem was what to do with Malaysia from that point forward because I didn't want to hurt her.

Since I, my stepmother, and my brother all live in different states, we'd decided on a virtual reading of the will this morning, instead of getting together and doing it in person. So, I left the house, climbed behind the wheel, and set off for Randle's office, feeling light as a feather. My father's lawyer would read the will and determine what everyone was entitled to. That was one of the issues Pops had addressed when he'd come to town a few months ago. On that occasion, Pat had forbidden him from staying at our home, and I would never forgive her for that. Pops had told me that he was switching the order of the beneficiaries and making my brother the second one because of his reckless lifestyle. Pops had said he wanted generational wealth to accumulate in his family, which he couldn't see happening if he left everything to my brother and not me.

Gliding through Texas traffic with ease, I put my truck on cruise control, because I was in no particular hurry. Although I was in an extreme financial bind, I didn't want to appear desperate, so I certainly didn't not want to arrive early to the meeting. After maybe forty-five minutes of driving, I finally arrived to hear my fate. When I walked to Randle's office, I kept my head held high and my chest stuck out. I greeted the doorman, the secretary, another client, and even the janitor. My mother had always taught me to be kind to everyone, no matter what their status or income level was. Plus, I was just extremely happy, which I figured had something to do with the great sex with Tiffany and the money about to come my way. That thought alone made me chuckle. It was funny how money had a way of making people feel happy, confident, friendly and, especially, powerful. I was on top of the world, and nothing on earth could spoil the mood I was in. At least until I opened Randle's door and I caught sight of Patricia sitting there with Kim, an old friend of hers. I ignored Pat and Kim and hurried over to Randle, who was sitting at the head of the table.

Trying to speak quietly, I interrogated Randle. "Man, what's going on here? What the hell is she doing here? And why didn't you call and give me a heads-up?" I asked, my face probably as red as a beet, despite how black I was.

In fact, I was sure they saw smoke coming from the top of my head, because that was exactly how heated I was.

"Terrence, please have a seat. Let's address this calmly, okay?"

"No, there's no having a seat until you tell me what she's doing here. This is *my father's* will reading, which *she* has nothing to do with."

Randle got up and pulled me over to a corner of the room. I saw Patricia gawking and whispering to Kim when I peeked at her out of the corner of my eye.

"Terrence, look, I know you were hoping I could do something to settle y'all's divorce without going to court, but the truth is, I couldn't. And since you're still married, I had to share what might happen today with her lawyer. That's when she demanded to be a part of this meeting, and I couldn't decline. And by the way, we have a little more trouble than I imagined. Now, I need you to be straight up with me. Can your wife prove any inappropriate behavior between you and any other woman?"

"What? No, no, not at all," I said, already kicking myself for ever posting anything on social media.

"Are you sure?" he asked, possibly to give me an opportunity to change my answer.

"Randle, I said no. So how fast can we get them out of here? And, anyway, are you even sure Kim is a legit attorney? Because I've never known her to be one. Plus, you don't know my wife the way I do—or hell, maybe you do—but either way, she always has tricks up her sleeve. After the fight we had a week ago, and then her coming by the house this morning, there's no telling what she's up to."

"Listen, as far as I know, her attorney is legit, but that should be the least of your concerns. Patricia claims she has proof of your infidelity, so you'd better start hoping and praying that she doesn't. Because, honestly, if she does, I can guarantee that you can pretty much kiss that million bucks away. You won't be seeing a dime of it when the divorce is final." He patted me on my shoulder and went back to the table, leaving me standing there. If I hadn't realized it before now, I definitely did now: my wife was always up to no good and could be as heartless and cruel as any man alive.

How the hell did I marry this bitch? I thought.

A few minutes later the meeting got underway. I paid attention to every word my attorney said but made sure to keep an eye on my wife and Kim. Finally, after all the particulars had been laid out, it was time to get down to business. To my brother, my pops had left his clothes, tools, and two trust funds, one for my brother's son and one for his daughter, which couldn't be touched until they graduated high school. Then came the moment I'd been waiting for.

"And to Mr. Terrence Montgomery, your father has left two trust funds for your twin daughters, to be released to them upon successful completion of high school. He also leaves you his wonderful collection of old-school records, family pictures and, finally, a building he recently purchased for your future restaurant, upon the dissolution of your marriage to Mrs. Patricia Montgomery," Randle announced. "He also has cash holdings totaling two million dollars, to be rewarded to, and split equally between, you and his loving wife of the past twenty-seven years. However, he included a special notation just recently, right before his passing, that you will not gain access to those funds until you and Mrs. Patricia Montgomery have been divorced for at least an entire year. That will conclude the reading of this will."

I didn't have the words in me to address anyone. I simply pushed away the stack of papers sitting in front of me and barged out of the room into the hallway. I could barely breathe as I attempted to digest what I'd just heard. Randle came running out of the room after me.

"Randle, is this some practical joke? All I get is some damn records and pictures?"

"Terrence, did we not just hear the same thing? You're getting the million that you've been banking on and a building for your restaurant. What's wrong with you?"

"Yeah, but I won't get the funds until I'm divorced from Pat for a least a year. But, man, I'm struggling *right now*. What am I supposed to do *now*? Hell, I don't even have money to get a damn divorce."

"Look, we'll figure out something, all right?"

After I left the building and hopped into my truck, I was tempted to head straight to the casino. I was longing for a fix and for the possibility of winning some extra cash. But then I realized it was too risky. I had to think things through. I no longer had my job with the Texas Department of Transportation. I'd barely been to the school as of late, because of all that I had going on. There was this whole mess with Patricia. And now I needed money and somewhere to stay until I found another home, because I refused to go back to the house. I wasn't getting anything from my father's estate, at least not yet. Everyone I knew was already struggling in their own way, so I didn't have anyone to loan me anything. . . .

Then it dawned on me that maybe Malaysia wouldn't mind loaning me some cash. Maybe I could come up with something that sounded desperate enough and just promise to pay her back. However, as quickly as the thought came, that was how quick it left. I prided myself on being a man who didn't depend on others. There was no way I could ask a woman, especially one that I'd just met, for some money. Besides, I'd already had her under the impression that I was this highly successful, soon-to-be very wealthy man. I couldn't taint my image now.

After sitting there, contemplating a bit longer, I pulled out my phone. *Bingo.* I'd received a text from the one person I was sure I could count on.

I hope everything goes well at your meeting this morning, Terrence. I love you.

"Perfect timing." Ever since I'd met Tiffany, we'd both been there for each other. True enough, I hadn't gone as far as to ask her for any money, but now I figured that was what friends were for. In any case, I would be there for her if she needed some financial help, and I had the intention of paying her back in the end anyway. With that in mind, I headed her way with a new sense of hope in my spirit.

CHAPTER 21

PATRICIA

"You really mean to tell me I have gone through all of this for some records and pictures? So, you're really telling me that I'm not getting a million dollars?" I yelled in Randle's office right after Terrence stormed out. Randle and Kim kept trying to calm me down. Especially when his secretary came running in to make sure everything was all right. But it wasn't going to be that easy.

"Patricia, why don't you get your things so that we can leave, all right?" Kim said, trying to hush me and hurry me out of the building.

I was furious, though. Not only was I staying in a small-ass room in my father's home, but I also had two boys to care for, all on my own. I wasn't working, and my only income came from my good-for-nothing husband, who neglected his whole family. I couldn't even pay Kim for what she'd already done or for a divorce that I really didn't want. And the only gun in my pocket was that Terrence was cheating with Tiffany, but other than some mere Facebook posts, I couldn't actually prove that. On top of it all, my now deceased father-in-law was even trying to control things from his fucking grave. Who the hell did he think he was, saying that the only way Terrence would get anything was when his divorce was settled and over with for at least a year! I felt so hopeless.

It was obvious that Kim felt sorry for me too. When I got to my car and burst into tears, I could feel her hand caressing my back.

"Everything's going to be okay, Pat. It's not the end of the world," she told me as we stood there.

"Yeah, well, maybe for you it's not, but I'm losing everything that I love, so for me, it is the end."

"Don't say that. Just look at all that you do have. You've got your health, your strength, your right state of mind, and two loving boys who are growing into men. And trust me, one day you will have a man that loves you as much as you do him. So, I'll say it again. It's not the end of the world. And if you've forgotten, you still hold all the cards, sweetie, because that man cheated on you."

"But I can't honestly prove that he did, Kim. And how am I going to find a man who wants to put up with me and two children that aren't his? I did that with Terrence, and you see how things have turned out."

"Listen to me, you're not the first woman who will be divorced, with children, and you surely won't be the last. And I know this because I did it. Once I let go of my ex-husband and all the toxicity of our marriage, I freed myself of all my pain and insecurities. I started loving on me, and in due time, God sent me who I needed, honey, with *four* children that wasn't his. That's why I took your case, Pat. Because I know exactly what you're going through. But the key is to not go looking and controlling things yourself. Find Patricia first, and the right man will find you."

I shook my head in agreement. In just a few minutes, she had given me the encouragement, support, and love that I'd been longing for, for quite a long time. After a few minutes of silence, she wrapped her arms around me and gave me a long, tight sisterly hug.

"Hey, consider today on me. You don't owe me a dime so far. And when you are truly ready to part ways with Mr. Montgomery, then just call and we'll figure something out. I'll be here for you." She turned and walked to her car. For several minutes, I remained standing next to my car there in the parking lot. When I saw Kim drive away, I got behind the wheel.

Instead of driving to the place that I now called home, I decided I needed a little time to myself. I turned on my car stereo, a tune that my mother used to sing all the time came on. It was "Can't Give Up Now." As the artist sang the words, I joined in. "I just can't give up now. I come too far from where I started from. Nobody told me the road would be easy. And I don't believe He's brought me this far to leave me."

Tears came rushing down my face as I thought about me and Terrence. I'd made so many mistakes in our marriage, but so had he. Still, all I truly wanted was his love. I wished he could see it. However, as much as I didn't want to let go, it was beginning to seem like I had no other choice. Terrence had made it clear that he no longer wanted to be with me, and all I heard in the back of my mind now was my father asking the very question I now asked myself. *Why do you want to be with someone that doesn't love you?*

As I sat there with my eyes shut tight, bobbing my head to the music, all of a sudden I heard someone tapping on my window. My eyes flew open.

"Randle," I exclaimed as I let my window down.

"Hey, Patricia. I hope I didn't scare you, but I saw you sitting here, and I wanted to make sure you were all right."

"Yeah, I'm okay. And I apologize for the scene I made in there. You must think I'm some crazy woman, huh?"

He smiled a very charming smile, one that I hadn't noticed until now. "I wouldn't say crazy. A little high-strung maybe and challenging, but not crazy."

We both laughed, and for the first time in a long time, it felt good just to enjoy a sincere and genuine moment with someone.

"Hey, I don't mean to overstep my boundaries or anything, but if you could use a bite to eat, I would love it if you joined me for lunch. Only as friends, of course. And we can't talk about anything regarding you and Terrence. It will just be two friends having lunch."

"Randle, you are speaking my language, sir." I hopped out of my car, and he took my hand to escort me to his.

I didn't know exactly what this meant, but as I sat in his passenger seat, I decided that it didn't matter. I was simply going to enjoy the moment, without any concerns about my husband.

CHAPTER 22

TIFFANY

Monica had left an hour ago, and I must have passed out on the sofa during the middle of watching *The First 48*. For as long as I could remember, I'd had an infatuation with investigative-type shows, and *The First 48* was at the top of my list of favorites. Let anyone who really knew me tell it, and they would say I had worked for the FBI in my former life.

Anyway, although I'd been very embarrassed, I'd shared with Monica pretty much everything that had happened at Terrence's home. She'd laughed until she'd cried at the thought of me hiding in the man's basement, about to piss on myself. However, I didn't see anything the least bit funny. In fact, I was still shaking from almost getting caught. Of course, Monica had scolded me for going there in the first place. She'd said whatever was done there could have been done here in the comfort of my own home, which were my sentiments exactly. She'd added that if she were Patricia and she'd found me there, she would have seriously hurt me, and she would have been well within her rights. I'd agreed and promised to never go back.

Now that she was gone, I got up off the sofa and started cleaning up the mess she and I had made. We had left a couple of empty wine bottles, glasses, and the bowls from our salads in the living room, and my slight OCD prodded me to get everything straightened up. So I told Alexa to turn on some good ole Anthony Hamilton and started cleaning to his tunes. As I glided around the kitchen, I danced and sang into the broom like it was my microphone, crooning the lyrics to "Comin' From Where I'm From" along with Anthony. *Forget working for the FBI. I should have been the fourth member of Destiny's Child*, I thought. I swayed and whirled around like I was auditioning for a part, until my cell phone scared the crap out of me when it vibrated in my pocket. I lifted it out and looked at the screen.

"Hey, girl," I answered, out of breath.

"Hey, where on earth are you? Sounds like you're at a club or something."

"Oh no, just dancing during my cleaning, that's all. Now, hold on," I said. I told Alexa to turn down the music. "What's up with you? You must miss me already, huh?" I joked.

"Honey, please, I am totally enjoying the quiet and solitude again in *my* home."

"Yeah, yeah, whatever."

"But, no, really I just received a weird phone call from the Ritz-Carlton."

"Really? What was wrong?"

"Well, it seems that the cleaning lady found a pink diamond locket inside the hotel room after you left. She gave it to a gentleman who came to the room that morning, looking for you. They were calling to make sure you received it."

"Damn. I took it off while sleeping and must have forgotten all about it. But they gave it to someone who came to the room?"

A few seconds later, we both said in harmony, "David."

"Didn't I tell you?" Keisha exclaimed. "That man does not have cancer. He came there to the hotel with an agenda, Tiffany. To mess up your night with Terrence. Now he has your locket, and he's probably going to use it to hold over your head or something."

"Keisha, calm down already. If I know David, he's going to contact me sooner rather than later, and I'll deal with him then. But right now, I have other issues to tackle."

"Issues like what? Is Patricia still calling?" She had abandoned her anger over David, and now her voice told me she was concerned.

"No, I haven't heard from her, thank goodness. But I did something that I'm feeling a little guilty about. Last night I went to Terrence's house, and we had sex there."

"What the hell do you mean, you had sex in the man's home? Where was his wife, his *crazy-ass* wife?"

"She wasn't there, and to tell the truth, I don't think she lives there anymore. The house was almost completely empty. He had a pallet on the floor, with candles all around, because to be honest, I don't think his electricity was on."

"Wait, Terrence is out here living foul like that?"

"I wouldn't say living foul, Keisha. But we haven't talked about things, so I don't know what's really going on with him or between the two of them."

"Okay, but if she doesn't live there anymore, then what's the problem?"

"Keisha, the problem is it's a house that he shared with his wife. And I haven't had the chance to tell you that she showed up."

"What?" she yelled in my ear.

"It was after we'd had sex, and Terrence had me hide in the basement until she left. Girl, I felt so crazy, being a grown woman and hiding in another woman's basement."

"I'm sorry, Tiff, but you should have felt crazy. And Terrence never should have put you in that situation."

"Yeah, me and Monica both agree." I had let it slip out, and before I knew it, there was a strange silence on the phone. I knew Keisha hated that I shared things with Monica before her, but I just did, and I didn't want to keep apologizing for it. I tried to redeem myself now, though, because I was about to tell her something that I hadn't shared with Monica yet.

"There's something else too," I said, to break the awkwardness. "I looked at his Facebook page earlier, and I don't know if I'm overthinking things, but some female made a comment on his page."

"Really? What did she say?"

"She said something like, 'Enjoyed my time with my new, old friend, and I'm here for whatever you need.' And she put a heart and the kissing emoji behind it."

"I don't know . . . It doesn't sound too bad. His father passed away, so you have to expect that all kinds of women are going to post things like that on his page," Keisha responded.

"Yeah, but what's weird is that it was only there briefly, like Terrence had deleted it or something. Out of all the other comments on his page from various women, why would he delete that one? And what was even stranger was that before the comment was deleted, I tried going to her page, and I found that I was blocked. Now, are you still thinking it's only a coincidence, or do you find that strange too?"

"Oh yeah, now I see. That's definitely strange. What's the woman's name, so that I can keep a close eye on her myself?"

"Her name is Malaysia Cole, and believe it or not, Keisha, she's also from St. Louis."

"No. Are you serious?"

"Dead serious, and for the life of me, I haven't been able to stop thinking about this. Something in my gut is telling me that there might be more to this Malaysia chick than I know, but I don't want to say anything about it to Terrence and end up appearing just as crazy as Patricia."

"Okay, well, don't go getting your pretty panties all in a bunch," Keisha warned me. "You're probably just a little overly suspicious because of everything that's happened in your past. Truth be told, I feel like you have every right to be. I mean, David did have you moving your entire life, only to go live in another woman's home. So, for now, let's give Terrence the benefit of the doubt. And like I said, if there's some funny business going on with Ms. Malaysia, your best friend will find out all about it."

"Okay, girl," I said, my mood much lighter now. Keisha was able to put a smile back on my face, as always. After shooting the breeze a little while longer about much of nothing at all, I let her go so that I could shower and relax. I wanted to get back into reading my Word, because to be honest, I hadn't done much of it while I was back home. I had a ton of catching up to do.

After I ran my bathwater and went through my ritual of adding all my scented oils, I turned out the lights in my home and lit a few scented candles in the bathroom. "Perfect! Just the way I like it," I sang.

I slid my naked body into the steaming hot water and immediately laid my head back. I absolutely loved days like this, quiet, peaceful, and relaxing. A second later, I told Alexa to softly play songs by one of my new favorite artists, H.E.R., and then I grooved the evening away right there in the Jacuzzi. Enjoying the peace and tranquility, I no longer focused on David, Patricia, and Malaysia—or whatever her name was—and not even on Terrence. For the first time in a long time, my mind was clear, and it was all about me.

"God, I truly thank you for things being as well as they are," I whispered.

After closing my eyes, I dozed off in the water. I slept for the next twenty minutes or so, until I heard a knock at my door. I wasn't expecting anyone, and Monica had already come by, so I had no idea who it could be. Then it dawned on me that I had never picked up my packages that had been delivered to my neighbor's home while I was away, so I figured it was probably my neighbor. I got out of the Jacuzzi, and without fully drying off, I rushed to slip on my robe and slippers.

"One moment. I'm coming," I yelled as I tried to get to the door without falling.

After making it to the front door, I slowly opened it while standing behind it. "Hey, you can just leave my packages on the porch. And thanks so much again for grabbing them while I was gone," I said without actually looking at the person standing there.

Silence.

I peeked around the door. "Terrence! How did your meeting go?"

Instead of answering me, he stepped inside and handed me a dozen long-stemmed red roses, which he'd been holding behind his back. Then he pulled me to him and held me tight. I practically melted in the man's arms. At that moment, I wanted him just as much as I did last night, but I also couldn't seem to erase Malaysia from my mind. I knew I'd told Keisha that I would hold off on questioning him about her, but now that we were face-to-face, I couldn't. Slowly, I wrestled my way from his embrace.

"Terrence, we need to talk." I turned my back to him.

"Baby—"

"No, listen to me. There's a lot that we need to discuss . . . the night at the hotel, last night, your father, Patricia, and others. I've been quiet, patient and, I believe, extremely understanding about your situation. But I have to be honest, I'm a bit confused about where things stand with us. We haven't been communicating about things."

"*You're* confused?" he questioned, turning me back around to face him.

"Okay, listen, if you're talking about David, then I can explain." I wrapped my robe around me tighter and motioned for him to have a seat on the sofa. "Baby, what you saw that night in the hotel room was only a friend trying to be there for a friend. That's it. Nothing more happened between us."

"So, what you're saying is, you and David are friends again now? Is that really what you're trying to tell me because I don't get it. How can you be friends with the man after all he's put you through?" he quizzed as he took a seat.

"All right, maybe I used the wrong verbiage, because I don't quite know how to label what we are. But, Terrence, all I know is that I don't want to hang on to a grudge for what he did to me or waste my energy hating him. Besides, he told me that he was sick, and, well, I was trying to do what I felt was right in my heart to do. But that's it. And what you walked in on meant absolutely nothing. Not to me anyway. I was merely giving him a hug to send him on his way."

"But that's just it. He never should have been there in the first place. That was supposed to be our special night, Tiff."

"I know, and I'll never forgive myself for allowing him to mess it up, but you have to believe that it meant nothing to me."

I went on explaining to him everything regarding the situation with David, including the fact that Keisha and I believed he'd been on a mission from the very start to come between me and him. Although I could see the anger rising inside him, I needed him to know that he could trust in my love and loyalty. I would take care of David in my own special way. But now I needed for him to be straightforward with me.

We both allowed what we'd just discussed to sink in, and at the same time, I attempted to find a way to address the topics of Patricia and the unknown woman from St. Louis, Malaysia. I didn't want to come off as pushy or possibly insecure, but I also couldn't hide the fact that I was bothered by both women's actions.

"Why don't I get us something to drink?" I suggested before tackling either subject. I walked into the kitchen, and he got up off the sofa and followed right behind me.

"Tiff, why do I get the feeling that there's something more you're not telling me?" He leaned against the island while I poured the remainder of the red wine in one of the bottles Monica and I hadn't finished off.

Finally, I took a deep breath. "Maybe because there is. Terrence, I haven't been sure what to make of it, but your wife contacted me."

"Patricia?"

"Do you have another wife, one that I don't know about?" I said sarcastically as I glared at him.

"No, but how? When? What did she want with you?"

"She called me through Facebook Messenger and basically wanted to accuse me of destroying your relationship with your two sons." I handed him his glass and moved back to the living room.

"You have got to be kidding me, right?" he said as he trailed behind me.

"No, I'm not. But I have to admit that even though I was angry at first about her calling, Terrence, I really felt her pain and desperation. I mean, have you truly considered how this might be affecting your sons?"

"Look, don't worry about Pat or the boys. Trust me, they will be all right. Besides, she's pulled enough stunts these past few days, or years even, that all her whining and crying doesn't faze me anymore. So, the same way you're going to deal with David, I will handle my wife. Is that all that's been bothering you?"

I sat down at one end of the couch, and he took a seat at the other end. "Uh, not quite. I, um, went to your Facebook page earlier. I was going to offer my condolences for your father, since we haven't talked much about him," I said, trying to be delicate in the way I asked about this strange woman. I didn't want him to feel as if I was questioning him.

"I'm sorry I haven't talked much about his passing. I've just been dealing with a lot when it comes to him. So, I apologize, baby."

"It's all right, but you had a comment that looked a little strange, from some woman named Malaysia. She said something about enjoying her time with a new but old friend," I said nonchalantly, then took a sip of my wine and peeped over the top of my glass to weigh his reaction. He didn't flinch or get fidgety or anything.

"Malaysia?" he asked, as if he had no idea whom I was referring to.

"Uh, yeah, your new friend, whose post is mysteriously no longer there," I said, not mentioning that she also had me blocked from her page. I simply wanted to see how he would respond.

Next thing I knew, Terrence gave a slight chuckle as he took a sip of his wine. Although he found it all pretty humorous, I didn't. "And I guess you're wondering who Malaysia is, right?" He looked at me as I smirked, pressing my lips together.

"Well, I'm definitely not questioning you or anything, but she did kind of seem to pop up out of nowhere."

"Baby, Malaysia is an old college friend that I bumped into while in St. Louis. Nothing more, all right? But your slight jealousy is a little cute." He laughed again.

It was killing me that I dared not ask why she had blocked me or if they had become a little cozier than old friends.

Terrence had found so much humor in my asking about her, but then he suddenly turned serious on me. "But, hey, speaking of social media, I needed to talk to you about all of that," he said solemnly.

"What's wrong?" I couldn't figure out exactly what we needed to address.

"Well, seeing that Pat pretty much blames you and infidelity as our reason for divorcing, and because I can never guess what her antics will be, I was thinking that maybe, um, I should take you off my accounts for a little while."

"Remove me from your social media? Like I'm some type of secret now? The way I had to run and hide in your basement?"

"No, baby, no. It's just that I never know what she's going to be up to next, and I don't know what her shady-ass lawyer might do either. For all I know, they could use things from my social media accounts to try to prove infidelity, and well, Randle and I—"

I cut him off. "Randle? Who the hell is Randle?"

"My lawyer. Anyway, Randle and I figured this would be the easiest and most harmless way to deal with things. Besides, baby, social media doesn't define us, and it could be better for us in the long run."

"Really? How so?" I asked, not sure whether I believed what he was saying at the moment, especially since I didn't have answers to why I had been blocked from Malaysia's page.

"Well, in my opinion, social media is the number one reason that a lot of couples break up today. It's all a trap, like the way you misunderstood the post from Malaysia. I just think that you and I are much stronger than what we post on Facebook or Instagram, and we don't need those kinds of problems in our relationship. Anyway, the minute I'm all done with this divorce, everything will go right back to normal."

I wasn't sure how I felt about all of this, but the last thing I was going to do was beg this man to keep me on his social media. So, with that said, I had to go along with things as he wanted. However, I kept in the back of my mind the notion that if something wasn't right, then it would eventually come out in the open. Everything done in the dark always had a way of coming to light.

Without warning, Terrence moved down to my end of the couch until he was sitting right next to me, then took my wineglass out of my hand and stood it on the coffee table.

"What are you doing?" I asked softly as his hand made its way inside my robe and began to massage one of my nipples.

"Trying to make up for lost time and pick up where we left off last night." He looked at me, and before I knew it, his tongue found it way in between my lips, making its home inside my mouth. He caressed my tongue with his, and just like that, I instantly became wet.

"Didn't you miss me?" he inquired, kissing and licking his way to my breasts.

"Yes. Yes, Terrence, I missed you." My words came out slowly between heavy breaths and moans. My nipples now stood erect as he cupped both my titties and licked and sucked all around them. I wanted to cum that second, but I also fought to savor the moment, because I didn't want him to stop.

Out of nowhere and without being given a command, Alexa, who must have been sensed the energy and vibe in the room, started up where she'd left off by playing "Every Kind of Way" by H.E.R.

Terrence laid me on the floor in my living room and gave me all the foreplay I could possibly stand, licking and sucking every single crevasse of my body. The song's words, melody, and bass controlled our bodies as they intertwined and became one.

He gazed at me, looking deep in my eyes, and whispered that he loved me before sliding his tongue down the middle of my body to my clit. I almost couldn't hold back when he took it inside his mouth. The moisture and motions of his tongue almost made me scream. Then he flipped me over, putting me face-to-face with his manhood. I slid him into my mouth as he resumed tasting me. My body gradually began to tremble as he played my clit like a violin. Suddenly, spinning me back around, Terrence placed his giant body on top of mine and thrust his dick inside me. I gave a slight groan as every pound of him pushed deeper and deeper. I was almost ready when he stopped and flipped me over yet again, this time putting me on my knees. He pushed my torso down and my ass up, putting the perfect arch in my back for his liking. Every lunge from him caused my ass to slap his body as he reached in and grabbed my breasts all in one motion. Our bodies were both moist with pleasure and sweat as we made beautiful music with one another.

I could no longer hold back when I felt his nature rise inside me. Every inch of him pulsated inside me when I screamed, "Terrence, I'm, I'm, I'm cumming, baby." My body exploded from satisfaction. I could tell the feeling was mutual when he pulled out and passed out right there on the floor. Just like last night, it was what we both had wanted and needed, and this time I didn't have to go hiding in anyone's basement from their wife.

CHAPTER 23

TERRENCE

I tried to steady my breathing to come down from the high I felt. I'd felt nervous from the conversation about Patricia and Malaysia, and I'd realized I needed to do something to shift the energy in the room. From the looks of her lying there peacefully, with a smile on her face, my job was done. However, now I had to be on a totally different mission, as I still needed some cash and a place to stay. I didn't want to interrupt our solitude, but something told me it would be best to ask while she was still so relaxed and on a natural high.

"Baby?" I sat up on the side of her.

She opened her eyes slightly, moaning, and rolled over to face me.

"I kind of need to talk to you about something, something rather important," I said.

"Right now?" she questioned.

"Yeah, I can't seem to relax, because I keep thinking about it."

This time she forced herself to sit up and rested her head on one hand while looking at me with seriousness, all sense of pleasure gone. "What's wrong, honey?"

"I'm sort of in a real bind from things not turning out the way I had hoped this morning. Under normal circumstances, I wouldn't come to you like this. I'm a man, and I take full pride in being one and not depending on a woman for anything."

"Okay," she said in a tone that indicated I should go ahead and get to the point.

"And, like I said, this isn't something I've ever done before, so it's extremely hard for me to come to you this way."

"Terrence, would you please spit it out already?"

"All right, here's the thing. All this time I was under the impression that if something ever happened to Pops, I would get a certain amount of money from his estate. But I found out this morning that there's a stipulation involved."

"Really? What's that?"

"Well, it looks like to receive anything, I have to be divorced from Pat for at least a year. When that happens, I get half of his total estate, and he even purchased a building for me to open a restaurant."

"Terrence, that sounds great to me." She sat up straighter, with pure excitement in her eyes. "I mean, you want a divorce anyway, right? So, what's the problem?"

"There's several problems," I said, hating to practically burst her bubble. "Um, first, I don't have the money to even get the divorce process started. Now, of course, Randle is a good friend, but that's also how he makes his living. I can't ask him to wait for an entire year to get paid. Then there's the fact that I don't know in which direction Patricia is leaning. She will either stop us from getting divorced, so that *I* can't get the money, or she'll find a way to get around this stipulation and file herself, so that *she* will get some money. And the last thing I want is for her to have a single cent from Pops's estate."

This time she had the same expression on her face that I had had on mine in Randle's office. "I don't understand, though. Why would your father make a stipulation like that?"

"Well, my assumption is because neither of them really cared for the other, and so he didn't want her to benefit from something coming from him. She practically threw him out like yesterday's garbage when he came to the house, so I can't blame him."

"Wow." She got up, put on her robe, and went into the kitchen. I got up and trailed behind her.

"I can't say that I don't understand and agree, especially with all that she's done, but don't you think that's rather severe?" she went on. "To control things like that from his grave?"

"I guess you could look at it that way, especially since this thing is between me and Patricia and no one else." I immediately saw where she was coming from.

"So, have you told her about this?" she inquired while putting on a pot of water for tea.

"That's the crazy part. I didn't have to. She showed up at Randle's office today, trying to see what *she* would be entitled to. It was a huge shit show, and I walked out before it was officially over." I went into the cabinet and grabbed two mugs for the tea and handed them to her. She put tea bags in the mugs.

"All right, but what does all of that have to do with whatever you want to ask me?" She leaned against the island while we waited for the water for the tea to boil. I was much more nervous than I had thought I would be because I didn't want her to think any less of me. But at the moment, I had to do what I had to do.

"I guess the only thing for me to do is just come right out and say it. Baby, I'm really strapped for cash. I was kind of depending on the money from Pop's estate. Then there's all this nonsense between Patricia and me. She didn't even tell me that we were receiving foreclosure notices the entire time I was staying in a hotel. And, as you saw for yourself, when I made the trip to St. Louis, she moved everything out of the house and moved into her father's."

"I'm sorry, Terrence, but your wife is crazy." As she filled the mugs, she almost spilled the water as she laughed at Pat's behavior.

Nothing with my wife ever shocked me, though, because I'd learned that was just who she was. "I wish I was kidding, baby, but I'm not. So now I pretty much don't have a home, I'm strapped for cash, and I'm stuck in this *situationship* of a marriage."

"How much cash are you actually talking about?" She removed the tea bags from the mugs, handed me my mug, and started to blow on hers as we walked back into the living room.

"Whatever you could help with," I said as we both took a seat on the couch. "And, baby, I promise, whatever you do give me, I'll give right back to you once I get on my feet. This will only be a loan. I'm nothing like these guys out here that basically live off the women in their lives."

She didn't say anything. Instead, she got up and went into her bedroom. I felt on edge, wondering what was going on. I started to think all kinds of craziness, like what if she was going to get a gun or something to throw me out? Or maybe she went to call Keisha or Monica to ask their opinion on what she should do. But then, a second later, she came out, carrying her purse in her hand. After sitting back down on the couch, she pulled out what looked like her checkbook and began to write a check. I hadn't even given her an amount, and instantly I started sweating in anticipation. Then she handed the check to me. I looked down at it, and although I wanted to jump right out of my skin, I tried to remain calm.

"Oh, wow, Tiff. Baby, I can't take this. It's way more than I anticipated."

"Listen, you helped me so much when I first moved out here. In fact, you and Monica were the only two in my corner. I wouldn't have made it without you. So, even though it's not a lot, I want you to take it and do what you can with it. And don't worry about when to pay it back. Whenever you get back on your feet, then don't forget about me."

"Baby, I could never forget about you, and thank you, thank you so much. I swear, they just don't make women like you anymore. You are truly cut from a different cloth."

"Terrence, I love you."

Neither of us had said those words to one another since before she ran off to St. Louis. So much had happened since then, including Malaysia, who had just texted me for at least the tenth time. I felt torn as to what to do. I did love Tiff, but I also didn't want to lead her on. But on the other hand, she had just made a major move for me, and I couldn't leave her hanging.

"I love you too, baby."

"And please know that if you need somewhere to stay until you get your living arrangements in order, then my home is open to you," she said, and it was music to my ears.

"Woman, don't tell me that. I just might need to take you up on your offer," I joked, but I was dead serious. Only thing I needed to figure out was how I was going to live with her while dealing with Malaysia too. On top of that, I couldn't let Patricia find out, either, or she would definitely have the proof she needed to show infidelity. At that moment, though, all I could focus on was the check in front of me. What had happened earlier didn't seem like nearly enough of a reward for this.

"Why don't we take a shower?" I suggested.

CHAPTER 24

DAVID

One month later . . .

Feeling as if I would pass out at any moment, my hand shook as I rang my mother's doorbell repeatedly. All bent over, I could hardly breathe, and my ribs felt inflamed. She finally opened the door, and I fell over the threshold onto the floor.

"David, what's wrong, son? What happened to you?" she asked as I lay there, all beat up, with cuts and bruises all over me. "I'm calling the police and an ambulance!" she yelled.

"No, no, Mama, don't," I begged her between bouts of coughing up blood on her foyer floor. "I'll be all right. Just leave the police out of this."

"But, David, honey, you need an ambulance." She knelt beside me, not knowing exactly what to do. "Son, what happened to you?"

"Mama, I was beat up, all right? But like I said, I'll be fine."

"Who did this to you, David? What's going on?"

"Mama . . ." I really didn't have the strength to yell, but I had to get her attention. "I don't know who they were or what's going on. But just leave me here. I'll be fine."

I could see out the corner of my eye as she got up and ran toward the kitchen. That was where she kept her first aid kit, but I knew my cuts were a little too deep for some minor Band-Aids plastered here and there. I struggled to stand, then made my way to her favorite recliner, sat down, and tried to catch my breath.

"Oh, baby, look at you," she cried while cleaning the cuts and scratches on my face with alcohol and then applying antibacterial ointment. "I don't know what you've gotten yourself into, but I still think you need to contact the police or at least go to the emergency room."

"Mama, I said I don't want to involve the authorities, and if I go to the emergency room, that's definitely what they're going to do. I just need to treat these cuts and take a few pain pills. I'll be okay."

"I don't understand this foolishness, David, but you're a grown man, so I'm going to leave it at that. I'll get you some water and a couple of muscle relaxers."

She left the room as I fought to sit up straight. I had heard her say that she was going to leave it at that, but knowing my mother, I figured it was far from over with.

As I sat there, I thought back to yesterday, when I'd received a strange phone call, and something told me that this wasn't some random incident. Someone had set me up. The call yesterday had been about meeting up with someone regarding a business opportunity. I hadn't found it odd at the time, because of the line of work I was in. With driving tour buses, a lot of business came directly by word of mouth, so I had figured it was a third party recommended by someone I knew. With that in mind, I had agreed to meet up this morning. However, when I first tried to leave, my car wouldn't start. I didn't have time to figure out what was wrong with it, because I didn't want to be late to the meeting. Instead, I hopped on public transportation and went to the Starbucks. I waited there an entire hour and a half, while calling this person over and over again, before realizing they weren't going to show up. Then, when I was returning home, right up the street two guys jumped out of the bushes in broad daylight and beat the holy crap out of me. I had never seen them before and didn't have a clue who they were, but my gut continued to tell me that this was connected to Leslie.

A month ago, Mrs. Smith had refused to point me in her direction, so I had ended up going to the police after receiving that text that said only, *Die*. They did a slight investigation and told me that Leslie had an alibi for each instance when the texts came through. They also stated that the texts were coming from a burner phone, which she was not in the possession of or in the vicinity of. No matter what they had claimed, I knew it was her, because no one else could be behind this. And now, since it appeared she had enlisted some help, I needed to as well. Immediately, I thought of the one person was was just as sneaky and conniving as me: Patricia.

Peculiarly enough, we hadn't spoken since that day she called off our whole mission. Yet I believed she still owed me for my services, and it was time she paid up. Not being able to wait until I healed, I called her right then and there. She answered, sounding a little weird.

"Hello?" Her breathing was heavy and fast. Maybe I'd caught her while she was exercising or taking a jog.

"Patricia, it's David."

"Oh," was all she said, not sounding the least bit thrilled to hear from me, but little did she know the feeling was mutual. "How can I help you, David?"

"I'm calling because we need to meet up. There are some things I need to discuss with you and could use your help on. And seeing how I helped you out before, I'm sure you wouldn't mind returning the favor, right?"

"You helped me out? All you did was go to St. Louis on *my* dime. Anyway, I don't know about this. I'm not sure that whatever you're up to, I want to be involved in."

"Well, sorry, but I'm not taking no for an answer. So, meet me at the Starbucks on Tenth tomorrow at noon. I'll see you then."

I hung up without giving her a chance to contest anything. And by tomorrow, I would have myself all cleaned up, would figure out a way to get back at whoever did this to me, and would see where things stood with Patricia and her million bucks. She may have thought I'd forgotten all about it, but naturally, I hadn't. And that money might very well be my ticket to paying back Leslie for her foolishness.

CHAPTER 25

PATRICIA

"Ooh, baby, faster, harder. Oh, my goodness, Randle. I'm about to cum!" I screamed before releasing every bit of anxiety and tension I had bottled up inside me. Especially after getting that phone call from David, who'd had the nerve to bring up *my* one million dollars, or the one million that I wouldn't have. Anyway, I couldn't believe him or the fact that he was seeking my help with something that he was involved in.

"Who was that on the phone? It wasn't Terrence, was it?" Randle questioned, rolling over onto his back and trying to settle his breathing. I guessed I'd really taken him for a ride.

"It wasn't anyone important. But why are you so afraid of Terrence finding out about us?"

"I'm not afraid, but he's a friend as well as a client. I don't need him thinking I'm mixing business and pleasure with his soon-to-be ex-wife."

"Soon-to-be ex? Who said anything about me divorcing my husband?"

"I guess I assumed that with what's been going on between us for the past month, you would be over that part of your life, Pat."

"Well, I'm sorry if I've led you on, but Terrence is still my husband, who I love deeply."

"I see," was all he said, sitting up on the side of the bed.

I had other concerns on my mind, though, and no time to worry about his feelings or his ego. "But, Randle, I do have a legal question for you really quick."

"Right now?" He looked at me sideways.

"Yes, baby, right now. Anyway, when it comes to verbal agreements, how do those hold up in a court of law?"

"Well, if one or both of the parties can prove that they had an agreement from the start, then that agreement is just as legally binding as a signed contract."

"And how can anyone actually prove a verbal agreement?"

"Uh, some people have recordings of their agreement or maybe even text messages or emails affirming that something was in place," he said before getting up and heading for the bathroom.

I knew that David and I didn't have any recordings, but he might very well still have my initial Facebook message reaching out to him. And I was positive he still had the numerous texts we'd sent back and forth when he headed to St. Louis. Needless to say, I knew I'd gotten myself into a real pickle, which I had to figure out how to get out of by tomorrow. I wasn't going to let David scare me, though. This ball was still in my court, and he'd learn at this so-called meeting tomorrow whom to fuck with and whom not.

Randle came walking back in, buck naked, and I was more than ready for round two. I guessed I was making up for all the time that Terrence had been out doing his thing with Ms. Tate. But now it was my turn, and I couldn't care less that Randle was his friend and attorney. He made me feel good. Unlike Terrence, Randle was interested in me. He asked about my likes and dislikes, he encouraged me, and he made me feel beautiful and, most of all, desired. We'd spent almost every day with one another after leaving his office that day. He'd bought me flowers, taken me on dates. He courted me like a man was supposed to. But just when I thought that things were great, he had to go and sour the entire mood.

"So, if you're done asking your questions, I have a question of my own. Are you really still in love with your husband? Is love what's stopping you from starting the divorce process, or is it that you don't want him to end up with the money and be with another woman?"

I couldn't believe he was asking these things, because I thought I'd made myself clear when we discussed it the other ten times before. I got up and put on my robe, because I could already see that there would surely be no round two.

"Didn't we talk about this already?" I replied.

"Yes, we tried, but you didn't give me an answer then either, so I thought you might be ready now."

"Look, it's all just complicated, all right?"

"No one is making it complicated but you and Terrence, and you two don't even want each other. I mean, you're having sex with me, and he's with—"

I cut him off with rapid-fire questions. "With whom? Has he confided in you? Has he told you about him and that coworker of his?"

"Why the hell are you so obsessed with that woman anyway? Damn," he yelled at me.

I'd never seen that side of Randle, and I wasn't sure if I was upset or turned on more by it. "It's not that I'm obsessed, Randle. He's my husband, for goodness' sake."

"So, what am I? Just some good dick to keep you company until you and Terrence figure out what you're doing? Because I'm not going to be the side dick or rebound brother, Pat. That's not where I am in my life. I thought we might have been on the same page." He grabbed his jeans and started to slide them on.

I couldn't believe that after having such an amazing time with each other, things were turning out this way. I crawled up behind him and threw my arms around his neck. "Randle, please, would you stop being so dramatic! You know that you're not my side dick or rebound. But I just thought we were having fun, without complicating things."

"Oh, fun. *Fun* is what you want? So, you mean you want a brother that has sex with you and then you bounce? You want someone that doesn't call or text just to see how your day is going? You want someone that's not concerned about building a home for you and your sons? You want *fun*? Well, Patricia, maybe I'm not the *fun boy* that you want, because I'm a grown fucking man. I had fun in my twenties. Now it's about building a life and a future. So, I guess when you're out of the fun stage and you're finally ready to let go of a man that's clearly showing you he doesn't want you, then give me call. I *might* still be around."

Randle grabbed his shirt and left me sitting there, looking foolish. I got up and walked over to my mirror and took a good look at myself. "What's wrong with you, Pat? Here you are with a wonderful man in your life who's wanting to do all the things you've been begging your husband to do. Yet you're trying to hold on to something that's not there just to get revenge and make Terrence as miserable as he made you. What are you going to do?" I asked myself, speaking aloud.

Next thing I knew, I walked over to my cell phone and started to dial a number. Although there was a small part of me that still didn't want to do it, the rest of me knew that I *needed* to do it. I took a deep breath when I finally heard her voice on the other end of the line.

"Hey, Kim. It's Patricia. You told me to give you a call whenever I was truly ready to start the process."

CHAPTER 26

TIFFANY

I was starting to think that the minute I'd put that check in Terrence's hands a month ago, I'd created a monster. He'd ended up staying with me only for maybe a week and a half before finding a decent enough house to rent. Although I personally felt it was a bit pricey, the home was beautiful and in a perfect location. I saw it as the perfect place for us to one day begin building our little family together, once his divorce was final, especially since we'd officially labeled ourselves a couple.

Of course, I didn't want to rush things, and I knew he still had a lot that he needed to resolve with Patricia, but he had assured me that this part of his life was over. He continually told me that he was ready to establish a home and a family for his two biological children. His twin daughters meant the world to him, but their mother refused to allow him to see them outside of her parents' home. He had explained that this was why it was so important that he had a home, a place where he could truly build a relationship with them. Only thing he had requested was that I give him at least six months of living on his own before I moved in, because after all the craziness with Pat, he just needed a little time to himself to breathe. I completely understood, so there was no pressure from me at all. However, strange things had started to happen, things that to me weren't adding up, and I was beginning to feel like Terrence was playing games and taking me for some type of fool.

"We better get up, baby, and get our day started." He hopped up right after getting some morning sex and prepared to shower.

"Yeah, I guess you're right. Did you want me to grab you something from Starbucks too? I'm going to stop and pick up something for me and Monica on the way in."

"Uh no, actually, I'm not going into the school today. I might be heading out of town in the morning, and I have a few things to handle before I leave."

"Out of town? Where are you going?" I asked.

"Uh, probably St. Louis. I don't know if I told you, but my best friend, Greg, lives there. He has some work to do on a house that he's renovating and asked if I would come and help him out."

He kissed me on the cheek and headed for the bathroom, his way of saying the discussion was over. Yet for me, it was far from that.

"Why didn't you tell me about this before?" I yelled just as he closed the bathroom door.

"Oh, I don't know. I guess I didn't think it was a big deal." He walked back into the bedroom and grabbed his cell phone.

"I see. Well, if it's all right with you, I'm going to leave a couple of things here so that I won't have to pack on a weekly basis," I told him. He must have thought I was asking for permission. Next thing I knew, he stopped in his tracks and turned to face me.

"Baby, maybe you shouldn't do that right now."

"Why not? You have things at my home and even a key to the house."

"I know and you're going to have a key here once you move in, but right now I don't want to confuse things, all right? It's nothing personal, and you know I love you, but we have all the time in the world for stuff like that."

He went back into the bathroom, and a minute later I heard the water running in the shower.

You don't want to confuse things, huh? I thought at the very moment my eyes suddenly caught a glimpse of something that looked like shoes peeking out from under his bed. When I bent down to get a better look, the items were exactly what they had appeared to be. "Now, what the hell are you doing with a pair of women's sandals and house shoes under your bed, Mr. Montgomery?" I muttered aloud.

I picked up the sandals, contemplating whether I should go and throw them into the shower with him. Instead, however, I decided to put them in my bag. One thing I was sure of, whomever the sandals belonged to, they would surely come looking for them, and when they did, Terrence would have some explaining to do to both of us. "Serves you right, Mr. I Don't Want to Confuse Things."

I left his house while he was still in the shower. I couldn't wait to get to the school and talk with Monica.

Thirty minutes later, I asked Mrs. Washington if Monica was inside her office and if I could go in. Monica must have smelled her Starbucks through the door, because she opened it up and told me to come right inside.

"Girl, give me that coffee quick. I just had a one-on-one meeting with Mr. Taylor, and I thought I would have to fire the man. He better be happy I had my latte on the way to help calm me down."

I didn't say anything but simply sat down in one of the chairs in front of her desk.

"Hey, what's wrong with you?" Monica asked.

"It's Terrence, as usual as of late."

"Oh, boy, let me sit down for this." She took the chair right next to me. "Now, what's going on in lovers' land?"

"I'm not exactly sure, Monica. It's almost like he changed the minute I gave him that check to help him out and he got the house."

"Girl, I still can't believe you did that, because that's a grown man, and he had no business asking you for any type of help, especially not financial help. But what's going on?"

"It's just that ever since he got the house, he's been so different with me. I normally stay there a couple nights out of the week, but it seems he's starting to have an is-sue with that. Then today I asked if he minded me leaving some items there, so I don't have to pack this spinnanight bag every week, and he had an issue with that too. Not to mention, he's still asking for money here and there, be-cause he claims he's falling short all the time. And on top of it all, I've been finding a lot of feminine items at his home that *don't* belong to me."

"What? Like what?"

"Well, it started with female body wash and body sprays. Then I found a pink-ass toothbrush and a pink umbrella. Twice, I've found feminine products in the cabinet under the bathroom sink. And just today I found these." I reached down and pulled the ugly-ass sandals out of my bag for Monica to see.

"Yep, those are women's sandals, but they sure are ugly too. But, Tiff, girl, why do you have them with you? And how did you get them out of there without him knowing?"

"He was in the shower, so I just took them. I want Terrence to have to come and ask me about them, if he has the nerve, because I'm sure the owner knows that she left them there. She'll wonder where they went."

"And do you really think he's going to do that? Because we both know that no matter how guilty a man is of something, he'll take it to the grave before coming clean."

"Yeah, I know. I just want him to address it, because I know I'm not crazy, and he's trying to make it like I am."

"I guess I don't understand why you two are even playing games like this with one another. I thought you wanted to be together?"

"Well, I still do. I mean, you know how much I love that man. But I'm not quite sure if he still wants the same. His mouth says it all the time, and everything is great whenever we have sex, but other than that, his actions are telling me that his mind and heart are somewhere else. I swear, it's like he's turned into someone that I don't even know anymore and honestly don't like. It's really starting to scare me, Monica."

"Listen, try not to overreact, okay?" She placed her hand on my knee. "Maybe his behavior has a lot to do with him still grieving his father. And then there's the fact that things didn't go how he thought they would with his father's estate. And I'm sure he's still dealing with a bunch of drama from Patricia. So, maybe he's dealing with everything the best he can, and it's coming off a bit strange."

"I hear you, but I don't think that's it at all, Monica. To be honest, Terrence doesn't seem as torn up about his father's death as I would have imagined. He's far more torn about everything with the estate. And believe it or not, Patricia has been oddly quiet lately. He hasn't heard a peep out of her. So, I hate to even think like this, but I get the feeling that his recent behavior has a lot more to do with St Louis and a woman named Malaysia, who lives there."

"No." Her eyes danced around, betraying her shock.

"Yeah. I mean, we've been with each other for the past couple of days, and he never once mentioned that he was taking a trip to St. Louis this weekend. Then, when I asked him about it, he suddenly has a best friend that lives there and needs his help working on a house. It just doesn't sound right, and call it my woman's intuition or whatever, but I have a real suspicion that this woman is much more that some old friend he bumped into."

"So, you think he's dealing with her? Long distance?"

"It's possible."

"But why, when he has you? Why, if he has everything he can ask for in a woman in you, would he risk it by playing around with some heffa all the way in St. Louis?" She got up and started walking around, as if with each step she took, she was trying to put together the pieces of the puzzle in her head.

"That's what I would like to know."

"All right, so I guess my next question is, what are you going to do? Because you can't go on letting him get sex and money from you while he's playing around with someone else. And didn't I see you putting together a menu, a logo, and other stuff for his business in the library the other evening?"

"Yeah, he wants to have it all done so that the minute his divorce is final, he can get the building and won't have to worry about things like that," I explained.

"No, I don't believe that. He just wants you to do it for him so that he doesn't have to pay anyone else to do it. And I don't care how long Terrence and I have been friends . . . Right is right, and wrong is wrong. He's not about to have you as his lover, ATM machine, secretary, graphic designer, housekeeper, or anything else if he wants to run off and go play with little Ms. Mayonnaise, or whatever her name is."

"Monica, it's Malaysia," I said, trying to keep a serious face.

"I don't care *what* her name is. Terrence has another thing coming if he thinks he's going to play my girl. Hell, he better be happy I haven't said, 'Let's head to St. Louis and find out what he's *really* up to.' But no, we don't have to go running behind him, because one thing I know for sure, what's done in the dark always has a way of coming to light."

She put her hand up for a high five, and I quickly obliged. Whatever Terrence was up to would surely be revealed, sooner or later.

CHAPTER 27

TERRENCE

Malaysia met me at the baggage claim and kissed me on the cheek. "Hey, baby. How was your flight?"

"I thought I told you to just pull the car up and I would be out."

"Yeah, I know, but I couldn't wait to see you." She was all lovey dovey and googly eyed, like she'd been of late.

"Even if it was going to take only a few more minutes?"

We laughed and headed toward the car. Once we got there, she jumped in on the passenger side, leaving me to drive. I got behind the wheel and headed in the direction of what had become one of my favorite places to go whenever I was in town—the cigar shop, to pick up my favorite cigars. After I bought the cigars, I realized I was famished.

"Terrence, where are you going? This isn't the direction of my condo."

"I know, babe, but I want some Lee's Chicken."

"No, you can't fill up on that, because I was thinking we would go to Ruth's Chris tonight."

I knew she had her heart set on Ruth's Chris. It was one of her favorite restaurants, especially when I came to town. However, seeing that I was a little low on cash for the entire weekend, picking up some chicken seemed like a much better option to me.

"Baby, I feel like we waste so much money on dining out. Can't we get the chicken this time and have a quiet, relaxing evening at home?"

"No, we can't. Terrence, you've been putting off coming here to see me for the past couple of weeks, and now that you're here, we can't go out and enjoy each other?"

"So, what, we can't enjoy each other unless we go out and waste money?"

"Okay, that's what this is about? Money?"

"Baby, I already explained to you everything that's going on with me. And because of that, I'm just a little tight on cash right now, that's all," I said, knowing I hadn't fully been honest about *everything*.

"Okay, I can understand that. So, when are you getting the money from your father's estate anyway? Or the building for your restaurant, so we can bring in some real cash?"

I remained quiet instead of answering her questions, because honestly, I didn't know how to answer without starting a huge altercation. I hadn't found it in me to tell her that I wasn't getting anything from my father's estate until I was divorced, mainly because she had no clue that I was even married. All this time, I'd just allowed her to think whatever she wanted. And it seemed she believed that we were going to have a future together, and that we'd be millionaires and own a restaurant chain. Well, it sounded good, damn good. That was why I didn't have the guts to come clean with the whole truth about things.

I noticed how quiet she'd become, and her smile had faded from her face. Rather than stop anywhere, I headed straight to her condo. When we got there, she sat there waiting for me to open her car door, so that we could go upstairs together. However, I needed to handle my business in Texas first.

"Hey, baby. Can you go ahead and go up? I need to make a business call, and then I'll be right there."

She glared at me, letting me know her displeasure, but didn't say a word. Then she climbed out, slammed the car door, and went upstairs to her condo. I knew she was pissed, but I also knew how to make it all better. A few seconds later, and after making sure she was inside her place, I dialed a number.

"Hello?"

"Hey, sweetie. I just wanted to call and let you know that I made it here safely."

"Oh good. And how's your friend?"

"My friend?" I had no idea who she was talking about.

"Yes, your friend Greg. The one you said you were going to help renovate a house."

"Oh yeah, Greg. I'm sorry, babe. My mind was on getting some food in my stomach because I'm starving. But Greg is good, and he told me to tell you hello."

"Tell him I said hello, and I can't wait to meet him whenever he comes to Texas."

"I sure will, baby, but I was calling because I had a quick question too. Um, I thought I had a little more in my bank account than I do. It seems that something I'd forgotten all about was automatically withdrawn, and it's left me a little low. And since I didn't want to be out here all weekend depending on Greg, I was hoping that you would help me out."

"Terrence, are you serious? I thought this was a paid job. He isn't paying you?"

"Yes, baby, he is, but he's my best friend, so I didn't want to charge him what I would anyone else. Plus, we're not going to get the money until the end of the job."

"So, how much are you talking about?"

"I don't know. Maybe three or four hundred should be all right until I get back, and then I can pay you back from whatever I get from the job."

"I don't know, Terrence. I need to check my account first."

"That's fine, baby. Just send whatever you can. And if you can Cash App it or Zelle it to me, that would be great."

"Yeah, okay."

"Thanks, baby. Listen, I have to go. I'll give you a call or something a little later. I love you."

"Yeah, I love you too."

I'd hung up with Tiff in just the nick of time because Malaysia had made her way back outside and was heading my direction. Lucky for me, right as she approached the car, I got an alert that I'd received a Cash App for three hundred bucks.

She approached the driver's side of the car and said through the window, "I guess you're still on your *business* call, which you couldn't take *inside* the house, huh?"

"Are you really trying to act upset with me because I had some business to handle?" I asked as I climbed out from behind the wheel.

She poked her lips out, folded her arms, and didn't say anything.

"Okay, well, will I be able to erase that frown from your face by telling you we're going to Ruth's Chris this evening?"

She looked at me with curiosity, and I immediately saw a hint of a smile coming back around.

"I thought that you were low on cash and that we didn't need to be wasting money on dining out?" she asked softly.

"Well, that's what my business was about, so I could make sure I was making you happy."

She reached over and started kissing me all over my face. "You always make me happy, Mr. Montgomery."

We went upstairs together, but the minute we stepped inside her condo, she threw another dagger at me, which I wasn't ready for.

"Baby, while it's on my mind, did you grab my sandals that I asked you to bring with you?"

"Uh, nope, because I checked up under my bed before I left, and I didn't see anything. Are you sure you left them there?"

"Terrence, I'm positive I did. Why is it that every time I leave something at your house, it suddenly goes missing?"

"Baby, look, maybe you should look for the sandals here again, because they weren't at my house, all right?"

"I don't have to look for them, Terrence, because I know for sure I left them there, so you need to find them." She went into the bathroom and slammed the door.

I sat down on the sofa, thinking how I hadn't been in St. Louis a whole hour yet and all we'd done was argue here and there. True enough, she had more than likely left her sandals at my place, but for the life of me, I had no clue where they could be. I'd searched my home up and down before leaving. Then it dawned on me. *Tiffany.* I hopped up and ran over to the bathroom door.

"Baby, I have your keys, okay?" I called. "I'm going to run to the store and grab me some beer. Did you need anything while I was out?"

"No," was all she said, and I knew for sure she was inside pouting and probably even crying.

"Baby, listen, I'm sorry, okay? Maybe I was rushing so much that I overlooked your sandals. If you said you left them there, then I'm sure they are there. And if they have somehow disappeared, then I'll just buy you another pair."

She still didn't say anything, so I knew at that moment I needed to get right down to the bottom of things. Heading to the car, I dialed a number on my cell phone while trying to figure out exactly what to say.

"Hello?"

"Hey, baby. I wanted to call and thank you for the money you sent."

"You're welcome, Terrence. But to be honest, I can't keep taking care of my responsibilities and giving you two, three, or four hundred dollars on a whim whenever you need it. I think when you return, we should sit down and talk about things."

"Yeah, you're right, and I totally agree. But, hey, I have a quick question. You didn't happen to see any sandals under my bed when you were there, did you?"

"Sandals? I didn't know you wore sandals, baby. Are you trying something new?"

"Uh, no. Actually they are, um, women's sandals," I replied, hoping I didn't just get myself into something that I couldn't lie my way out of.

"Women's sandals? Why would women's sandals be under your bed, Terrence?"

Dammit. Please let me think of something quick, please, I begged the universe. "Oh, well, see, the other night I let my cousin and his girlfriend spend the night because they didn't have anywhere to stay. And well, my cousin said his girlfriend got dressed in my bedroom, and she forgot her sandals underneath my bed."

"Wait, so you have a full bathroom upstairs, two other bedrooms besides yours, an entire basement downstairs with a half bathroom, but your cousin's girlfriend chose to get dressed inside *your bedroom* and that was cool with you?"

"Baby, I thought it sounded crazy, too, when he told me. But now she's looking for her sandals, and I couldn't find them anywhere before I left."

"And you thought about these sandals while you're in St. Louis, helping your friend renovate a house, and you figured you would call and ask me?"

"Well, he just called and asked me about them again, so I thought I would just check with you. So, have you seen them?"

"Nope. I think I would remember seeing a pair of women's sandals under your bed. That's something I don't recall."

"All right. Well, I guess I'll get back to work. I'll talk with you later."

"Yeah, okay."

We hung up, but my gut told me Tiffany knew way more than what she was letting on. It struck a nerve, though, because I couldn't recall a time when I felt like Tiffany had been dishonest with me. But I knew that she knew about the sandals and that I'd lied about where they came from. Only thing was, I had no clue what I was in for with her when I returned home or what to say to Malaysia either.

CHAPTER 28

MALAYSIA

"Girl, he claimed he was running to the store to pick up some beer, but I know Terrence is lying about something." I had hurried to call Toni while he was gone.

"But what do you think it is?"

"I don't have any proof, but my gut is telling me that it has something to do with that crazy ex-girlfriend he had me block from my social media. I got a funny feeling that she's behind all my things coming up missing that I left at his house too."

"Look, I sure don't want to say, 'I told you so,' but it was strange to me that a nice-looking man that has so much going on for himself is single."

"Yeah, and I'm really beginning to question everything he's saying about the money and the restaurant from his father too. I mean, if it was all true, then why hasn't it happened yet?"

"I don't know, but what are you planning to do about it?" Toni asked me.

"What I'm not going to do is stick around and have him continue lying to me. From here on out, if he wants me in his life, he's going to have to prove it. First, I'm going to let him know that I'm tired of feeling like a secret. We need to be out in the open, especially on his social media. If we're going to do this long-distance relationship thing, then at least every woman in Texas needs to know that I exist. Then I plan on unblocking that friend of his, and I'm going to make sure that she gets an eyeful."

"All right now, Malaysia. You're playing with fire, you know that, right? He might just get so upset about the ultimatums that he cuts things off completely."

"I know, but I'm rolling the dice on this anyway. I think I hear him coming, though, so I'll give you a call later," I whispered. I hung up right as his key was entering the doorknob.

When he walked through the door, he glanced over at me on the sofa, trying, I assumed, to see if I still appeared upset. "Baby, I know you said you didn't want anything, but I picked up your favorite wine." He smiled and held it up.

I still gave him the silent treatment while trying to decide how to enter this conversation of ultimatums. He put the alcohol away and fell on the sofa next to me, then rubbed his head on my shoulder like a puppy dog.

"Is my baby still mad at me?" he whispered.

"Stop it, Terrence. Because the cute stuff is not going to work right now." I pushed him away. "We need to talk." I ignored his expression, which said that I was getting on his last nerve. We were going to have this conversation whether he liked it or not.

"What's wrong now? Because if it's still about those damn sandals, then I told you I would get you a new pair."

"Terrence, it's about the sandals, my body washes and perfumes, my feminine hygiene products, and everything. It's about social media and the fact that I can't post anything personal about us. It's about me being here and you being there. I'm just frustrated about it all. I need to feel like the lady in your life and not some huge secret," I said all at once, without thinking about everything I was saying. It all just kind of fell out of my mouth, and he only sat there, taking it all in. To tell the truth, there was a nervous feeling inside me, and it basically sealed the deal on our fate.

"Baby, you're right," he said shockingly a second later. "You're not a huge secret, and I'm sorry if I've made you feel that way. I will do whatever possible to figure out what happened to your things, and from this day forward, you can feel free to post whatever you like on social media."

"Are you sure? Because I don't want you to do anything that you really don't want to do."

"I'm positive," he said while I studied his face for any doubt. He still looked as if he was thinking, though.

It was beyond me what had gotten into him all of a sudden, but I loved it. In such a short time, I had fallen head over heels in love with this man, and I wanted the world to know, especially his crazy ex-girlfriend. She needed to know that Terrence had someone in his life and that she should leave him completely alone. If he wasn't going to make sure she knew, then I would.

CHAPTER 29

TIFFANY

"Do you see what I mean? Did you hear the lies he had the nerve to tell me?" I asked Monica, who was sitting across from me, with her mouth hanging wide open.

We'd left the school to grab a bite to eat for lunch. Terrence had called the minute we sat down at our table, and I had put the phone on speaker so that Monica could listen in and would know I wasn't crazy.

"Wow. It's like the lies just slid off his tongue with ease. He didn't even sound like he had to think about them."

"Right. But what gets me is that he must really think I'm foolish enough to believe his cousin's girlfriend got dressed in *his* bedroom."

Monica nodded. "Yeah, that was a bit of a stretch, if I say so myself."

"And did you see how he kept calling and getting off the phone in a hurry, like someone was going to catch him?"

"Yep, I sure did." Monica nodded in agreement again. "But like I asked you earlier, Tiffany, what are *you* going to do about this? Because Terrence can't continue to think that he can get away with any of it. You've got to say or do something."

"I know, but I'm not exactly sure what to do."

"You're not sure?" She spoke loud enough for the whole restaurant to hear. I gave her a look, and she lowered her voice when she said, "Tiffany, we both know now that Terrence is trying to play you for some kind of fool, and you can't let that happen. Hell, what are you afraid of by confronting him about the sandals, the body wash, or any other crap you've found at his house? And, more importantly, lying to your damn face?"

"Maybe because I've allowed myself to fall in love with him, and I'm a bit scared of losing him forever," I confessed.

"To hell with that, Tiff. I understand about being in love and all, but you're my girl, and I'm not going to let you go out like this. Love doesn't consist of a bunch of lies and mistruths. And it's not going to allow you to be disrespected either, honey, because that's exactly what Terrence is doing. He's lying, possibly cheating, and disrespecting you. So, if you're not going to confront him about all of this, then please, at least just leave him alone. Start loving on yourself and focusing totally on you. And believe me, the second he realizes you're not around to play his little ATM machine or anything else for him, he'll be singing a much different tune."

We started to dig into our salads, which the waiter had brought over to the table while we were conversing. It was extremely quiet as we concentrated on eating, but I was also allowing what Monica had said to sink in. She was right. Terrence was disrespecting me, and I was the only one who could put a stop to it. When I was right in the middle of my thoughts, Monica picked up her cell phone, brought it closer to her face, and froze.

"Monica, what's wrong? You look like you've seen a ghost."

"Tiff, are you and Terrence still Facebook friends?" she asked hesitantly.

"No. I thought I told you that he gave me some crap about having to delete me for a little while, until the whole divorce process is final."

"Is that what he said? Because from the looks of it, it might be because of an entirely different reason." She turned her phone around to let me see a picture that had been posted within the past twenty minutes. It was her, his *friend*, the one whose post had been deleted from his page before he took me off. She and Terrence were all hugged up together, and the caption read, I LOVE WHEN MY BABY COMES TO TOWN.

I looked at this woman, who was grinning from ear to ear, with a dry-ass face with no makeup on and a weird-ass haircut. And then I looked at him. His expression gave the impression that he was happy and at peace with her. I fought hard to hold back the tears that were making their way into my eyes as I continued to look at them together in the picture. As much as I wanted to, or even needed to, I couldn't stop looking, while my heart sank further and further into the pit of my stomach.

"Tiff, why don't we get out of here and go back out to the car?" Monica grabbed my arm and pulled me out of the restaurant without me having to say a word. It seemed the minute we made it to the car, I broke down all the way.

"How the fuck could he do this? He had sex with me over the past two days. I just sent his ass three hundred dollars. And he's out in St. Louis, living the good life, on my dime with some trick. Really? Who does that to someone they claim to love?" I screamed as tears came gushing out of my eyes.

Monica took me in her arms. "It's all right Tiff. Everything's going to be all right," she said softly while rubbing my back.

But at that very moment, consoling wasn't what I needed. I wanted to speak to Terrence that very second. I couldn't wait any longer. After pulling out of Monica's embrace, I grabbed my cell phone.

"Oh goodness, Tiff! What are you doing? What are you about to do?" I could hear the fear in her voice.

"I'm calling him. He's going to talk to me right now." I dialed his number, but my call went right to voicemail. I called again, and the same thing happened.

"Honey, why don't you try to calm down and just address this when he returns home?" She tried taking the phone out of my hand, but I wasn't having it.

"No. I don't give a damn who he's with, he's going to talk to me now." After maybe the hundredth call, just when I was thinking about giving up, Terrence finally answered.

"Why do you keep calling my phone like this?" he yelled at me.

"Why? Why? Are you really asking me why right now? Who is she, Terrence? Who is the lowlife-looking-ass trick on the picture with you?" I shot back.

"You don't ask me about another woman that I'm with. And what the hell are you doing anyway? Stalking me?"

I could feel Monica nudging me to hang up.

"*Stalking you*? Oh, so now I'm stalking somebody that I'm fucking? And you know what, Terrence? I always thought that if you were going to cheat on me, that it would *at least* be with someone that halfway looked like something."

"And what the hell do you think you look like without your makeup, Tiff? You don't look so cute either," he retorted.

"Really? You didn't have a problem with my looks the past couple of nights at your house. And who the hell are you trying to impress, anyway, right now by talking to me like that, Terrence? Is she there? Is she sitting right next to you? Who is she, Terrence?"

"You don't need to concern yourself with who she is. Just know that I'm getting everything I need from her, and she doesn't remind me of Patricia, the way you do. I finally have someone that stands on her own two feet."

Before I was able to take a jab back at him, Monica snatched my phone out of my hand and pressed END.

"Stop it, Tiff. Just stop it. You are a full-grown woman, and the last thing I'm about to let you do is sit here and act like some average-ass chick by cursing Terrence out. Now, I know you're pissed, but the point of the matter is, he has shown you exactly who he is. It's time for you to believe it and walk away with your dignity. Let him have whoever he is with, because one thing I know for sure, no other woman is going to be as good to him or do half the things you did for him. So, as much as it's going to hurt, it's time to walk away."

I knew she was right, even if I didn't want to admit it. My heart ached, and this was honestly the worst feeling I'd ever felt. I couldn't even remember feeling this way with David. Terrence had had my heart, and I felt like he'd just thrown it down and stomped all over it. And for her. Who was she, and where did she even come from? What was she doing for him that I hadn't? I was no longer able to be strong at that point, so Monica held me close as I released everything I felt on her shoulder. I cried for what seemed like an hour or more, knowing that after this, I didn't want to cry anymore.

"It's all right, Tiffany. Let it all out, and just know that a man reaps what's sown. Terrence will *not* get away with any of this."

CHAPTER 30

TERRENCE

I wanted to yell at the top of my lungs over what had just happened. Quickly glancing at Malaysia when I ended the call, I saw that her face read satisfaction and vindication all rolled into one. However, I couldn't remember a time when I had felt worse in my entire life. Tiffany hadn't deserved what I'd done or the things I'd said, and all I could think about was how I needed to fix this.

"I'm so glad you told her off, baby," Malaysia said. "Maybe now she'll leave you alone and go find a man of her own, one that wants her."

There was no way that I could respond to Malaysia or how she felt, when I felt so bad. Part of me wanted to hop on the next flight back to Texas, but I knew that would only unleash a ton of confusion with Malaysia. If only Tiffany hadn't questioned me the way she had or gone snooping in my personal business, things could have turned out completely different.

"Baby, are you all right?" She must have noticed my sour disposition.

"No, not quite, Malaysia. See, you don't know Tiffany the way I do. She has a really good heart and didn't deserve the things I said to her."

She looked at me with her nose all turned up, like she couldn't believe what I was saying.

"Baby, don't feel bad about how you had to address her. I may not know her personally, but from what you've told me, along with her behavior today, it had to happen. Some women just can't seem to understand when it's over and when a man has moved on. You needed to talk to her that way because saying things delicately wasn't getting through to her."

"Yeah, I guess so. If you don't mind, though, I'm going to go for a drive, but I'll be back shortly."

"Wait a minute. You're leaving?"

"Malaysia, please don't start an argument with me right now. I just need to clear my head, all right? Is that too much to ask?"

"You're damn right it is, if it has something to do with a woman you said you wanted nothing else to do with. I mean, if it's affecting you like that, then maybe you need to be with her and not me."

"Please do not push me, because you may not get the outcome that you're expecting. Now, all I asked for was a moment to myself."

"And all I'm saying is, if you leave this house, then you may as well head back to Texas," Malaysia barked.

I wasn't about to be pushed around by anyone, not by Tiffany or Malaysia. Calling her bluff, I threw her car keys on the coffee table, grabbed my bag, and headed for the front door.

"Where the hell are you going, Terrence?"

"Back to Texas, like you said. I'll wait on an Uber outside to take me to the airport. Maybe you'll calm down by the time I make it back home, and we can talk then." I tried opening the door, but she had run over and was blocking my way.

"So, you're choosing *her*? Over me? Because if so, then we won't talk when you get home. We won't talk ever again, Terrence." The expression on her face told me she demanded some type of reaction out of me, but I wasn't giving it to her.

"Suit yourself. I'm out of here," was all I said.

I skirted around her, walked out the door, and sat outside until the Uber I called showed up. Thinking back to that morning, I realized that I had woken up feeling on top of the world, and now I was feuding with both of the women I cared for. For the life of me, I couldn't understand how I'd gotten myself in this predicament. And I certainly didn't know how to get out of it. One thing I was grateful for, though, was that Patricia was nowhere in this messed-up equation. She had been quiet as a mouse, although I had to admit, her silence still made me tense.

CHAPTER 31

PATRICIA

David should have been happy that Starbucks was one of my favorite places, because I'd been sitting there for the past thirty minutes, waiting for him. I planned on giving him only another ten or fifteen minutes before I left.

"Ma'am, can I get you something to drink while you wait?" the barista asked me.

"Sure. A trenta-sized Strawberry Refresher with lemonade. Three pumps of pineapple ginger added would be great."

"Coming right up." She smiled and walked away.

"If you're not here by the time my drink is up, then I'm out of here," I said aloud, angry that I'd even given David the time of day.

While I waited, I decided to try Randle once again. I called his cell phone, but it went straight to voicemail. Next, I called his office, to no avail, and his secretary offered to take what must have been the sixth or seventh message from me. I fully accepted the fact that he was angry, but what I didn't get was how he'd shut me out ever since he left yesterday morning. It wasn't the same as when I argued with Terrence. He pretty much fed into my foolish behavior and argued back with me. Randle wasn't doing that, and I didn't know how to respond. I thought about calling his cell again and leaving a message, but then I saw David coming inside. He wasn't looking like the man I had first met. His beard was all scruffy, his clothes were extremely wrinkled, like he'd slept in them, and he had scratches and bruises all over his face.

"Hey." He pulled up the chair across from me.

"What the hell happened to you?" I questioned. "You look a mess."

"Wow, Thanks for the compliment, Patricia."

"I'm only saying." I shrugged. "What happened to you?" I repeated.

"Listen, that's kind of what I'm here for. I've gotten myself in a bit of a bind, and I need my share of whatever you were going to give me from the money, and then I won't bother you again." He spoke softly and kept looking around, like someone was after him.

"Are you all right?" I had to ask. "What's going on with you? You're making me nervous."

"Pat, listen, I don't have time for games, okay? Are you going to give me the money or not?" he said, raising his voice slightly.

"Um, *not*. First of all, you have a lot of nerve demanding money for a job you didn't complete. And secondly, there's no money to give, David."

He looked at me, searching my eyes to see if was lying. "What do mean, there's no money?"

"Just what I said. Terrence didn't get what he thought he would, so there's no money to give you."

"You mean, had we continued on with your antics, I would have been lying to Tiffany and messing with your husband all for nothing?" he muttered, raising his voice even more.

"Look, I don't know what's bugging you, but you need to lower your tone with me. Anyway, don't sit there and act as if you weren't going to get something out of it either. You hate my husband, remember? And you wanted your sweet little Tiffany all back to yourself, or has that changed?"

"I already told you. I just wasn't feeling good about lying to her anymore. It didn't feel right."

"Aw." I wiped fake tears from my eyes, as if I felt his pain.

"Real funny, Pat," he said, and I couldn't help noticing again how he kept looking around.

"Are you going to tell me what's got you shook? Because we could have talked about the money over the phone. So, what more is it? What's really going on with you, David?"

He waited a few minutes before answering, his voice low again. "Okay, I think—no, I know—that someone is after me."

"What?" I asked, in a manner that brought attention to us from those sitting nearby.

"Hey, lower your voice please. Now, back when I met Tiffany, I was kind of already engaged to someone else—"

"Are you serious, David?" I seethed, cutting him off. "And you have the nerve to call *me* the sneaky and conniving one? That's real funny."

"Listen, are you going to let me tell you or not?" he answered, pressing.

"Okay, okay, go ahead." I sipped on my Refresher because I could already tell this was about to be juicy.

"Anyway, I was engaged to a woman named Leslie. And before you ask, I honestly have no idea why I proposed to Tiff, since I was already engaged. But then Tiffany pushed for us to live together, and I suggested she moved here instead of me moving to St. Louis. But, Pat, I never thought she would actually do it, because that meant giving up everything she had in St. Louis."

"Damn. Engaged to two women at once? Is your dick made of platinum or what?"

"Yeah, wouldn't you like to know," he shot back, giving me a look as if to say, "Shut up and let me finish."

So, I did just that.

And he went on. "So, at the time, I was kind of living with Leslie, but since she was a flight attendant, I let Tiff move in there until I figured out how to get her back home."

"Hold up. You let another woman move into another woman's house? How crazy are you?"

There was that look again, so I motioned that my lips were zipped shut and there would be no more interrupting.

"Anyway, Leslie came home from a trip earlier than expected and found Tiffany there. And ever since she discovered the truth about it all, I've been getting threatening messages that I'd better watch my back. I even got a strange feeling that she might want me dead."

I covered my mouth with both hands, shocked, and did my best not to barge in again.

He continued. "I mean, it has to be her, because I've already canceled out the theory that it's Sonya."

This time I had to say something. "Who the hell is Sonya?"

"She's the woman I was kind of using for somewhere to stay and some cash when Tiffany and Leslie found out about each other. Only thing is, she ended up pregnant in the time that I was there."

I gasped, almost unable to breathe and feeling like I was going to pass out.

"Anyway, I suggested an abortion, and needless to say, she started hating my guts, too, so at first I thought it was her, but it's not."

"But you're sure that this Leslie woman or someone is after you?" I asked him.

"Yeah, because of all the texts. And then yesterday, before I called you, I was set up and beat up by two unknown guys. And I'm positive they are working for her. I'm not sure how far she's going to take this."

"David, if this has gone as far as two men beating you up, then maybe you need to get the police involved. I mean, they could have killed you."

"Don't you think I've already tried the police? But they're telling me that Leslie has nothing to do with it, that she has an alibi. That's why I just want to handle this myself. I was hoping to get some cash from you, to pay her off, and then maybe all this nonsense will stop. But I have to do something, because I can't keep being paranoid every time I leave the house."

"Oh, wow, David. I have to say, you really have my head spinning. I didn't think it was possible, but you're worse than my husband."

"Oh, thanks a lot," he answered sarcastically.

"And you honestly think that money is the trick?"

"I don't know if it is or isn't, but it's worth a shot. I'm willing to try just about anything because I believe my life is on the line."

"Well, I'm sorry about the money that I promised and not being able to offer you anything. I'm a little limited financially too. Well, a lot limited. But maybe we can put our heads together and come up with something else to keep this woman off your back."

"Yeah, that sounds good in theory," he answered, pretty much looking defeated.

With that said, we agreed on another time to get together to see what either of us had come up with. David wasn't my favorite person in the world, but he had become someone that I could talk to, and he was someone I was growing to care for. I didn't want anything to happen to him. However, I spoke too fast.

After I paid for my drink, we walked outside. We exchanged goodbyes, and David stepped off the curb. As I looked on, a black car came speeding from out of nowhere and hit David as he crossed the street.

CHAPTER 32

DAVID

"Help, help! I've been hit." I lay in the middle of the street, trying my best to move one of my legs. After my body hit the ground, it took a second before I felt the pain, but then my whole left leg felt like it was on fire. Lying there, I could hear several people screaming, including Patricia, who came running over and knelt at my side.

"Somebody, please call an ambulance," she yelled out. "Don't worry, David. You're going to be fine. Just hold on. We're getting you some help," she told me, trying to reassure me.

I wasn't so sure I would be fine myself. I literally could not move my leg at all, and if getting beat up wasn't enough, now I was really afraid for my life.

"Patricia, whatever you do, please don't leave me," I struggled to say.

"I'm here, David, and I'm not going anywhere. Just save your energy, though. Don't try to talk. An ambulance is on the way."

It was crazy that I couldn't be happier that Patricia was there with me. There we were, one minute unable to stand each other and both trying to get our ex's, and the next bonding over my misfortune. The more the pain took control of me, the more I had to admit to myself that she'd become much more to me than someone to devise devious schemes with.

"Patricia," I called, feeling weaker and weaker.

"David, please just try to relax until the ambulance arrives."

"Thank you for being here for me." I didn't hear her say anything back, which made me think I was fading into the afterlife or something. Then she finally answered me.

"You're going to be fine, David, I promise. And I'm not going anywhere."

CHAPTER 33

MALAYSIA

"He left. He just up and left, Toni. I don't know if he went to apologize to her. I don't know if he and I will ever talk again. I don't know anything because he just left." I walked around Toni's living room. I had so much nervous energy that I hadn't been able to sit still in the twenty minutes I'd been here. After filling her in over the phone on everything that had happened, she'd suggested coming over to my house so that I wouldn't be alone. However, needing to go outside and get some fresh air, I'd told her I would go over to her place.

"Girl, I don't understand. Is he with the woman or not? Because if not, then why is he feeling regretful about how he had to address her craziness? She had no right questioning him about anything he's doing if they aren't together anymore."

"That's exactly what I thought, but he continued to say how she didn't deserve it and how bad he felt for talking to her the way he did."

"Okay, would you have a seat already and try to relax? I'll get us something to drink." Toni got up off the living-room couch and went into the kitchen.

I sat down on the couch finally, but my nervousness hadn't subsided. My mind was all over the place, yet all I could seem to think about was whether he had gone to be with her. And if so, what did that mean for me and him? He might have thought she was crazy, but I was prepared to show him crazy—crazy enough even to head to Texas just to see where things stood between us. Toni came back in with two glasses of red wine, handed one to me, then took a seat in her oversize chair.

"Didn't you tell me, though, that he has her blocked from his social media account?" she inquired. I could basically see the wheels in her head spinning.

"Yeah."

"So that means she must have been spying on your account, eh?"

"I really don't know. I guess so," I answered, not seeing where she was going with this line of questioning.

"Well, if she wants to spy, then why not give her something to look at?" Toni suggested, with her lips all turned up.

"What do you mean? She already saw that he was here with me."

"But I'm saying give her more. Post the pictures all the way back from when you two bumped into each other. Post the ones from when you went with him to make arrangements for his father. Girl, post them all and give her exactly what she's looking for. And in the meantime, and between time, you go and get your man back."

I had heard the words that came out of her mouth, but I wasn't sure I understood them. "What do you mean, go and get him back? He left me to run to her."

"So, what if he did this once? That man has traveled hundreds of miles just to see you several times since you two met. He took you, not her, with him during one of the most important and fragile times in his life. And, Malaysia, he does whatever he can to make you happy. So, I'm not telling you to ignore tonight, but if he is truly who you want to be with, then fight for it."

"But *I'm* not the one destroying us or allowing someone else to come in. *He* is."

"Honey, okay, but sometimes men just need a little *push* in the right direction. So, go ahead and let him feel bad for how he spoke to her. That just means that he has a heart of compassion. But, deep down, his heart is really with you. Remind him of that."

I tried to let what Toni had said sink in. Going back in my mind, I realized that maybe I had pushed him in her direction by giving him an ultimatum. I probably had even come off as bitchy and nagging or, in some way, just like her. And now I was the only one who could turn that around, so maybe I did need to go and get my man. Maybe I did need to fight for him. And that was exactly what I planned to do.

"Toni, how do you feel about taking a quick trip with me?"

"As long as we're headed for Texas, I'm down." She gave a devilish grin.

I'd never really been a spur-of-the-moment type of girl, but this time I was going to take my chances. Only thing I was positive of was that I didn't plan on leaving Texas without my and Terrence's relationship pinned down. And although I didn't plan on giving him another ultimatum, he would have to keep his crazy ex in her place and out of our lives.

CHAPTER 34

TIFFANY

Instead of my going back to work at the school, Monica dropped me off at my truck and I went home. I still hadn't been able to get past any of the horrible things Terrence had said to me or the fact that he'd been cheating on me with this woman in St. Louis. I wanted to call Keisha and tell her everything that had happened, but I knew how crazily she would react. Keisha was the type of friend who would find a way to the girl's home and would confront Terrence and beat the crap out of the girl too. I didn't need those kinds of problems, so I decided against telling her for the moment.

As I was going into my kitchen to make a cup of tea, I suddenly heard my cell phone alerting me about several text messages. I took it out of my pocket, gazed down at the screen, and saw that all the texts appeared to be from him. I read the first one.

Can we talk?

As my eyes took in those three simple words, which meant so much and so little all at the same time, I wondered how I was going to respond after the things that were said. Could we possibly move on from this? Those were the two questions that stood in the way of me answering as quickly as I wanted to. I walked around my living room, studying the text.

"All right, Tiffany. You know you want to respond, but what exactly do you say?" I asked myself aloud. I started to weigh my options. I already knew that this conversation could either go badly or really badly, but either way, I needed to choose my words very carefully. Slowly, I begin to type my reply as I took in a deep breath.

I thought we said everything there was to say, Terrence, and I thought you were enjoying your friend?

Please. I'm trying to apologize. I said some awful things out of anger, and I'm so sorry, Tiff. And I'm on my way back home. I left Malaysia's right after the call to get back to you. Will you meet me at my house?

I didn't know why but my heart felt relieved that he was on his way back home; however, my mind told me there had to be something more to this for him to leave so soon. I had to know why.

Why are you coming back so soon? I figured you were enjoying her company.

I already said it's because I need to make things right with you. Plus, I realized that she has some issues that only God can help her with, and she's just not cut from the same cloth as me. I'm done with her, I promise.

Done? I thought to myself. "Hell, you never should have gotten started with her," was what I really wanted to say to him, but I chose to go a different route.

What happened?

I really don't want to go into all of that, he shot back.

Then I waited before asking the one question I really wanted to know the answer to, the one that scared me most. I debated if I truly wanted to know the response to it. Curiosity was eating away at me, though, so before I knew it, I started to type.

Can I ask you something?

If it has something to do with her, this will be your one and only chance. After this, I don't want to discuss her any longer.

Little did he know I had at least a million questions that I wanted the answers to, but if I asked everything that was on my mind, we'd be here at least a week. So, I picked out a couple that I felt were most important. And I started with the one I really wanted answered.

Do you love her, Terrence? I cringed as I awaited his response.

I thought I was growing to, but like I said, I'm done.

Why are you doing this to yourself, Tiffany? I wondered after his response practically crushed me. Just the idea that he felt he was *growing* to love this woman tore me apart.

All right. But where did she come from, and how long have you been with her?

It hasn't been long, was all he said.

Although I could go on and on, I chose to stop at that point. Nothing that I asked was going to make me feel any better about the situation or explain why he had gotten involved with her in the first place. Part of me wondered if it was me. Had I done something wrong, or was there something I wasn't doing for him? But the more I thought about it, the more I was convinced that there was no reason for him to cheat. If he didn't want me, he could have said so. And now I wasn't even sure I could go back to trusting him at this point.

Can you please come to the house, so we can talk face-to-face? he asked.

Yeah, that's fine.

Great. Be there in about three hours.

I was mentally exhausted from it all, but I agreed that we needed to talk face-to-face. Although I was still unsure about where things stood between us, I was extremely happy that he was coming back home.

Before I freshened up and got dressed to head his way, my fingers almost had a mind of their own and di-

CHAPTER 35

TERRENCE

Upon making it to my seat on the plane, I threw my carry-on in the overhead and made myself comfortable. I was glad to have a window seat and no one sitting beside me, because I was hoping to wind down mentally before getting home. Thankfully, Tiffany had agreed to come over and hear me out, to let me straighten out this entire mess. But then, I wasn't totally sure where things stood between me and Malaysia. Deep down I knew that maybe I needed to just call things off with her. Yet it was strange. I loved her energy when things were right and we weren't doing all this fussing and fighting. Not to mention, I simply did not want to hurt her. Closing my eyes, I continued thinking about the two women in my life. My thoughts were interrupted a few minutes later by a soft, gentle voice.

"Excuse me, sir. I think my seat is next to yours."

My eyes popped open, and I saw a tall, slender woman standing there. Immediately, I could tell that she was some type of physical trainer or workout junkie because her muscles were popping out everywhere. She also appeared to be a bit older than me, maybe in her mid-fifties or so.

"Oh, I'm sorry. I didn't think that anyone would be sitting here." I grabbed my magazine from the center seat and stuck my hand out for her to indicate that she was free to sit down. "By the way, I'm Terrence. Terrence Montgomery."

"Hi, Terrence. I'm Roslyn. It's very nice to meet you." She sat down and made herself comfortable.

The next ten or fifteen minutes were quiet, with both of us playing around on our phones while waiting for takeoff. But when it came time to turn off our phones, she looked over at me.

"So, Mr. Montgomery, do you go to Texas often, or do you have a layover there?"

"Um, actually, I live in Dallas, to be exact. I was visiting a friend here in St. Louis."

"Girlfriend?" she inquired without any hesitation.

"Uh, no. Just a good friend."

"Well, maybe you should come back to St. Louis soon to hang out with your *new* good friend."

"Wow. You get right to the point, huh?"

"Honey, I'm fifty-seven, and I've learned that when you see what you want, you go after it."

"Is that right?" I said, incredulous. I was almost at a loss for words.

She burst out laughing, lightening the mood.

For the rest of the flight, we talked nonstop about a little of nothing and a little of everything. We discussed our careers, traveling, our hobbies, and whatever else came to mind. She even showed me pictures of her children and grandchildren. Of course, finally, she disclosed that she'd been divorced twice and that she was simply looking to meet someone new and fun. I supposed I was *something new*, because after we landed and taxied to the gate, she refused to let me out of my seat without my offering her my phone number. I had to admit that it was kind of attractive being the pursued one and not the pursuer. Plus, I loved her sophistication and independence.

She didn't come off as the needy, clingy, or emotional type, and that was like a breath of fresh air. I liked Roslyn and looked forward to getting to know her more, as a friend, of course.

I'd been home for at least thirty minutes when I finally heard Tiffany's truck pulling up outside. Before I'd left, I'd given her my garage opener, in case of any emergencies here at my house while I was away, so I waited for her to let herself in. I knew she still had a ton of questions to ask, yet all I wanted to do was move past this and move on. On the plane, while conversing with Roslyn, I had realized that moving on more than likely wouldn't include Malaysia in my life and that this just might be all for the best. That way I wouldn't have to go through the dramatics of trying to explain to Malaysia that I was still married or why I had lied to her to begin with. And I wouldn't need to keep trying to juggle her and Tiffany, which had become tiresome and confusing anyway.

Grabbing the remote to my TV, I plopped down on my living-room sofa just as Tiffany came walking in.

"Hey," was all she said. Knowing her as well as I did after all this time, I knew that tone meant that this wasn't going to be an easy exoneration. However, I extended my hand, and when she took hold of it, I pulled her down on the sofa with me and started kissing her all over.

"Wait, Terrence, wait. It's not about to be that easy, not after the things you said to me."

"Baby, I said I was sorry, and a lot of it was said in the heat of the moment. I didn't mean any of it."

"Yeah, well, I want to believe that, but what about this Malaysia woman? Where do things stand between you and her?"

"Sweetie, sweetie, I told you already. I messed up, okay? But I'm done with her. I can't risk losing you, because I love you," I said as she gazed back at me, and I could tell she was eating up every word. And it wasn't like I didn't mean any of it anyway. I did love her and didn't want to lose her. "Can I make love to you now, or are you still going to focus on a woman that I'm no longer focused on?"

Slowly, she stood up and slipped off her little summer dress, revealing her nakedness in all its glory. She was absolutely beautiful, and as we walked upstairs, I flicked off the lights and told Alexa to play "Break Up to Make Up," by the Stylistics.

I have to be a fool to have almost let this woman go, I thought.

CHAPTER 36

TERRENCE

I was awake when Malaysia's name scrolled across my cell phone screen. Glancing at the clock, I saw that it was almost six in the morning. Not wanting to wake Tiffany, I got up and went downstairs in the basement to talk. Maybe this was my chance to call things quits. I didn't want to prolong things any further. I dialed her number, and she picked up on the first ring.

"Hi. You never called to tell me that you made it home safely."

"Uh, Malaysia, look—"

"Terrence, I'm sorry for everything," she said, cutting me off. "I never should have given you an ultimatum, and I should have been more understanding about how you were feeling."

I didn't say anything, as I was attempting to figure out which direction she was going with this.

"Are you still there?" she asked when nearly a minute had passed.

"Yeah, I'm here, and I accept your apology. But maybe we should talk some other time, you know, to give us a little more time to think things through."

"Baby, I don't need more time. Do you?"

"Malaysia, so much was said yesterday, and things are not how they were when we first met. I don't like arguing all the time, and last night I started feeling that maybe this isn't right for us."

"Oh, so I don't even get the opportunity to make things up to you?"

"And how were you planning on doing that?" I asked playfully, trying to see where her head was.

"I don't know. How about my showing up at your front door, with your favorite dress on and ready to do whatever you would like for me to do?"

Fully enjoying where she was going, I decided to play along. "Really? Wouldn't that be difficult, with you all the way in St. Louis and me here?"

"No, because I'll actually be there in the next forty-five minutes or so."

"Be where? Be *here*?"

"Yeah, silly, at your front door. Surprise! I came to Texas."

"What?" I knew there was no way she could really be on her way here, but something told me that she was. All I could think about was how I was going to get Tiffany out of the house before Malaysia got here.

"Damn, what a wonderful surprise," I managed to get out. "So, baby, why don't I go and get cleaned up before you get here, okay?"

"Okay. That sounds good. I'll see you soon."

I ran upstairs as fast as I could, almost breaking my neck on the steps. Luckily for me, Tiffany was just waking up and stretching.

"Good morning, you. I was wondering where you ran off to," she said.

"Oh, I had to take a call from Randle and didn't want to disturb you," I told her, thinking fast on my feet. "Baby, I am so sorry to cut things short, but Randle wants me at his office in the next twenty minutes or so."

"Oh, okay. Do you just want me to lock up whenever I leave?"

"Uh, no. Instead, if you could leave when I leave, because I lost my other garage opener, and since you have my other one . . ."

"Oh, all right. Well, say no more, sweetie."

I went through the whole charade of showering and getting dressed so that I could leave when she did. Twenty minutes later, I kissed her outside and waved goodbye while watching her drive off. And ten minutes after that, Malaysia pulled up. I hurried inside my house, and shut the door. When I slowly opened my front door, I found her exactly as she had said she would be—in one of my favorite dresses, one she'd worn before.

"Your wish is my command, Mr. Montgomery." She pulled me inside the foyer, closed the door, then unzipped my pants and dropped to her knees. If this was what came after an argument with her, then maybe we needed to argue more often, I thought. However, as I enjoyed her way of making things up to me, I couldn't help but be thankful I had showered. I also prayed that Tiffany didn't have to come back to this house for anything.

What have I done? was all I could ask myself as my eyes stared at the blank ceiling. Malaysia was nestled under my arm, with her head lying on my chest, sleeping peacefully like a newborn baby. Just that quickly, an hour after her arrival, we were right back to where we had started. So, here I was, once again trying to decide what to do with the two women in my life. As my mind kept roaming from woman to woman, I felt Malaysia start to squirm beside me.

"Hey, sleepyhead," I said, hoping to wake her completely. Since she'd popped up unexpectedly, I needed to find out how long she planned on staying.

"Hey." She acknowledged me while looking around the room, as if she'd forgotten where she was. "How long have you been up?" she asked through yawns and stretches.

"Only a few minutes. Did you have a good nap? And you didn't even give me the chance to ask about your flight here."

"My nap was great, baby, but I always sleep better when I'm with you," she made sure to throw in. "My flight wasn't bad either."

Crawling out of her embrace, I got up and threw my boxers on to go and shower. "So, baby, how long do you plan on being here?" I asked, putting my feet into my slippers and moving around the bedroom.

"I don't know. I guess that depends on you." She sat up and covered herself with the blanket.

"What does that mean?"

"How long do you want me here?" she asked, but I wasn't sure where she was going with it.

"Malaysia, did you get a round-trip ticket, or did you decide to try to figure me out first?"

"Okay, okay. Actually, Toni and I came out here together. She's in a room over at the Marriott. And yes, we purchased round-trip tickets. Our return flight leaves tomorrow afternoon. But, baby, I really don't want to leave. I mean, I don't know about you, but I'm tired of this distance between us. And look what we had to go through after having a minor disagreement. I had to hop on a flight to come all the way out here just to make up. That makes no sense to me if we both know that we want to be together."

"Maybe I'm not understanding what you're trying say." I took a seat on the edge of the bed. She crawled up behind me and threw her arms around my shoulders.

"Baby, what I'm saying is, let's stop all this foolishness and be together. Here in Texas *together*."

"So, wait, you're trying to move here? Relocate your entire life to be with me?" I turned and looked directly at her to be clear.

"I love you that much, Terrence. And you said you love me too." She stared back with puppy dog eyes.

"I do love you, but relocating and living together takes money and compromise, and our relationship still needs to be built. I don't know if we're quite ready to make that type of move."

"Terrence, maybe you're unclear about what I'm saying. I don't want to just live with you. I want to *be* with you. I want to be your *wife*."

I tried to focus my eyes on her face to read if she was serious or not, and something told me she was, without my having to see her expression at all. *Married? There's no way I can marry her when I already am married. I have to find a way to get that whole scenario out of her mind*, I thought.

"Baby, marriage is such a huge step, and I've been there and done it, and it's hard. I mean, things were great in the beginning, like they are with us now, but we started arguing over money and finances, social media, her children, and all sorts of things. It just didn't work, and I'm still repairing my life from our breakup, so I don't know about this."

"But, honey, your problems with the last woman don't have to be ours. We won't argue over my son, because he's practically a grown man, and his father is in his life anyway. And you already know I'm not going to worry about anything I see on social media. And when it comes to money, I believe we'll be just fine. You're getting the money from your father's estate, I have a substantial amount of savings in the bank, and we'll start the business to bring in even more income. Baby, we can be one of Texas's power couples and live the best life possible."

She was still talking, but my mind was stuck way back on her having a substantial amount of savings in the bank, because to be honest, I was still lacking in the financial area. Getting my hands on some real cash could be a lifesaver for me.

"All right. So, say we were to do this, baby . . . I can't say exactly when I'll get the money from my father's estate. There's been a lot of legal red tape to go through, and it's taking a lot longer than expected. So, when you say you have savings, how much are you talking about? And are you willing to part with it until the restaurant is up and running and I'm able to support us solely?"

"It's not much. I have at least two hundred and fifty thousand in my account. And the vows say for better or worse, and for richer or poorer, so yes, I can take care of us if I need to."

Little did Malaysia know, she was singing music to my ears the minute she said 250 grand was in the bank. The wheels in my head turned faster as I tried to figure out just how I could pull this off.

Maybe I can agree to the marriage and get my divorce before things become official, or somehow pull out of this at the last minute. Only thing I still need to figure out is Tiffany. But right now, what she doesn't know won't hurt her, my mind told me.

"So, you're absolutely sure about this?" I asked her.

"I'm positive. Baby, I've never been so sure about something in my entire life."

"All right, then." I got on one knee right there in my bedroom. "Malaysia Cole, will you do me the honor of being my wife?"

Before I could get the question out good, she shouted yes and threw her arms around me.

As we embraced, I said, "Listen, now, you know your friends are going to be asking about a ring. What do you plan on telling them? Because I can't afford that right now."

"Terrence, I'm not worried about a ring, so I won't tell them anything. This is between you and me, and just knowing I'm going to be Mrs. Terrence Montgomery is enough for me."

She couldn't stop hugging and kissing me, and I tried to return the sentiment. However, my gut told me that I needed to play every single day right from here on out, or things could go drastically wrong for me and everyone else involved.

"I'm going to get cleaned up and head over to the Marriott and tell Toni. I'm so excited," she yelled, dancing her way to the bathroom. I knew if she ever found out the truth about me, I'd be dancing my way to an early grave.

Then, on top of all, I received three text messages from Roslyn.

CHAPTER 37

MALAYSIA

"I did it, girl. I am going to be married to Terrence Montgomery." I whirled and twirled all over the hotel room.

"Whoa, whoa. Sit down, Ms. Dancing Machine, and tell me exactly what happened."

Toni sat on the bed, and I pulled one of the chairs over to face her and plopped down in it.

"My mind is all over the place, and so I don't even know where to begin," I confessed.

"Well, try to calm down. And why don't you start with showing me the ring first?" She waved her hand at me so that I would show her my ring finger.

"Uh, well, there's kind of no ring right now."

"What do you mean, no ring?" Her nose was all turned up in true Toni fashion. "How the hell is there an engagement with no ring?"

"Because that's not what this is about. The ring is only something materialistic for others to see. We don't need that to express our love to one another."

"Yeah, I guess that's usually what a man says when he doesn't have the money to buy a ring. But are you trying to make me believe this or yourself?"

"Toni, please."

"No, Malaysia, don't *Toni, please* me. Now, I'm going to go along with this whole charade because that's who you want to be with. But Terrence is pretty much treading on thin ice with me, just so you know. I mean, did he even explain this entire situation with the ex-girlfriend of his?"

"Damn, girl! I came in here with the news of my life, and you just brought my energy and emotions all the way down."

"I'm sorry, all right, but I'm trying to bring you down to *reality* before you get yourself excited about a mere pipe dream."

"Maybe I don't want to be in reality. Maybe for once, I want to live in my fantasy world. And that's being with Terrence. Can't you be a friend and be happy for me?" Tears rolled down my cheeks.

"Okay, girl. I'm sorry." She came over to me, bent down on her knees, and started wiping the tears from my face. "I know how you feel about him, and I know that this is important to you. But I don't want you getting hurt over it. You just recently came back into this man's life, a man that you haven't seen in years. From what you told me, he wasn't even interested in you back then. He's all the way here in Texas, and you're in St. Louis. He claims he's single, yet there's some crazy ex-girlfriend that just pops up out of the woodwork. You can't post y'all's relationship on social media. He keeps telling you he's going to be a millionaire and restaurant owner, but there's nothing to show for it. So, please try to understand why I'm being cautious and overprotective of you. It's because you're so in love that you can't see the signs. The point is, there's a lot not adding up for me, and I don't want you hurt in the end."

"I hear you completely, and you're right. There are things that haven't added up. But I believe Terrence is being totally honest. And, Toni, everything about this *feels* right."

"All right. Then say no more." She threw up her hands. "My lips are sealed, and I am happy as long as you are happy."

We hugged one another, but I felt a little uneasy about the fact that I hadn't quite shared everything with her. Pulling away from our embrace, I tried to find the best way to say what I'd avoided sharing, hoping there would be no judgment.

"Uh, there's one minor thing I haven't told you yet."

"Uh-oh," she said as she sat back down in the chair across from me. "Go ahead and spill it."

"Well, Terrence sort of believes I have at least two hundred fifty thousand dollars in the bank."

She covered her face with her palms, to let out a silent scream, I believed. "Why does he think you have that kind of money? Better yet, why are you guys even discussing *your* money?"

"Because he's going through a ton of legal stuff when it comes to his father's estate. Which I believe is because of the amount of money he's due to receive. But I may have let him believe that I could and will hold us down until he gets it."

"And what's going to happen when he looks to you for something financial and you can't do it?"

"Well, I suspect that he'll have his father's money way before I actually have to come out of pocket for anything, and then he'll forget all about my money. Anyway, once the restaurant opens, we'll bring in enough money together that we won't need to focus on *his* money or *my* money. We'll be married and business partners, so it will be *our* money."

"You mean, *your* money, the money that you don't have," she reminded me.

"Listen, like I said before, this feels right to me. And all I'm doing is exactly what you told me to do. I'm doing what I need to get my man."

"Yeah, but I never told you to come out here and tell a bunch of lies and pretend you're rich."

"You know what? You're such a Debbie Downer about this that I'm almost considering changing my mind about having you as my maid of honor. I might just have to ask Larisse."

Next thing I knew, she grabbed the pillow off the bed and started hitting me with it.

"All right, all right, I was only joking about that," I assured her, holding up my hands in mock surrender. "But on a serious note, I'm going to need your help, because this wedding needs to happen within the next couple of months."

"Two months? Girl, are you crazy? What did Terrence say about that?"

"Honey, at this point, I think he'll go along with anything I suggest. And no, I'm not crazy. I don't want to be away from him any longer than a couple of months. And if we can pull this off sooner, that will be even better."

"Chile, I swear, I don't think I've ever seen you so determined about something. So, if it's a wedding in two months that you want, then that's what you'll get. Just call me superwoman maid of honor. I'm at your service, Mrs. Montgomery."

Merely hearing the name Mrs. Montgomery sent me floating on a natural high, which I never, ever wanted to come down from.

CHAPTER 38

DAVID

"So, neither of you got a look at the person who was driving? You're not sure if it was a man or a woman?" the detective asked me and Patricia as we sat in his office at the police station.

"No, Detective, but I can almost assure you that it was a woman," I insisted. "Her name is Leslie, Leslie Wright. I mean, what's taking you all so long to put her behind bars or something? I've shown you all the texts, and I've told you why she has it in for me. It doesn't take a rocket scientist to put the pieces of the puzzle together to know that it's her. Do I have to wait until she kills me?"

"Mr. Allen, I totally understand, but we've told you that it's not Mrs. Wright. Are you sure there's no one else that it could be?"

"Um, Detective, do you mind if I speak to my friend alone for a second?" Pat asked.

The detective nodded. "Uh, sure. I need to take care of something anyway. I'll be back in about five minutes or so."

The minute he walked out of the room, Pat looked at me. After I'd been transported to the hospital yesterday, the doctors and nurses had checked me over and determined that I had no broken bones or internal bleeding. My left leg still caused me a great deal of pain, despite the painkillers I'd been given, along with orders to take things easy for a couple of weeks. Patricia had made sure I got home safely and then had picked me up again this morning to take me to the police station.

"All right, Pat. What are you thinking that you had the detective leave the room?"

"Well, I never thought about it until now, but you said that it's not Sonya for sure. The detective is saying that it's not Leslie for sure. So, I hate to say it, but that leaves only one other woman."

"Who? Tiffany? What? No way! Tiff wouldn't do something like this to me."

"David, all I'm saying is she has a legitimate reason to hate you. All the things you've done to her. And what if she knows that you lied about the cancer too? And then you told me that her best friend hates you. And not to mention, my husband hates your guts. She could very well have anyone assisting her in this."

I sat there wondering what if Pat was on to something. I didn't want to believe it, but I had to be honest with myself too. Tiffany could very well be behind it all, in an attempt to get back at me. And the fact that I hadn't heard from her since I'd left the hotel was suspicious, too, considering that she had gone on and on about how she would be there for me no matter what. Then I wondered if the hotel had called her and told her they gave me her diamond locket. Tiffany was the last person I wanted to consider, but truth be told, I had to. A few seconds later the detective came back in his office.

"Okay, so did either of you think of anyone who might help us figure this case out?" he asked.

We looked at one another, and I couldn't believe I was saying it, but the next words out of my mouth were, "Tiffany Tate, Detective. She's my ex-fiancée, and she might want me hurt just as much as the other two women."

"All right. Well, do you have a phone number or address for Ms. Tate, so I can ask her a few questions?"

I wrote down Tiffany's number and address on a piece of paper, although I wasn't completely sure if she'd already returned home. But then again, maybe she wanted me to believe that she was still in St. Louis, rather than here, attempting to hurt me. I handed the detective the paper.

"Well, Mr. Allen, we will investigate this," he said as he studied the information I had supplied. "I will get back with you should anything come up with Ms. Tate, all right?"

I agreed, and Patricia and I walked out of the office.

"I think you did the right thing, David, by giving him Tiffany's name. I know you don't want it to be her, but you and I both know that the woman is not as innocent as she tries to make herself out to be."

I heard Pat say that I had done the right thing, but it sure didn't feel that way right now. In fact, I was beginning to wonder if this was just another one of Patricia's plots to keep Tiffany away from Terrence.

CHAPTER 39

TIFFANY

Making it home from the grocery store, I was more than ready to unwind and be a couch potato for the rest of the weekend. Besides putting away the groceries and tackling a couple of weeks of dirty laundry, my schedule was totally free and clear. I threw my purse down on the sofa and started undressing the minute I walked in the door, leaving a trail of clothes on the floor. Heading toward my bathroom, I instructed Alexa to play some jazz music. Today I didn't want anything with lyrics, only some nice, mellow music. I put some different oils in my bathwater as I ran it, and then I went into my bedroom to fetch my bonnet and robe. While I was there, I heard my phone ringing inside my purse.

"Damn, who could this be?" I wondered aloud as I pulled out my phone. When I looked down at the screen, I saw that it was Keisha. "I'm sorry, girl, but whatever it is will simply have to wait until tomorrow. The rest of the evening is for me, myself, and I," I said aloud, pressing IGNORE. Once I was back in the bathroom, however, she called three more times, the phone vibrating in my hand. Although I didn't want to be bothered, I knew it had to be something important for her to call numerous times, back-to-back. I dialed her back, but before the call could go through, she was calling me once again.

I picked up. "Hello?"

"Hey, girl. How are you?" she asked in a melancholy sort of way. "Are you busy?"

"I'm okay, Keisha. It's just been a long week, so I was about to soak in a bubble bath, have a bottle of wine, and read a book until I fall asleep. What's going on with you?"

"I'm good. But, hey, I wanted to know, are you and Terrence still involved with one another?" she asked cautiously.

I wasn't sure how to respond since something appeared to be a bit off about her questioning. She was almost acting as if she knew something that she didn't want to come right out and say. Then I remembered I hadn't told her about the whole incident when he was in St. Louis with the young lady, so I figured that was what she was referring to.

"Uh, yeah. We've had some different things that we needed to work out, but we're still hanging in there. I haven't spoken to him in a few days or so, because he's been taking care of some business with Randle and his stepmother."

"Oh," was all she said. Then there was a deafening silence on the phone.

"Keisha, girl, are you all right?"

"Look, if you're not sitting down right now, I think you better, because there's no easy way for me to say what I need to say."

"Okay, but you sound so serious, like someone has passed away or something. What's going on?"

"Tiffany, Terrence is . . . he's, um . . . I really don't know how to say this."

"By just going ahead and saying it. Terrence is what?"

"Well, remember when I told you that I would make sure to check this strange woman's page from time to time?" She continued to beat around the bush, instead of coming out and saying whatever she needed to say.

"Yeah. Her name is Malaysia."

"Well, it looks like him and Malaysia are . . . Well, they're engaged."

I stopped in my tracks and tried to take in her words, but I knew I must have heard her incorrectly. "Wait a minute. Did you say that she and Terrence are *engaged*?"

"Yeah, Tiff," she answered matter-of-factly. "He must have asked her very recently, but it doesn't look like she hesitated to announce it. Girl, she even started a page on the Knot website. But I knew you couldn't have known because I was positive you would have told me."

Keisha kept talking, but the last thing I heard was the word *engaged*. She was right, though. I needed to sit down, because instantly my entire body felt numb and weak. The word *engaged* kept playing over and over again in my head. And this time, surprisingly, I had no desire to burst into tears. Instead, my blood began to boil, and I felt like I wanted to hurt the man. Lately, he'd done so much that left me an emotional wreck, but this took the cake. I wanted Terrence to feel the exact same pain that I was feeling at that very moment. I couldn't listen more to Keisha ranting and raving about how much of a jerk Terrence was or how much hostility she felt toward Malaysia, so I decided to end the call. I needed to be alone, with nothing more than my thoughts, to figure out how I was going to address this.

"Hey, Keisha. I'll give you a call back later, all right?"

"Tiff, wait. Are you all right?"

"Yes, I'll be fine." I hung up without any further conversation.

Immediately, I went to the website that Keisha had told me about. There in big, bold red lettering were their names and their announcement, smacking me dead in my face. *Malaysia and Terrence. A black-tie affair, coming soon in St. Louis, Missouri.* Before I knew it, I'd become so queasy that I ran into the bathroom and hung my head over the toilet. It seemed like everything I had inside me came out. Once nothing was left, I sat there and cried my heart out. Here I was, still helping him financially, still being his support system when it came to Patricia, still being his shoulder to cry on about his father's passing, still there for his intimate pleasure, still encouraging, still loving, still enduring, still, still, still. And all of a sudden, I felt hopeless. I truly felt as if this woman had taken the life that I was supposed to have. I felt betrayed, disrespected, and foolish for trusting this man, who had said he would always love and protect me, yet the one I needed protecting from was him. And the one thing I hated the most was even at this very moment, I still had love in my heart for Terrence Montgomery.

As I sat there, the running water caught my attention just as it was about to spill over the edge of the tub onto the floor. I had forgot that it was even running. I rushed to turn it off, then sank again to the floor. As I looked at the water lapping the tub's edge, I thought how, metaphorically speaking, it was my life. Things were on the brink of spilling over and causing a huge mess, and I needed someone to shut off the faucet, yet I knew it wasn't that simple. Nothing was that simple when it came to love and matters of the heart.

Anyway, I went into my bedroom and curled up in my bed. I didn't want to see anyone, talk to anyone, or think about anyone. I closed my swollen, tear-filled eyes and began to talk aloud to the one I knew could ultimately take away my pain. It was the most honest, vulnerable, and sincere moment that I could recall having in my entire life.

"God, I need you. If you hear me right now, please tell me why this happened. Tell me what I did wrong to deserve this from Terrence. Tell me why he can't see how much I truly love him. And tell me how I'm supposed to move on without him."

CHAPTER 40

TIFFANY

I struggled to open eyes when I heard someone ringing my doorbell repeatedly, as if the police were after them.

"All right already! I'm coming, I'm coming," I yelled while throwing my robe over my naked body. On the way to the door, I glanced at the clock, which read twelve noon, and I couldn't believe I'd slept so late. Normally, I was up and moving no later than seven or eight each morning, even on the weekends. Then I noticed my home was a mess. Walking past the bathroom, I saw the tub was still filled with water. Then, moving into the living room, I heard Alexa still playing jazz. And the clothes I'd worn yesterday made a trail on the floor from the front door to the bathroom.

After cracking open the front door, I peeked out and saw that it was Monica. I wasn't totally in the mood for company, but knowing I couldn't hide from her too long, I went ahead and let her in.

"Hey, Monica." I said, hoping I didn't sound to dry or sour, but I was sure I did.

"Tiffany, I'm sorry for popping up like this, but I've been calling you since yesterday evening. I got worried when your voicemail became full. Is everything all right?" She looked at me from head to toe, then gave the living room a once-over. I was positive that my home and I were in such disarray, something she was not used to seeing. I also realized she was more concerned about my well-being than me finding out about Terrence, which made me wonder if she even knew. I dragged my feet into the kitchen to throw on a pot of coffee, and she took a seat on the sofa.

"Would you like some coffee?" I called.

"Uh, sure, that's fine. But again, is everything all right, Tiff?"

"Yep, everything is just perfect," I said as I came back into the living room while the coffee brewed.

"Um, I hate to say it, but it doesn't quite look that way." She looked around once more. "So, do you want to talk about it?"

"Not really, but I'm just curious . . . with you being a friend to Terrence . . . Do you plan to go to the wedding?" I asked, trying to feel her out.

"Wedding? What wedding?"

"The wedding of your coach and his fiancée." I tried to say it with a straight face while I took a seat at the other end of the sofa.

"Girl, what are you talking about?" she asked, like I was the crazy one.

But rather than answer her question, I had her go to Malaysia's Facebook book page and then to the page on the wedding site.

"Oh, my goodness!" Her mouth hung wide open. "How? When? What?" She couldn't seem to make any more sense of it all than I could. "Tiffany, how on earth is Terrence engaged when he's with you? And better yet, how can he get married when he's already *legally married*?"

"Those are the exact same questions that I have."

"Well, have you talked to him? What does he have to say for himself?"

"Nope. I haven't talked to Terrence, and I don't plan to. Or at least I don't plan on letting him know that I know anything about this engagement."

"What? You can't be serious." I must have sounded like a complete lunatic, the way her eyes bulged out at me.

"Monica, look, I've thought about this all night. What would be the point in me saying anything, only for him to turn around and try to lie his way out of it? And clearly, it's real enough that this woman is posting it all over social media for the world to see. I just can't fight for this anymore, at least not for someone that's not fighting for me as well."

"So, what do you plan to do? I mean, do you ever plan on revealing that you know?"

"In a perfect world, I would hope that Terrence would care enough about me to approach me in an honest and truthful manner and let the chips fall where they may. But realistically, knowing that probably won't happen, I haven't fully decided what I'm going to do. Part of me is telling me that I have the right to show up at that damn wedding and reveal it then."

"Tiffany, you wouldn't."

"Girl, the way I'm feeling right now, yes, the hell I would, and I'm not letting anyone talk me out of it." I finished by giving her a look that said, "Including you."

"Hey, I don't know how I would react in this situation, so I'm definitely not going to tell you what to do. But if I can be a small voice of reason, I'm asking you to think about how that would affect *you* in the long run, not him. Besides, he's already done enough to hurt you. Don't let him destroy the beautiful spirit that you have by leaving you bitter."

There was that one word that I never wanted to be in my life: *bitter*. Although I had been able to dodge being the bitter ex-girlfriend with David, here it was, slapping me in the face with Terrence.

"I hear you, Monica, but so much of me wants him to feel the same pain and embarrassment that I feel," I said, picking up my cell phone and throwing it over to her. "I mean, look at the number of voice messages and texts that I have. And I'm sure they're all about him and this announcement. I just feel humiliated that he's broadcasting this woman for the world to see in front of people who knew we were together."

"Well, don't feel humiliated. Those same people have undercover issues of their own and can't say anything about you. And as for Terrence, don't allow him, or any other man, to have that kind of power over you. Besides, trust me, if there's one thing I know for sure, it's that every dog has his day, and karma will eventually bite him in the ass. You wait and see. And don't worry about little Ms. Thing either. She may think that she has a prize, but her turn is coming too. He cheated on his daughters' mother with Patricia, he practically cheated on Patricia with you, and now he's cheating on you with her. So, she's not exempt from it, and her turn is surely coming." She stopped and took a deep breath.

Hell, if you ask me," she went on, "I don't think this whole getting married business is real anyway. I know Terrence Montgomery, and he's never dealt with someone that he hadn't mentioned to me first, and he's said nothing at all about this Malaysia woman to me. Something about all of this doesn't feel right, and the truth will be revealed soon enough."

I was sure she was right, but soon enough still wouldn't be fast enough for me. Either way, I had to hold firm to my word to myself. I wasn't going to let on that I knew anything at all about this engagement. I would continue as if I was clueless and would let Terrence bury himself in his own ditch of lies.

A few minutes later there was yet another knock at the door, and this time it made me wonder if he had the nerve to show up at my home. Monica and I looked at one another. I walked over, peeked out the window, and saw a strange man standing there. Something in my gut told me not to open the door until he identified himself.

"Who is it?" I called.

"Detective Miller. Are you Tiffany Tate?"

"Can I see your badge first, Detective?" He flashed his badge where I could see it, and I opened the door. "How can I help you?"

"You are Tiffany Tate, correct?"

"Yes, yes, I am."

"Would you like to come down to the police station and talk with me for a bit?"

"No, not until you tell me what this is about and if I'm being arrested for something."

"You're not being arrested yet, but your name was given in relation to a possible attempted manslaughter investigation. I just have a few questions for you so that I can rule you out."

"Attempted manslaughter? Of who? Please don't tell me this involves a woman named Patricia Montgomery."

"Mrs. Montgomery is somewhat involved, but this has to do with Mr. David Allen. So, can you come into the station, or do I need to put handcuffs on you?"

Monica approached the door. "Uh no, Detective, that won't be necessary. I will bring Ms. Tate myself, if that's all right with you. We'll follow you there. She just needs to get dressed."

He agreed with what she had said, and the next thing I knew, we were headed to the police station to try to clear my name. What a nightmare this was all turning out to be. First, I had found out that the man I was in love with was engaged to another woman. And on top of that, I was practically being arrested for something that involved his crazy wife and my good-for-nothing ex.

CHAPTER 41

PATRICIA

I stormed into Kim's office without her secretary giving me the okay. "Call off this whole divorce process now."

"Hey, let me give you a call back. I just had a client come in," Kim told whoever was on the other end of the line. However, I could tell she was flustered by the way she turned beet red.

"Hello, Patricia. Would you like to calm down and tell me what I can do for you today?" She got up and closed the door behind me.

"I can't promise I can remain calm, Kim, but I'm here because I want you to stop the divorce process. I'm not ready anymore."

"Can I ask what brought this on all of a sudden? The last time we spoke, you clearly stated that you were more than ready."

"This. This is what changed my mind," I said, showing her a text I had received early this morning. It was a photo of a post made on Facebook.

"Oh, wow. I see. Um, where did you get this?"

"Someone who's a friend to me and him."

"And it isn't anything that's been photoshopped or something?" Kim asked me.

"I highly doubt it," I answered, watching her continue to study the picture.

"Okay, so your husband does know that he can't get married until he's divorced from you, right?"

"Clearly, he doesn't care, Kim. But I'm going to make him care. I'm going to make sure he doesn't get to marry anyone else until I'm good and ready to release him from this marriage."

"Patricia, now let's try to think about this logically. This is basically the proof we need to stand up in court if you go ahead and file for divorce. And your dear old, deceased father-in-law can have stipulations all he wants. But once a judge finds out that Terrence not only committed adultery but was also going to try to get married to another woman while being married to you, all bets will be off, honey. You'll get enough money to last you for life. Besides, why would you want to stay in this just to keep him from marrying someone else? I thought you told me you were ready to move on with your life?"

"Well, that was before he did things like this behind my back. And I don't even know who this woman is. I've never laid eyes on her before in my life."

"But is that a reason to block him from marrying her?" She looked at me suspiciously.

"Kim, look, if my husband came in here right now and said he wanted to try to work this out, I would be all for it. What I'm not for are these random women entering his life, thinking they're going to take my spot. If they want it so bad, then they'll need to fight for it, just like I am."

"Girl, you act like he's a piece of property or something, Pat." She looked at me and chuckled, but I gave her a look back that said I was dead serious.

"Until we have a dissolution of marriage decree, Terrence is mine. So, she can make as many social media posts as possible about whatever fantasy world Terrence has her living in. But like I said, I'm not going anywhere until I'm good and ready. And nobody is changing my mind, not even you, Kim."

I could tell that she wanted to say more, but that she didn't know exactly what to say. It didn't matter. She didn't have the words that would change my mind.

"All right, Patricia. If this is your decision, then I will stop things as of right now. I hadn't got to the point where I sent his attorney anything yet anyway. So, you let me know when you're ready to move forward."

"Thank you," was all I said as I walked to the door. The thing was, the minute she mentioned Terrence's attorney, Randle, something struck me in my gut. Suddenly, I was reminded that the longer I stayed married to Terrence, the longer it would take before I could be with Randle again.

I hope you understand, Randle, that right now this is just the way things have to be.

CHAPTER 42

TERRENCE

"Man, what is this nonsense I'm seeing on Facebook? You're getting married?" my best friend, Greg, asked as we spoke on the phone. He laughed so hard, I thought he was about to cough up a lung. He and I had been friends since we were both ten years old. Let him tell it, I was always up to something, and from the post Malaysia had made of our recent engagement, in which she'd tagged me, it appeared things hadn't changed.

"Man, I guess you could sort of say that," I replied.

"Naw, that wasn't a *sort of* kind of question. It's either yes or no. And if the answer is yes, how the hell are you getting married when you're already married to Patricia? And what happened to Tiffany? Aren't you still *sort of* seeing her?"

I filled Greg in on everything that had taken place in my life from the time I went to St. Louis for Tiffany and found out Pops had passed away, up until now, including Malaysia and Roslyn. After saying it all out loud, I decided he was right: not much had changed.

"So, that's where I am," I said after telling him everything. "I'm still legally married to Pat, and Malaysia is looking to get married within the next couple of months, although I'm hoping to extend that to more like a year. Not to mention, Roslyn has entered the picture, and believe or not, I'm still in love with Tiffany."

"I'm curious. Will your divorce be final by the time Malaysia wants to get married, if you can't hold out for a year? And why are you dealing with her, anyway, if you're in love with Tiffany? She sounds more like the perfect one for you, if you ask me."

"I don't know, man. Somehow, I just got caught up in all of this, and I'm not sure how to get out of it. And to be honest, Pat and I haven't even started the whole divorce process yet."

"Do you hear yourself right now? You're talking as if getting a divorce is as easy as signing some loan papers or something. My man, this is a *divorce* we're talking about."

"I get that, all right? I just need to figure this all out," I told him.

"And Tiffany? What about her? Have you figured out how you're going to tell her you're marrying another woman and not her?"

"No, unfortunately, I haven't. See, things are a bit more complicated when it comes to Tiff, because I don't want her out of my life completely."

"Terrence, have you lost your mind or something? Do you really think this woman is going to stick around while you run off and marry another woman? Because if so, I need to have a sip of whatever you're drinking," he said, joking around.

"Man, Tiffany still loves me, and I love her too. It's just her, Malaysia, and now Roslyn and this whole mess going on in my life, all happened at the wrong time."

"And you think you're going to be able to keep this a secret from Tiffany until you pull off this wedding, huh?" I could tell Greg was totally perplexed now.

"Look, there's no way she can find out. I gave her some crappy excuse as to why I had to remove her from my social media, and I had Malaysia block her from hers. So, unless she and Malaysia somehow come face-to-face with one another, there's no way she will ever find out."

"Man, I hope for your sake she doesn't. But just let me know if you need me for anything."

"Well, now that you mention it, I would like to ask if you would like to be my best man in the wedding."

"Man, if this wedding happens, trust me, I wouldn't miss it for anything in the world." He cracked up laughing before hanging up with me.

I couldn't let on to Greg or anyone else that I was dragging my feet when it came to starting the divorce process. I had personal reasons for this. Plus, a huge part of me was still thinking of a way I could possibly get out of this wedding with Malaysia at the last minute. Or, better yet, make her pull out of it, *after* we used a good portion of her two hundred fifty grand.

CHAPTER 43

TIFFANY

My quiet and lazy Saturday spent relaxing in my sweats had been shot to hell the minute that detective had knocked on my door. A couple of hours later, Monica and I finally returned to my place.

"Can you believe this? David accusing me of attempted manslaughter?" I grumbled.

"No, and even though I can't stand the man, something tells me that this is more Patricia than him. We both know that she'll do anything to hang on to Terrence."

"No matter who it is, it's crazy. And to try to have me arrested is even a stretch for Patricia. That woman can't possibly be that insane."

"Girl, she's already showed us that she is, so nothing at all surprises me anymore. But I'm just glad that we were able to resolve everything at the police station. Hopefully, you can rest, relax, and enjoy the rest of your evening now."

"Yeah, I hope so too."

"Were you thinking of contacting David?" Monica asked me.

"Oh hell no. I'm sure the detective will tell him everything he needs to know, but he can never contact me in life again. I do still hope that he finds out who's threatening him, though."

"Chile, you are better than me, because I would care less about anything concerning that man. Anyway, I'm going to go and get home to my husband and children. But please, should anything else happen, don't hesitate to call me. Better yet, why don't you just turn your phone off, take a nice hot bath, and crash? I love you, all right?"

"I love you too." We hugged one another before she left.

After I closed the front door, I looked around my home, which was still a complete mess. A nice hot bath sounded great, but I decided it was time to pick up some of this mess and bring some order back to my home and my mind. Call me a person with OCD or whatever, but I'd never been one to be able to think straight among a bunch of clutter.

I told Alexa to play some tunes, and as I cleaned, I sang along. I sang my heart out when Alexa played "In the Morning," by Ledisi. The lyrics reminded me so much of me and Terrence that I couldn't help myself. I hadn't been able to remove from my thoughts the fact that he was marrying that woman from St. Louis. Or, better yet, that he hadn't even had the decency as a friend to tell me this. Instead, he'd been strangely silent. I had left it that way. In fact, since finding out, I'd been able to maintain a tough outer shell and not reveal to him that I knew anything, but in all honesty, it was tearing me up inside.

After getting my home back to the way I liked it, instead of soaking in the tub and falling asleep, I grabbed a glass of wine and walked into my office as I told Alexa to turn up the music. Sitting down at my computer, I decided to do some online shopping, hoping that would somehow relieve the pain I felt. As I explored the new merchandise on the Coach website, I got the urge to peek at Facebook. I knew there wouldn't be much to see, since both Terrence and this woman had me blocked, but I wanted to do some searching anyway.

Going to my page first, I decided to replace my profile picture and cover photo with more recent ones. Then I posted a couple of spiritual quotes, just to let people know that I was alive and well. After that, I did a little surfing to see what was trending. Then I logged off and got back to my shopping. I kept getting a weird urge, though, to look at Terrence's fiancée's page. As I keyed in her first name, I tried hard to remember her last name, but suddenly her page popped up, and I was able to see her pictures. "Oh, so you unblocked me, huh? Okay," I said out loud.

The first thing that slapped me in the face was her most recent post. It contained a picture of her and Terrence, and it had a date on it. The caption read, THE DAY WE'LL FINALLY SAY I DO. #MONTGOMERYSFORLIFE. After seeing that, my eyes went directly to the very next thing that stood out. According to the information provided about her location, she *lived* in Texas and was from St. Louis. "Oh wow! Did you move her here with you, Terrence? I don't believe this," I exclaimed. I looked at the other pictures of them that I was able to view on her page before I decided to log off. That was, until a chat message popped up for me.

Hey there, stranger. Long time no hear from.

I hesitated, trying to decide whether to respond. It wasn't that I didn't want to. From what I could remember, Andre was a great guy. We'd met a long time ago when Monica and Todd introduced us. She had been trying to take my mind off Terrence, but just like now, I had felt too emotionally drained to deal with anyone. However, out of nowhere, I began to hear Monica in my ear now. *Honey, when you least expect it, God is going to send the perfect man into your life, and you won't even see it coming.*

"God, could this be my perfect man? I guess I won't know unless I give it a shot, huh?" I asked aloud.

After a few more minutes of staring at the screen and dwelling on whether to make a move, I started to type a response.

Hi, Andre. How have you been?

His response took no time at all, almost like he'd been waiting with his fingers on the keyboard.

I'm great. And what about yourself? I've been thinking about you a lot lately, but to be honest, I've been a little nervous about reaching out.

I've been good as well, and there's never a reason to be nervous. I'm still the same ole Tiffany.

So, what's been up with you? Are you married yet?

Uh, no, not married yet.

Maybe that's because you let your soul mate slip through your fingers.

Oh, is that right? And I guess my soul mate was you?

Hey, you said it. I didn't it. Anyway, if I'm not being too aggressive, I was hoping that I could call you and we could finish conversing on the phone instead of by chat message.

Damn. The very minute I'd become comfortable with the idea of communicating over chat, he was pushing me for more. However, I wasn't sure I had *more* to give of myself, because I'd already given Terrence *more*, and look how things had turned out. But then the picture of Terrence and Malaysia flashed right in front of my eyes.

"Tiffany, he has clearly moved on, and it's time you did the same. Besides, it's only a conversation with an old friend. How much can than hurt?" I asked myself aloud.

Sure, you can call me.

Great! I'm really looking forward to it.

We exchanged numbers, and it seemed as if he called the second I typed the last digit of my cell number.

"I can't believe I'm on the phone with you right now. It's been a long time, and we have a ton of catching up to do," he told me as soon as I answered the call.

"I guess we do. But I'm curious. What made you reach out now?"

"I don't know. I would see your pictures or posts from time to time and would always think about reaching out. But then I would always assume that you were more than likely involved with someone."

"Well, not yet, so I guess you could say I am free and clear."

"Wow. Sorry to all those other men that might be scared of approaching you, but lucky for me, huh?"

We both found humor in his last comment, which kind of cracked the ice between us. From there we talked about everything that had been going on with us since that day we met, except for relationships, that was. To my surprise, the conversation was free flowing and refreshing. I'd always loved a man with a great sense of humor, and Andre had me laughing, until he came to the subject that I was most afraid of, the future.

"This has been great, Tiffany, talking and catching up with you like this."

"Yeah, I have to agree that it's been nice."

"So, where do we go from here? I mean, I'm not trying to be too pushy or anything, but I would love to see you and take you out, but only if you're cool with that."

"Um, how about we just stay in touch and continue to talk? And then we'll see where things go from there."

"That sounds good. You have to promise we'll stay in touch, though."

"Of course, I promise."

"Good night, Ms. Tate. It was a pleasure talking with you."

"Good night, Andre."

We disconnected, and the strangest feeling came over me from out of nowhere. I honestly felt as if I'd cheated on Terrence. Here he was, with a wife *and* a fiancée, yet I felt bad for merely talking with Andre. At that moment, I became even more determined to continue talking with Andre. I had to get Terrence out of my head and my heart, especially since someone else had his. Nonetheless, I didn't plan on letting him get off that easy for just walking out of my life, with no explanation. And before he exchanged wedding vows in a couple of months, Terrence was going to learn that I knew all about him marrying Malaysia Cole, even if I had to show up at the wedding myself and confront him.

CHAPTER 44

PATRICIA

I kept looking at the picture of Terrence and this woman. "How the hell do you think you're getting married when you're already married to me?" I screeched. My husband had pulled many stunts in our time together but never anything this drastic. He had to be out of his mind to even consider bigamy. I wasn't sure what had come over him, but I was dead set on Terrence not marrying this Malaysia woman. I thought about everything I could do to stop him and realized that contesting the divorce just might not be enough. I had to do more, and since I'd been helping my friend David of late, it was time he did one more thing for me. I called him.

"What's up, Pat?" he said when he picked up. I guessed he had decided to skip all the preliminaries.

"How are you feeling?"

"I've been better, but the painkillers are doing their job. What about you?"

"Honestly, I'm not so good, David."

"What's wrong?"

"It's Terrence. He is, uh, engaged."

"Wait! To Tiffany? How is he doing that if you and him are still married?"

"It's not her. It's someone else. And, in fact, I've been doing a lot of digging and found that there are actually two other women who think they're with my husband besides Tiffany."

"*Two?* Are you kidding me?"

"No, I just recently found out about both from social media. Anyway, I need you, David."

"Oh no, no, Pat. We've already been down this road with Tiffany, and I can't do it again, especially not in my condition."

"Listen, it's only once more, and I will pretty much take care of everything. All I need is for you to show up with me," I told him.

"Show up where, Patricia? What are you thinking of?"

"Well, I think it's time my husband comes face-to-face with all the women in his life. I'm going to send a message to all of them from a fake account, inviting them to a hotel room. They'll believe they're going to have a romantic evening with Terrence, but in actuality, it will be one big party, and the honoree will be my husband."

"Pat, I really don't think you should do this. Someone might get hurt, and I don't mean physically."

"Yeah, I know, they all might be hurt in the end, but like I told you, it's time for my husband to get his just desserts. You owe me, David," I insisted.

"I guess I do, but I'm telling you, after this, I'm wiping my hands clean of all these games."

"Okay, great. I'll be in touch."

After I hung up with him, it was time to handle my next line of business. I hadn't been able to reach Randle by phone, so I decided to surprise him with a little lunch. It was a beautiful day out, so I figured we could go to the park and enjoy the scenery. There I would tell him how much I truly desired to be with him and would assure him that all I needed was a little more time to deal with things with Terrence. Then it would be all about me and him.

Once I arrived at his office, I saw that his secretary had up her GONE TO LUNCH sign. I did an about-face to walk back toward the lobby, but then I noticed Randle's office door was cracked open, and I could clearly hear him talking. What made me nervous, though, was the sound of a woman's laughter. I walked closer to the door and peeked inside the office. There she was, sitting in the chair in front of his desk. Her back was to me, but I could see her fair skin and long auburn-colored tresses. She seemed very comfortable, because her heels were off and were lying on the floor next to the chair. Then my eyes watched him. He was sitting on the edge of his desk, in front of her. His suit jacket was off, his tie loosened, and his top shirt buttons were unbuttoned. He was extremely relaxed, and I saw him brush her hair from her face. There was no way my eyes could be seeing Randle enjoying himself with another woman. I almost ran away, but I felt he owed me an explanation for this.

Slowly, I pushed the door open farther to reveal my presence. I stood there, picnic basket full of goodies in hand. At once, his eyes connected with mine, and her head swung back and she looked at me. Both their mouths were wide open, until he tried to speak.

"Patricia."

I didn't bother answering him because my eyes remained pinned on her.

He tried again. "Patricia, what are you doing here?"

"I could ask you the same thing, or maybe I'll ask, what is *she* doing here?"

The woman bent down and picked up her heels. "Um, why don't I leave you two to talk? Randle, I can give you a call later."

"No, please stay," he insisted, addressing her, and then he looked at me. "Pat, can I please call you later?"

"No, you can't call me, ever. You two can get back to enjoying your lunch together." I dropped the picnic basket right there on the floor and walked as fast as I could out of the building to my car. I could hear him behind me, continually calling my name and trying to catch up with me.

"Pat, wait a minute. Would you wait please? Hold up and talk to me," he yelled just as I reached my car.

"Talk to you? Talk to you about what, Randle? I've seen everything I need to see. You just throw me to the side and then take up with some other woman? You sure do work fast, don't you? So, what could we possibly have to say from here?"

"Listen, what was I supposed to do? Keep waiting around until you finished playing whatever game this is you have going on with your husband?" He was standing in front of me now.

"I expected you to care enough to wait. Just wait for me and not latch on to the first woman that caught your eye and threw herself at you."

"Look, she didn't throw herself at me. And besides, how long was I supposed to wait, Pat? Because even with you finding out that Terrence has intentions of marrying someone else, you still won't let go. Yeah, I'm the one that sent you the post about their engagement and the other woman he's with. I thought that would make you finally wake up, but clearly, it hasn't. So again, how long was I to wait?"

"You're right, Randle." I tried leaving it at that by opening my car door, but he closed it.

"Patricia, I care so much about you, I do, which is the very reason I can't stand by and watch you play all these foolish games just to get back at Terrence."

"So, how long have you been with this woman? Have you been with her the entire time you were fucking me?"

"Don't do that, Pat. You know what type of man I am, and she came by today only for lunch. That's it."

"Well, lunch is how things started with you and me, remember?" I retorted.

"Of course, I remember, like I remember every day after that. But you're the one that cut it off Pat, not me."

"You know, what's funny is she doesn't even look like your type."

He shrugged. "My type, huh? Well, she's a wonderful woman, beautiful, intelligent, classy and, most of all, *available*. And, well, you're not available."

"Wow. So just like that, you're going to be with her and not me?"

"Pat, I don't know who I'm going to be with. I will be completely honest with you, though. I do plan on asking her out, as any free and *single* man would. I mean, unless you're ready to start your divorce process. And if so, then I'll wait for you."

"Randle, it's much more complicated than that."

"No, it's not. Why don't you tell me and yourself the truth? You don't want Terrence to move on with anyone else other than you. But whether you choose to realize it or not, sweetie, he already has."

"Listen, I'm just not ready yet, and that's it. So, if you're not willing to wait, then do whatever you feel you need to do. I wish you the very best, Randle."

Leaving him standing there, I hopped in my car and drove off as fast as I could. My nerves were shot, and I felt anxiety creeping in. Little did he know, I wanted to let go of Terrence, but right then, I simply couldn't. I wished with all my heart that I could explain it, but I could hardly make sense of it to myself, let alone anyone else.

Instead of allowing my emotions to get the best of me any further, I thought about my plan. Now I was even more determined to follow through with it.

CHAPTER 45

TIFFANY

One week later . . .

After I showered, I debated with myself about wearing my formfitting black summer dress or some simple ripped jeans and a cute off-the-shoulder top for tonight. Since my indecisiveness was taking control, I laid both outfits out on my bed. One of them suddenly felt right. I sat down on the edge of my bed and massaged my shea butter cream into my skin. I thought about how tonight was going to be the first date I'd had in a while, and I was kind of looking forward to it. At least until my mind slowly drifted back to the first time Terrence took me out.

I had been excited yet afraid all at the same time because I hadn't wanted to cross any lines with him, even though my body had said something totally different. Even now I could see what he'd worn, could smell how he'd smelled, and could feel the way my heart had skipped a beat when he'd looked at me. Cracking a slight smile, I couldn't help but remember how his eyes had practically said he wanted to eat me up, and little had he known, I'd wanted him to.

Then I recalled how his strong body had felt next to mine when we'd danced the night away to Lalah

Hathaway and her live band. It had been so amazing that I hadn't wanted it to end, which was why I'd made the unwise decision of inviting him to my suite for a nightcap. At the time Terrence was still very much with Patricia, and I was 100 percent vulnerable from my breakup with David. For those reasons alone, neither of us desired to complicate things for the other. But call it fate or destiny, the unthinkable happened, and we ended up sharing the most beautiful experience to be had between a man and a woman. Although it meant everything to me, we vowed that it would never happen again—unless things were right for both of us.

I thought we were there, Terrence. I truly believed we would finally have our happily ever after. And now, soon enough, you'll be someone else's husband, I thought now, as I finished with the shea butter cream.

I fought off my desire to cry and attempted to focus my thoughts on something other than him and his wedding. Luckily for me, Monica called at that very moment, and I welcomed the distraction. I picked up my cell phone, answered her call, and tried to turn on a happy voice.

"Hey, girl! What's up?"

"Hey, Tiff! How are you? I'm headed to Bible study, and Todd stayed home to do some studying. So, I wanted to see if you wanted to ride with me tonight."

"Oh, I forgot to tell you. I'm not going to Bible study tonight. I kind of have a date."

"A date? With who?"

"Um, I kind of don't want to say right now."

"Wait, is he there with you?" she whispered, as if someone could hear her.

"No, but I don't want to jinx myself if things don't quite go right. But he's taking me to dinner."

"Wow. So, this must be someone you're really into, huh?"

"Honestly, I don't know yet. I mean, don't get me wrong. He's a wonderful guy, but something's blocking me from liking him the way I should. We have great conversations, he keeps me laughing, we have tons of things in common, and not to mention, he's a very nice-looking man. Yet I can't seem to think of him any more than as just a friend. He doesn't give me butterflies or goose bumps or anything. He's just available."

"Well, honey, I don't why you don't know what the problem is." She chuckled, like I'd told her a practical joke.

"What do you mean? What's the problem?"

"Uh, Terrence Montgomery is your problem. Now, you can try to fool me and even try to fool yourself, but, Tiff, we both know that you're not over him, no matter who you try to date. But that's just my opinion."

"Well, Terrence has moved on, and so should I. Besides, this man could very well be my Boaz."

"Girl, look, you know I'm going to always be real with you if nothing else. If mystery man was truly your Boaz, you wouldn't still be focused on Terrence's ass. He's just here filling a void, and that's not fair to him or you. I just don't want you wasting your time, or his, for that matter. If you're not ready, then you're just not ready. There's nothing wrong with being single and taking some time for you. But the worst thing you can do is hop into something before you're ready, no matter what Terrence is doing."

"I know, and I hear you, which is why I've been trying to take things as slow as possible."

"Okay, okay. Well, all I will say is that I hope things go good tonight, and I can't wait to hear all about it."

I hung up, but in the back of my mind, I knew that Monica was right. Whether I tried fooling her or even myself, deep down I had to admit that I was nowhere near being over Terrence, and it wasn't fair to Andre. As I started to get dressed, I needed to decide if this would be the first *and* last date with him, because the last thing I wanted was to string him along.

An hour later, I sat at the bar of Fleming's Prime Steakhouse and Wine Bar, where we had agreed to meet. Andre had kept insisting that he pick me up from my house, but being an extremely private person, I had told him meeting up would be best. I had also wanted a neutral location just in case I decided to let him down. Looking around, I saw that the restaurant was very classy and upscale, which I liked. However, I could have used a more private place, one that wasn't packed with wall-to-wall people. I was glad, though, that I'd decided on my dress instead of jeans. I would have hated to be underdressed.

While waiting for him to show up, I ordered a vodka and cranberry and enjoyed the ambience. My sitting alone must have given the impression that I was possibly there looking to pick someone up. At least two gentlemen approached me and offered to buy me a drink. That was why I was more than relieved when a few minutes later, I heard a familiar deep voice in my ear from behind.

"Hey, beautiful!"

"Andre." I turned around and found his arms extended for a hug. As we embraced, I immediately noticed how I didn't feel anything—no tingling, no warm sensation, and especially no feeling of wanting to remain in his arms. So, I quickly pulled back and tried to gather myself.

"I hope I didn't have you waiting too long," he said as he gazed at me.

"Uh, no. I was fine," I responded and then smiled.

After sitting down on the barstool next to me, he tried to make small talk, but my mind was someplace other than there. I kept looking at him and wondering what I had seen in him when we first met. He was still a very handsome man, but he just didn't have the swag or charm that I liked. I couldn't take my eyes off his attire either, as his style of dress wasn't to my liking. We were at an upscale restaurant, yet he had chosen to wear some jeans and a simple button-down shirt, with no blazer. I had also noticed when he hugged me that I hadn't inhaled the scent of any type of cologne. He'd smelled clean, of course, but I would kill for a good-smelling man. Anyway, after we finished our drinks, the maître d' came over to escort us to our table.

We got to the table, and I thanked Andre for pulling out my chair. As I sat down, he immediately started talking.

"I can't believe it. After all this time, you let me come and take you out."

"Yeah, I figured it was time that we saw each other face-to-face. It's been a long time," I responded.

"Yes, it has, but you look as beautiful as ever."

"You don't look so bad yourself," I told him, and he smiled from ear to ear.

After a couple of minutes or so of his small talk, I didn't even hear him anymore. My mind was on Terrence, who was everything that Andre wasn't. Terrence's looks, personality, charm, and being were what I was attracted to, not Andre. The more I sat there, the more I wondered what was happening in my life. The man I was in love with was about to marry another woman, and I was sitting here with someone who I was hoping and praying didn't try to kiss me at the end of the night. Then, out of nowhere, I heard Monica's voice.

If you're not ready, then you're just not ready. There's nothing wrong with being single and taking some time for you.

"Andre," I said, interrupting whatever he'd been going on and on about for the past ten minutes. "Uh, I really hate to cut the evening short, but I'm not feeling so well."

"Uh-oh. What did I do? Because you felt sick and left the night that Monica and Todd introduced us. Am I talking too much? Does my breath stink? Are you just not attracted to me? What is it?"

"Andre, no, you've been great. Well, maybe talking a bit much, but honestly, you've been great. It's really nothing to do with you. It's me. I think I'm trying this whole dating thing a little too soon, and I need some time to me."

"Okay, I understand that. But just like before, I'm going to wait until you're ready, because, Tiffany, I like you. I like you a lot. And I just want a real opportunity, so that we can see where things could go. Anyway, no pressure. How about we just continue to communicate, and when you're ready, then you let me know?"

"That sounds great."

With that said, I left the restaurant and headed home. I was glad I'd made a point for us to meet at the restaurant instead of him picking me up. This way I was able to leave without feeling obligated to speak soon. After making it home, though, I decided to check my social media before relaxing for the rest of the night. Immediately, I saw that I had a message from Terrence in my in-box.

Tiffany, my love, I love you, and I want to show you just how much. Please meet me at the Ritz-Carlton on McKinney Avenue tomorrow night, at seven p.m. I'll text you the room number an hour before. And, baby, wear something sexy.

I read his message a couple more times and couldn't believe that he had the audacity to think he was still going to be with me while he was engaged to marry another woman. *Do you really think I'm that stupid, Terrence Montgomery?* I had a mind not to show up and all and leave him there by his lonesome. But even that would let him off too easily. So, I decided I was going to go, and this would be it. Finally, I was going to get off my chest everything that I'd been holding in for the past few months, and then I would be done, completely done. I wasn't going to listen to any more lies, hand out any more cash, or worry myself about what he was doing and whom he was with. He owed me an explanation for all the pain I'd endured, and tomorrow night he was going to give it to me. Terrence was going to face me before he said, "I do," to anyone.

CHAPTER 46

MALAYSIA

Lying on my sofa, I held the latest novel from Carl Weber's The Family Business series in my hands, yet I couldn't concentrate on one single word. There were so many other things that occupied the space in my mind. I wasn't sure if Terrence and I would be able to pull off the wedding financially without getting help from my parents. On top of that, he was becoming more and more distant with me. Lately, he'd been behaving as if any discussion regarding the wedding was annoying and a pure waste of his time. His whole attitude made me afraid that he might not even show up when the day came. I didn't want to tell Toni or anyone else about my fears. I just felt it best to pray that everything would turn out okay.

Please, God, if Terrence is the man for me, then give me some type of sign.

After sticking my bookmarker in between two pages, I got up to get a glass of wine to soothe my nerves. A second later, I heard my cell phone buzzing from the coffee table in the living room. I retrieved my phone and saw that it was an in-box message from Terrence. I hesitated to open it, wondering if he'd sent me a message to call things off, instead of facing me directly. *Well, let's see what you have to say for yourself, Mr. Montgomery.*

Malaysia, my love, I love you, and I want to show you just how much. Please come to Texas and meet me at the Ritz-Carlton on McKinney Avenue tomorrow night, at seven p.m. I'll text you the room number an hour before. And, baby, wear something sexy.

"Well, hot damn!" I exclaimed. "God, I didn't know you were going to answer that fast. Oh, and I'm sorry about the D word."

Terrence hadn't given me any time to get everything in order before I had to leave, but he could rest assured that I would be on the first flight to Texas to meet him at that hotel.

"I knew you still loved me, Terrence, and I promise to show you tomorrow night how much I can't wait to be your wife," I said aloud, a broad smile on my face.

CHAPTER 47

ROSLYN

Roslyn, my love, I think I'm falling in love with you. I want to show you just how much. Please come here and meet me at the Ritz-Carlton on McKinney Avenue tomorrow night, at seven p.m. I'll text you the room number an hour before. And, baby, wear something sexy.

When I opened the text message, that was the last thing I thought I would see. It hadn't been long since Terrence and I met, and it was good to know that the feelings were mutual, because I felt like I was falling in love with him too. I was so excited that I almost picked up my phone to call and tell him I had received his message. Until I realized that this was some type of surprise and I had to play things cool. However, I had to tell somebody, so I called my best friend. Danielle answered immediately, like she'd been waiting on me to call.

"What's up, girl?"

"Chile, you will not believe what I just got."

"What? Whatever it is, you sound like you're about to jump out of your skin."

"Maybe, because I am. Girl, remember the handsome young guy that I told you I was flirting with on the plane?" I said.

"Uh, Terrence is his name, right? I mean, I should know as much, as you've been going on and on about him since y'all met."

"Danni, whatever. Anyway, he just sent me a text message inviting me to Texas for a romantic night at the Ritz-Carlton."

"Does this man know that he doesn't have to go through all that trouble and spend that kind of money just to get some? Hell, I'm sure you would have dropped those drawers for a Happy Meal in a McDonald's dining room."

"You're damn right I would have, for his fine ass," I agreed. We both laughed about it.

"Well, I guess I don't have to ask if you're going. So just tell me what time your flight leaves and what time I need to take you to the airport."

"Thanks, Danni. See, that's why you're my girl. As soon as I look up the first flight out, I'll text you the info. Love you, boo."

"Love you too, Roz. And please, be careful, okay? You haven't known this man that long."

"I know, but I promise, this is love at first sight. And he's assured me that he's tired of all the relationship games just as much as I am. I'm telling you, girl, I think this man is the one. I can feel it."

CHAPTER 48

TERRENCE

When I'd received a text from a private number with an invitation to spend the night at the Ritz tonight, I'd figured it had to be from Tiffany. That hotel was our special place. I'd also decided that she wanted to make up for the night in St. Louis. I'd checked in fifteen minutes early so that I could decorate the room with the red roses I'd brought before she arrived. After arranging the roses, I made sure the champagne was chilled. Then I dimmed the lights. I wanted everything to be perfect from the minute she walked into the room.

So much had been going on in my life that lately I hadn't had much time to spend with Tiffany. I was dealing with Malaysia and this wedding business, and Roslyn was becoming more and more attached to me. And only God knew what Patricia was up to. So, tonight was going to be a much-needed night with the woman I loved most.

I stood in the center of the room and waited, expecting Tiffany to appear at any moment. But the minutes ticked by, and still no Tiffany. I looked over at the clock and saw that it was 7:10 p.m. I couldn't help but wonder what was keeping her. Tiffany was a very punctual person, and her text message had told me to be here promptly at 7:00 p.m. I figured I would call her and make sure that everything was all right. I dialed her number as I walked into the bathroom to start filling the Jacuzzi tub. Just then, I heard the door to the room open. Immediately, I hit END on my cell phone.

"Hey, baby. I was just calling you to make sure everything was all right. I know it's not like you to be late," I yelled from the bathroom.

She didn't say anything, and I knew this had to be some type of sexy game she was playing. I quickly removed all my clothes and walked out into the bedroom to see her beautiful face.

"Oh shit," I said under my breath.

"Hey, baby," Malaysia said, standing there in a black nightie.

"Malaysia? What?"

"I made it, and I wore something sexy, just like you said."

"What do you mean, just like I said?" I asked just as someone knocked on the door. I ran back into the bathroom to get a robe to see who it was. I felt Malaysia's eyes following my every move. When I opened the door, I almost closed it again when I saw Roslyn standing there.

"Hey, you," she said, posing in a formfitting red dress and six-inch heels.

"Uh, Roslyn. Oh my God! What are you—"

"Terrence, who is this?" Malaysia asked, interrupting me.

"Yeah, Terrence, who is this?" Roslyn asked, walking into the room without being invited in. And just when I was about to close the door behind her and try to think of some lies to tell, Tiffany approached in a sexy black dress of her own.

"Terrence, what's going on here?" she questioned, looking at me, then at Malaysia, and then at Roslyn as she entered the room.

Suddenly, it dawned on me that this had to be the handiwork of my damn wife.

"Uh, ladies . . . Uh, listen, I can explain all of this," I said, having no idea what the hell I was about to say.

As they all stood there looking at me with stank faces and waiting on an explanation, Patricia and David came walking up to the door.

"Hey, everyone," Pat called as she and David stepped into the room. She smiled from ear to ear, clearly taking pleasure in every bit of this. "Why don't we all introduce ourselves? I'm Patricia, Terrence's *wife*."

"Wife?" Malaysia and Roslyn said in unison.

"I'm sorry. You're his *ex-wife*, right? Because he's engaged to be married to me," Malaysia added.

"Engaged? But you told me you were single, Terrence," Roslyn said.

The only one that wasn't saying a word was Tiffany. She stood there looking at me in pure disbelief.

"I'm sorry, Ms. Malaysia, but my husband can't marry you, honey, because he is still legally married to me. Here's the proof if you need it." Patricia stood there waving around our marriage certificate.

My blood was boiling so much that before I knew it, I lunged in her direction. I was ready to kill the woman, but David grabbed me before I could get my hands on her. We started to tussle.

"Get off me. Get off me, you punk! I should have hurt you when I had the chance before," I yelled as I broke free of his grasp.

By now the ladies were screaming, and Patricia was laughing. Suddenly, Malaysia passed out and collapsed on the floor. At once I took my focus off Patricia and David and ran over to Malaysia to try to wake her up. As she slowly started coming to, I could hear the commotion in the room but was unable to make out what anyone was saying. All I knew was that Patricia kept laughing and Roslyn was using every curse word possible. When I looked back to see where Tiffany was, I saw her leaving the room. I didn't even know who had called the paramedics, but the next thing I knew, they were entering the room with members of the hotel staff.

In a matter of twenty minutes or less, the whole night, along with my whole life, had become nothing less than a shit show, and it was all due to my crazy-ass wife.

CHAPTER 49

TIFFANY

"Oh, God, please help me," I begged Him as I ran out of that hotel as fast as I could, trying to catch my breath. I couldn't believe I'd been in that hotel room with him, Patricia, David, Malaysia, and that Roslyn woman, all the people he'd been dealing with. It made me sick to my stomach the more I thought about it and pictured it in my mind. "How could you do this, Terrence? After everything we've been through! How could you be so low-down to do something like this?" I cried out.

And to realize that Patricia had put this all together . . . She'd been up there dancing around like a fool with their marriage certificate in her hand. She really thought that she'd done something major, but it hadn't dawned on her that she was playing with the hearts of others, and that this would one day come back on her. And to top it all off, David had just stood there, with some dumbass expression on his face. He hadn't been able to look me in the eye. It was all too much, and I had to get far, far away from there as quickly as I could.

I wasn't even sure where to go. I didn't want to go home, because I was afraid Terrence might come there to try to talk to me. I didn't want to go to Monica's, either, because I didn't have the energy to tell her about this. Besides, it was way too embarrassing to even talk about. I thought about calling Andre, but truthfully, I didn't want to deal with any man at that moment in my life.

After riding around in my truck for at least an hour, I found myself in the parking lot of my church. I wasn't sure what I was doing there, but that was where my truck had led me. There was only one other lonely truck sitting in the entire lot, and I knew it belonged to my pastor. I didn't want him to see me, especially not in my emotional condition. So, hurrying to start up my car, I figured I'd go home and drink my problems away until I passed out. However, before I was able to pull off, I heard a tap on my driver's side window.

"Tiffany? What are you doing out here, all alone, so late?"

I lowered my window. "Um, Pastor Miles, um, I really don't know, to be honest with you. I was driving around, and somehow, I ended up here," I said, praying that he couldn't see the tears building in my eyes.

"Oh, well, I was just finishing up some business. Is everything all right with you?"

I could see the concern on his face. It took me some time to answer, because I really didn't want to involve him in my personal affairs. But in all honesty, I needed someone like him to talk to. Pastor Miles had become a major part of my life after Monica had introduced me to his church. I liked him because he was a vibrant young pastor who knew the Word of God and taught it with passion. He also loved people and the community. And more importantly, he was real and down to earth.

"I'm . . . I'm . . . I'm fine, I think, Pastor." I could barely get the words out.

"Listen, I'm not trying to pry, but I can sense that something is not all the way right. Why don't you come inside the church for a moment? Even if you don't want to talk right now, you can come in and get yourself together before driving home."

Reluctantly, I raised my window, turned off the ignition, got out of my truck, and went inside with him. He led me into his office.

"Why don't you have a seat, and I can grab us some bottles of water from the fridge, okay?" he said.

"Yes, please. That would be nice," I replied.

While he went to get the water, I almost wanted to get up and run out. It wasn't that I didn't feel like I could confide in him. The truth was I didn't want him to know how foolish I'd been for a man.

"All right, here you go. I brought you two just in case." He handed both bottles to me and sat down in the chair in front of me. "So, was there anything you wanted to talk about?"

"Pastor, I really don't want to waste your time with my personal problems. I'll get over it all soon enough."

"Well, like I said outside, I'm definitely not trying to pry, but sometimes it's good to have a listening ear, just to get things off your chest. And maybe I can even give you some scriptures that might be helpful to you."

I thought about it for a quick second and figured talking to him wouldn't hurt, especially since he was so willing to listen. "Pastor, it all has to with a gentleman that I met some time ago. We were coworkers and quickly became good friends. Then, after he separated from his wife, we became a lot more than that."

"Oh, I see. And I'm assuming you all are having some issues?"

"You could say far more than *some issues*." Next thing I knew, I started to pour my heart out to him. I started from the beginning, telling how I had met Terrence right after David and I broke up. I shared how things had seemed great between us until Terrence started asking for money, and how out of nowhere, he had switched up on me when he began living alone. Then I revealed that

I had found things in his home that belonged to another woman, and that was when I'd found out about Malaysia. I even shared with him that I had discovered he'd asked the woman to marry him, and I mentioned that I didn't know how he would pull that off since he was still legally married to his wife.

To top it all off, I told him about tonight, including about the woman I knew nothing about. But what I hated the most was revealing that despite all the negative things Terrence had done, in my heart, I *still* loved him. After I'd shared all the gritty details, Pastor looked at me, dumbfounded.

"Wow. I have to be honest, Tiffany. I don't even know where to begin. I guess if I can start anywhere, I would like to set Terrence aside for a moment and ask you a very important question."

"Sure, of course," I answered, but I had no idea what he wanted to ask.

"How do you feel about yourself?"

"I don't understand, Pastor. What does that have to do with anything?"

"It kind of has everything to do with it. So, I'd much rather you try to answer my questions first, and then I'll elaborate."

"I love myself, Pastor Miles. But I'm still not putting together what that has to do with my problems with Terrence. I mean, he's the one that's doing all the lying and cheating. So, what on earth does the way I feel about myself have to do with that?"

"Tiffany, I really don't see this being about Terrence more than it is about you. Now, you say you love yourself, but I want you to take some time and do some soul-searching. I want you to think about how you truly feel about yourself, to get to the root of why you pick the type of men that you do. More importantly, why you choose to stay involved with these men when it's clear that you should leave. See, although David's or Terrence's behavior wasn't right or appropriate, they can do to you only what *you* allow, nothing more and nothing less. And please, I don't want you to think I'm defending either of them, either, because I'm not. They both have their own crosses to bear and will have to answer for their actions.

"But when all is said and done, my focus is to make sure you walk away from this healthy and truly happy. Once that happens, who knows who God has in store for you. It could end up being someone completely new, or it might very well be Terrence. Only God knows who and what's best for you. However, it seems that Terrence clearly has a lot of work to do on himself, and you have work to do on you, before either of you can make the other happy. You can't keep trying to be someone's peace while leaving yourself in pieces. So, I say find peace within yourself, and in the meantime, pray that they find theirs, and then let God do the rest. Take your hands off it all and put it in God's hands."

Pastor thought for a moment, then continued. "It's not for you to hate those that mistreat you or to wish that harm or negativity comes to them, Tiffany. 'Vengeance is mine,' says the Lord. What you need to do is remove yourself from the equation, which is causing you pain, and pray for him at the same time. Pray for his spirit, his soul, his prideful ways, his deceitful tongue, and whatever else. Then let God deal with him, because we don't know what type of spiritual battle he may be fighting. What we do know is that this could be the very reason God sent you into his life, that is, to get you to the point of praying for him, since he is obviously unable to pray for himself. And remember, Tiffany, someone prayed for you too."

"Pray for him, Pastor? Really? You did hear me tell you that he was dealing with me and two other women and asked one to marry him, right?"

"Yeah, I did. I still believe he needs prayer, though, as much as I feel you do too."

Sitting there, I was at a total loss of words. When I had first sat down, I was sure Pastor Miles would take my side after I'd pointed out all the things Terrence had done wrong. Yet in the end, it all boiled down to me, and he wanted me to pray for the man, when all I wanted was to smack him across his face.

A second later, Pastor snapped me out of my thoughts. "Now, I know I laid a lot on you, Tiffany, but I have faith that you will be all right and everything will turn out good for you. Will you allow me to pray for you before you leave?"

"Oh yes, please. I would love that."

We stood, and the two of us joined hands, bowed our heads, and he began to pray. So much was going through my mind as I tried to concentrate on every word he said. Although I was still confused about everything, at that very moment, I knew for sure that it was God that had led me to the church. I had needed to hear all that Pastor Miles had to say.

When his praying ended, we headed toward the door. As we went, he began to laugh to himself.

"What's funny?" I asked.

"Oh, I was just thinking back to when Rochelle and I first got together. I guess you could say I was a lot like Terrence, and she was a lot like you. I wasn't anywhere near ready for what Rochelle wanted and needed, and I played all kind of games in the beginning."

"And she still chose to stay with you?"

"Heck no. That woman put me in my place quick and told me if I ever wanted to be with her, I'd better get myself together. And she was dead serious about it. She even broke up with me, and we were apart for almost two years."

"Well, how did you two end up back together?"

"I missed her so much that it literally drove me crazy. After trying to be stubborn and trying to prove a point, it finally hit me that I wasn't hurting anyone but myself. Rochelle had gone on with her life, happy and free. So, I woke up one day, and I knew exactly what I needed to do. I was determined to spend the rest of my life with her, so I did the work that it took to get her back. Luckily for me, she was still available. So, either Terrence will come to that same realization, or he may not be the one for you. But, as I said, it's going to be up to you to decide what you're going to put up with and what you're not. You have to set your boundaries and make him respect them, Tiffany. Are you ready to release this chapter of your life and turn the page, Tiffany?"

We had reached my truck by that point. He hugged me, and I got in, overwhelmed mentally and emotionally. However, I finally felt a sense of hope, as I knew exactly what I needed to do.

The car ride home was quiet. I wasn't in the mood for any type of music or anything. I simply rode with my window down, allowing the night's breeze to hit me in my face. Instead of focusing on Terrence and what had happened earlier, I recalled everything that Pastor Miles had said in the church. This was about me now, not Terrence.

As I dwelled more on his words, I realized I couldn't explain why I picked men like David and Terrence, or why I chose to stay with them. Of course, in my heart I loved Terrence more than life itself, but love wasn't enough anymore to make me stick around and be lied to and cheated on. True love just shouldn't hurt like that, and I was tired of hurting.

Upon arriving home, I entered my house with a whole new mindset. First and foremost, I felt like I couldn't move further with my life until I brought closure to this chapter of it. I slipped out of my dress and heels, threw on my robe and slippers, and went into my kitchen. Pouring myself a glass of red wine, I leaned against my island, still thinking about Pastor's words. *Are you ready to release this chapter of your life and turn the page, Tiffany?* Heaving a huge sigh, I figured even if I wasn't, I had to be.

From this point forward, all I wanted was to relax and not think about certain things anymore. I didn't want to think about love, relationships, marriage, wives, fiancés, and especially not Terrence Montgomery. I was angry with him and felt that whatever he got, he deserved. Wineglass in hand, I walked into my living room, placed the glass on the coffee table, then lay down on my sofa. I closed my eyes and decided to nap. However, instead of dozing off, I tossed and turned, got up, and lay back down. I had such trouble finding a comfortable position. Then it struck me that it wasn't my body that was restless or even my heart that was in agony. My soul was unsettled, and this issue was spiritual, not corporeal.

Instantly, more of Pastor Miles's words entered my mind yet again. *It's not for you to hate those that mistreat you or to wish that harm or negativity comes to them, Tiffany. "Vengeance is mine," says the Lord. What you need to do is remove yourself from the equation, which is causing you pain, and pray from him at the same time. Pray for his spirit, his soul, his prideful ways, his deceitful tongue, and whatever else. Then let God deal with him, because we don't know what type of spiritual battle he may be fighting. What we do know is that this could be the very reason God sent you into his life, that is, to get you to the point of praying for him, since he is obviously unable to pray for himself. And remember, Tiffany, someone prayed for you too.*

I thought about everything my pastor had said, and all at once, things became clear. Although I didn't like Terrence's behavior, I still chose to believe that he had the potential to be who I once knew him to be, or possibly better. I also didn't have to have any ill feelings toward him or the women he was with. We all had choices in our lives, and my choice was to free myself completely from that situation. There would be no more answering his calls or texts, arguing with him, or listening and trying to understand him. It was time I did what I needed to do.

I got up from my sofa. I knelt on my knees. I prayed that Terrence would come to see his wrongdoings, acknowledge them, and repent. Also, I prayed that he would no longer lie or cheat and would finally get his life and personal affairs in order with God. I even found myself praying for the other women involved, that God would protect their hearts from pain. Then, at last, I prayed for myself. I wanted God to close this chapter of my life and prod me on to bigger and better things. Also, to help me fall in love with myself, so that when He did send true love into my life, I would be open and available to receive it. Upon finishing my prayer and wiping my last tear away, I was at peace again.

"Thank you, God."

I went inside my office and sat down at my desk. As hard as I knew it would be, I was ready to put an official end to Tiffany and Terrence's love saga and begin a new chapter in my life. I opened a blank Word document on my laptop. I wasn't so sure where to start, but in lieu of letting anxiety or frustration build, I allowed my imagination to lead the way. In the middle of the first page, I typed the words *I Didn't Think You Existed.* I knew it would be a long road from that moment on, yet

I was willing and ready for the challenge. It was a part of my life that was long overdue, and even if it never went anywhere, it would provide the healing and the release that I needed.

CHAPTER 50

TERRENCE

There was such a commotion in the hotel room that I hated that this night had ever happened, any of it. Tiffany had run out of there like a bolt of lightning. I had wanted so badly to go chasing after her, but my feet had felt like they were stuck in quicksand. It had seemed like I couldn't move an inch. Patricia, I assumed felt vindicated. She had grabbed David and had left, with nothing more to say. Roslyn had cursed me out with every word in the book before she'd taken off. And the paramedics had taken Malaysia to the hospital for observation, just to make sure she was all right.

Needless to say, I felt horrible about it all and was left sitting on the bed alone, with my head in my hands. I wasn't as torn up about anything as much as I was about Tiffany. The look in her eyes had made me cringe because I had literally felt the pain that she was feeling. Although I was positive she hated me now and wanted nothing more to do with me, I at least had to tell her how sorry I was.

Swallowing the lump in my throat, I began to dial her number on my cell phone. With sweaty palms, I held the phone in one hand, while wiping my head with the other. Part of me hoped and prayed she answered, but then the other part almost wished she didn't, just to save me from the embarrassment of it all. Then it happened.

"Hello?"

I didn't say anything at first; I was basically searching my heart, trying to find the right words to say.

"Hello?" she said again, and I knew if I didn't respond quickly, she would disconnect the call.

"Tiffany, it's Terrence."

That time, she didn't say anything at all, but I could hear her breathing.

"Tiff, are you there?"

"Yes, I am."

"Um, do you have a second? Can I talk to you for a moment?"

"I'm listening, Terrence," was all she said.

"Tiff, I need to apologize to you for everything—" I began, but she didn't let me finish.

"Really? Everything like what, Terrence? Because I need to know what you're honestly apologizing for. Is it for cheating on me for who knows how long in our relationship with not one but two women? Is it for taking money from me to pay for yourself and these other women? Is it for asking a whole other woman to marry you? Or could it possibly be for not being the friend to me that you promised always to be? Which one are you really calling to apologize for?"

"Baby, I'm—"

"No, don't 'baby' me right now. I need you to be honest for once with me and yourself and answer my question. What exactly are you apologizing for?"

"For everything, Tiff. You have to know that I never meant to hurt you or betray you. I just lost control of things and didn't know how to fix them."

"You fix it by stopping the lies. You fix it my being honest with yourself and everyone involved. You fix it by asking God to help you and deliver you from whatever has control over you and your actions. That's how you fix it, Terrence. Not by digging yourself deeper and deeper in a ditch and hurting others in return," she answered me, and I could clearly hear the pain in her voice.

Neither of us said a word after that, and I assumed we were both letting everything sink in. She broke the silence when she asked, "So, what is really the purpose of your call, Terrence? If it is only to apologize, then okay, I accept your apology. But there's nothing more for us to talk about from here. Have a nice life, Terrence Montgomery."

I could tell she was about to hang up, but I had to stop her. There was so much more that I still needed to say. "Tiff, please, don't hang up on me, please."

As quickly as I said it, though, was how fast she was gone. She'd hung up, and I was positive that we would never speak again.

"I love you, Tiffany Tate, with all my heart, and I always will," I said aloud.

Then I got down on my knees on the side of the bed and did the only thing left to do. "God, please, I don't know how I got myself all caught up like this, but if you would just help me, Lord. Help me turn my entire life around, and please help me to one day get Tiffany back."

CHAPTER 51

PATRICIA

"Did you see the look on their faces? Especially Terrence's. Oh my God. That was amazing," I screamed when David and I hopped into my car.

"Damn, if I didn't know any better, I would think you're having an orgasm off it or something."

"And if I am, then I deserve to for all the times my husband didn't make me have one."

"Look, I don't need to know about any of that, all right?" He turned his head and looked out the window, as if he was disgusted by the thought.

"And what's bothering you? You don't feel amazing after getting back at your worst enemy the way we did?"

"You mean, the way *you* did. And no, I don't feel good about it, Pat. To be honest, I'm feeling bad about the whole thing tonight. We never should have done that."

"Oh, David, don't be such a damn party pooper. I did what I had to do, and that's that. It's not my fault that my husband is a liar and a cheat and had more women than he could keep up with. So, if you want to blame someone, blame him. This was all his fault."

"Yeah, whatever makes you sleep at night, Patricia, but it still doesn't make it right, okay? Maybe you weren't paying any attention, but I looked at every one of those women, and all of them were hurt by this."

"You mean, your little Ms. Perfect Tiffany was hurt, because she's the only one you're actually concerned about." I turned my nose up at him.

"Whatever, Pat. Either way, I don't think you should be celebrating like this. In fact, we shouldn't have done this at all."

I was glad that we were pulling up to his house because he was killing my entire vibe from what had just happened in that hotel room. I was sure the second he got inside, he was even going to call little Ms. Perfect to make sure that she was all right.

"Well, despite how you're feeling, I appreciate you helping me with this, David. I couldn't have pulled it off without you."

"You just better be happy I was there, because had I not held Terrence back from you, he probably would have killed you tonight."

"My husband wasn't going to do anything, and like I said, he got exactly what he deserved." I reached over to give him a hug before he exited my car. I couldn't wait to get home and continue my celebration. However, the second I pulled off, another car came speeding past me, and suddenly, I heard gunshots. There was no way they were shooting at him, but then something in my gut told me they were.

Immediately I whipped my car back around, then drove the short distance to his house. I pulled over, and before my car had come to a complete stop, I hopped out and ran over to David. He was lying on the ground and was all bloody. His neighbors started to come out of their homes, and they walked over and gawked at the sight. Some even began shooting live videos.

"Someone please call the police!" I yelled at them. "David, just hold on. It's okay, honey. You're going to be all right."

He didn't say anything back to me, just lay there, not moving at all. I was afraid that he might not make it to the hospital alive, yet I couldn't say that to his mother when she came running out of the house.

"My baby, what happened to my baby?" She fell beside him.

"Someone already called an ambulance, Ms. Allen," I told her. "Everything is going to be all right. It has to be."

CHAPTER 52

MALAYSIA

One year later . . .

"It's been an entire year, Toni, and my heart still aches like it just happened yesterday," I told her when she called to check on me.

"That's exactly why I keep trying to tell you that you need to get out of that house. You need to be around other people. People that can make you laugh and smile. And who knows? Maybe you might even meet someone new, someone who can take your mind completely off Terrence Montgomery."

I heard what she was suggesting, but my mind wasn't on meeting anyone new. I still needed answers as to why he had done this to me, and I was determined to get them.

"I wonder which one of the women he's with now. His actual wife, Tiffany, or that other woman, what's-her-name," I mused.

"Girl, why do you even care? The point is, he's not married to *you*, and from the looks of it, he never had intentions on doing so. That's all that matters."

"Look, Toni, I get it, all right? I know I should be angry and hate his guts and all, but I still have so many unanswered questions. Plus, he's still the man I fell in love with and was about to spend the rest of my life with."

"All right, but who do you think is going to answer your questions? Not his *wife* and certainly not him. Hell, after what happened, you shouldn't believe a single word that comes out of that man's mouth. And I don't want to say, 'I told you so, Malaysia,' but I told you when you first ran into him that he *had* to be involved with *someone*. He was so busy spilling that mess about some crazy ex-girlfriend, but not once did he mention that he had a whole, entire wife."

"Damn. Thanks for not saying, 'I told you so.'"

"I'm sorry, girl, but you know what I mean."

"Well, you're right. Maybe I can't go to him or his wife for any answers, and I'm sure that Roslyn woman didn't have a clue, either, because she seemed just as shocked as I did. But there's still one person that I can possibly go to."

"Wait a minute. Who the hell are you talking about? I know you're not thinking of contacting that Tiffany Tate woman."

"Why not, Tee? She might very well be my only source for getting some type of answers. Besides, all I want to know is the extent of their relationship and why they broke up."

"Really? And you think she's going to come right out and tell you anything about her relationship with him? I mean, think about it, Malaysia. Would you spill your heart out to another woman? Especially another woman that's been with your man?"

"But he did this to both of us. Hell, all of us, for that matter. Me, Tiffany, Roslyn, and even his wife are all victims of Terrence's lies and betrayal."

"Which is why I think you need to leave this alone and say good riddance to him and this entire situation. Besides, what do you plan on doing? Becoming best friends with the woman and swapping sex stories?" She laughed as she said it, but I was dead serious. "I'm sorry, but it sounds crazy. And I think you're doing way too much for someone that hurt you the way he did. Please, just dismiss all thoughts of him and allow that to be the closure you need."

The phone went silent for a few minutes after that. My friend had to know that despite what she had said, I was not about to give up that easily.

"All right, Malaysia." She sighed. "Say that I went along with you on this, how would you contact her? It's not like you have her number stored in your cell phone, or do you?"

"Of course, I don't have her number in my phone, Toni. But honestly, I have gone to her social media page a couple of times. It seems Ms. Tate recently released her first novel, and she's touring from city to city, having book signings. St. Louis was her home, and she'll be here in a few weeks. Maybe I can show up."

"Malaysia, you wouldn't. Not at the woman's book signing."

"Toni, the more I think about it, that's starting to seem like the only way to handle this. Tiffany Tate and I need to talk woman to woman, face-to-face."

"Lord, help us," was all that Tee said before we exchanged our goodbyes. I knew deep down she wished I would let this go, but I just couldn't. I wanted to talk to Tiffany first, and then soon enough, Terrence and I would indeed meet again.

CHAPTER 53

PATRICIA

I rolled over and faced him, then laid my head on his chest. He was still sleeping peacefully as I thought to myself how much my life had changed in a matter of a year. All at once, my mind traveled back to the very day in that hotel room with Terrence and his concubines. I could still see the expression on his face when David and I entered the room. The man looked as if he could crap on himself at any moment, with everyone's eyes staring directly at him. Clearly, he had no idea what to do, and for once I had the ball in my court. I was finally the one in control, and it felt good.

At least that was until his poor little bride-to-be passed out and he and David got into a minor tussle. It was all a complete mess, to say the least. There they were, trying to pull the two men apart and attempting to snap the bride out of her daze, while I sat back, laughing hysterically at the theatrics. And instead of showing any remorse whatsoever, Terrence tried his best to blame everything on me. But the truth of the matter was, no matter how wrong my actions were, they didn't outweigh his one bit. All of it was his fault, and for once everyone got a chance to see the real Terrence Montgomery versus who he'd been portraying himself to be.

Laughing inside now, I shook my head at the notion that my now ex-husband honestly thought he could pull off marrying another woman while still married to me. Anyway, after that day, things went exactly how I had figured they would. We divorced in little to no time. I didn't put up much of a fight or requested any spousal or child support, because to be honest, it was time. I was finally ready to be free and clear of him and whatever it was I thought we had shared all those years together. It was time I let that part of my life go and move on with my future. My boys were no longer small children, and other than living with me, they basically cared for themselves. They no longer needed a father figure in their lives the way they had when Terrence and I were married.

The crazy part of it all was that Terrence had the nerve to file a restraining order against me so that I couldn't come within so many feet of him. I guess he thought I would always be chasing after him. Yet little did he know, my heart had grown fonder for someone much better than him, someone more exciting and spontaneous, and someone I was much more compatible with than he and I ever were.

As I rubbed my fingers through the very hairs on his chest now, I was still stunned how falling for him basically come out of nowhere. At first, I had hopes of my future possibly including Randle, but I soon found out that he'd asked another woman to marry him instead. Of course, my heart was crushed when I heard the news, but that was when I got the shock of my life. I ended up finding comfort in the one person who I would never have imagined being with. My hand made its way now from his chest to under the covers to massage his manhood, and immediately it became rock hard, and his eyes popped open.

"Well, good morning, sleepyhead," I said and smiled.

"Hey, good morning," his groggy voice mumbled back. "You don't get enough, do you?"

"Honey, I am a newly divorced woman enjoying life. Why should I get enough?"

"Well, as much as I would love to indulge, we may have to take a rain check on this morning."

"Why?" I whined in a little girl's voice. "It's only a little after ten, and neither of us has anywhere to go."

"Damn. Ten? I didn't mean to sleep so late. I'm sorry, Pat, but I have to get dressed and get out of here. I need to run over to my mother's."

"Really? Your mother's, David?"

"Yes, my mother's. What's wrong with that?" He sat up, perched on the side of the bed, and slipped his joggers on.

"It's just that, well, you're a grown-ass man in his fifties, yet every time you come over and stay a little while, you rush off early every morning. And you always blame it on your mother, but I know better than that. I know the games men play when there's someone else from the very actions of my ex-husband. Besides, your mother is a big girl, and I'm sure she can take care of herself. She doesn't need you running over there every morning. I mean, don't you think it's probably time for you to get off her titty?"

"Listen, Patricia, for one, I'm not on my mother's titty. And two, let's get something straight this very minute. Don't you ever compare me to or talk to me the way you did that ex-husband of yours. Because believe me, if you do, then we can end whatever this is we're doing. But, anyway, I have to go."

"David, David, wait a minute." I got up and ran over to him, stopping him before he headed for the door. "Look, I didn't mean to compare you to Terrence or upset you, okay? I just think that we have something good going on, and it's like you're always blocking things from getting too serious."

"Yeah, well, I think you're moving a little too fast and getting too serious for someone who just got divorced a year ago. Not to mention everything that happened with me getting shot and almost dying. All I want is for us to keep enjoying one another's company and to have some good-ass sex, that's it. Can we do that?"

He kissed me on the cheek and hurried to the door as fast as he could. Next thing I knew, he shot out of there like his pants were on fire, so I knew wherever he was rushing off to must have been urgent. However, something inside me still told me there was much more going on than his morning date with his mother. I really didn't want to go back to my old habits of not trusting and lurking, the way I had with Terrence, either, but I couldn't help myself. I'd gotten to know David pretty good from the time we had spent together, and one thing I'd learned was how to detect when he was lying about something. And there was not an ounce of truth in his words before he left.

"If it's one thing I hate more than anything, it's for someone to lie straight to my face, David. I know there's more to what you're telling me. And you better believe that I plan on finding out what it is," I muttered under my breath.

CHAPTER 54

DAVID

I couldn't leave Patricia's house fast enough. The past couple of months I could sense that she was becoming attached and wanting more from me than I could give her. Although I enjoyed our time together, and the sex was great, I had so much more to think about than forcing some relationship between the two of us.

For one, I was just happy to still be alive, and I didn't want to be tied down to anyone right now. Last year—getting shot and then finding out the one person I would have never considered had done it—was such an eye-opener for me. The detectives had told me it was all Mrs. Smith's doing. She had hated me so much for what I'd done to Leslie that she'd wanted me dead. And she put her grandsons up to do the deed. She'd told the police that Leslie was like a daughter to her, and I reminded her of her good-for-nothing ex-husband. She'd wanted to do to me what she'd never done to him. Of course, the police wanted to lock her away for planning a murder for hire, but I couldn't allow that to happen. Although I hated what she'd done to me, there was no way my spirit would be settled with an old lady rotting in some jail cell for the rest of her life. I chose not to press charges. The police did, however, charge her grandsons with attempted murder for committing the act, and now they were behind bars, where they belonged.

My attention at this very moment was focused on someone who was more important than anyone else in my life, even Pat. That was the very reason I'd run away from Pat's first thing every morning. Today I had to race just to try to catch a glimpse of him. As I pulled up and parked my car behind the same bushes I hid behind every morning, I looked at the time and took a deep breath. I'd made it with only a couple of minutes to spare. Three minutes later I saw her front door open, and the two of them came outside. Normally around this time, she would leave the house with him. So, I made it my goal to park behind the bushes across the street from her home. I wished more than anything that I could simply walk up to Sonya and say something, or ask to see him, but I knew the outcome wouldn't be good if I did. She still acted as if she hated my guts. And she'd threatened to make sure a judge never gave me visitation with my son after everything I'd done to her. So, to stay out of any legal trouble, I'd basically settled for this. This way, I was able to get little glimpses of him growing up without things turning crazy.

After a few more minutes, I couldn't help but realize that something appeared different about this day, though. Any other morning, she would have left by now. I would watch her pack everything into the car, tuck him in the back seat, and they would be on their way. This morning, however, it was taking much longer than usual. Part of me wondered if something was wrong, and I almost took my chances and went over to make sure everything was all right. But that was when I saw *him* come out of her home. Squinting my eyes a bit harder to see them better, I watched Dante' playfully smack her on the rear, tongue her down right there in the driveway, and hop in the car before they sped off with my son in the back.

After starting my car back up in a hurry, I sped down the block to follow behind them. This guy bobbed and weaved in and out of traffic, as if no one else was inside the car but him, and especially not a child. After fifteen minutes of my trying to keep up, he finally pulled up to some strange house. The building itself looked abandoned, and it was in one of the worst neighborhoods possible. Music was playing loudly from one of the other cars nearby, and several men were hanging on the corner. It didn't take me long before I realized this was nothing more than a trap house. My eyes watched as Dante' got out of the car and gave man hugs to the five guys who were standing outside.

"Why the hell would you have this guy around my son, Sonya?" I muttered. Before I knew it, I jumped out of my car and began walking in their direction.

The only man who should be around my son is me, yet you act like I'm not good enough. But then you go and choose a punk like this. All right, well, I'll show you exactly what I'm going to do about it, even if that means catching a case, I thought as walked.

Inching my way closer to them, I was prepared to muscle my little one away from him, until I saw the weapon he had strapped on his waist. It was the same one from the day I went to her house. Stopping in my tracks, I realized that there was no way I could approach him without getting seriously hurt or possibly killed. And having just gone through the scare of my life, I wasn't about to take any chances. With a huge feeling of defeat, I walked back to my car, got inside it, and pounded my fists against the steering wheel.

Never had I thought that I could create a child. In all my fifty-some odd years on earth, it had never come about with any woman that I'd been with. Yet here I was with a son of my own, and I'd sacrifice my life before I allowed Sonya to keep handing him off to some young jerk trying to play Daddy. I knew that I had to think of a way to get full custody of him, and it had to be sooner rather than later. A second after that, it dawned on me. Patricia wanted a future together, and I needed to prove to a judge that I could provide my son a stable family-type environment. I felt like Patricia owed me, anyway, for getting me involved in that whole mess with Tiffany and Terrence.

Maybe I can make this work with Patricia, after all, to get what I need. It's exactly what she'd done to have someone in her sons' lives, so why not? I thought.

"All right, Pat. If it's more that you want, then it's more that you'll get," I declared.

CHAPTER 55

TERRENCE

It was funny, the turns that life could take all in a short amount of time. After I hung the last picture on the wall of my office, I looked around in utter shock at where I was now compared to just one year ago. No one would ever believe me if I told them now that I'd been married to one woman, engaged to another, and dating yet another all at the same time, while the woman who truly had my heart waited in background. In all honesty, I still couldn't believe it myself. I'd done so much lying, cheating, gambling, and deceiving that I hadn't even known what was real or fake. And in return, I'd basically lost everything: my family, my home, relationships with the people that I loved. And most of all, I'd lost myself. No longer had I had any concept of who I was or what I wanted in my life. And the saddest part of it all was that I'd had no one else to blame but me.

As I thought back to that day in the hotel room with all those women, the thing I remembered most vividly was the looks on all their faces. Pat had worn a look of satisfaction, Malaysia's face had read that she could kill me with her bare hands, Roslyn had been confused by it all, but Tiffany's face had been the one that stood out the most. Behind her eyes had lain all the pain and betrayal that I'd put her through that entire time. Of course, ev-

ery single woman had turned their back on me after that
night. However, although I expected it from all the rest,
it wasn't until the moment that Tiffany did the same that
I realized how out of control of my life I truly was. For
some strange reason, Tiffany was the one that I thought
would always be in my corner, no matter what craziness
I put her through. And when it became clear that she was
ready to walk completely out of my life, I knew it
was time for a drastic change.

After sitting down and speaking with Pastor Jones, my
first line of business was this whole situation with Pat.
She and I both knew that a divorce was long overdue, so I
made no more excuses to prolong things, and to my surprise, she didn't fight it. Still, I decided to go ahead and
file a restraining order against her so that she couldn't
come within so many feet of me ever again. I'd become so
sick of her shenanigans, especially that night in the hotel
room, that it seemed like the only logical thing to do. I
still couldn't believe that she and David had drafted that
whole plan just to keep me and Tiffany apart from each
other.

Anyway, after that, I immediately filed for divorce.
There was no more hesitation, no more worrying about
whether she could take all my money and leave me with
nothing, and no more waiting on something to slap me in
the face to do it. I just did it, and freeing myself from her
was something I should have done long ago, no matter
what the consequences were. Not to mention, I was no
longer willing to put my life on hold. That chapter of my
life *needed* to be closed once and for all, especially after
I found out she'd slept with Randle. True enough, by the
time it happened, things were completely over between
her and me, but I still felt there were some lines not to
be crossed. I would never have slept with anyone she
trusted and called a friend, or I suspected was her friend.

But realizing who I was dealing with, I should have known there was no putting anything past her.

Thankfully, though, the divorce process took no time at all and went a lot smoother than I had ever imagined. We didn't have any businesses together, she finally stopped holding her children over my head, which was ridiculous since they were now considered adults anyway. And she gave up on the whole spousal support idea. So, with that, it was over and done with in no time and quite painless. Honestly, once it was over, my only hope was that she found a man that would love her exactly the way she needed to be loved, and exactly the way I couldn't.

Next on my list was Malaysia. I was sure that having Patricia barge in that night, waving around a marriage certificate and revealing she was married to the same man Malaysia was engaged to had to be as embarrassing and humiliating for her as it was for me. Probably more, to be honest, because I had allowed her to believe the wedding would happen in the first place. If looks could kill, I would have surely died that day were it not for her passing out a second later. I would never forget the pain and anguish written all over her face once she came to. What was supposed to be the best and most memorable time of her life turned out to be the worst, and it was all because of me.

Although I knew Malaysia would probably never accept it, I kept trying to find a way to apologize and ask for her forgiveness. However, I simply never found the words or even the courage to do it. Instead, I figured that for both of us, it would be best to leave well enough alone. Especially because since that night, I'd been receiving a ton of backlash from her friends and family that I'd come to know. They'd all pretty much threatened that if I ever contacted her again, I would live to regret it.

Then there was Roslyn. For the life of me, I couldn't
explain why I had got involved with her in the first place.
Well, actually, I did know. She was simply someone who
took my mind and focus away from the other things going
on in my life at that time, especially the situations with
Patricia and Malaysia. True enough, Tiffany played that
role in my life, as well, but I knew she wanted the type of
relationship that I wasn't ready to give her. Roslyn, however, was mature, independent, and very self-sufficient,
which was why I had thought we could have fun together
without any commitment or attachment at all. She'd said
she was divorced, was focusing on her and her grandchildren, and was not at all looking for anything serious.
But how quickly that whole tune changed in a matter of
a couple of months. All of a sudden, I became the love of
her life and the man she'd always dreamed of being with.
Seeing that she was investing far more in our friendship
than I wanted to, I'd already planned to break things off.
But the situation at the hotel happened before I ever got
the chance.

I guessed I should have looked at that night as a
blessing in disguise. However, I hated that it had left
her practically hating me. For days after, almost an
entire month, in fact, she had called, texted, and private
messaged me from social media, using every foul and vial
word in the book. The only woman I'd ever let talk to me
in that manner and get away with it was Tiffany, but I'd
figured I'd suck it up and just take it. The whole situation
was all my fault, and I knew she was only speaking from
hurt and pain. Somewhere down the line, though, I still
hoped we could one day be friends, because to be honest,
she was a great woman with great qualities, just not the
woman for me.

Of course, that left only my sweet Tiffany. Out of all
four women, I felt the worst about her. She had always

been a true friend and had been in my corner no matter what, and she didn't deserve any of what I'd done. In fact, she deserved so much more than what I've given her since we'd known one another. But I guessed, like Pastor Jones said, out of my own selfishness, I assumed that she would always be around, at least until I was ready to settle down.

As I stood in my office now and searched in my mind for a way to make amends with her, suddenly I heard a tap on the front door. My eyes lit up and a smile adorned my face when I saw them through the glass window.

I rushed to the door and swung it open. "Monica, Todd. What are you two doing here? The grand opening isn't until tomorrow," I said, hugging both of them.

"We know, but I thought it would be best to stop by today, before there's wall-to-wall people in here and you'll be too busy to talk. Plus, I wanted to give you this." Monica handed me a gift bag. I peeked inside and saw that it contained a beautiful black-and-gold picture frame. "It's to frame your first dollar bill made here at Montgomery's Barbecue and Soul Food."

"Wow, this is great, Monica. I can't thank you guys enough."

"Everything looks good too, man," Todd commented while his eyes danced around the room. "So, are you ready for the big day?" He rubbed his hands together, like we were in the final play of a championship game.

"Hey, as ready as I'm going to get. I just put the finishing touches up in my office."

"Cool. Do you mind if I finish looking around?" He started to walk around before I even gave him the okay.

"Go right ahead," I said. Monica pulled me to the side, with a sudden seriousness in her eyes, as Todd meandered around the space.

"So, Terrence, there is another reason I stopped by here today besides bringing that gift," Monica whispered.

"Really? What's up?"

"Well . . ." She held up a book and then handed it to me. "It's titled *I Didn't Think You Existed.*"

Although I had known without a doubt that this day would eventually come, I couldn't believe I was holding Tiffany's first novel in my hands. It seemed so surreal.

"Wow! She finally did it, huh? She wrote and published her first novel."

"Yeah, she did, and I couldn't be prouder of her, Terrence. She has everything her heart desires, except . . ."

"Except what, Monica?" I asked, but deep down I had a gut feeling I knew what she wanted to say.

"Listen, it's nothing, okay? Anyway, she's having a book signing at Barnes and Noble today . . . in a couple of hours. That's where Todd and I are headed, and I was thinking that maybe you could stop by. You know, just to show your support and congratulate her."

"Naw, you and I both know that that wouldn't be a good idea. She wouldn't be expecting me, and seeing the way things ended between us, my showing up there would probably ruin her entire day. I don't want to do that."

She looked around, as if she was gauging whether Todd was headed our way. Satisfied that he wasn't, she whispered, "Truth be told, I don't think it would ruin her day at all. In fact, you showing up there could possibly stop her from ruining the rest of her life."

"What? What do you mean? Ruin her life how?"

The minute I asked, however, Todd came walking back over to us, and Monica immediately went mute.

Regaining her composure, she said, "So, Terrence, again, we only wanted to stop by and bless your new restaurant and wish you nothing but success with your grand opening tomorrow."

"Yeah, man, everything looks great, and I can't wait to get some of that good soul food of yours," Todd added.

"Thanks, you two. It means a lot to me that you came by today."

"Well, I hate to rush off, but you know how traffic out here can be, and we have to get to our next destination. Keep in mind what I said, though, okay?" Monica announced. She winked at me as she and Todd prepared to leave.

They headed out and I waved from the doorway until they were out of sight. While locking the door behind them, however, I couldn't stop thinking about what Monica had said.

You showing up there could possibly stop her from ruining the rest of her life.

For the life of me, I couldn't figure out what she had meant. And although my mind told me not to go to that book signing, my heart said the total opposite.

CHAPTER 56

TIFFANY

One of my favorite passages in the Bible now was Ecclesiastes, Chapter Three.

There is a time for everything, and a season for every activity under the heavens. A time to be born and a time to die, a time to plant and time to uproot, a time to kill and a time to heal, a time to tear down and a time to build, a time to weep and a time to laugh, a time to mourn and a time to dance, a time to scatter stones and a time to gather them, a time to embrace and a time to refrain from embracing, a time to search and a time to give up, a time to keep and a time to throw away, a time to tear and a time to mend, a time to be silent and a time to speak, a time to love and a time to hate, a time for war and time for peace.

In the past year I'd truly learned that our timing was not God's timing, but when we waited on Him, everything somehow turned out perfect. Yet it wasn't until I had surrendered my life fully to God and had placed Him above everything and everyone that I truly saw for myself just how perfect He was. It was not that I hadn't believed in His omnipotence before, but I had realized that my own choices weren't allowing me to see His goodness manifest in my life, that was, until now.

As I looked around the bookstore, I felt a sense of pure amazement and an awareness of just how good He'd been to me. No one could have told me a year or so ago that when I declared my desire to one day be a published author, wrote it down, and prayed night and day about, my dream would eventually come true. But here I was, having realized that dream. Not only that, but I was also able to say that my work had been published by my favorite author and now mentor, Mr. Carl Weber. It was all still so surreal, and at that very moment, it didn't matter to me who might be watching as I threw my hands up, looked to the heavens above, and told God thank you. Right there, all alone, I gave Him the highest praise that He was due.

After completing my very first novel within seven months, I sold close to a half million copies, and Barnes and Noble had named me their Newest African American Contemporary Romance Author of the Month. Now I stood here, preparing to have a book signing in their store in less than an hour. My heart was filled with so much joy that it was hard for me to contain myself. Not to mention that as the time for things to start got closer, my nervousness grew a bit. I took a deep breath. Of course, all I had to do was speak about my journey and then sign books and take pictures. However, I felt my mission and purpose were so much bigger than that. I wanted to do my part somehow in helping women who found themselves in unhealthy relationships, one after the next. I wanted to express to them how first loving God with all their heart and soul and then loving themselves would ultimately prepare them for when He sent their earthly love.

This was why I'd already begun working on my podcast, called *The Love Still Exists* podcast. This podcast would hopefully allow me to sit down with single women and men and meet them exactly where they were, just as my pastor had with me. We would discuss single life, dating, spirituality and, most of all, healing and self-love, which would aid in their quest for true love. I couldn't wait to get it all up and running, and I prayed it would be a huge success, just as the novel was.

As I wiped the happy tears from my eyes, they suddenly lit up when I saw a few of my favorite people heading my way.

"Monica, Todd, I'm so happy you made it." I called.

"What? Girl, now, you know I wouldn't have missed this for anything in the world. I'm extremely proud of you, Tiffany, and you deserve all of this and so much more," Monica replied and hugged me first.

"Yeah, we're both very proud of you, Tiff. And Dallas and Austin can't believe they have a *famous author* as an aunt," Todd said as he and the boys gave me a small group hug.

"Well, that's flattering, but I wouldn't consider myself *famous* by a long shot just yet," I laughed. "I think I still have quite a long way to go for that."

"Hey, hey, what did I tell you about the words you speak from your mouth? They have power. With almost a million books sold, you are definitely famous in our eyes," Pastor Miles reminded me as he walked up and reached in to hug me too.

Pastor Miles had become not only my pastor and friend but almost like a second father to me too. I couldn't see where my life would be without his spiritual love, guidance, and leadership. With that in mind, I took a few minutes to hug him tight and thank him for all he'd done for me.

While my team finished setting things up, Todd and the boys made their way to seats on the front row. I continued to talk to Monica and Pastor Miles as women of all ages and ethnicities poured into room. Seeing the excitement and anticipation on their faces, I almost wanted to fall to my knees in gratitude. All these people were there simply to support little ole me, and I couldn't believe it. I tried my best to gather myself and remove any traces of fear and inhibition. I had written a novel from my heart of the perfect, imperfect love story, and their presence made me feel that people still believed in love as much as I did. After a few more minutes, the store manager walked up to the podium, and a sudden hush fell over the room. Monica and Pastor Miles hugged me once more and then rushed to take their seats next to Todd.

"Good afternoon, everyone. First, I want to thank you all for coming out today. We are in for such a special treat, so I hope you all are as excited as I am. Before our guest comes to the podium, though, I would like to invite you to partake in the hors d'oeuvres and champagne and make yourselves as comfortable as possible. Then, shortly after, we'll hear from none other than our newest best-selling author of African American contemporary romance, Ms. Tiffany Tate."

All at once, I watched attendees hurry to grab some hors d'oeuvres or simply mingle with others. A few sat quietly and kept to themselves as they waited for me to begin. Standing there, trying to take it all in, I thought about how this was such a complete dream come true. My only wish was that one certain person was here to share it all with me. As I started to picture him in my mind, I couldn't help but wonder where he was and what he was up to. Monica had even suggested that I invite him, but as much as I had wanted to, something inside me had made me decide against it. After that night at the hotel, it seemed we had both gone on with our lives and had drifted in opposite directions. So, no matter what my heart said, my mind and my gut had told me to leave well enough alone.

After a few more minutes, the store manager snapped me out of my daze when she told me it was time to begin. I made my way to the podium, trying to savor every single moment, while my team quieted the room until you could almost hear a pin drop. Until that very moment I'd been praying for God to remove all fear inside me, and the second I stood behind the podium, He did just that. Any uneasiness I'd felt slowly faded away, and I felt completely in my element. Glancing around at all the beautiful and handsome faces, it struck me that this was where God wanted me. This was my purpose in life, and there was no turning back. With that realization, I took a deep breath, cleared my throat, straightened my back, and began to speak.

"Wow. Hello, everyone. First, I truly want to thank each and every one of you for coming out today. This has been a long time coming, but it's here, and it's because of all of you who've supported me with this first novel. Now, I would love to stand here and tell you how this entire journey has been a breeze, but the truth is, I can't. There have been many sleepless nights, some loneliness, and a lot of sweat and tears. What kept me going is this book right here." I picked up my journal, which I'd kept over the years, and held it up.

"I started this journal a few years ago, at a time in my life when I was feeling low and unsure of the direction I was headed in. I needed to know my purpose and what I could somehow offer to make this world a better place. I began to pray, study my Word daily, and really build my relationship with the creator. That's when it came to me to buy this journal and write down the vision I saw for my life. Let me tell you, I went into detail, too, wrote about my career, my home, my health, and even the man I wanted to share my life with. I made every single detail plain to God, and then with faith, I waited. Now, trust me, waiting wasn't easy either. There were times when I almost lost hope and my desire to continue pursuing my dreams. Yet God remained faithful and always sent a small reminder that I was right where He wanted me to be. He showed me that the life I dreamed of could exist, and, well, here we are today witnessing His glory."

As I continued to speak about God and His desire for my life, I looked around, and there was not a dry eye in the room. Suddenly, I remembered my mother always saying that what came from the heart reached the heart, and I realized I was sharing not only my journey but also my heart with all the people there on this day.

As I connected more and more with the audience, there were moments of pure joy, laughter, seriousness, and more tears. For two hours, it seemed everyone had become one big extended family, talking about life, love, and all the things wrapped up in my novel. Faith and fiction had brought us together, and I was at the very center of it all. This was what I was created for. This was what God meant for me.

Before wrapping up my first book event, I autographed hundreds of copies of my novel, posed for pictures and social media posts, and got to know the readers. It was an amazing day, but by the time I posed for the last photo, I could feel my stomach rumbling from starvation. I hadn't eaten much of anything, because of my initial nervousness. However, now that it was all over, I felt like I could devour an entire seven-course meal. After saying my goodbyes to Monica, Todd, and the boys, Pastor Miles, and other family and friends, I commenced removing the clutter from the table I had used to sign books. By now everyone had cleared out. With my back turned to the door, I suddenly heard a voice behind me, and I assumed a straggler must have left something behind in the room and had come to fetch it.

"I didn't think you existed," was all the voice said.

The voice was very familiar, and it sounded melodic to my ears. Slowly, I turned around. I froze in place, with my jaw hanging wide open, unable to move when our eyes finally met. He cracked his usual smile as he stepped forward to embrace me. Once he pulled me in close to him, I inhaled his scent, and in an instant, all our time spent together came rushing back to me. He held me tightly in his arms for at least the next few minutes, and I didn't want to let go.

"Terrence." I struggled to pull away and gazed at him. Everything about him was still as perfect as could be, I thought as I admired him in his navy-blue suit and clean, crisp white shirt. His skin was still as pure and smooth as milk chocolate. There was not a hair out of place in his full beard. And although he must have lost a few pounds, his body was still strong and rock solid as could be. His dark eyes still pierced right through the very essence of my soul as he stared back at me. I didn't want to appear all googly-eyed or anything, but something told me, it was already too late for that. I was sure he could see I was practically drooling, and once again, I was putty in his hands.

"So, you finally did it. You wrote and published your first romance novel. And from the looks of it, it's just as amazing as I always knew it would be," he told me.

I covered my mouth with both hands as tears welled up in my eyes.

"What's wrong?" he asked, removing his handkerchief from his suit jacket and wiping away the lonely tear that slowly crept down my right cheek.

"I can just remember the night at the hotel when we first met. When I told you about my dream of becoming an author. You believed in me, Terrence, more than I believed in myself back then."

"Of course, I did. I could see in you what you didn't see in yourself at that time. That's what friends do, right?"

He took my hand and gently massaged it. I wanted to pull my hand away, or at least I knew that I should, but truth be told, his touch was what I needed and wanted most.

"Wow. I can't believe we're both standing here right now, especially after all that's happened between us," I said.

"Yeah, me either." He brushed my hair away from my face with his other hand. "But you know that I wouldn't have missed this for the world. My friend, once my lover and always my heart, is a whole published author. You've made your dreams come true, Tiff, and I'm so very proud of you."

I watched his lips the entire time he spoke and daydreamed about them kissing me and working their way from my lips down my entire body. I had to admit that the chemistry between us was still electric, although my mind quickly started to tell me to pull away before I got burned.

"Thank you, Terrence. I really appreciate that," I said, removing my hand from his and stepping back a few inches. I squirmed a bit as stillness filled the room. We both suddenly appeared awkward and anxious all at the same time in each other's presence.

"Um, listen, I also came because I wanted to apologize again for everything that happened, Tiff. I'll never forgive myself for how I treated you, and I just want the opportunity to make things up to you."

I heard his words, but I wasn't quite sure if I believed them. Deep down I wanted to, but my mind kept reminding me that I'd heard it all before. Folding my arms and walking a few steps away, I tried to bring some closure to this.

"Listen, there's no need to make up anything to me. What happened, happened, and it's all over now. We've both moved on, and we're happy. That's all that matters."

"Speaking of moving on, I would like to share something with you." I felt him step a little closer to me as he spoke.

"Oh really? And what's that?"

"This." He held up a piece of paper, a certificate of some kind. I took it out of his hands, and as I examined it closely, my jaw dropped from utter shock.

"Terrence, oh my goodness. This is the deed to Montgomery's Barbecue and Soul Food Restaurant. Wow! This is amazing," I screeched.

"Yeah, I finally got my own building about a month ago. I'm all done with fixing it up, and the grand opening is tomorrow. I had wanted to share it with you before now, but I wasn't sure if . . . well, you know."

"Well, congratulations. I'm so happy for you."

After closing the remaining space between us, I threw my arms around his broad shoulders in excitement and pressed my lips against his. Without hesitation, he kissed me back. It reminded me of the very first time we'd ever kissed, and just like then, I got lost in his affection. The kiss was so tender and passionate, and his lips tasted so good to me, that I didn't want to stop. Our tongues played melodically with each other as our lips found their home. Until I suddenly realized what was happening.

"Oh my God! I'm, I'm, I'm so sorry I did that. I guess I got a bit caught up in the excitement of it all," I said, pulling away from him nervously.

"It's okay, baby. I've missed that, your lips and their softness next to mine. I could tell that you missed it too."

At once, our eyes met, and his were practically undressing me. Although my body longed for him as well, my mind said no, especially with what was taking place in the next few days.

"Terrence, there's something I need to tell you."

"Sure, of course, but there's a couple of other things I wanted to share with you first. Now, I don't know if it will change things with you and me, but—"

"Terrence, wait, please," I said, cutting him off before he went any further. "What is all of this even about? I mean, showing up here today, congratulating me on my book, telling me about the restaurant. What does all this mean? Because it's been an entire year, and so much has happened that you're not aware of. And besides, it's not like anything that you say or do right now is going to change what happened in the past."

"Baby, look, I know I made some stupid mistakes back then. I realize that. But you're right. It's been a whole year, and I've changed during that time. I'm a completely different man than who you knew before. I'm a better man, a healed man, and I just want the chance for us to have what we should have had back then."

"Oh, I see. And I'm supposed to simply run back to you with open arms just like that, right? I'm supposed to believe what you say now when you made the same promises then? Do you remember, Terrence? You promised that you would love me, protect me, and prove to me that there were still some good and decent men left. You promised that I would never feel the same pain I felt with David. And we even made a pact not to let anything or anyone come between us.

"But out of nowhere, you allowed all those other women into your life, your bed and, most of all, your heart. And in return, you treated me like I never meant shit to you when I was the very one giving you my heart and soul unconditionally. I lost myself, Terrence, while I practically made you God in my life. But what hurt the most out of everything was that you didn't even have the decency to be the *friend* that I thought you were." I turned my back, remembering the promise I had made to myself that I would never allow him, or any other man, to see me cry over him again.

"Tiff, please." I felt his hand touch my shoulder. "You have to understand, I couldn't love you the right way back then, because I didn't even know how to love myself. All I did was go from toxic relationship to toxic relationship, without allowing myself to ever heal and find me again. And out of my own selfishness and stupidity, I made some fucked-up choices. I wasn't fair to you, those other women, or even myself. But, baby, when you left my life, things finally became clear to me. I knew what I needed to do."

It was in that moment that I turned to face him.

"So, things didn't become clear until I left? You couldn't see what was staring you in the face until I was no longer available to you? All the mess you took me through with this woman and that woman, only to realize what you had when it was too late. And now you come back? When everyone else has walked away? You come right back to silly, gullible Tiffany, right?"

"Listen, I know you're still upset. You have the right to hate me, and I deserve everything that you're dishing out right now. But the fact is we can't go back and change what happened. Tiff, I can change only my future, our future, baby. That's why I wanted to show you these today."

"What, Terrence? What on earth could you possibly have to show me that would make any bit of a difference?"

"Honestly, I don't know if it'll make a difference, but I at least hope they'll show you how serious I am about the fact that I've changed. This one is my certificate of dissolution of my marriage. I officially divorced Patricia. And just so you know, I never went through with marrying Malaysia. I was never in love with her, and that relationship never should have happened."

I stood there with my arms folded and my lips curled up, as if to say, "So what?" And then I waved my hand at the other document in his hand. "And the other piece of paper?"

"Well, this one is what I'm proud of most. It's my certificate of baptism. I rededicated my life to Christ and got baptized. I'm trying to live my life for me and God now, and that's all that matters. I want to elevate myself in every way possible. I have my business, my home, joint custody of my girls. The only thing that's missing, Tiff, is you."

Part of me wanted to scream. I couldn't believe Terrence had the audacity to show up here today, of all days, and throw all of this on me right now. His timing was way off, and I was furious at him, and at God even, for this practical joke being played on me.

"Terrence, I—"

"Baby, don't you still love me? I can see it in your eyes, and I felt it in our kiss. So, just tell me that you still do."

"But you don't understand, Terrence. It's been an entire year."

"Listen, I get that, all right? I know we've both made a lot of changes, but I know our love for one another hasn't changed. I mean, can you really stand here right now and look me in my eyes and say from your heart that you no longer love me? Because if you can do that, then I will apologize for coming here today, and I will promise I'll never bother you again. But I need you to look at me and say those words, because I still love you, and I'm *in love* with you. My feelings never went anywhere and never will."

He walked closer to me and took my hands in his again. With everything circling my mind, I put my head down, feeling as if I was going to pass out at any second. Then I looked back up at him as three words were about to leave my lips. Suddenly, I was brought back to reality.

"Hey, baby. I have everything packed up, if you're almost finished in here," he said as he walked up behind me. Terrence quickly dropped my hands and took a few steps back.

"Oh yeah, sweetheart, I'm pretty much done. Just signing one last book here for an old friend of mine. Uh, Andre, this is Terrence Montgomery. Terrence, this is my, um, fiancé, Andre. Honey, he's having his grand opening of his restaurant tomorrow, and he stopped by to tell me," I said nervously while smiling and trying my best to play off what had almost taken place between Terrence and me.

Terrence didn't utter a word as they both shook hands.

"Really? What kind of food will you serve, man?" Andre asked, not noticing my or Terrence's discomfort.

"Uh, barbecue and soul food mainly."

"Oh, that sounds great. Tiff and I have been looking for a good soul food spot out here. Unfortunately, we can't make it tomorrow, with all the craziness of the wedding, but we'll definitely stop through and see you very soon."

"Uh, yeah, that sounds good. I look forward to having you two there." Terrence didn't crack a smile, but as he glanced at me, his eyes said everything he couldn't.

"All right, well, I'll let you finish up your business here with your friend, and I'll be outside waiting, okay? And, Terrence, man, it was nice meeting you. Take it easy and good luck on your new business." Andre kissed my cheek and rushed out.

Once he had left, the moment I was afraid of was right back upon us.

"Wow. So, you're engaged?" Terrence asked, looking down at my ring finger.

"Uh, yeah, I am. Andre asked me about three months ago, but we've been together for some time now. My, uh, ring is a little too big, so I won't be wearing it until after the wedding."

"I see. And when is the wedding?"

"It's actually in three days."

"Whoa. Three days." A somewhat pained look came across his face. "I guess it's true what they say, then, huh?

That it doesn't take a man long to know when the right woman has entered his life."

"Yeah, I guess so."

Terrence turned around and started to walk away. Then his footsteps stopped, and he looked back at me. "Are you happy, Tiff?"

"What? Why would you ask me something like that? I mean, you saw for yourself how things went today. Plus, I have a whole new start on life, a book deal, thousands of readers, and I'm about to marry a wonderful man. So, what more could I ask for?"

"All right. Then if you're happy, it would be easy to say so. So, say it. Just tell me you're truly happy and you're no longer in love with me, and I'll walk away." He threw both his hands up, as if he were surrendering.

"All right." I took a deep breath, stood up straight, and looked him square in the eyes. "So, you promise to walk away for good and never disrupt my life again?"

"Yeah, I promise."

"Okay, then, I am happy, Terrence. And . . . and I'm not in love with you anymore."

He looked at me as if I'd given him the shock of his life. In fact, neither of us said anything else from that point on. In the silence Terrence turned around and walked away from me. The second he reached the doorway and stepped through it, though, my breathing became heavy and rapid. All the feelings that I'd held inside for the past year came crashing down on me, and I wanted to stop him, but I knew that I couldn't. Then my eyes shifted away from the door and connected with the one copy of my book still lying on the table. The words *I didn't think you existed* stared back at me. I reached over, picked up the book, and held it close to my heart.

"I do still love you, Terrence, and I always will."

CHAPTER 57

TERRENCE

"Married, Monica? Really? And in three days? Why didn't you tell me before I went over there and made a complete fool of myself?"

"Hey, wait a minute. When Todd and I were here earlier, I tried to tell you, but you refused to go to the book signing. How was I supposed to know you would show up there, after all? But now that you do know, what do you plan to do about it?"

"What do you mean, what do I plan to do? What can I do? The girl is getting married in three days, dammit. Besides, she said she's happy and doesn't love me anymore, so there's nothing I can do."

"You know that's a lie, Terrence. You know it."

I pulled out a chair at one of the tables, sat down, and put my head in my hands. After leaving the book signing, instead of driving home, I had come right back to the restaurant and had had Monica meet me here. I was hoping that she could somehow help me make sense of everything, but the truth was, this was all my fault. I'd made such a mess of things last year that I had practically pushed Tiffany into the arms of another man, and now she was marrying him.

"Look. " I heard Monica pull up a chair next to me and felt her hand on my knee. "I know she cares about Andre, but she's not in love with him, not the way she is with you."

"Yeah, well, that's not what came from her mouth. Where did she even meet this character anyway? Does she know him well enough to marry him?" I asked. When I didn't hear Monica say anything, I looked at her with suspicion and asked again. "Monica, where did she meet him?"

She hesitated a few minutes longer, looking around and bouncing her knee, and then she stood up and spit it out. "I introduced her to him, okay?"

"You what? Why would you do that? How could you?" I jumped up.

"Listen, hold up, Terrence. It was a long time ago, all right? You still had so much going on with Patricia, and you weren't giving her a definite answer on the two of you. I only wanted her to have something, or *someone*, to take her mind away from you."

"Oh, well, thanks a lot. She sure has someone to take her mind completely off me now."

"Look, don't go blaming any of this on me when you've had woman after woman in your life. I was only looking out for my friend. Hell, as far as I knew, she didn't even like Andre when they first met. She hadn't even told me that they got together until they were several months in."

"I'm sorry. I'm not trying to blame you. I just don't understand." I sat back down and tried to collect my thoughts. "But earlier you said that she might be making the mistake of her life. Why would you say that if you introduced them? What is it that you're trying *not* to say, Monica?"

"I have to go, all right?" She threw her purse on her shoulder and headed toward the door. "Just think about everything I said. I know Tiffany still loves you just as much as you love her. All I want is for both of you to be happy, and as crazy as it is, that's with each other. So, you have three days. Exactly three days to get her back."

She gave me a wave and walked out, leaving me to my thoughts.

"Three days to decide if I'm about to do something that will turn both my and Tiffany's world upside down, all while I have a grand opening tomorrow," I said aloud to myself. As I headed to lock up my office, I heard the door open again.

"What did you forget, Monica?" I called while turning off the light in my office and locking the door. I headed back up front to see why she hadn't answered me. I stopped in my tracks when I saw the woman standing there.

"Oh, hey there. What are you doing here? Where are the girls? Did I miss my weekend or something?" I asked.

"Uh, no, they're with my parents."

"All right. Well, is everything okay?"

"Kind of." Kayla stood there, obviously needing to say something.

"What do you mean, kind of?"

"Terrence, I'm sorry for stopping by like this, but I wasn't sure how to approach this with you."

"I don't understand. Approach what?" I pulled out a chair for her to sit down, and when she did, I sat across from her and waited for her to spit out whatever she needed to say.

"Well, I know a lot has happened between us over the years, and when we first divorced, I could never see us getting back together. But I've been thinking lately, and I find it strange that I'm single now and so are you. And I guess it made me wonder if things were supposed to turn out this way. You know, if maybe this was all a part of God's plan for us."

"I don't think I'm following what you're saying."

"Look, there's no better way for me to do this than to just come right out and say it. I came here today hoping that we could talk, Terrence, about us. I would love to give our daughters the opportunity to have a real family again, with both their parents. And the truth of the matter is that I never really stopped loving you. Even while I was married, sometimes I wished it was you."

Her words caught me completely off guard. Never would I have expected her to approach me this way. Now that it was happening, I wasn't sure how to respond, especially with the state my personal life was in. She was right about the fact that it was strange we were both single at present. And I agreed that we owed our daughters a chance to have a real family. Not to mention, Tiffany had made it very clear that she was moving on without me. So, with all that in mind, I decided maybe it was time for me to step up and do what I needed to do. If for nothing else than for the sake of my girls.

CHAPTER 58

TIFFANY

The wonderful feeling I'd had from the day's events had completely disappeared. Ever since Terrence had left the bookstore, he was all I'd been able to think about. I couldn't deny how much I had wanted to throw my arms around him and declare my undying love. But then there was a part of me that hated him for showing up at my book signing, especially since I had thought I was so sure of everything in my life.

Andre and I had made it home all of thirty minutes ago. The ride itself had been oddly quiet. Normally, we would be laughing and talking about anything and everything or singing along with whatever oldie but goodie was playing on Sirius. However, not this time. Instead, I had gazed out the window, thinking of everything related to Terrence Montgomery, including the kiss we had shared earlier. Of course, Andre had no clue about it, so I had assumed his silence was simply an effort to leave me to my own thoughts about the day. Either way, all I had wanted was get home, close my eyes, and try to forget what had happened between me and Terrence. I also needed to prepare somehow for the wedding in three days, one that now I wasn't so sure needed to happen.

After stepping into my steam-filled bathroom, where I'd started the water for my shower the second we walked through the door, I allowed my pink satin robe to fall off my shoulders and hit the floor. I closed the bathroom door, then wiped the foggy mirror clean to reveal myself. Looking at the reflection staring back at me, I wondered who the woman in the mirror really was. Never would I have imagined kissing another man while I was engaged to Andre, especially when that other man was Terrence. Now I was even having second thoughts about saying, "I do."

What are you going to do, Tiffany? Are you really going to marry this man, knowing your heart is truly with someone else? I asked myself.

Seconds later, I got into the shower and allowed the water to shoot into every crevice of my body. As I took it all in, I prayed that it would wash away all the doubts in the back of my mind. But with my eyes shut, all I could picture was Terrence, and my lips against his. Slowly but surely, tears started to force their way down my cheeks.

God, why is this happening right now? Please tell me what to do.

As I continued to talk to God in my mind and succumb to the water pouring down my head, I felt Andre's body press against the back of mine. I could tell that he wanted my affection, but there was no way I could give it to him, especially not in the state that I was in. At once, my eyes shot open, and I stopped his hands the minute they gripped my breasts.

"I'm sorry, baby. I'm really not in the mood tonight, okay?" Without giving him an opportunity to offer a rebuttal, I pushed his body away from me and hopped out of the shower. As quickly as possible, I grabbed my towel, wrapped it around my body, and went into the bedroom.

How can I let this happen? I thought. *Here I am supposed to marry this wonderful man in the next few days, yet I can't pull my thoughts away from Terrence.*

My thoughts were interrupted by the sound of the water being shut off in the bathroom. Not wanting to discuss anything, I hurried to lie down and throw the covers over me before he came into the room. A few minutes of complete silence went by before I finally felt him take his side of the bed.

"I know you're not asleep, Tiffany." He waited, but I remained quiet. "Tiffany?" he repeated.

I started to moan and move about, as if I had fallen into a deep sleep and was on the verge of waking. "What's wrong, baby?" I whispered, never turning over to look at him.

"Okay, so we're going to play this 'I'm fast asleep in two seconds game,' huh?"

"Andre, honey, it's been a long day, and I'm extremely tired. Can we just get some rest and talk in the morning?"

"This is because of him, isn't it?"

"What? Who is him?" I questioned, trying to buy some time to figure out how I would approach this conversation he was so determined to have.

"You know who I'm referring to. Your friend Terrence."

The minute I heard his name come from Andre's mouth, I could practically feel my bladder threatening to fail me. That was how nervous I was. I wasn't sure where this line of questioning was going, but I was positive I wanted it to end fast.

"Honey, Terrence is just an old friend, like I said at the bookstore, okay? He stopped by to support me and tell me his news about his restaurant. That's it. I mean, I know you're not jealous, are you?" I gave a slight chuckle, basically to say that would be insane.

For a second, he didn't respond, but everything inside me knew he was staring directly at me. That was when he said the one thing that would make me sit straight up and confirm his suspicions that I was, in fact, awake the whole time.

"No, I'm not jealous. But just so that you and I are on the same page, I want you to end your friendship with Mr. Montgomery. Oh, and I hope you didn't have any plans on attending his grand opening."

I sat up straight in the bed. "You're joking right, Andre? So, now we're saying who each other's friends can be?" I replied, my voice strong.

"And I thought you were extremely tired. I guess you found enough energy to talk from somewhere, huh?" The sarcasm in his voice started to piss me off.

"Don't play with me, Andre. Now, I'm not sure if your ego has been threatened or something, but Terrence and I have been friends for a long time now. I'm not going to turn my back on him."

"Turn your back on him? Look, I don't care how long it's been. If you're going to be *my wife*, it ends now," he shouted while getting up and snatching the blanket and his pillow off the bed.

"Where are you going? We're not done talking about this." I jumped up, too, and followed right behind him.

"Yeah, we are done, because now I'm the one that's extremely tired. So, it's your choice from here, Tiff. It's either me or Terrence." With that said, he marched into the guest room and slammed the door shut in my face without another word.

Walking back to our master suite, I thought how as long as I'd known Andre, I'd never seen him that angry, and he'd never talked to me or yelled at me in such a manner. But the scariest part of all was the look in his eyes. If looks could kill, I would have already been dead. Crawling back into our king-sized bed, I felt a teardrop fall from my eye and hit the pillow.

I cried out to God. "Lord, please tell me what to do. If this isn't for me, let me know before I make the biggest mistake of my life."

CHAPTER 59

TERRENCE

"Terrence? Terrence?" I suddenly heard Monica's voice but had no idea when she'd come into my office or how long she'd been standing there. "I stopped by your house, and when I saw that you weren't there, I figured I might find you here. The door was unlocked up front, so I let myself in. Are you okay?"

Without answering her question, I looked at her from head to toe. Her face was adorned in shades of soft pink and shimmers of gold. Her hair was in pin curls. She wore a white T-shirt with bold lettering that stated MATRON OF THE BRIDE and some ripped jeans.

"Today's the big day, huh? Don't you think you should be headed to the church instead of standing here harassing me?" I muttered as I sat in my chair behind the desk.

"*Harassing* you? That's a stretch. I only came by to see how things went with the opening and, well, to make sure you were all right, so you don't have to take that tone with me."

"I guess the opening was as good as can be expected. It seemed like I kept my eyes on the door, thinking that she would show up at any minute, saying she'd changed her mind. And, of course, that never happened. So, you want to know if I'm okay, Monica? No, I'm not. I screwed up so bad last year and over the years before that, and I've hurt both women I've ever really loved in my life. Now today one is vowing her life to another man, and now that I've been given a second chance with the other, I don't actually want it."

"What? Who? What other woman are you talking about?"

Realizing I may have been talking too much, I tried to brush off what I'd said. "Just forget I said anything, all right? You have a wedding to attend, so maybe you should go and leave me to myself."

The room was silent, and I realized that she had caught sight of the half-empty bottle of alcohol on my desk. She went over and picked it up. "Or leave you to this, you mean? Drinking on the job now, Terrence?"

"Look, I'm a grown man and the owner of this establishment, if you didn't remember. I can have a drink anytime I damn well please, okay?"

"Dammit, Terrence. I'm not the enemy here. I've tried nothing more than to be a good friend to both you and Tiff. Now, I may have made a mistake by introducing her to Andre. I realize that. But I plan on talking to her once more before she walks down that aisle, and I needed to come by here and speak with you too. However, I won't be yelled at or spoken to disrespectfully for trying to make both of you stop this madness before she makes a huge mistake. But, Terrence, if you'd rather sit here and drown your sorrows in this bottle, then you go right ahead. I'm wiping my hands clean of this entire situation." She set the bottle down and headed toward the door.

"Monica, wait!" I jumped up from the chair, grabbed her arm, put my arms around her, and hugged her. "I'm sorry, okay? Everything is just all messed up, and I don't have a clue how to fix it."

"Honey, call her, text her or, hell, go to the church with me. But if you love her the way I know you still do, then please stop this wedding."

"You don't know how bad I really want to do that, but I already hurt Tiff enough last year. If she's truly happy, then I don't want to disturb that, not for the sake of my own happiness."

"You know, you and her are two of the most stubborn and bullheaded people I know. That's why I'm positive you belong together."

"I wish you were right about that, Monica. But the more things play out, the more I'm thinking that maybe it's not in the cards for us, especially now. I mean, in a few hours she'll be the wife of another man. I have to respect that."

"My mother used to always tell me not to put my trust in what I see or hear, and to only trust God's hand. You just never know what He has in store, despite what it looks like. Now, you might see that in a few short hours she'll be married, but I refuse to say that until I hear the minister pronounce them husband and wife."

"I hear you, but I also don't want to force anything, either, by trying to stop it. If it's meant to be, then I guess we'll have to see how this all plays out. But I will say that you didn't hear the tone of her voice or see the look in her eyes when she told me she was happy and not in love with me anymore. That right there was pretty convincing for me."

"Well, I didn't have to be there to hear anything of the sort to say I still don't believe it. If I know Tiffany the way I believe I do, she accepted the proposal in the first place only to try to get over you. Now, of course, I'm not suggesting that she doesn't care about Andre, but I know who her heart is really with."

Her words suddenly reminded me of something. I went over to my desk drawer, opened it, and pulled out a small blue box with a white ribbon tied into a bow. "I was debating with myself whether or not I wanted to get this to her, but since you're here, would you please take it for me?" I held it out for her to take.

"I can do that, but only if you're absolutely sure you don't want to take it yourself."

"I'm positive, Monica."

She took the box from my hand and put her head down in disappointment.

"Please, tell her that I wish her all the best and I'm happy for her," I said.

At first, Monica didn't say anything else and turned around and walked to the door, ready to head out. But then she turned back around in the doorway. "By the way, who is this other woman you mentioned?"

I debated with myself whether I wanted to tell her about the girls' mother and the proposition she'd given me. However, knowing Monica as well as I did, I knew she would never understand, so I decided against it.

"Trust me, it's not important, all right?" was all I said.

"Okay, if you say so, but I hope Patricia is not coming back around with any of her devilish schemes. Although you don't want to admit it, you know you had a soft spot for that woman." She stood in the doorway, refusing to leave until I reassured her that Patricia was not in the picture again.

"No, Monica, it isn't Pat. But trust me, if anything should come about, then I promise you'll be the first to know. Right now, though, there's nothing to talk about."

She looked at me once more with suspicion in her eyes, but not wanting to press the issue any further, I assumed, she finally turned to leave. I didn't let her leave until I had hugged her once more. When I was alone again, I locked the front door so that I wouldn't have any more unexpected visitors.

Back and forth from Tiffany to Kayla my thoughts went. I loved Tiff with all my heart, but the fact of the matter was she was beginning a whole new life with a different man. I had to let her go. Then there was Kayla.

While I was married to Pat, I had always felt that if only I had the opportunity to go back and do it all over again with Kayla, I would. Yet now I wasn't so sure if I even needed to open that can of worms, especially since the only reason for it was the girls.

I picked up my cell phone and looked at the picture of my daughters plastered across the screen.

"Maybe I should at least try. You two deserve that much."

CHAPTER 60

TIFFANY

Today was officially the day, and for the first time in the past two days, I felt on top of the world. Although there was still a small bit of tension between Andre and me, I'd already promised myself that nothing or no one from this point forward would get in the way of my happiness or future with him, not even Terrence. I had realized last night that I had to be out of my mind even to consider giving up what I had with Andre. Especially with it being based on one encounter with the very one who had caused me so much heartache the past couple of years. So, if Andre felt it necessary for me to end my friendship with Terrence, then as his soon-to-be wife, I had to respect it, and I was ready to do just that. My only hope was that Terrence would respect it as well.

Upon opening both my eyes, I looked over, hoping to give my fiancé a huge kiss on the lips. However, instead of finding him there, I found a breakfast tray with a little card on top addressed to Mrs. Williams.

"Tiffany Williams, Mrs. Tiffany Williams, Mrs. Tiffany Tate-Williams." I let the name roll off my tongue several different ways to see how it sounded. However, none of them had a ring to it in the way that Tiffany Tate or Tiffany Tate-Montgomery did. Nonetheless, Williams was about to be my new name, so I needed to find some way to adjust.

My mouth began watering the minute I uncovered the tray to find scrambled eggs, fluffy waffles, bacon, fresh fruit, and glasses of orange juice and water.

You are absolutely amazing, Andre Williams. But do you really think I'm going to eat all of this on the morning of our wedding? I thought while opening the card.

> *Good morning, beautiful,*
> *First, I want to sincerely apologize for our mis-understanding the other night. I never should have yelled at you the way I did. I'm sorry, and I hope you can forgive me. I also want to say that if I haven't expressed it already, I am overjoyed by the mere thought of becoming your husband. I love you, Tiff, and I look forward to showing you how much every day for the rest of our lives. So, if you'll still have me, then please get ready to meet me at the altar, and don't be late.*
> *Hugs and Kisses,*
> *—Andre*

If there were still any lingering doubts in the back of my mind, he'd made sure to remove them all with this. I had started to nibble and peck at my breakfast when someone knocked on the door and made their way inside the room, without giving me a chance to say, "Come in."

"Hurry up, girl! Today's the day, and we need to get you over to the church," Monica yelled as she plopped down on the bed.

I couldn't seem to stop smiling after she said that. "Okay, okay. I'm just having a quick bite to eat, and I'll be ready to go in a second. Is my husband still out there?"

"He's not your husband yet, and he might not be if you continue sitting here, trying to eat that entire breakfast," she joked. "You won't even be able to fit into your dress, let alone waddle down the aisle. But seriously, he already left for the church when he let me in."

"Okay. Good." I turned serious all at once. "Mon, can I ask you something?"

"Of course. What's up, girl?" She appeared concerned.

"Did you have any anxiousness and jitters, and did you second-guess yourself on your wedding day?"

"Uh, a little nervousness? Sure. I think that's natural. But, Tiff, if you're second-guessing your entire decision, then maybe—"

I didn't let her finish. "Maybe what?" I asked. "You think I should call off this wedding, don't you?" I looked her square in the eyes, trying to search for the truth of her words.

"Honey, no, I never said that. All I'm saying is, if you're not absolutely sure that Andre is the man you should spend the rest of your life with, then maybe you should hold off a little while, until you *are* sure. I mean, things did move pretty quickly with you two." Her words were mumbled toward the end.

"I can't hold off a little on the morning of my wedding, Monica. And Andre *is* who I want to be with. I only said I was feeling a bit anxious. Besides, if not Andre, then who? Terrence?" I said sarcastically.

"Look, I never said Terrence's name. You did."

"You know, he stopped by the book signing the other day." I got up, slid my white robe on, and walked over to the window. "He came to congratulate me on the book and apologize again for everything that happened in the past. He even had the nerve to suggest we try to start over. At least that was until Andre walked in, and luckily, it was after we kissed."

"What? You and Terrence kissed? He never—" Her words immediately came to a halt, as she realized what she was saying.

"Wait a minute." I slowly turned around to face her. "So, you already knew? All this time you knew that he planned on coming there, and you never said a word to me? Did you invite him? Did you and he set all of this up?"

"Tiff, no, no. Listen." She hopped up, walked over to me, and grabbed both my hands in hers. "I'm not going to lie to you. Did I suggest to Terrence that he should stop by? Yes, I did. But it's only because I know how much you still love him, and he loves you."

"And you also know how much he hurt me over and over again last year. Why would you want me to go back to that?"

"Because people change, Tiff, especially when they allow God to change them."

"I guess he's gotten to you, too, huh? Because that's the same piece of garbage he said to me."

"Look, I see the change in him, just like I've witnessed the change in you over the past year. You have to admit that you're definitely not the same person who went lurking outside his home in the middle of the night."

"Oh wow! So, what? Now we're blaming everything on me?"

"Of course, I'm not. But all I wanted was for both of you to get to know the people you are today, and to put aside the ones who made all those foolish mistakes back then. I mean, you two were truly your own worst enemies, but you've grown and matured and healed, Tiff. And I'm sorry. Maybe I went about things all the wrong way, but I didn't mean any harm, okay? But look, if you're completely over him and truly want to be Mrs. Andre Williams, then who am I to say any different? This is your life, and only you know what makes you happy."

"Thank you. Because I am happy, Monica. I really am, and it's all because of Andre." We looked at one another, both with tear-filled eyes.

"All right, well, then, stop second-guessing things. If there's one thing I do know for sure, it is that Andre adores you. I can tell. And if he didn't, then he wouldn't be here. So just let everything else fade from your mind and focus on marrying your man. Can you do that for me?"

"Yeah, I think I can," I whispered as we hugged one another.

"Good. Now I will start loading some things into the limo, while you hurry up and get dressed so that we can get to the church. Oh, but before I forget, please don't hate me for this, but I'm supposed to give this to you." She pulled out a Tiffany-blue box with a white ribbon wrapped around it and handed it to me.

I looked at the box sitting in my hand, and I instantly knew exactly who it was from.

"Are you going to open it?" she asked, wanting to know, I assumed, what was inside it as much as I did. So, without any further hesitation, I untied the ribbon and opened the top. All at once a rush of tears began to stream down my face as I pulled out the key inside and read the engravement.

YOU WILL ALWAYS HOLD THE KEY TO MY HEART—TERRENCE

Monica gazed at me with a flushed face full of tears. "Okay, I'm only going to say this one last time, and then I'll leave it all alone. If you're having any doubts at all, Tiff, then it's not too late to call things off."

"Monica, I'm okay, really. Just a little caught off guard, but trust me, I'm fine."

"Okay, then I won't say anything else. But if you feel, for any reason, that you need to back out before you say, 'I do,' then just do it. I'll handle everything, I promise."

I hugged her one final time, assuring her of my decision. "Trust me, I'm fine. I'm ready to marry this wonderful man of mine. So, can we please hurry up already and get me down that aisle?"

"Of course, sweetie."

I tried not to let her apprehensive words or Terrence's gift bother me. Instead, I hurried to take a shower so that she and I could head over to the church. In just a few short hours, all my dreams would come true, and I would be Mrs. Andre Williams.

A few hours later, I heard beautiful music begin to play softly in the sanctuary of the church. That was my signal that it was almost time.

"You can do this, Tiffany. Andre loves you, and you love him. Your forever starts now," I whispered to the nervous woman staring back at me in the mirror. Yet it seemed that no matter how much I had tried, I still hadn't succeeded in removing the events of the other night completely from my mind. It wasn't so much that Andre had given me an ultimatum to choose between him or Terrence or that he had yelled at me that way. All of that I could get past. But it was the look in his eyes that night that still made me fearful and gave me chills every time I thought about it. With such dismaying thoughts on my mind, the knock on the door a second later made me practically jump out of my skin. Monica peeked in.

"Okay, girl. They're playing your song out there." She walked over to me and fixed my veil one last time. "Are you good? You ready?" she asked, looking into my eyes.

"I think I'm as ready as I'm going to get," I said, hoping that she couldn't sense my fear. "And Andre, is he—"

"Standing at the altar, waiting patiently for you," she said, cutting me off. Then she kissed the side of my cheek, as it was time for her to go out before me. As she led the way, I took one last glance at myself in the mirror before pulling the veil over my face.

When the pianist began playing the traditional wedding song, I took a deep breath and made my way into the sanctuary. Immediately, at the entrance, I could hear gasps and chatter from everyone in the audience. As I stood there for a moment or two, I looked around and took in the gorgeous sight of all my and Andre's family and friends. The church itself was breathtaking and was pretty much decorated for a princess. That was when it suddenly dawned on me: I was that princess.

I stared straight ahead down the long aisle garnished with red and pink rose petals, and I saw Andre waiting for me. The look on his face finally set my spirit at ease and told me I was doing the right thing. Now I didn't see the evilness that had lain within his eyes the other night. Instead, I saw a man that loved and adored me and was just as nervous as I was to take the leap of faith we were taking. At once, I knew that Monica was right. If he didn't want to be here, then he wouldn't be.

The music played as my eldest brother took his position beside me—in place of my father, now deceased—to lead me to my king. He, along with all the other groomsmen, looked dapper in his all-black tux. Monica and my bridesmaids looked simply classic and elegant in their black dresses. Andre and I were the only ones dressed in white. As I looked ahead at my beautiful wedding party, I realized that one person was missing—Keisha. She hated that I wasn't marrying Terrence and felt that I barely knew Andre enough to marry him. She hated even more that Monica was my matron of honor, and I'd asked her to be only a bridesmaid. Given that, she had chosen not to be here, but I still held her close to my heart. I knew she would soon get over it and one day would regret that she hadn't shared in this moment with me.

Now the moment I'd been waiting for was here. Our pace was slow and steady as we stepped down the aisle.

I tried my best to savor every single second. As I looked around the sanctuary, I exhaled upon witnessing all the smiles, tear-filled eyes, and camera flashes. This was the very moment I'd longed for all my life, and here it was, only a few more footsteps away.

Once I made it to the front, my brother handed me off to Andre, who took my arm in his while whispering softly in my ear, "Thank you for choosing me."

The ceremony started, and we partook of all the normal elements of a wedding: the singing of the Lord's Prayer, the opening remarks, and the charge to the couple. While all this was taking place, I couldn't seem to let Andre's words escape my mind. What exactly did he mean by *choosing* him? Was he referring to the other night and his ultimatum that I choose between him and Terrence? Or was I simply overthinking this and his words were genuine and sincere?

That was the only thing I could seem to concentrate on. Time must have gotten away from me, too, because out of nowhere, the exchanging of our vows was upon us. After Andre and I joined hands, I set my eyes on him and saw little beads of sweat form on his forehead when the officiant looked at him. Then the officiant began.

"Andre Williams, do you take Tiffany Tate to be your wife, to have and to hold from this day forward, for better or for worse, for richer or for poorer, in sickness and in health, to love and to cherish, till death do you part, according to God's holy law?"

Andre stared at me and remained awkwardly quiet. I had no idea what was going on, as it seemed as if he was struggling to get his words out. But a second later, he smiled at me and open his mouth to speak, and all my tensions again eased.

"I do. For the rest of my life, I do."

"Uh, you only have to say it once, young man," the officiant joked, and laughter echoed throughout the sanctuary. Then the officiant looked at me.

"Tiffany Tate, do you take Mr. Andre Williams to be your husband, to have and to hold from this day forward, for better or for worse, for richer or for poorer, in sickness and in health, to love and to cherish, till death do you part, according to God's holy law?"

I heard the words from the officiant, but before I could answer a strange feeling came over me. In my mind Andre was saying that I needed to choose between him and Terrence, and at that very moment I realized I couldn't. Slowly, I gazed over at him. He appeared anxious and angry from my lack of a response. Then, out of nowhere, I noticed that same look in his eyes that he'd had the other night, a look that conveyed that he would kill me if I made the wrong choice. I began to sweat a little and to squirm as I glanced at all the faces, which were silently asking me if I was okay and were encouraging me to say, "I do."

"I . . . I—" I couldn't get the words out.

"C'mon, baby, and say it. Don't you dare do what I think you're doing!" Andre whispered through a fake smile and gritted teeth.

"I . . . I—" No words followed.

Andre tightened his grip on my hands. As he squeezed my fingers, my breathing became labored, as if I was fighting for air. It was then that I knew something wasn't right and I had made a very wrong decision.

"I'm sorry, Andre. I can't," I whispered.

"Tiffany, don't do this. Whatever is going on, we can fix it after the wedding. Baby, c'mon and just say, 'I do.'"

"I can't. I love you, I really do, but my heart belongs to him." I pulled away from his grasp and looked back at Monica.

She grabbed my arm and whispered in my ear, "I already have the limo and driver out there waiting for you and ready to take you to the restaurant. Go, go. Get out of here."

I took off down the aisle, and as I went, everything was such a blur that I wasn't fully sure what I'd done or what to do next. As I left the sanctuary as fast as I could, all I could hear was the commotion going on behind me. Andre's voice yelling my name, along with the screams and frantic chatter of the guests, faded away when I finally reached the limo. Whatever was happening inside that church no longer mattered to me. All I wanted and needed was to get to Terrence.

After I got in the limo, the driver confirmed Monica's instructions. I wasn't sure how she had known that I would do this, but I thanked God that she had followed her first mind and had not listened to what I'd said before the wedding.

"I am to take you to a restaurant, correct, ma'am?"

"Uh, yes, that's correct. Can you please get me away from here and get me there as quickly as possible?"

"Of course." He nodded his head in acknowledgment and pulled off without any other questions asked.

A few minutes after driving off, he let down the glass that separated the two of us and handed my cell phone to me, informing me that I had a phone call. I guessed Monica must have given him that as well.

"Hello?"

"Hey, Tiff. It's me."

"Monica, I—"

"Honey, look, don't try to explain. I told you, I already knew deep down what might happen, and I have you covered. Now, I've made an announcement to all the guests, and slowly but surely, they've started leaving. Your family, of course, has a million questions, but I've been able to satisfy everyone's curiosity with a simple, 'She'll be in touch.' But just know, this isn't going to be easy."

"Yeah, don't I know it. And Andre?"

"Well, you and I both know that he's not happy at all. I was able to get Todd and the other groomsmen to take him somewhere to try to calm him down. But, trust me, he's pissed. Eventually, he'll be all right, so don't worry about him. His ego is bruised, I'm sure, but he's a man, so he'll bounce back quick. My only concern right now, however, is you. Are you okay?"

"I think so. I just feel so horrible for what I did, but something wouldn't let me go through with it."

"Yeah, well, I think we both know who that *someone* is. That's why I've already given the driver the address to Terrence's restaurant. I'm positive that he is more than likely there. Honey, go to him and tell him how much you love him. And please, stop trying to control everything and just allow God to be God. He knows what's best for you and Terrence."

"I don't know how to thank you for this, Mon. I really don't."

"Look, there's no thanks needed. This is what sister friends do. But I'll check back with you later, all right? That is, unless you and Terrence sneak away to get your groove on. And in that case, just text me." She laughed, and for the first time since the start of the wedding, I was able to crack a real smile.

We hung up, and I planned on doing exactly what she had said: allow God to be God. And in my heart and soul, He was telling me at that moment to go to Terrence, express my love for him and how much I didn't want to do life without him. Thinking about seeing him in my white wedding gown and kissing him the way we'd done the other day, I allowed my mind to drift far into never-never land. I was so much in my own fantasy world that I didn't even notice when the driver slowed down the limo all of twenty minutes later.

"Should I wait for you here, ma'am?" he asked, snapping me out of my reverie.

Just as I was about to answer, my eyes caught a glimpse of a couple coming out of the restaurant. They were both smiling from ear to ear and were hugged up with one another like they were in love.

Oh my God! I can't be seeing this. Terrence? And the girls' mother? What is going on? I felt like my eyes had to be deceiving me. *Maybe I'm reading way too much into things. Maybe this is something harmless. I mean, he does have two children with the woman, so this could very well mean nothing at all.*

But then as I continued to gawk at them, I saw him take her face between the palms of his hands and kiss her. Right away, I turned my head as my heart sank into the pit of my belly.

"Sir, go, go. Please drive. Please get me away from here as quickly as possible."

"But—"

"No buts. Please get me out of here."

Promptly, the driver did exactly what I said, and luckily, without Terrence ever seeing us. I assumed the driver sensed my pain, because right after driving away, he let up the middle glass and left me to my own inner space. I was confused more than hurt, and I wondered if there was some reasonable explanation for what I'd seen. But the fact of the matter was he had kissed his daughters' mother, as if they were madly in love. For me there was no other way to explain that.

"What is going on, Terrence?" I whispered.

At that very moment, I was completely unsure of everything in my life. I didn't know whether to call Monica, where I should have the driver take me, if I should call Terrence and interrogate him over what I'd seen, or even if I should go back to Andre and beg for his forgiveness. All I did know was that what I had dreamed would be my perfect day had turned into a complete nightmare, one that I prayed desperately to wake up from. I felt like a total fool, all in the name of love.

CHAPTER 61

TERRENCE

Business was booming at the restaurant, and it had been busy all week long. That was why I couldn't seem to explain the awkward feeling that I had inside. The past seven days had been somewhat stressful, to say the least, and it all had to do with the women in my life. Here I was, practically trying to force myself to have feelings for the girls' mother. We'd been spending time together as a family almost every day, and I could tell that she and the girls loved it. However, no matter how much time we'd spent together, I wasn't feeling the same chemistry with her that I had once felt, or that I felt with Tiffany.

On the other hand, I'd been pretty much torturing myself with my constant thoughts of Tiffany and her wedding day. Part of me wished I had gone and sat far in the back of the church. I wished I had seen her in the fullness of her beauty as she walked down the aisle. I wished I'd seen the smile of happiness that I was sure had graced her face. And more importantly, for myself, I had *needed* to witness her saying, "I do," to another man, to somehow move on with my own life. Yet my pride hadn't let me show up and give the impression that I was some wounded ex who refused to let go. I only prayed her day was all that she had hoped and dreamed it would be.

Now, as I hid away in my office, the knock on the door quickly shot me back to reality. I knew it was time to put my issues with the women in my life on the back burner and get back to being the owner of a successful restaurant. There was always some issue to handle or fire to put out, and I was sure this was nothing less.

"Come in," I called.

My lead waitress, Ebony, peeked her head inside. "Hey, Mr. Montgomery. Uh, there's a gentleman out here requesting to see you. I told him I would see if you were available."

Oh really?" I stood from my desk, walked over, and peeked out the door, wondering who it was. "Where is he?"

"He's sitting at the table over there in the corner."

Looking in that direction, I was damn near startled when I saw who it was. There Andre sat, with an odd expression on his face and a strange disposition about himself. I swore, there was something about that man I didn't like and never would.

What the hell is he doing here? And without Tiff at that? I asked myself. *Maybe he only stopped by to be nosy and rub it in my face that they're married.* I almost dreaded having to go out there and wear some fake-ass smile, like it was cool that he had stopped by.

"Just let him know I'm a little tied up right now, but I'll be out in a second," I instructed Ebony, deciding to let him sit and simmer for a bit.

In the meantime, I picked up my cell to call Monica and see if she had any idea what this was all about. However, once again, my call went straight to her voicemail, as it had all week. I'd figured she and Todd were on some couples' trip with Tiffany and Andre; however, now I knew that wasn't the case. Anyway, a few minutes passed, and with no response from Monica, I figured I would bite the bullet and go ahead and see what this character was up to.

I left my office and approached the table in the corner. "Hey, uh, Andre, right?" I said when I was a few feet away.

"Yeah, Terrence. How are you? Your place you got here looks great, man." He stood and shook my hand.

"Oh thanks, thanks a lot. But as much as I would like to, I really can't take credit for finding this place. Tiffany found it a while ago when I first talked about having my own business. I guess I must admit that she was right. This is the perfect spot," I said, watching him closely to judge his reaction.

He only sat back down and took a sip of his water, basically ignoring what I'd just said. That was when I decided to cut out the small talk and get right down to the reason for him being here.

"So, Andre, I have to be honest. I'm curious to know what brings you by today, especially without Tiffany. I assumed that you two would be somewhere overseas on your honeymoon or something."

"So, are you trying to tell me you haven't spoken with her, Terrence?" His question came across as more of an accusation.

"No, I haven't, not since that day at her book signing," I answered, confused.

He laughed under his breath, as if he didn't believe me. "All right, well, let me just say what I came here to say, then. Tiffany and I didn't get married last week. She left me standing at the altar, basically for you."

"What? No way." I didn't believe what he had said, but I prayed there was some truth to his words. However, if that was the case, I couldn't help but wonder where she was and why I hadn't heard from her.

"Yeah, she did. And made me look like a complete fool in front of all my family and friends."

"Okay, but what does that have to do with me and with you coming here today, Andre? I mean, I already told you that I haven't talked to her, and you don't see her around here, so—"

"Listen, I only came to tell you face-to-face, man-to-man, that Tiffany and I *are* going to work through what happened and will be getting married, just like I planned. But, as for you, I need for you to stay the fuck away from my wife, for good, and let her finally be happy."

It took everything inside me not to pick this joker up by his collar and throw him the hell out. However, he knew exactly what he was doing, because I had to maintain my composure with a restaurant full of guests. Instead, I quietly let him know that he'd met his match as I looked him straight in the eyes.

"First, let's get something straight. Don't you ever come into my establishment making any kind of threats or demands on me. And as for you telling me to stay away from your wife, it looks like Tiffany isn't *your wife*, is she? And I will go around whoever I please."

Upon hearing that, he stood up, drank the rest of his water, and threw a hundred-dollar bill on the table.

"Consider yourself warned, Terrence. And feel free to keep the fucking change."

To Be Continued . . .

About the Author

After attempting several different career paths, Hazel Ro embraced her God-given talent as a fiction romance writer and entrepreneur and followed her passion.

Her love for writing started at an early age, when at times she felt misunderstood and found an outlet in journaling her thoughts. Hazel Ro would take whatever negativity was around her and would build her own *world* by drawing from her imagination and creativity.

However, never in a million years did she imagine that her writing would lead to her first self-published novel, *For Better or For Worse*. This story deals in an effective yet entertaining way with serious *real-life* issues, such as cheating and adultery, betrayal, lies, broken relationships, spirituality, and so much more. Hazel Ro's ultimate objective in this novel and others is to promote and encourage healthy African American relationships.

Aside from writing novels, Hazel Ro coproduced her first stage play, *For Better or For Worse*, in 2012. She is passionate about all facets of the arts and loves poetry, music, and singing.

Hazel Ro is a graduate of Lindenwood University, where she earned her MA in mass communications. She earned her BA in sports and entertainment management from Fontbonne University.

Hazel Ro is originally from St. Louis, but she has called Chicago home since April 2015.

~~Ro Chamberlain~~

Find *I Didn't Think You Existed 2: Fool for Love* and other novels by Hazel Ro by visiting www.hazel-ro.com.

There, the author can be contacted to arrange discounted book purchases for large orders, group discussions with book clubs, speaking engagements, and more!

Thank you again for your support!
Hazel Ro